The shining splendor of our Zebra Lovegram on the cover of this book reflects the glittering excellence of the story inside. Look for the Zebra Lovegram whenever you buy a historical romance. It's a trademark that guarantees the very best in quality and reading entertainment.

SAVAGE POSSESSION

Night Hawk drew Callie over onto her back and just before he dipped his head to nuzzle her neck she glimpsed the raw hot need in his eyes.

His hand moved down, his fingers searching, finding.

"You're so beautiful," he whispered. "Let me soothe you."

Sensual voice, skillful hands, and she *did* like how he set her afire. Far too much, she suddenly realized, but she'd never let him know it.

"I told you I wouldn't touch you unless I thought you'd welcome my caress. If you want me to stop, I will," he said.

She couldn't seem to make herself say the words.

"Take one spunky heroine, add a dash of devastatingly sexy hero, and you've got one highly entertaining read. Mary Martin is an author to keep your eye on."
Romantic Times

MARY MARTIN

WILD TEXAS ANGEL

ZEBRA BOOKS
KENSINGTON PUBLISHING CORP.

ZEBRA BOOKS

are published by

Kensington Publishing Corp.
475 Park Avenue South
New York, NY 10016

First printing: December, 1992

Printed in the United States of America

This book is dedicated to my brother John F. O'Neill III, his wife Patty and family — in special honor of their baby's birth. And to my dearest aunt and uncle, Connie and Thomas Coad, with much love.

I'd like to acknowledge the following people for their help and unfailing support during the creation of this book: My son James Martin, and Kevin La-Fata; thanks guys for seeing me through the computer blues. My son Thomas Martin, who keeps the home fires burning, making my life easier. Mom, my biggest fan and best promoter. My "Leo" buddies: Donna Julian, my amiga, through thick and thin you are always there; Anna Eberhardt, your scorching pen keeps me highly entertained and your wit never fails to make me smile; Joan Buckman, for your input and tireless efforts on my behalf.

And, as always, Blue Eyes. Love you all.

The Night of the Hawk

Texas, 1861

Naked and majestic he stood alone in the moonlight. His broad-shouldered form and untamed raven hair were dusted bronze by the pearly glow of the moon as it crept steadily upward over the towering canyon wall. High on a jagged bluff — overlooking a blood-colored river that roared far below his remote aerie — the warrior stared out at the rugged land where the Comanche reigned supreme.

The surface of the cliff where he stood was smooth but, on its face, green moss clung amid stunted cedars nestled in rocky crevices. It was the highest of several knolls, rising in pyramidal outline beneath the full moon like a sacred altar ablaze with fire. Only those who knew it well, or who were unaware of the perils, ventured through it uninvited by its host, the Comanche.

"A la cola del mundo . . . To the tail end of the world," he stated almost reverently, finding the early Spanish explorers' depiction of the canyon and the

Llano Estacado—the vast flat-topped plateau that bordered it—an accurate description.

Bright rays of revealing moonlight washed across the smooth planes of Night Of The Hawk's face, glinted off the polished chips of jet that dangled from one ear, and filtered through his flowing mane. Garish wolf rings encircled his expressive eyes and black paint slashed his high cheekbones and chiseled jaw.

He was what he appeared—dangerous and deadly—an equal to the predators who roamed here. But he had not come to the sacred canyon to seek *puha* to make war. He had come for a vision to guide him on his mission for peace, and he knew that this night he would receive it.

During the revelation, he would hear a voice and then be shown signs; he believed very strongly in this ceremony. His superstitions were rooted in centuries-old tradition—although he wasn't certain if man actually had the power to conjure magic—but it was the Comanche way, and it gave him the confidence and inner strength that he needed for the uncertain road that lay ahead.

Patiently he watched and waited.

Soon the first sign appeared.

He forced himself to remain motionless and stared trancelike as a yellow-tipped hawk glided gracefully into view—not more than twenty feet over his head—and issued a shrill call. He felt a kindred spirit with the wolf and the hawk, and with all manner of creatures that roamed this land tonight, but he was saddened by the sense that an era unlike any other was passing and might well be lost forever.

Sometimes it was impossible to imagine that men, being what they were, would ever succeed in changing the world with their warfare. The Comanche in him differed, for they had always been a warlike people and had fought to the death to protect land and family. A task that was becoming exceedingly harder for, even though he stood here far removed from any civilization, he felt the winds of change upon him, and knew that the road ahead lay twisted, and as yet, without an end in sight.

A shiver of apprehension snaked along his spine. What if his mission for peace did not succeed? Would only their voices remain to linger on the wind? An entire civilization wiped out by another because of greed. He could not allow that to happen, and he searched desperately for answers.

By ritual, he turned first to the east, then the south, west and north.

"I, Night Of The Hawk, call the winds now to this sacred place, and I ask that the spirit gods come forth and join me."

He repeated the prayer until he'd relayed his message four times, and the sound of his voice filled the canyon.

"The People need the white eyes to hear their voices and concerns. There is no one who will listen, who seems to care, and for the first time that I can remember our courage is faltering. This warrior seeks your blessing before I set out on this uncertain road. For the People I will journey over this twisted path. Give me strength and wisdom, spirit, hear my prayer."

Even as he spoke the words, he wondered whether he was really strong enough to make the required sacrifice. It would be no easy task, and he was only one man against many enemies. Did he have the courage? Was he a true believer? He had seen his life shattered and his loved ones taken away. It had left him embittered and doubtful. He didn't think he'd ever again be the man he'd once been. In thinking this, self-doubt and confusion warred with his sense of righteousness, and his voice began to falter.

Closing his eyes he tried to calm the storm of emotions within him. Suddenly, feeling trapped by something insidious and consuming, he threw back his head—long hair splaying around his bare shoulders—and gave a low, ululating cry. And hearing him, perhaps sensing his torment, his brother the wolf returned the mournful call from somewhere farther out on the plain.

He took this as a sign that the gods were listening. And turning his face up toward the heavens, he called forth Mother-Moon and the ever-present spirits who existed here in the dark places, for they had always guided him on uncertain journeys.

Sharply etched rocks and winding gorges faded to gray, and the fitful wind joined his spirit song, moaning through the canyon passages like some devil phantom seeking lost souls to claim.

The taunting zephyr, as if to distract him, sighed around his tall, lithe form and caught his ebony hair—free of feathers or band except for three golden hawk feathers secured above one ear—and set it streaming like a war banner behind him. At last finding the herald he sought, he suddenly relaxed tense shoulders and drew around him the magic born on this night of the full moon. With his face still turned heavenward, he began to chant his medicine prayer, his faith restored.

"Oh, Great Spirit, grant my prayer, and as you look down upon the Comanche, protect them, shield them from their enemies so that they might continue to live in joy and peace.

"Send my brothers the hawk and the wolf to stand guard over my people, and guide me wisely throughout my journey.

"Help me . . . spirit . . . hear my plea."

He voiced his concerns and his hopes. When at last he had finished, he waited quietly and tried not to think about the possibility that a vision would not come to him.

Then, as if in response to his prayer, the night sky slowly began to deepen in color, and the cadenced harmony of the night creatures stilled. An unnatural calm settled over the canyon, and the warrior knew his prayer had not gone unheeded. The bright Comanche moon, tinged crimson, cast the land and river below in hues of scarlet and gold; the stars, like jewels, shone brilliantly against a velvet-black sky.

It was just around midnight, with the moon at its highest point and the wind keening through the treetops, that his ghostly shape leaped and whirled around a blazing fire. Curious wild eyes peered from their lairs and stared at the strange vision as if hypnotized.

He danced in a circle, his rhythmic cries piercing the night, the hawk's feather he held in his right hand pressed against his heart. As was his custom, he'd dressed in a breechcloth, knotted on one narrow hip, and a necklace of smooth bear claws — taken from a huge grizzly he'd killed as a young hunter of sixteen summers — adorned his chest.

He wore his parfleche around his neck, and among the contents were blades of sweet grass, herbs, an eagle's claw, and several quartz crystals. They were his most sacred possessions.

A band of sleek black otter fur — affixed with tiny bells — encircled his ankle and made delicate music whenever he moved. As he danced his focus remained centered on his purpose, and for a long while he kept up this relentless pace without tiring.

His mind, his entire body, seemed to absorb power and strength from his prayer song. He felt his muscles stretch and grow stronger. Then when his energy finally waned, and he felt the time was right, he stood quietly on the bluff once more. With only a sense of primal instinct to guide him, he summoned forth the very special *puha* to carry forth from the canyon.

Slowly, he opened his closed fist, and there glimmered the crystals that the old shaman had given him after his first vision quest. With a sweep of his hand, he flung the stones over the cliff, and prayed aloud.

"Let the gods bestow their blessing upon this Comanche. Send a sign that I might interpret for our future course in life . . . tell me what it is I am to do, and help me to be strong." His voice was vibrant with urgency, and he stood watching as the stones tumbled down through the night-draped sky like a shower of stars and then were swallowed up by the canyon. He knew there could be no harm in using this very special source of power, and he felt a strange sense of excitement as he quietly waited to see what the spirits would reveal.

He gazed far below, where hundreds of conical lodges were but pale shadows on the floor of Palo Duro canyon. It was the village of the Nermernuh, The Only People, as they had thought of themselves for centuries, and he was proud to be one of them.

The glow of embers from the evening fires seemed to dance like fireflies among the trees, but each year he'd seen their numbers diminished. The white man and the diseases he carried were slowly destroying the People.

Once, this had been their kingdom. Then the white invaders began to transcend the Comanche's boundaries, and the fight for the mother earth began. The warrior knew that the white eyes were migrating westward in ever increasing numbers; he'd seen their tracks and the homesteads they were building on Comanche land. What would become of the Comanche when the buffalo vanished and the open land disappeared?

Just thinking about the People losing the only way of life that they had ever known brought fire into his ebony eyes. He still held hope that the white eyes would never conquer the Comanche, although he well knew the bitter struggle that lay ahead and the lives that would be sacrificed on both sides.

Night Of The Hawk stood there for some time with his focus centered on a vision, but none came to him. He felt hopelessly defeated, and he bowed his head and sighed. The spirits knew he didn't believe in himself, so why should they reveal anything to him? *Suvante!* It was finished.

"Have you so little faith that you give up so easily!?" Night Of The Hawk swore he heard someone shout. He whirled in astonishment and looked around him. There was no one, but he knew he had heard something.

"You are doubtful, but it will pass if you truly believe in yourself," the intrusive messenger said. "What you seek is within your reach, but you must want to hear the words and be willing to change your life."

Night Of The Hawk felt his heart racing. He knew then whose voice he'd heard. His own. The inner voice that had guided him through every crisis in his life, the voice he had so recently chosen to ignore. It was time to face the future once more. He stood there on the cliff's edge and for the first time he realized that he'd been the one fighting change because he hadn't wanted to let go of his past and the memories that were so bittersweet. He wished to help his people, but he hadn't been willing to make the necessary sacrifice. He knew he must; he had to.

Once again he waited, but this time his mind was firmly set.

Images, faces, bits and pieces swam before his eyes. He saw his past flash before him, and then it disappeared like the mist after sunrise.

Finally there was nothing but darkness and a terrible void. Then suddenly, he caught a glimpse of his future, and he knew the man he would become. He envisioned the tall, lithe form of a pale-skinned beauty with shining russet hair, and violet eyes so lovely and bewitching that it made him tremble; he sensed that one day soon she would take her place by his side.

He was stunned. He was angry. This was not what he had expected. He must have prayed for the wrong medicine. Unable to bear the sight of her another minute, his deep voice called out, "I have no need of you in my life, and I want no other by my side! . . . Leave me . . . leave me now!"

He sought yet another vision, but it remained the same.

Then, in the still of the night, he heard a heart-rending sound and prayed it was only the wind, but the sound lingered and he could not will it away.

His eyes grew moist, and he fought furiously against the humiliation. He could not weep; warriors did not shed tears. But his gaze blurred despite his strong will, and he whispered brokenly. "Please . . . do not taunt me so . . ."

But the sound came again, and oh, how it tore at his heart!

It was a woman weeping.

17

Her tears almost brought him to his knees, for he knew who she was and why she cried. How he hated to remember that time over a year ago, when his world had come crashing down around him.

"Morning Star . . . what do you want of me?" He lifted his face and saw his lovely Indian wife and their baby daughter. They looked exactly as they had on that ill-fated day he'd ridden away from their village with the other hunters. It was a very bitter memory. One he hadn't wanted to face and had kept suppressed. This time he forced himself to recall everything in painful detail.

Morning Star had been so beautiful. Young, willow-slim, her luminous dark eyes always shining with love for him. And his precious baby daughter, asleep in the cradleboard strapped to her mother's back, innocent and so trusting. They had not deserved to die so violently.

His handsome features twisted, remembering their brutal, senseless deaths, and pain overwhelmed him once more, the kind that ate deep down into his soul. He clenched his fists so tightly the sinewy muscles of his arms quivered and the scars from wounds he'd self-inflicted during his mourning ritual glistened beneath his mahogany skin. It was the only imperfection on his splendid form, but he cared naught and bore the scars proudly in memory of his slain family.

He would not forget that they'd been murdered, or how he had not been there to protect them. What haunted him more than anything was the fact that his baby daughter, Precious Flower, had been screaming before she'd died. Despite her piercing cries, no one in the village had been able to reach them in time.

Precious Flower had been torn from her mother's back and, perhaps in order to still her frantic cries, had been thrown into the bathing pool, where she had drowned. Morning Star had lain on the sandy bank, badly beaten, unable to come to her baby's aid. How horrible that must have been. Then, his kind, gentle wife had been raped and, finally, strangled.

It was an image he carried into his sleep each night.

There could have been no worse death for his beloved wife. The Comanche believed the spirit floated from their mouth at the moment of their death and on to the land beyond the setting sun. However, because Morning Star had been strangled, her spirit had been trapped inside of her body and she would never rest in peace. She was doomed to wander in darkness for eternity.

Night Of The Hawk swore her attacker would meet the same fate whenever he found him. And he *would* track him down. The man might think he'd gotten away before anyone could identify him, but Morning Star had managed to slash him with her knife, ensuring he wear the brand of murderer. Her bloodied skinning knife had been found lying beside her. The killer had left a scarlet trail in the sand, but even their best trackers had not been able to find him. He'd vanished without a trace.

Night Of The Hawk had been overwhelmed with

guilt and rage. And because his loved ones' last moments had been at the hands of a crazed madman, Night Of The Hawk had made certain before they'd been laid to rest that he was the only one to prepare their bodies for burial. He wanted them to remember only the touch of his loving hands.

Cradling Morning Star in his arms, he'd dressed her in soft, white elk skin and wrapped her in ermine fur. Then, he'd carefully painted her face with vermillion, and had sealed her eyes with red clay. He repeated the ritual with Precious Flower, then for the last time, lashed his baby to her cradleboard. Placing her in Morning Star's arms, he had lifted them onto the back of his wife's silver mare. Swinging up behind Morning Star's body, Night Of The Hawk had held her gently against him.

The entire village had turned out for the funeral procession, wailing and weeping; even the heavens had cried, the dark clouds opening up and the rain upon his face mingling with his own tears. The pain everyone said would diminish with time was still fresh inside him and, to this day, he wasn't certain how he coped. Physical agony was one thing. He was a strong man and could withstand even the most excruciating kind of torture inflicted by an enemy, and had many times. But this was beyond even his endurance. To give himself the will to go on another hour, another day, Night Of the Hawk thought about how this man would suffer before he killed him. The Comanche was well versed in ingenuous ways to make a man die slowly and screaming for the end. Night Of The Hawk knew the man could not hide forever and one day he would find him. The trail might be long and tortuous, but it would only be a matter of time before the wolf at his heels found the way to his door.

The terrible memories faded at last, and he stood there for some time chanting, seeking another vision, but the only one that came to him was the same one of the flamed-haired *herbi* with the violet eyes. The path for his life was there for him to see, and this woman would somehow become a part of it. He knew that Morning Star wept for what they had lost and would never have again.

As the first hint of dawn came, he murmured, "Don't cry, my beautiful Morning Star . . . I would give my life to take your place, for love does not end with death, and even if another is to walk by my side she will never have my heart, for it can belong only to you." He added one last request as well. "Oh, great and generous spirit, please listen to this Comanche's voice. Let Morning Star join our baby daughter in everlasting peace. Grant this, and I will vow this night to pick up the pieces of my life and walk the path that has been chosen for me."

He did not really expect an immediate response but, moments later, he swore he heard familiar soft laughter and his heart lightened, for there were no more sounds of tears.

Then he was amazed at the sight of a beautiful silver hawk — something he'd never seen before — soaring free before him, winging gracefully upward to vanish in the high white clouds.

"Beloved?" he questioned, his voice hushed.

Night Of The Hawk, whose features were usually darkly brooding, almost smiled beneath his grim mask of black paint.

"Be free and at peace," he murmured huskily, and turning away, felt a sense of joy for the first time in a long while.

Chapter One

Mardi Gras, New Orleans

Sheer lace curtains fluttered against leaded-glass, and beneath the partially opened window a warm moist breeze scented with seduction sneaked in, and drifted across the sweat-sheened bodies of a man and a woman.

Together they'd lazily explored away the hours after midnight and did not notice, or give care, to the watery gray light of dawn filtering through the airy bedchamber of the opulent mansion, condensing dewlike on the couple's entwined limbs. They were only intent on each other, the marvel of finely chiseled bones and sculpted muscle, the pleasure to be had from hands that roamed with skill.

Leather boots, a discarded blue uniform, a crumpled and naughtily brief white costume, lay forgotten on the polished wood floor beside the four poster bed draped in filmy netting.

The woman, audaciously bare-breasted, inclined her silky blond head to one side, her gaze sliding over him hungrily. She was wearing a satin demi-mask adorned with sequins and rhinestones — it was Mardi Gras, after all — but eschewed the need for anything else.

"Your uniform doesn't do you justice, *cherie*," Lily LaFleur murmured throatily, bold shameless eyes following the path of her agile fingertips, enjoying, absorbing the barely leashed power beneath the hardened muscles. "You are a beautiful man . . . perhaps too much man for some, but not for Lily." On impulse, she suddenly leaned over him and pressed her lush mouth to the hollow of his throat, her small white teeth nipping him in almost desperate need. He was what she wanted, what she needed; she never seemed able to satisfy her hunger for him.

His lips twisted in a half smile. With him, she was as free with her compliments as she was with her charms, but he'd never minded being the recipient of either. Yet he drew the line when it came to bearing her love bites and, reaching up, his fingers sliced through her tangled blond mane and gently, but firmly, dragged her head back. "Patience, love, the hour is young, there's no need to rush such a pleasurable interlude," he said, his voice low and coaxing.

"*Oui* . . . patience . . . a very difficult thing to ask when I am in your arms," she said dreamily, feeling weak from the need that only he inspired.

"Shh, just relax and let me show you how rewarding patience can be," he said, and drawing her head down, their lips met.

24

He lingered in the kiss, enjoying the warm sweet taste of her. He'd always thought there was nothing quite as satisfying as the smell and texture of a woman caught in the throes of her own dark desire.

His hands moved, and before she realized, had spanned her waist, and lifting her, pressed kisses along the smooth flesh of her belly and thighs.

She writhed against his tender assault, feeling consumed by his mouth and out of control. Lily rarely lost her control, but with him she did each time they were together. He made her say and do things that should have shocked her, but nothing they ever did together disturbed her. He was a consummate lover, and inventive as well.

"Now . . . please . . . I need you so," she breathed, fingers clutching at his shoulders as he tumbled her beneath him and moving lower, nestled between the sleek tense legs that greedily claimed him, his lips gently parting dewy curls.

Her mouth opened slightly as if she needed to draw in a reassuring breath, but she could only moan instead. "Yes . . . oh, yes . . . kiss me there," she sighed, her whimpers of ecstasy and the pattering rain on the roof lost in a rumble of thunder that shook the walls.

Pale cream sheets rustled on the thoroughly rumpled bed as the woman twisted and turned, overwhelmed by the deliciously carnal things his mouth could do to her.

He was the only man who'd ever truly made her feel like a woman. Despite how everyone said he was destined for a bad end — that if some irate husband

25

didn't kill him, a jealous hussy surely would — Lily La Fleur knew that no other man would do for her lover. Although even she had to admit he'd changed considerably since his daring escape from Camp Sumter, aptly renamed Camp Death by the Federal prisoners, a hastily built sixteen-and-a-half-acre prison stockade in Andersonville, Georgia. From everything she'd heard about the place, Lily knew it must have been dreadful for him, even though he wouldn't discuss his confinement there with anyone, not even her. Everyone said the camp was crowded and badly managed and, because of inadequate diet and poor sanitation, disease ran rampant claiming many lives. Lily hated to think of the trials he must have endured, the horror he'd seen.

Rafe was not as quick to laugh anymore, and while he'd always been an enigmatic man, he was now given to black moods and long periods when even she didn't know what she might expect from him. But she stuck by him despite those trying times, and if not for Rafe, Lily felt certain she might have succumbed to her grief after her husband was killed in the battle at Hampton Roads.

When she was with Rafe like this — and he was being so attentive — she imagined she could forgive him anything. What a difference from her earlier mood, when she'd been ready to think that he'd left her this time and would not return.

Lily remembered how she'd returned to her lonely mansion after the Mardi Gras ball at the Dumond estate on the edge of the city. While it had been nice to mingle with old friends, the ball had been undeniably subdued in contrast to past years, and there was a forced gaiety in the air that had never been a part of Mardi Gras before the war. Now it seemed evident in every facet of their lives. Still, everyone had seemed to thoroughly enjoy the afternoon social, followed by a costumed ball and late night supper.

For Lily and her Creole neighbors it had been a chance to gather together, to briefly forget how much they'd all sacrificed to the war and, sadly, how their city remained firmly under Federal control.

Since the occupation in '62, the Mystic Crewe of Comus had encouraged the Creole people to celebrate the season in private and they had, although the invaders had seemed to have good reason to rejoice and did so with enthusiasm.

This year, despite the Southerners' protests, there were over a hundred ballrooms scheduling festivities, and the St. Charles theatre had promised a lavish production. There would be noise and laughter and Yankees in Jackson Square. But there would be few who really belonged there.

So much had changed since those longed-for days, Lily thought, and Rafe was the only person in her life who could make her feel better. Most importantly of all, he could make her forget.

Lily had only gone to the party to escape her empty house. Her escort had been a perfect southern gentleman and had attended to her every need. Yet it had been Rafe's strong arms she'd longed to have hold her and his voice whispering the words she so needed to hear. He was the only one who could chase her doldrums away.

Rafe had not been to visit her in weeks. Lily could only hope there was no one else, but she knew she could never really be sure of him — couldn't be, for there were any number of women who would eagerly share their bed with him.

Her heart heavy, Lily had pleaded fatigue and left the party early. She was back home well before midnight, sending her escort on his way again with a chaste kiss and a polite thank you for a lovely evening.

As soon as she turned the key in her door and entered the foyer, the walls began to close in on her. Thunder rumbled ominously and the wind moaned through the spreading limbs of the ancient live oaks that towered over the house. She hurried up the wide center staircase, her long velvet cloak billowing around her, and entering her darkened chamber quickly shut the door on the world.

"Damn you, Rafe," she grumbled to herself. "Why, when I need you the most, aren't you with me tonight?"

The room lay in heavy shadows but someone, (certainly it had to have been her faithful housekeeper Delcey), had lit a fire in the stone hearth. A crystal lamp sat on a polished rosewood table next to the bed, the wick turned down low, its golden glow dancing against the rose silk wall.

Standing before the cheval mirror, Lily dropped her cloak and began removing her costume — a daringly revealing one-piece white catsuit, enhanced by fur trim around the collar and cuffs.

Rafe still flitted in and out of her thoughts . . . how he looked, the way he entered a room, the way he could draw attention with merely his presence. Most especially, she remembered how he could make her feel when they were together, just the two of them.

Lily stared at her image in the glass and had to admit that her costume was daring. She knew her designer, Madame Rue, would be delighted when she learned what a stir it caused. Even Julienne Mc-Clure's Salome costume—with its frothy veils that left her semi-naked beneath them—had seemed pale by comparison, Lily mused.

The southern beauty coolly assessed her image in the mirror, running her hands over her body. There was no denying that she looked magnificent. She recalled the sensation that she'd caused earlier. How when she'd swept into the ballroom, every male head had swung to stare, and then it had sounded like a buzz of angry queen bees had invaded the room.

The women glaring, whispering to each other in such shocked disapproval.

"Scandalous! Can you believe the audacity of that woman?"

"I knew she had nerve . . . but I never thought she'd go this far . . ."

"Henry? . . . Henry! You'd better put your tongue back in your mouth, someone's liable to step on it," Lily had heard a plump matronly woman standing next to her exclaim in a huff.

If looks could kill, Lily knew she would have been struck dead on the spot.

"Meow . . . meow," Lily purred playfully to the cat-woman in the mirror. But nothing they said had bothered Lily. A girl just had to do what she must to survive and to make the best of such trying times. And Lily knew better than most how to capitalize on her stunning looks.

She swiped one long-nailed hand through the air, and as easy as that, she erased them from her mind.

After unfastening the tiny pearl buttons along the front of the suit, Lily casually tossed the costume aside, but hesitated before removing her satin mask and hood. *Mon Dieu!* why did she suddenly have this strange sensation that she was not alone?

Quickly glancing over her shoulder she caught a brief movement behind her, and noticed the faint silhouette of a man sitting in a chair next to the fire.

Lily was never more aware of the fact that she was wearing only a white fur hood over her pale blond hair and the demi-mask of white satin. She felt his penetrating gaze. She did not realize that in the firelight something glittered in her navel against smooth, alabaster skin—a pear-shaped diamond winking in the flickering firelight that gilded her body.

In the years prior to the war, Lily would have proudly flaunted diamonds from head to toe. But the South no longer boasted of its idle rich, and even one's own neighbors might rob you of your last penny should they know where to find it. So Lily kept the most valuable possessions that she'd managed to retain, hidden away — sometimes in the most unlikely places.

He smiled at her and she heard his soft laugh. Lily couldn't think of anything else but that beautiful mouth as she caught a glimpse of even white teeth.

"You could break a man's heart dressed like that," he said huskily, unfolding his long lean body from the chair with wolfish grace. "You look ravishing, Lily."

His presence seemed to dominate Lily's world, and she gasped, her small hand fluttering to her throat. "Rafe . . . you startled me. How . . . long have you been sitting there?"

"Long enough to appreciate your performance."

Lily never blushed, but she did then. All the way down to her scarlet painted toes.

"It must have been a memorable evening," he drawled.

"Yes . . . well . . . there are some who will say so, I feel certain," she replied, biting back a smile.

He never took his eyes off her as he closed the distance between them, and he made no apology for the invasion of her bedchamber or for scaring her half to death. "And now I'd like to make a few memories of my own."

It had been so long, so terribly long since he'd come to her like this. But she didn't want to readily admit that she was thrilled to see him for she was annoyed as well.

He expected her to tumble into his arms just like

that — no explanations, no apologies, just another night of wonderful sex. Yet afterward, she'd still be alone. She drew a ragged breath. "What do you want me to say, Rafe?" she asked, confused by her turbulent emotions. Why did he have to be looking at her in that warm familiar way? Her heart was hammering against her ribs and she didn't know how to answer him . . . but she knew she wanted him with her very much.

This was so typical of Rafe, to come here tonight not knowing what plans she might have or considering that she might have promised her bed and the night to someone else — although this she rarely did, for no other man could compete with him. Rafe was as wild and unfettered as she was, but there were times when even Lily began to wonder what it might be like to belong only to one person again, and to share every moment together. Yet she doubted whether this was something Rafe ever considered.

He came and went in her life whenever he pleased and, although their relationship was unfailingly passionate, there were times when even she did not think she really knew him at all, that he'd always keep a part of himself aloof and free from any emotional entanglements. He would give her his nights but she should not expect anything more.

"It's not a difficult decision, love. Do you want me to stay with you, or would you prefer that I leave?"

Lily hesitated only briefly, studying him in the firelight. His full mouth was set in that usual reckless slant, but she noted a subtle, yet definite change since she'd last seen him. His features bore the harsh stamp of a man who'd been spending too much time on the edge and perhaps, for the first time, found it consuming him. She reasoned that he must need her tonight as much as she needed him, but damnit, she'd never hear such words from him. Lily's eyes narrowed slightly behind the almond-shaped holes of the mask. "Would you even care if I did send you away, Rafe?" she blurted, needing some reassurance, just a small measure to salve her tortured soul.

"I care about everything you do, Lily, and I have to admit I thought about you a lot while I was away." His smile was heartstoppingly sensual and those incredibly sexy eyes were looking at her in a way that set every nerve in her body screaming for him to touch her. "But even I couldn't have imagined you looking more beautiful. . . ."

She was lost and she knew it. Beneath his assessing gaze her skin tingled, and she felt the smoldering heat of desire stirring. She wanted to resist the temptation to yield to his arms, but Rafe made such an option impossible. Just being near him was always her undoing.

Still, Lily was trying to remember that it had been weeks since she'd last seen him, but what frustrated her most was the fact that she'd never know where he'd been, what had kept him away for so long. She'd learned long ago there was no sense in questioning him.

He'd been gone so long that she'd begun to suspect he might not come back to her. Then she'd imagine him lying wounded in some distant field hospital, cut off from all communication, or lying dead upon a battle field. What worried Lily most of all, and accounted for her sleepless nights, was the niggling suspicion that he might have found someone else he desired more than her.

Lily had become accustomed to living alone—following her husband's death she'd had little choice—and had grown quite independent of having a man dictate her life. But since Rafe had become her lover she'd become addicted to sensual pleasure, and she'd damned him for it, even as she couldn't stop wanting him to possess her in the way that only he could.

His night-black eyes met hers. She thought he had the most seductive eyes she'd ever seen, fathomless as the darkest night, framed by long thick lashes, and glinting with a dangerous attraction that held Lily enthralled.

"You are a scoundrel, Rafael . . . and you would deserve it if I sent you away," she said.

Reaching out, he took her hand and kissed her fingertips. Then, glancing up at her with the light of the devil in his eyes, he said, "Sometimes, sweet Lily, we don't always get what we deserve."

As soon as he touched her, and Lily had never longed more for him to touch her, she willingly surrendered. Slipping her hands inside his tunic and freeing the buttons up the front, she began to undress him before the fire.

"Am I to interpret this as an invitation?" he asked, a smile curving the strong lines of his mouth.

Lily stood up on tip-toe and slid her arms around

34

his neck. *"Oui . . .* I am yours," she whispered, thinking that this was still Mardi Gras, after all, and Ash Wednesday was soon enough to atone for her wickedness this day.

Lust, as sinful as it was delicious, was simply irresistible with Rafe and as close to heaven as Lily figured she would ever get. "Make love to me, *cherie,"* she urged, and molded her firm young body against his hard frame.

And he had again and again throughout that long sultry night.

Callie Rae Angel's amethyst eyes flew open and her head snapped up. She brushed one slender hand across her sleep-drugged eyes, forcing them wide as she straightened up in the hard hospital chair. She'd been putting in too many long hours as a volunteer nurse and she just had to take a day off soon.

She was losing control.

She'd had that dream again.

The one about the dark-haired stranger and the beautiful woman . . . or was she a cat? She sat there puzzled for a moment before she realized what she was doing. Oh God, she didn't know night from day anymore, she was so tired. And now she didn't even know if she'd been dreaming of a woman or a cat?

Glancing out of the window, she noted the full moon shining down on the Mardi Gras revelers filling the street. She thought then that her strange longings and dreams were probably because of the moon and the noisy celebrations that had been going on for days. Nothing seemed real when shadows became masked demons and cats' faces loomed everywhere.

This year every man wanted to be a spawn of the devil, and every woman a feline of incredible beauty.

She blamed the outrageous costumes for her fantasies and, she reasoned, her unbidden dreams would vanish with the advent of Lent and she'd be glad. She didn't understand the dreams *or* the way they made her feel. But a little voice inside her head taunted . . . *Callie, that's not true and you know it. You don't want your soul to burn in hell, so you pretend . . . but you can't pretend with me. I'm your conscience and I know you . . . I know you well.*

Her heart pounded and her palms grew damp. She sat frozen with embarrassment, knowing her face must be brighter than the red of her hair. She felt even worse when she thought about what Father O'Brian would say when she went to confession tomorrow morning. She didn't realize that at eighteen her body and mind were maturing faster than she might understand, and her longings were quite natural. But temptation was a subject the good sisters at the convent avoided well and only its evils had ever been explained to the girl. Callie had never considered herself easily tempted, but that was before the dreams had begun. She was no longer so certain.

Swallowing, she patted the dampness from her neck with her lace handkerchief and brushed back a strand of red hair that clung to her moist cheek. Although every window had been thrown wide, there

36

was little air circulating through the ward, and she could only imagine how the patients in the over-crowded room must feel.

She castigated herself for having the devil's own thoughts, and refocused her attention to the injured man lying on the bed beside her.

She'd become obsessed with saving Sam Matthews. Of course she really wanted to save all of them. The nuns said she was God's own messenger, and through her healing touch she had managed to save many whom everyone else had given up on. But Matthews still had a long way to go before he recovered . . . if he ever did.

"Miss Angel?"

"Major Jones." Callie looked up to find one of the doctors paused at the foot of Matthews' bed. "Is there something I can do for you?"

He smiled gently. "You look so tired I hate to ask you, but one of the nurses went home sick. Can you cover for her until we find someone to take her place?"

"Of course," Callie answered unhesitatingly, "for as long as you need me."

"Thank you. I don't know what we'd do without volunteers like you."

She knew he was just as weary as she was, and had probably been in the operating room for the better part of the day. His face was lined with fatigue and the white apron covering his uniform was smeared with blood.

He favored her with a grateful smile and then, noting a newly arrived stretcher, he sighed. "Well, back to the trenches," he said, and trailed behind the ambulance carriers bearing the wounded soldier.

There were just too many wounded and too little help, although everyone did as much as they could. Callie took the care of the patients in her charge seriously; she made certain that their dressings were changed every few hours, and watched closely for any signs of putrefaction.

This was the most crucial period for Matthews, when the risk of gangrene was of primary concern. The wound was fresh and had to be kept scrupulously clean. She disinfected everything that came in contact with his shoulder wound. She believed it saved lives and was well worth the extra time it took. But many of the doctors didn't share her concerns regarding disinfection, and she shuddered every time she thought about the surgical instruments that were barely rinsed between operations — amputations of limbs sometimes running as high as a hundred or more each day depending on the intensity of the battles. Men needlessly lost their lives to infection that might have been prevented if cleanliness had been the rule.

But this was 1864. Perhaps someday a medicine would be discovered that would halt the spread of infection but, for now, she could only prescribe cleanliness. She wished that she had her bag of herbs and medicines but they were watching her, waiting for her to defy them and, she mused, they might yet see her famous temper if they persisted in their foolishness.

There were a few Yankee doctors who'd already warned her not to practice her healing arts inside their hospital again or she'd be relieved of her nursing position.

"The fools," she grumbled under her breath, "their prejudice comes from nothing more than superstition. It isn't witchcraft, it's a healing skill that would ease the suffering of these men."

She noticed Sam Matthews' eyes blink, and he turned his head to stare up at her. "Don't they ever let you go home, Miss Callie?" His husky whisper was rough with pain.

"You can't get rid of me that easy, Lieutenant." Callie smiled, and sat forward to stretch the soreness from her cramped muscles. She was dressed in a simple day gown of lilac muslin, and she had her hair pulled back from a face that was striking enough to grace a cameo. "Can I get you anything?"

"I don't think so," he managed weakly.

"You didn't touch your breakfast. Surely you must be hungry. Would you care for something to eat?"

He shook his head. "I don't have much of an appetite. I'd just as soon forego dinner if you don't mind." Even the slightest movement made him wince in discomfort, and she knew that his pain must be almost unbearable, although he rarely complained.

Sam Matthews had been a patient in the New Orlean's hospital for three days and in that time Callie had grown quite fond of him. He was the least demanding of the many patients she tended for, though hers was only a volunteer position, the number of sick and wounded had more than doubled since the Federal takeover of the city.

"At least have something cool to drink," she encouraged him, touching a soothing hand to his forehead. It was hot as a firebrand. She filled a dipper with water and held it to his lips. But he only managed a small sip before he grimaced and his head fell back on the pillow. Then he chuckled softly. "You know, ma'am, I suddenly have a hankering for something after all," he said.

"Indeed, and what would that be, Lieutenant?" Callie queried, glancing dubiously into his eyes.

"You think you might sort through a few of those bottles you're always toting around with you and see if you can rustle me up a stiff shot of bourbon?" he suggested, his voice laced with easy humor.

"Nice try Lieutenant, but it's unlikely," she replied dryly, feigning shock at his suggestion. But her eyes danced with amusement, for she knew he enjoyed their good-natured bantering. She reached for a dark bottle and a spoon on the bedside table. "However, I *do* have something for you."

His eyes followed her. "Now wait just a minute, that's not exactly what I had in mind."

"You know it's time for your medicine, and it will help the pain."

"Tired of my outrageous demands already, are you?"

She leveled a look of mock severity. "Lieutenant Matthews, how you can suggest such a thing when you know I have only your best interests at heart?"

She tipped the bottle and the laudanum puddled into the spoon. "Now, open wide."

"You're a hard woman, Miss Angel," he groaned in mock despair.

"So they tell me, Lieutenant Matthews," she said, and ever persistent, pressed the spoon to his lips. "Open," she stressed firmly.

With a sigh, he opened his mouth and swallowed, shuddering at the bitter taste. Callie shook her head, and couldn't help but smile. She didn't know where he found the energy but he was always the one trying to make her smile.

Not long afterward the laudanum took effect, and she noticed his eyelids begin to droop. She waited quietly while he drifted into oblivion. She hoped and prayed that her diligent care might provide a marked improvement in his condition soon. She knew that all they had was hope, and sometimes there wasn't enough of that, but she refused to think about the grave possibility that Matthews still might lose his arm. The next several hours were going to be the most crucial.

Chapter Two

"Pleasant dreams, Lieutenant," she whispered, "you've certainly earned them after everything you've been through."

Callie was unable to forget how he'd been shot while trying to help some of his men pinned down behind enemy lines under heavy artillery fire. Trapped out in the open, there didn't seem to be any hope for them, until Sam had taken up the charge alone. He'd advanced on the Confederates' flank, pouring out rifle fire, enabling the Union soldiers to make a break and scramble to safety.

Samuel Matthews' brave efforts had managed to draw fire away from his friends, but the heroic deed had nearly cost him his own life. He'd been gravely wounded but the fierce battle had raged for days, before his men could reach him. By that time he'd lost a great deal of blood and was perilously close to death. But he'd managed to survive the rough transport to the field hospital and the crude facilities they used as an operating room. It was apparent he had a strong will to live, and he refused to consider the fact he might lose his arm. She wanted to reassure him, but she knew the worst wasn't over for him yet.

Callie liked Sam Matthews. She enjoyed their camaraderie and his lazy Texas drawl. It reminded her so much of Galveston, although it had been many years since she'd been back to her hometown. Not since the day her father had been murdered.

It was still a painful memory, and she didn't care that the nuns had told her she must forgive the Indians who'd killed him. She couldn't. She hadn't even tried. And to this day she could not bear to remember that horrible day without tears coming to her eyes.

She'd been traveling with her father enroute to Galveston from San Antonio where they'd been visiting with her grandmother. The trip had been fun for them both but on the return journey, the Concord had been attacked by Indians and, after they'd killed both the driver and the guard, they went in pursuit of the coach.

"Indians! Lord have mercy, we'll all be killed!" the matronly woman sitting next to Callie cried, burying her face in her hands.

The brightly colored coach was the perfect target. Arrows thudded into the door, and one flew through the window and struck the man across the aisle in the chest.

Callie could still remember that strange, gurgling sound — as if the man's life was slowly seeping out through the hole in his chest—before he'd slumped over, blood trickling down the front of his spotless white shirt.

The three women were screaming; the noise and confusion and the Indian's war whoops were sounds that Callie thought she'd always remember. That and her father's last words.

"Listen carefully," Callie's father said, leaning over her and drawing her into the shelter of his arms. "The coach is a runaway, and the Indians will undoubtedly take over it any minute. I'm going to try and hide you. It's the only way I can think to save you."

Callie didn't want to listen, but he made her, and she promised him that she wouldn't make a sound. Tragically, her father wasn't able to save the other women—the Indians were delighted with their find after they'd converged on the coach—but he made certain that Callie wasn't captured.

He pushed her down in the seat, and quickly gathering their coats, he heaped them over her trembling form.

Even before her father leaned over and pressed his cheek against hers, kissing her that final time, shielding her as he'd done her entire life, Callie knew she was never going to see him alive again.

"I'll not let them take you, my darling child," he murmured. "Now close your eyes, and do not come to my aid no matter what you might hear. And remember . . . we shall meet again in a far better place."

The Indians came after the women first, and

44

dragged them out onto the ground as they pleaded for mercy. Her father tried valiantly to stop them, but he was no match for so many, and the savages easily overpowered him. Then, they made him stand and watch while they'd played out their brutal game.

Those poor women, how they'd begged and cried for a quick death, but the Indians, their blood lust aroused, only laughed and fell upon the women in a frenzy, intent on only one thing.

The coach was completely forgotten, and the horses, spooked enough as it was, bolted, carrying Callie away. She lay there sobbing, clutching the precious amulet that her grandmother had just given her. *Never take it off; it will always bring you luck.* Her grandmother's words had run in her ears.

The last thing she heard was her father's tortured cries. And she never forgot those awful sounds that drifted to her while she lay safe in her hiding place. She knew what the Indians were doing to the women, and to her father, how they made them suffer until the end, and she felt so terribly guilty because she knew they wouldn't reveal her hiding place, and that she would survive.

She didn't know how much time elapsed before a cavalry detail finally happened upon the runaway stage, and Callie was rescued. But they were too late to save the others.

The three women and Brett Angel had disappeared. They had either been taken captive, or killed, and perhaps what remained of their bodies had been carried off by the wolves and coyotes who roamed the area.

At least, this was the explanation the cavalry officer had listed in his brief report, and so the incident was forgotten, for even if they were still alive, captives were rarely found.

Callie had left Galveston right after the memorial services for her father. She'd been half crazed back then, and her mother, desperate to help her child recover, had sent her to the Ursuline convent in New Orleans, hoping the quiet tranquility and kindness of the nuns would help her daughter to recover from the tragedy.

Once at the convent, Callie found she didn't dwell on the past, and the nightmare scenes that had caused her so many sleepless nights began to fade. The quiet serenity of the convent, and the good sisters who had so lovingly taken her in, had become her refuge from the cruel world. It didn't take long for her to realize that she didn't miss Texas at all. One day perhaps, when the war ended and her services were no longer needed at the hospital, she thought she might return and face her past. She couldn't run away from it forever. And before she could go on with her life, she knew she'd have to come to terms with her worst nightmare.

Her mother had finally picked up the pieces of her life, and she'd recently married a military man. Callie was happy for her; she sounded content at last, but she couldn't bear to imagine her mother with someone other than her father.

For that reason, too, she thought it best to remain where she was, far away from the wild Texas plains and the memories that still haunted her. It was there she'd lost the only man who'd made life worth living. She knew he could never be replaced. She didn't really know how her mother thought he could.

Callie shook free of her brooding thoughts, and reached for the medicine bag beside her. Satisfied that Matthews was sleeping soundly at last, she opened it and withdrew a gleaming surgical knife.

She had to lance his shoulder at least once a day to drain the wound of any poisons, but she was grateful she could perform the procedure while he lay sedated, and hopefully, would feel little discomfort.

She hated inflicting pain, her hands were for soothing, healing. It was, Callie knew, what she'd been born to do.

Several hours passed while Callie sat, a cup of coffee in hand, her head nodding, allowing herself only snatches of sleep. Even in slumber, there was no escape from the busy ward that was overflowing with the wounded, and her sleep was disturbed by dreams. But this time she dreamed fitfully and awoke with a start to grim reality, and the moans of the wounded who filled the beds from wall to wall.

"And how is our patient, Callie?" The sweet lilting voice intruded on her silent reverie and the young woman couldn't have been more grateful for Sister Rose Margaret's timely intervention.

"I'm afraid he could be better," she replied solemnly.

The nun's round face sobered. "I'm sorry to hear that. I had hoped for an improvement by now."

"I know, and it's very frustrating Sister Rose. There's so little time to spare, and he's so weak."

The nun moved to stand beside the lieutenant's bed and immediately noticed his ash gray pallor. She frowned as she pressed the back of her hand to his brow. "He's burning up. I think we may have to summon the physician to examine him." She retrieved a cloth from the bowl of cool water and, wringing out the excess, she solicitously sponged his forehead. She pressed her cool fingertips against the feeble pulse at his throat. It throbbed weakly. "It's time we alerted the surgeon," she said. He hadn't responded to her touch at all.

Callie's fingers dug into her palms. "Please . . . not yet. There has to be something more we can do for him."

"There isn't any way we can spare them all, dear. The arm must be removed, and the sooner the better for this young man."

"I . . . don't think he's strong enough to withstand the operation," Callie said, her expression sorrowful.

Sister Rose placed a comforting arm around the girl's slender shoulders. "We'll all pray for him," she stated quietly. "There is nothing more we can do."

The nun studied her eighteen-year-old charge, the pained expression on the faultless features she'd come to know so well. Callie was unlike so many of the other girls her own age. She'd proven herself to be a tireless volunteer in the hospital, and one of the few Southerners who didn't seem to resent having to tend the wounded Union soldiers as well. The men were hurt — many far from home for the first time — what did it matter the color of their uniform? But the Federal administrators who'd taken over the hospital didn't always agree. They had made it a point to make the staff aware that the Union wounded came first and received preferential treatment.

But Callie insisted they should all be treated compassionately — whether their uniform was gray or blue — and she didn't care who disagreed with her. No one worked longer or fought harder for her patients' rights. There was something very noble about the girl, and Sister Rose was proud of the fact that Callie had matured into one of the finest women that she'd ever known. The Ursuline sisters stressed humility and love for one's fellow man, but Callie, always adventurous and headstrong, and a Texan by birth, was a staunch supporter of the Confederacy. Sister Rose Margaret had been apprehensive when the first Union patients had begun to arrive at the hospital, but Callie had managed to overlook her patriotic views, and had stayed on. To this day she'd never given the nun any reason to doubt her.

She loved her work and it was evident she was a natural healer. She wore an amulet around her neck that she told the nuns had been given to her by her paternal grandmother, a healer in her time. At first the sisters had been skeptical, and in the beginning there had been those who'd doubted her. But no more. It seemed the girl did indeed have the gift, and she wisely combined it with compassion.

This realization had come as a pleasant surprise to Sister Rose. For a long time after the girl had been put in her charge, she'd wondered if they'd made a mistake when they agreed to accept her. Callie had been almost impossible to handle back then — she'd been consumed with grief and bitterness — and she'd refused to accept direction from anyone.

In those earlier days, she'd constantly rebelled against authority, often donning unassuming clothing and climbing over the walls late at night, trekking unchaperoned about the countryside. The nuns were used to difficult children, but Callie was more than that. She was hurt and bewildered, and Sister Rose knew Callie might wonder if God had forsaken her.

The child's behavior constantly upset the Mother Superior, who'd finally thrown up her hands and had turned the girl's structuring over to the quiet, but equally willful, Sister Rose Margaret.

The nun had always had a special place in her heart for the sad-eyed little girl with the smoky violet eyes. So expressive and revealing, they were like windows to the girl's soul.

From the start Callie and Sister Rose got along famously. Yet, despite her chaperone's watchful eye and long arm, Callie Rae had still managed to slip away unnoticed, although she soon found she couldn't travel far before Sister Rose, astride her aging donkey, began scouring the countryside, leaving no stone unturned, even traveling deep into the bayou if necessary, in search of her wayward charge.

Over the years, the road that led into the bayou became a path the nun had frequented many times.

Callie acquired friends easily — with her outgoing charm few could resist her — and during one of her sojourns into the bayou she'd made the unlikely acquaintance of a Cajun woman who lived alone in a cabin next to the swamp. It was as if fate had led her there.

Of course, anyone who'd lived in New Orleans as long as Sister Rose had already heard the tales of the mysterious medicine woman who rarely ventured beyond the gray shadows of the bayou, unless she was summoned by some family in need of her skills. And the nun really didn't know whether she believed the stories of the woman of myth and medicine who was supposed to possess the healing touch, although the Creoles and Cajuns certainly did. But they'd always been a superstitious lot and knew who among them had "the gift," as they called it, and where they might be located.

Callie had been fascinated with the Cajun healer from the beginning, and Sister Rose had always known exactly where to look for the girl whenever she unexpectedly turned up missing.

For a moment the nun allowed herself to reflect back on her first introduction to Isadora. She hadn't quite known how to react when the eccentric swamp woman, with her tangle of black hair and soul-searching coffee-colored eyes had fixed her penetrating glare on them, declaring with startling certainty, "I knew as soon as I laid eyes on the child that she had the gift of healing in her hands. I've no doubt she'll learn the ways and save many lives."

Her hawkish gaze had riveted on the silver amulet that Callie wore around her neck and her voice had hushed. "Don't you ever lose it, girl . . . it is probably the most valuable possession you'll ever own. And it must be passed on when the time comes."

By then Sister Rose's gaze had flitted about the sturdy little cabin constructed from cypress wood, her sharp eyes cautiously probing every nook and cranny. After having made careful note of the ugly twisted roots that hung suspended from various wood beams, the jars of every size and description filled with dark murky liquid that seemed to move as if with a life of their own, the nun had snatched Callie by the arm. "Sweet Mother Mary, save us," she'd gasped, crossing herself. "'T'is the devil's work here. Come child, we're leaving this instant."

Callie, on the other hand, had stubbornly dug in her heels, and had admonished the wide-eyed nun. "Don't tell me you believe those old wives' tales, Sister Rose?" When the nun hadn't known what to reply, Callie had brushed aside her concerns. "Ask anyone . . . Isadora doesn't practice black magic . . . she does God's work, and we should be grateful instead of reproving."

"The child speaks the truth, Sister," Isadora had replied, smiling at the nun's dubious expression. Then holding up a small basket filled with suspicious looking berries, she said, "Look here, Sister. This is nothing evil . . . just berries taken from our myrtle trees. When mixed into a concoction, they ease all manner of pains. When the leaves are boiled for a tea it can be used to relieve a fever. Nothing the devil has a hand in, I assure you. But very beneficial to those who might be in need."

Then, setting it aside, she'd picked up a jar filled with a powdery substance. "Blazing Star, or Devil's Bit." She'd chuckled when Sister Rose had taken a cautious step backward. "Don't be alarmed . . . it is only the name that makes it sound like it was mixed by Satan's own hand," she assured the nun. "It can be used to check nausea and relieve pain . . . even want of appetite and dejection of the spirit."

She'd moved about the cabin explaining, showing, helping them to better understand her life's work in details. The nun and the girl had ended up staying for hours that day and, undeniably, Sister Rose had been as captivated as Callie by the fascinating things they'd learned. Later on the nun had become one of Isadora's faithful supporters.

Thereafter, Isadora had been an inspiration to the young Callie Angel, and over the years the tireless instructor schooled her pupil in the art of healing, as she herself had been taught by the generations of knowledgeable swamp people before her.

As Isadora had so wisely predicted, the slender young convent girl had found her natural calling. Since that time, Callie's life had taken a dramatic turn. Her burdens and grief eased, and the convent and Sister Rose had found peace of mind at last.

Later, as the word spread, it was always Callie who was called upon whenever Isadora was busy

53

elsewhere, to provide relief with a syrup for a bad cough, or a salve for a burn which, after treatment, miraculously healed and barely left a scar.

Callie apprenticed for many years under the medicine woman, and she never seemed to enjoy herself more than when she was with Isadora in her cozy cabin, practicing the healing arts.

It was the girl's healing skills that Sister Rose considered as she finished her shift and prepared to leave the hospital for the day. Callie walked with her to the front entrance.

"I've spoken with the physician who examined Lieutenant Matthews. He's scheduled the operation for tomorrow," Sister Rose explained gently. Noting the girl's bleak expression, she sought to ease her inner conflict. "The lieutenant won't survive without it, dear. There isn't any other way to save him."

"Isadora would know what to do," Callie stated quietly.

"I expect she might, child, but she is not here . . . and I can't let you take the risk of going to her."

The nun and the young woman lingered just outside the door for a moment. Sister Rose tried to bolster Callie's flagging spirits. "I understand how you feel, but the woods have become a dangerous place since the war. You know that as well as I do." She did not lecture, but she didn't like the grave expression marring Callie's smooth features. She knew it was difficult for Callie to stand by and watch so much suffering without being able to do more. But she no longer allowed her to make the journey to Isadora's. The bayou had become a haven for deserters with no regard for anyone but themselves, and with everyone desperate for money all manner of thieves watched the roads, waiting for the unsuspecting traveler.

Callie nodded solemnly. But she couldn't make her heart listen.

"Please . . . this is one time you just have to accept what must be," the nun urged, wondering if Callie even heard her words.

The young woman stood on the gallery as dusk settled, her gaze lingering on the nun's familiar figure as she strode briskly across the yard to fetch her little burro.

Sister Rose wasn't as young as she used to be, but Callie was glad that age hadn't seemed to diminish her spirit. Sister Rose was still a bundle of energy, and she kept busy at the hospital from dawn until dusk each day. Like Callie, she enjoyed helping others more than she did anything else in life.

Callie didn't think she'd ever known another more generous or loving person. Except perhaps for her father. He'd given his life for her, and she didn't ever think she'd forget his selfless act. But at long last she was beginning to forgive herself. The pain of his loss had dulled, but she'd always remember the special bond they'd shared.

Once she was seated sidesaddle, Sister Rose waved goodbye, and Callie stood watching after her as she rode off down the busy street, filled to overflowing with the noise and confusion of the Mardi Gras season.

For a brief moment, Callie allowed herself the

luxury of reminiscing about past years and how, when she'd been allowed to stay at the home of friends, she'd attended parties and enjoyed the Carnival festivities. Those had been such wonderful times. But no more, she feared. The South was never going to be the same again. So much had changed; she had changed. If experience were any indicator, she felt as though she'd aged significantly since the war had come to New Orleans, and she didn't think she'd ever feel young and carefree again. It was difficult to understand the political situation, why men were so intent on ruling one another, and how even the most gentle of men now talked of killing and conquering the enemy.

Troubled, Callie swung around with a sweep of her skirts, and pushed open one of the wide double doors. She stepped back inside, but as the heavy oak door swung closed behind her, she felt the hem of her dress snag on the splintered wood.

She knew she didn't dare make a sudden move. Just as she'd half crouched to free the fabric, a tall, intimidating figure swept through the opposite door and barely missed careening into her. She was caught unaware, and couldn't escape the long lean legs in dark blue.

It was as if her entire world had just been turned upside down as, with a small cry of distress, she stumbled backward.

Unbalanced, and teetering precariously back on her heels, her hands shot forward in a desperate bid to find an anchor. Instead, she grabbed hold of something that felt firm and powerful and muscular.

"Oh!" she gasped, her face flaming when she realized she was clutching a very masculine, well-formed shoulder. A deep voice came out of the shadows.

"You almost took a bad fall. I hope you weren't hurt?"

His hands had reached out from behind to steady her, and she gasped when she was suddenly whirled around and brought up hard against a whipcord-lean body. She struggled trying to free herself, too uncomfortable with that dark, dangerous-looking face so near hers. Her breathing quickened as she sensed the power underlying all of that firm muscle, and despite that cultured voice, she knew those compelling eyes weren't fixed on her in a gentlemanly way.

"I . . . don't believe so," she stammered, feeling suddenly woozy, as though the stays binding her rib cage were constricting her breathing more than usual. She was mortified when her knees began to buckle.

Feeling her sway against him, he said gruffly, "Christ, you aren't going to faint, are you?"

Dazed, Callie managed to shake her head. "Of . . . course not . . . you just startled me that's all." She'd never fainted in her life; the only thing she needed was for him to give her room to breathe. It was the way that those hands were holding her, and those long, supple fingers were pressed possessively against her skin, that made her feel as though he were doing something terribly improper. She felt herself gasping for air again.

Those all knowing eyes scanned her face, then lowered slowly to her heaving bosom, lingered, then inched their way back up again. "You seem out of breath," he drawled. "Maybe we'd better find a place where you can sit down for a moment."

Her gaze was ensnared by his, and she noted that he had the most beautiful eyes she'd ever seen for a man . . . midnight-black, glittering with a controlled sensuality. Caught in the flicker of the overhead lamp, warm amber lights danced in their depths, but failed to disguise the wickedness she noted behind that probing look. Oh, but he could be a devil, she just knew. Suddenly she felt out of her element and terribly confused as well.

"That really won't be necessary," she assured him, and instinctively took a step backward. It was as far as he'd allow her to go before the pressure of his fingers increased, and she knew she hadn't imagined that he'd stroked the smooth skin on the inside of her wrist. Her eyes narrowed. The situation was getting entirely out of hand. "I really don't need to sit down, and I assure you that I'm perfectly capable of taking care of myself," she stated more firmly, regaining her composure. She jerked on her imprisoned wrist. "Let me go, please."

She thought she noticed one side of his mouth curve slightly upward. It was decidedly suggestive, definitely not the sort of smile one should bestow on a genteel southern lady.

"I'll let you go, but first tell me your name," he ordered huskily, those fingers never still, igniting tiny fires along her skin.

Callie felt certain he was the type of man accustomed to crooking his little finger, flashing that lady-killer smile, and having every hussy in the Quarter ready and willing to go home with him. But all of that sensual charm and determined confidence was lost on her, she thought smugly, and in view of her impressions, she wasn't about to tell him anything about herself.

"Certainly not," she replied haughtily, "and I insist that you let me go right now or I'll . . ."

"Scream?" he finished for her, his lips quirking. When she tried to pull away he only settled her that much closer. "Surely you don't consider me a threat, *mademoiselle?* After all, I just saved you, and you must know a gallant knight never harms the lady fair," he said, those devilish lights glinting in his eyes.

Callie's wary gaze battled his. "I am not, nor will I ever be, the type of lady you're obviously fond of, sir," she replied, her voice dripping with sarcasm. "Furthermore, I am very busy, and I don't intend to stand here and waste another minute verbally sparring with you." Bright flags of color blazed in her cheeks, and her heart was thudding so hard against her rib cage that she felt certain he must hear it. She needed air. She needed to get away from him, but in her confusion she found she just couldn't seem to resist one last look at him.

Her eyes glanced upward, and she found to her dismay that she liked what she saw very much. He was a handsome devil, she thought. Lordy, maybe there was something to the way he crooked that finger after all.

Words seemed lost to both of them for the moment.

Her chin tilted higher as her eyes scrutinized his features in the shifting pattern of light and shadow. She was tall, but he must have stood well over six feet. She was amazed by his broad shoulders and the strength that seemed to emanate from his body. Fighting for control, she mentally shook herself and found she was standing eye level with a row of gleaming brass buttons. Yankee buttons! No wonder he didn't have an ounce of manners.

She felt his warm breath whisper across her lips and stir a shiver along her spine. Even though she'd lived a cloistered life at the convent she's interacted with all sorts of men through her work at the hospital, and she was puzzled that this one particular man should fluster her so. Perhaps it was the unexpectedness of that soft drawl coming out of the shadows that had unnerved her. It was so potently male. Everything about him was. And he was just as aware of her as well. Callie knew by the way his fingers had flinched on her arm that he had also experienced that tingle along every nerve ending. Although to look at him you'd never be able to guess she'd affected him at all. But she had . . . and she felt somewhat triumphant realizing it.

Uncomfortable beneath his close scrutiny, she finally glanced away. She could still feel her knees wobbling, but her insides were shaking even harder. She didn't know whether it was because of their collision or this unwanted, but undeniable, attraction, but she realized that he smelled wonderful, like fresh pine and the clear New Orlean's night. The heady assault was doing bewildering things to the sensitive peaks of her breasts, and to that other place she wasn't even supposed to think about. Things that shouldn't happen to a woman when a strange man puts his hands on her. Callie was absolutely aghast.

He had been studying her as well, and then suddenly, as if he found she didn't merit his flirtation, he released her with a soft laugh, and said, "Be on your way then, little miss, but remember the next time you're dashing through dark hallways, keep watch, for the big bad wolf may be waiting, and I don't have to remind you what he does with little girls."

Callie stared up into those wild, dark eyes and didn't think she cared to argue his logic. At that point she couldn't have even if she'd wanted to for her voice had fled along with her bravado.

Then he was gone, striding down the corridor before she could draw a calming breath, leaving her to compose herself before she tried to move. In the next instant, her eyes caught a glimmer of color trailing from his pocket and fluttering at his side.

That glimpse of lavender riveted her gaze.

She was so astounded she didn't once consider her own actions, and impulsively called after him, "Isn't . . . that my hair ribbon?"

She realized that other people around her had

heard so she stood there, utterly mortified by her outburst, and noticed two nurses observing her strangely.

She could only stare after the stranger's retreating back and long-legged stride, feeling as though a wild wind had just invaded her life.

Chapter Three

It had been a long and difficult day. By the time she had completed her duties for the night, Callie had regained a measure of her composure, but still hadn't managed to dismiss from her mind the embarrassing encounter with the Yankee officer. She'd never felt more humiliated. The feeling had remained with her throughout the evening, and she almost wished she might encounter him again, for this time she'd be prepared to tell him what she really thought of scoundrels like him.

Yet as soon as she began to imagine such a scene she shivered, recalling how those black eyes had undressed her and made her feel as though she'd been standing naked before him. Aghast, she experienced a frightening heat curl low in her belly and she had to press her fingers against herself to bank the flame. She knew she mustn't ever consider him again, but it wasn't easy to do. Be that as it may, she was finally able to put him out of her mind. Idle hands make for the devils' workshop, the nuns had always preached. Callie had never busied herself more.

By the time she'd finished lending a helping hand in the examining rooms, an hour had passed, and she was anxious to return to Sam Matthews' ward. Stepping over the threshold, she was surprised to see the dark-haired stranger standing beside Matthews' bed.

She thought it rather odd that a Union officer should have such obvious concern for a Confederate patient, but she could tell by the look on his face that he was undoubtedly distressed by the lieutenant's grave condition.

Callie observed him quietly, withdrawing to one side of the crowded room, pausing to fuss gently over another patient who had flung his bedcovers aside.

"I know you're uncomfortable, soldier, I'll try and get something for your pain." She smiled encouragingly at him as she smoothed the worn blanket over his thin body, her heart twisting when he managed to smile in return. They were so brave, and all so young. God, why wasn't there more that she could do?

He stared up at her with eyes glazed with pain. "Thank you, ma'am. I sure would appreciate it."

Callie went in search of a doctor and the one she found told her he was extremely understaffed but he'd examine the boy just as soon as he could. She knew that might well be a few minutes, or a few hours, depending on his priorities.

She spun on her heel, feeling more frustrated

than ever before. There just didn't seem to be anything more that she could do to alleviate her patients' suffering, and it was becoming harder for her to bear.

Returning to the hollow-eyed boy, Callie tried to reassure him. Needing to do more, she straightened his pillows and made certain he had a pitcher of fresh water at his bedside. As she tended to his needs she couldn't seem to keep her gaze from straying to the Yankee captain who was still at Matthews' bedside, his face set like granite.

She told herself it was only her curiosity that had drawn her back to him, but she didn't fail to define that he was broad of shoulder and narrow hipped, with a thick mane of hair that gleamed blue-black in the lamplight. He wore it a tad too long for her tastes, but judging from his profile, he wasn't altogether hard to look at. Dear God, she didn't want him to see her. That scene in the foyer had been embarrassing enough! Callie was just about to turn and flee when suddenly she froze. His head had swung around and she knew at any moment he'd see her.

Indeed, as if he had felt someone watching him, she saw his dark eyes shift and scan the crowded ward, never resting for long on any one person but carefully perusing the room. She recognized that he did this with a certain watchfulness born of war and of having had to make split-second decisions. She knew that at any second his gaze would pin her. She tried to gather her composure, but still wasn't prepared for the impact of those blazing jet eyes that bore into her with such force it felt like something physical passed between them.

Callie took a steadying breath and stepped forward. She had never been one to run from trouble and she knew just by the look of him that he could be trouble. She'd had that feeling ever since they'd collided in the foyer and she'd looked up into his starkly-chiseled face.

She drifted to stand behind Matthews' bed. Glancing down at him, she realized with a sinking feeling that his condition had deteriorated further. He wasn't even cognizant now of what was going on around him.

She glanced up and favored the captain with what she hoped was a calm appraising look. "Is there anything I can do for you, Captain?" she queried, forcing herself to be polite.

There didn't appear to be a flicker of recognition in his eyes. "Yes, Ma'am, there is." His words were clipped, and there was no warmth in his tone. "You can fetch Lieutenant Matthews' nurse. I'd like to have a few words with her . . ." He paused before adding tersely, "On second thought . . . maybe I'd like to have *more* than a few words with her if that's what it takes to get some decent care around here."

It was the disdain in his voice that made Callie flinch, and she could feel her face burning. How dare he! She longed to tell him exactly what a pompous ass she thought he was, but wisely, she decided to hold her tongue. He was a Union officer, and they carried weight in this hospital. She couldn't afford to anger him. He could see that she was dismissed. But she didn't have to take that kind of insult from anyone!

Callie drew herself up to her full height. They were standing almost toe to toe, glare for glare, although he easily towered over her. No matter to Callie. She'd had about all that she could stand for one evening. "Then you may as well just speak your mind right here and now, Captain," she disdainfully retorted, "because I am the lieutenant's nurse. Despite what you obviously think, he's getting the very best care I have to offer. And considering that this hospital is now run by a bunch of pig-headed Yankees who don't give a damn about anything but the color of a wounded man's uniform, it is a miracle that he's still alive at all."

She knew he would probably report her, but nonetheless, she was satisfied that her words seemed to have tied up his tongue momentarily. She was surprised to notice a glimmer of grudging respect cross his taut features.

He released a pent-up breath and some of his anger seemed to vanish. "Look, Miss . . .?"

"Angel," she supplied curtly, her features flushed rosily.

That seemed to give him another moment's pause. She felt the heat of his eyes as they assessed her smooth ivory skin, her flashing eyes, the prim way she wore her hair. She had a difficult time standing there while he studied her so intently, but she managed to keep her focus steady, determined not to weaken. She stared right at him, her gaze never wavering. His cold, impersonal eyes finished scanning her from head to toe—there was no heat in his perusal this time—and seemed to bore into hers before his eyebrow raised speculatively, and she swore he muttered, "Could have figured." But then she really couldn't be certain. His eyes were as dark as polished obsidian, and their challenging light never softened.

Callie's cheeks burned hotter, but she'd also noticed the lingering frustration behind that dark gaze, and understood well how he must feel. Perhaps his surly behavior was forgivable after all. Futility, anger, even hopelessness at times—these were emotions she faced here every day. He was faced with them now, and of course he was going to strike out at the first person he came across. She'd wanted to herself, many times, but propriety and her upbringing had never allowed her such a display of emotion before. Of course she'd certainly had her say today. Then, calling upon years of rigid training, she managed more calmly. "I wish there were more that I could do for your friend. Please believe that, Captain."

He sighed, and favored her with a weary smile. "I do believe you, ma'am, and I'm sorry you had to bear the brunt of my nasty temper. Sometimes I just get so . . ." his words trailed off, and he shrugged.

"Mad at the world you'd like to spit," she supplied with enough force to make him chuckle softly.

His smile widened. "I couldn't have phrased it any better myself."

He suddenly seemed less forbidding, and she thought perhaps even Yankees were human after all, though she still thought this one could use a lesson in manners. But this was the first glimpse she'd had of him without the pretense of flirtation between them, and it was startling how different a man he really was. "You should probably do that more often," she said before she could think to stop herself.

He looked at her questioningly. "Do what, ma'am?"

She blushed, but replied, "Try to smile. It's about the best medicine there is for whatever ails a person inside."

His eyes reflected a certain bitterness. The smile quickly faded and his mouth turned grim. "I guess it's something I've been finding harder to do in these crazy times," he said. Glancing over at Matthews' inert form, his face darkened. "And now finding Sam in such bad shape. I don't know what I was expecting . . . but it wasn't this." He swung around to look at her, seeking reassurance, but Callie couldn't give him any . . . she was fresh out of miracles.

"I know what you'd like to hear from me, but I'm afraid the news isn't good, Captain. You may as well hear it now as later. They plan on operating tomorrow. He's going to lose his arm."

"God, no . . ." he said, his voice hoarse, "There must be something more that can be done?"

She shook her head. "Believe me, he'll die otherwise," she said, and realized sickeningly how often she'd repeated those very same words—it seemed like entirely too many times.

The cloying scent of perfume drifted across the

room, and with it a soft feminine voice. "Rafe, darling, shame on you. I've been looking all over this hospital, and no one seemed able to tell me where you were."

Callie and the Yankee captain looked up expectantly. Callie noticed a flicker of annoyance cross his handsome features.

"What is it, Julia?" he asked, the harshness back in his voice.

The ravishing creature didn't seem to notice or care. She stood at the captain's side. She was diminutively proportioned and exquisitely beautiful. Her thick-lashed azure eyes sought his. "Darling, are you aware of the time?" She had barely cast Callie an accusing glare before she'd stepped between them and had rudely shown Callie her back. "We're going to be late for the theatre if we don't leave here this instant."

"I am quite aware of our plans, Julia, and I distinctly recall asking you to wait in the cab," Rafe shot back, frowning.

"You promised you'd only be a few minutes, and it's been over a half hour already . . ."

His cool look stopped her midsentence. "Go back to the cab, Julia," he ordered firmly, "and I'll be along when I'm good and ready."

In the next instant, Callie fully expected the young woman to stomp her elegantly slippered foot. But she must have reconsidered, and capitulated. "Oh, very well, if you insist," Julia replied petulantly. "But don't forget we're to meet the general in his box before the opening act. You know how

Father hates to be kept waiting."

She turned abruptly, and almost bumped into Callie. Bristling, her china-blue eyes assessed Callie reprovingly. "I hope you won't detain the Captain much longer, miss," she said stiffly. "Even *you* must know how difficult it is to get good seats during Carnival."

Her flippancy shouldn't have bothered Callie, but for the first time in her life, she became aware of the simple lines of her gown, her sternly backswept hair, and the fact that she hadn't even had time to run a comb through it since early morning. She knew she must smell of antiseptic and sickness, and she didn't like the way this woman made her feel on the defensive. Self-consciously she clutched the folds of her gown, remembering the rent in the material that she hadn't even had time to pin. But she managed to hold her head high. "I assure you, he's free to leave whenever he chooses," she replied coolly.

"And I will," the captain interjected, "Go on, Julia . . . I won't be much longer."

Rafe Santino had watched Callie's shoulders draw erectly proud as she'd squared off against Julia. He didn't know what to make of her at the moment, she seemed such a contradiction of emotion, but he knew one thing for certain. Sam had an angel in his corner—one who could no doubt give the devil his due—and suddenly, he just knew that his friend wasn't going to die. This sassy redhead was too damn stubborn to let him.

But it wouldn't hurt to speak with Julia's father about allowing him the use of the General's personal physician. Rafe knew he might raise hell, but he wouldn't deny the request. The General needed him to keep his spoiled daughter under control.

Julia wouldn't listen to anyone, and she generally did whatever she pleased. But she liked having Rafe as her escort — even though he'd made it clear from the beginning of their relationship that they'd never be lovers — so she behaved with him because she knew he wouldn't tolerate her highhandedness. She could have had any officer under her father's command at her beck and call. Rafe didn't really know why she'd settled on him, although he thought it probably had something to do with his indifference and the fact that Julia liked best what she couldn't have. She had everything else that money and her father's military position could buy. But Rafe had vowed she wouldn't have him. He was only involved with her because he liked challenge, and flirting with danger, and Julia presented a little of both. And he had promised her father that he'd keep an eye on her while they were in New Orleans; the poor man needed someone to help him out.

Turning his attention back to Callie, he never even bothered to watch the practiced motions of Julia's hips as she swept haughtily from the room.

He moved a few steps closer, and to Callie it felt like there were only the two of them in the room. Here, the silvery light from the moon poured through the wide windows and over him, defining high sculpted cheekbones and smooth mahogany skin. She was suddenly experiencing those same feelings that she'd had in the foyer when they had

72

been so close, too close, and her heart began to pound as before.

All at once she rather liked the idea of his having her hair ribbon as a keepsake of their first encounter—she'd considered mentioning it to him, but then she found she couldn't work up her nerve— and she'd thought of something else as well that almost made her smile. She rather hoped the hoity-toity Julia Davenport might discover the ribbon later, and wonder, and ask him. Callie received enormous satisfaction envisioning the other woman's face darkening with jealous fury, and could only wonder what his explanation might be. Who would he tell her the hair ribbon belonged to?

She was startled from her reverie when she felt the captain take her hand in his. Pressing it briefly to his lips, he almost made her jump out of her skin. "I'm sorry for having upset you before," he said, staring down at her. "I also insist on apologizing for Julia as well. She's had everything in life she's ever wanted, and I'm afraid it shows."

Callie's gaze met his, and turned smoky violet. *And does she have you as well?* she wanted to say, but of course she didn't dare. Instead, she tried to reassure him. "I . . . understand . . . and I know how upsetting it must be for you to come here and find your friend in this condition."

"Yes, it is. But I appreciate everything you've tried to do for Sam. I hope you won't hold it against him for having me as his friend." His eyes were smiling at her, and she couldn't help but smile as well.

"I think Lieutenant Matthews is very fortunate to have you as a friend, Captain."

"And you in his corner as well," he said, his words lightening her heart.

She felt mesmerized by his arresting jet-black eyes, and this more than before. She was actually beginning to like him, and it had been far easier on her nerves when she'd viewed him with disdain. "You'd better be going before you're late," she said, needing to put some distance between them.

He glanced hesitantly in Matthews' direction, but Callie quickly eased his concerns. "There isn't anything more you can do. I'll take care of him, I promise you."

He turned his head to smile at her again. This time his smile touched his eyes. It transformed his dark-bronzed face and eased that ever-present feral gleam from his gaze. "Thank you, that's good to know."

That look, that heartstopping smile, was electrifying, and his voice so deep and resonant. She knew she couldn't take another minute of their being in such close proximity. She just couldn't face the feelings he aroused. As casually as possible, Callie said, "Excuse me, Captain, but I really must see if I am needed elsewhere on the floor."

"Perhaps we'll meet again," he said, and allowed his gaze and smile to follow the gentle sway of Callie's skirts until she moved out of his range of vision.

Chapter Four

It was dusk; the work day was over; a throng of people left their work places, crowding onto the narrow streets; lamplighters went about their posts and Lily smiled as Rafe eased her onto her back and stretched out beside her on the bed.

Moonlight glistened on her soft full lips and bare lithe limbs. "I was surprised to see you again so soon," she said.

He placed a finger beneath her chin and lifted her face. "I'll be leaving again at the end of the week. I wanted to tell you so you wouldn't think I was skipping out on you without letting you know," he said.

"I'll miss you," Lily replied, "but then I always do."

Flecks of gold danced in his dark eyes as he watched her raise one shapely leg. The sheer stockings clung enticingly to mid-thigh, and she reached forward, intending to peel them down slowly. She felt his fingers exploring the soft scented flesh above the lacy garter. He caught her hand in his.

"Don't take them off," he commanded huskily.

"Why not?"

Lily noted his eyes followed every movement she made, and she felt as though she might melt from the heat in that dark gaze.

"Because I like the way they feel when you wrap your legs around me."

The stockings remained.

It was an evening that Lily was not likely to forget. She didn't question why he'd come; she didn't really want to know. She did have her suspicions. There was a hard tension about him, more than usual, and while their lovemaking had been wonderful, she knew he probably wouldn't come to her like this again. He might, in fact, have another assignment, but there was something more that would eventually keep him from her. A woman could just sense those things. And with a sinking feeling, Lily realized the undeniable actuality. He'd finally met someone else. If she knew him at all, though, he was fighting the attraction, and probably wouldn't even admit it to himself.

Who was she? Lily could only wonder. She knew it wasn't Julia Davenport. Despite her extraordinary beauty, Rafe enjoyed the company of women who had more to offer than just a romp between the sheets. He liked warmth, intelligence, and sincerity. Julia possessed none of those qualities. In fact, Lily felt certain he'd never been intimate with Julia. She knew him well enough to know that if he had, he would never have slept with her again. Rafe had this strange sense of loyalty; he was that type of man, and Lily knew he valued their friendship enough to tell her when their time together must end. She wasn't overly concerned that she'd have to give him up anytime soon, and she could only hope he'd visit her again when he returned. Perhaps she might worry if Rafe had more than carnal pleasure to offer a woman, but as yet, that was all he had to give. That, and his friendship, had always been enough for Lily. She looked up, savoring Rafe's handsome profile with her eyes.

Stretching sensuously, Lily abandoned herself and surrendered to the moment. She lay with her arms flung back over her head, envisioning silken bonds that agonizingly teased and tantalized, and softly restrained her. It was her own little fantasy, and she shared it with no one. Not even him.

"You set my blood afire," she sighed, eyes watching him explore the valleys and curves of her body with a connoisseur's skill. Lily followed his movements. The exotic contrast of his copper-hued hands slowly caressing her pale velvet skin caught for a moment in the subtle light, and she began to dream of different ways to please him. She wasn't selfish, and Lily knew many inventive delights to make a man feel like he was in paradise.

"You make me crazy when you do that . . ." she whispered, pressing closer to his seeking mouth. With a slight thrust of her pelvis, she moaned softly as his lips found the core of her need.

His warm breath touched dewy, pink flesh, and when his tongue penetrated her, the heat between her thighs burned out of control. No one had ever kissed her there with such exquisite thoroughness.

Her body began to convulse in shivers of passion, but then he drew back and wouldn't yet allow her to reach the pinnacle of pleasure she so eagerly anticipated. It was a ritual between them and, despite her whimpers of distress, she was enjoying herself immensely.

"Make me forget the uncertain tomorrows," she whispered.

He wanted to very much; he admired Lily tremendously. He knew he would never feel the kind of love that he should for her, love just wasn't in the cards for them it seemed, but Lily never really complained and he tried to spend as much time with her as he could. They helped each other to forget, to banish the pain of war and death and a future they knew was uncertain.

At the moment Rafe wanted very much to banish another image that had taunted him since their first chance encounter. But he couldn't. Even as he held Lily he felt guilty, because all the while he saw red hair as glorious as a sunset, wide smoke-violet eyes, and skin so soft a man might never tire of touching her. Sweet Angel. She'd made him feel things he'd forced himself to forget and had never wanted to know again. Deep, tender, disturbing emotions.

Go away, don't haunt me, he demanded of his wayward thoughts, even though he knew it was useless. He'd thought of little else but Callie since the night at the hospital. Thanks to her diligent care, Sam's condition had taken a turn for the better—the operation was delayed for now—but only time would tell if he'd continue improving. But Rafe still wasn't taking any chances and he'd prompted General Davenport to send over his personal physician. Of course, he'd done so strictly as a favor to Rafe. Rafe wondered how Julia would make him repay the debt.

Callie Angel—he'd learned her first name from another nurse—would never be the type of woman who'd put a price on everything she offered a man. But damnit, he knew it was Lily he should be thinking about at the moment. To make up for his straying thoughts, Rafe murmured words that helped absolve his guilty conscience. Lily was thrilled to hear his voice like a caress, yet oddly rough, and she knew he meant it as much at that moment as he ever would.

In truth, Rafe thought a lot of Lily, and he did consider her special. She could be a hellcat at times, but she continually risked her home, her happiness, and most certainly her life, to help people she didn't even know slip to freedom in the North. He had the contacts; she knew the shackled people. He protected her as much as he could, or as much as she would allow.

Lily didn't take kindly to having to live under a shadow of fear, she was about one of the bravest women he'd ever encountered. He had known a lot of strong, courageous women over the years and he never ceased to marvel at them. Such brave hearts they had, and they accomplished more with their quiet iron will than any ten men did with rifles.

He'd met Lily because of their similar views and, since then, he'd quietly helped her whenever she needed him. Lily's position, however, was becoming increasingly dangerous in a city with such single-minded patriotism. The North might have invaded New Orleans, but the people were far from conquered, and they condemned anyone who opposed their uncompromising opinions on slavery.

The issue over slavery was the most emotional of the war, and the dividing lines were clearly drawn on both sides. Lily had been a frequent face at many antislavery meetings, and he'd feared for months that she was becoming too visible.

Southern born and bred, Lily was a sultry beauty but she was no hothouse flower. She liked looking out for herself — and could, she'd reminded him often enough. As savvy as she was outspoken, she'd always believed — as he did — that no man should profit from the enslavement and misery of another. He knew that Lily didn't consider her activities disloyal to the South — she was a devout Southerner in every way — but she'd never owned a slave and she felt all people were equal. It was just as easy to pay a man for an honest day's work, and more profitable in the end, she'd said repeatedly, remaining undaunted by the furious outbursts such statements evoked from her neighbors. He wished he could remain in New Orleans on a full-time basis to better look after her, but duty called, and in his profession — he was a raider under General McNeal's command and fought wherever his type of skills were required — he'd rarely remained in one place very long.

These stolen hours, their mutual regard for each

other, were all that he could allow, and when the war ended he knew he'd resume his own cause once more. He'd come a long way from the man he'd once been, and he imagined that, should he return home, no one would likely recognize him. Not unless he grew his hair long once again and gave up his Yankee clothes.

And Lily? he wondered, gazing down at the pale blond beauty in his arms. What was going to become of her when the war ended? Suddenly, he didn't want to think of any of these concerns. It was the present drawing him, and the sensual smell and enticement of Lily's silken skin.

Lowering his head, a wave of black hair tumbling over his brow and brushing across her breasts, he kissed the valley between and felt his worries slipping away.

"Rafe," she murmured his name almost reverently, just the sound of it pleasing her and sending her pulses racing madly. "Please . . . I can't stand it much longer."

He knew that she really could, and would. His mouth and hands continued their languid exploration. Ignoring her soft protests his tongue caressed her breasts and nipples, until they became pebble hard and ached with sweet longing. She gasped, involuntarily arching toward him, certain she would burst into flame at any moment if he continued. But he did continue, much to her delirious distress. It was the most pleasurable pain she'd ever endured.

Rafe was a maddening lover, demanding more than she thought she could ever give to any man.

Yet, with him she found herself giving in; craving his touch, his hard body, allowing him liberties that she never had allowed to anyone, not even her husband. Every curve, every crevice, was his to explore. She yielded easily to his demands, and there was never any cause to wonder what he might think of her for being so hungry and in need when he came to her bed. He never rushed a woman, or left her immediately afterward. She liked how he held her and stroked her, making sure she was sleeping before he slipped out the door. Present company excluded, Lily hated goodbyes more than she did Yankees.

Rafe's arms offered her a wonderful haven from her dreary life outside these four walls. She did not really love him; could never love him in the true sense of the word, but when he left she would miss him. He was the only man she'd ever known who'd truly made her feel like a woman — whether in or out of bed — and for that she did love him in her own way. With some bitterness, she examined that thought. Did love even exist anymore? She thought not, for she believed the desolation and destruction of the war had stripped the survivors of emotions, leaving only death and despair. But she wouldn't be a slave to maudlin thoughts today. He was here at last, and knowing that it was only a matter of time before he'd leave her, for now it was enough just to be with him like this.

Sometime later, Rafe stood on the second floor gallery at the open French doors and listened to the sounds of the city. From outside the high walls of the courtyard he heard gay laughter, a foot-tapping melody strummed on a banjo, and above it all some religious zealot preaching of the evil and sin that festered in the wicked city of New Orleans. Despite the intrusive messenger and the ugliness of war, he found the city intoxicating, and marveled at how easily it could seduce him.

New Orleans, provocative and heavily perfumed with the smell of magnolias, beckoned him like a taunting lover. As did his thoughts of Callie. And he knew then that he wouldn't come to Lily again. It wouldn't be fair, not when he had thoughts of another woman. And he was definitely thinking a lot about Callie of late.

Beyond, the river, silvered by the moon lapped gently against the shoreline, and the throaty whistle of a passing steamboat echoed on the wind. The tightness in his chest eased, but didn't go away altogether. He knew what he wanted—another drink. Yet the half bottle of bourbon he'd consumed earlier hadn't relieved his mind of the nightmare visions and ghosts of war that faded with the daylight. As soon as he fell asleep, the haunting images came back to fight with him once again. He couldn't remember what it was like not to always feel tired and torn over his loyalties. The night air felt cool against his bare chest, but it was invigorating as well, and he stretched his lean muscled body in lazy contentment. He needed a drink and a good night's sleep, and he knew if he stayed here with Lily he wasn't going to get much of either. Lily's voice intruded on his silent reverie.

"Are you going to see your father while you're here? He isn't getting any younger, you know, and he's missed you, Rafe, he's missed you a lot," he heard her say from behind him.

He tensed at the mention of his father. "We'd only get involved in the same old arguments, we always do," he replied over his shoulder. "I'm tired of defending myself to him. As I imagine he's just as weary of having a son who's a disappointment."

"That isn't true and you know it," Lily said quickly.

"Well, I do know that he's never forgiven me for enlisting in the Union army."

"It was hard for him having to face his friends . . . to realize that his dreams for you were never going to be realized."

Pivoting, he saw that Lily was standing beside the bed, long silver hair flowing down past her softly rounded hips, the candlelight revealing lush blond charms barely concealed in a transparent wrapper of peach silk and French lace that had slipped off one creamy shoulder.

"I never did want his money or his plantation, and the only thing I did want, he couldn't give me," Rafe flared, despite his firm resolve to remain calm. "He's the one who insisted I go to Harvard to study law. I would have been content to attend the university in New Orleans, but he wanted me to obtain the best education that his money could buy." His expression darkened. "Well, I did. And I'm afraid I learned more than he ever wanted. I didn't know what a secessionist debate or the antislavery movement was about until I went North. Their message struck a chord. I could identify with their views, and I've always held sympathy with any human in bondage, whether they be white, black or red. My father never has understood, even though he claims the years that he spent with my mother and our people were the happiest of his life."

"He still loves her . . . I think he always will," Lily interjected softly.

Rafe's lips twisted and he said with irritable quickness. "He's never so much as mentioned her name to me, or spoken of his feelings toward Mother *or* me." He looked sullen and withdrawn, and Lily was sorry they'd drifted onto the topic of his prominent Creole family, who still lived in the Garden District on Philips Street.

"I'm sorry," she apologized. "I didn't mean to reopen old wounds. I just wish there was something I could do to end this rift between you two," she said. She didn't think she'd ever met two more stubborn men. It was the damned war, their differences of opinions keeping them apart. Her continual efforts to draw them together had once again been in vain.

"It doesn't matter. Not anymore," he said. "Nothing stays the same when there's a war . . . everything changes. The people most of all. If it hadn't been the war, it would have been something else that drove a wedge between us." He drew a deep breath and exhaled slowly. "It's getting late. I really should be leaving."

"Yes, of course," she replied slowly.

"I'm sorry . . . I wish we could have had more time together." He felt so very sorry for her, how terribly lonely and alone she was. But he had his own demons and he didn't think she deserved that burden. No woman did.

She read the unspoken message in his eyes. Was this his way of telling her goodbye. Lily's throat tightened. "I understand," she replied, and trying hard to keep her voice even, had to inquire. "Will . . . I see you again soon?"

"I don't know," he replied honestly. "My coming here like this is dangerous for you."

"Is that the real reason, Rafe?" Lily felt compelled to ask. She couldn't help herself. Her green eyes appraised his bronze back and the wide breadth of his shoulders as he leaned over and scooped up his clothing from the floor. A chill of premonition washed over her.

A log crackled on the fire and Lily flinched.

"See, my being here makes you nervous as a cat, you just won't admit it," he teased, trying to lighten the mood. He turned back toward her.

Withdrawing a cheroot from the pocket, she watched him place it between strong white teeth. He was purposely avoiding her question, but she would rather that than have him lie. Or perhaps even admit the truth. She wasn't ready to hear that from him yet. Forcing a brave smile, she said, "It keeps life exciting, darling. And I like danger just as much as you."

"That you do," he answered. Pulling on his trousers, Rafe left the top button incompletely fastened.

"But there's no sense asking for trouble, and I know a few people who wouldn't like the idea of your entertaining a Yankee in your home."

"But you aren't just any Yankee, Rafe," she said. "Besides, I never did abide with other folks telling me what to do." Lily's gaze readily swept over him, lingering, never quite able to feel satisfied unless she could touch him as well. Especially run her fingers through his hair. She did so love his rakishly long hair. Despite the cool evening it was still damp from their fevered lovemaking and gleamed like black satin in the wavering firelight.

Dressed in trousers and boots he stood away from her, in front of the French doors, and stared out at the misty wet courtyard. The flame from the match he struck against his thumbnail provided relief from the deepening shadows. After lighting the cheroot, he dragged deeply and filled his lungs with smoke before exhaling slowly.

The pungent odor of tobacco wafted through the room, the masculine scent dominating the scent of lavender and roses. But she did not mind. It had been too long since she'd spent time alone with him. However, Lily should have known her contentment would not last. The war and his duties always intruded and took him away from her.

"I could fix us something to eat before you leave. Are you hungry?" she offered, her voice hopeful.

He hesitated only briefly, then replied over his shoulder, "I'd like that . . . but then I wouldn't want to overstay my welcome."

Lily, ever playful, had other ideas. She sauntered

forward, hips swaying. "But, darlin', I've just gotten my second wind."

Rafe knew when Lily got in a mood, nothing short of a cannon blast was going to disturb her concentrated efforts. Thirty minutes later they sat together on the thick bear rug before a crackling fire and ate thick slices of homemade bread and cheese, sipping the vintage wine that Rafe had brought along. He managed to provide her with many fine things that she'd otherwise be forced to live without. It was his presence in her bed that she wanted more than anything; no man would ever be able to give her what Rafe did. He made the long nights easier to bear and her life less empty. Perhaps just one last go around on the sheets with him would keep her until she saw him once again. Lily's focus centered on that solitary button at his waistband that as yet remained undone, showing the shadow of dark hair in between. She couldn't prevent a smile as she found herself imagining her small hand sliding boldly under the waistband, exploring rock-hard sinew and muscle, stirring him to pulsing arousal once again.

"Is that a smile of satisfaction?" he asked, his dark eyes meeting hers over the rim of his glass.

She shook her head, the pale blond strands glinting in the firelight. "Anticipation," she replied throatily as she took his glass and set it on the tray with hers.

A smirk of acknowledgment played around his mouth as he leaned toward her. Noticing a droplet of red wine on her full, softly pouting bottom lip, he lowered his head. Long lean fingers reached forward and brushed the straps of her gown from her shoulders, spilling her lush rose-tipped breasts into his hands.

"Come back to bed . . . I want to touch you everywhere," she cooed, her fingers deftly working free the remaining buttons on his trousers.

Once more Rafe yielded, but couldn't help an inward smile. Perhaps the South had employed Lily as a sort of secret weapon? He didn't find the pace this gruelling even in the field, and it seemed she was intent on killing him before he got out of this room. But then he supposed a man couldn't find a more pleasurable way to die than with a smile on his face and a beauty like Lily snuggled up close in his arms.

Lily wasn't certain what it was that first woke her. Perhaps it had only been the remnants of a dream, or an unfamiliar noise that disturbed the silence in the slumbering house.

Turning over in bed, she reached out one arm, but the place next to her was empty. Rafe had gone. She really hadn't expected he'd stay the night, he never did. And she knew he'd wanted to be with Sam as much as he could. They'd been friends since before the war, and nothing but death would ever separate them for good.

Rafe always left without telling her goodbye. They'd made that promise to each other years ago. She never wanted to see him walk out the door, for she'd always feared if she had that image as a last memory, that he might not come back. A foolish superstition, but Lily remained firm in her decision.

She raised her head off the satin pillow. There was that sound again. "Rafe, is that you?" she called out.

Her bedroom door swung slowly inward. He hadn't left after all, she thought. Lily smiled, half expecting to see Rafe step over the threshold, and her lips froze. "You . . . !"

"Surprised to see me, darlin'?" The raspy voice came out of the frightening darkness, so near that she knew she didn't stand a chance of escaping.

The shadowy figure bent over her, and Lily clutched the covers to her chin. "Go away . . . leave me alone!"

Lust and death glittered in those eyes, and she knew what he meant to do to her. "Now that isn't any way to be."

"No . . . no . . ." Lily sobbed, eyes wide with acknowledgment and fear.

He grabbed both her wrists in one huge fist and forced her arms back over her head. Lily went rigid and could only stare up at him in disbelief. "I know how much you like to play games, and how you excel at everything you do." She could only stare as he began tying her wrists together. "Will you teach me what you've learned from him?"

After that, there was only the sounds of heavy breathing, and a violent struggle until the end.

When he'd first received Lily's handwritten note, Rafe had only thought of one thing. How fast he

90

might get to her house. The message had been brief but to the point. *Come as soon as possible. I'm in trouble and I need you.*

He knew right away that he would go to her. There wasn't any way he could not. But Rafe Santino had survived on his gut instinct for too long—it was the one thing he'd learned to trust despite everything else—and it was that part of him that cautioned him. He thought the situation over carefully as he stood outside of the LaFleur mansion. It was too quiet and still. The house was dark, and he knew he might be walking into a setup of some kind. Lily was involved with some shady people at times; any one of them could have turned on her.

Every nerve in his body urged him to turn around and leave. But he knew that no one had heard from Lily in a few days, not even him. He'd thought it strange. Now he knew that something wasn't right, and he couldn't leave until he checked and made certain Lily was okay.

He entered the mansion by way of the back entrance, and as soon as he knelt down on one knee and lowered the flaming match closer to the inert form lying in the middle of the kitchen floor, noting the awful bruises and the staring, lifeless eyes, he knew that Delcey's gay laughter had been silenced forever.

"What in the hell kind of animal would want to do something like this to you?" he groaned, then brushing the palm of his hand across her eyes, he closed them. Delcey had been Lily's faithful housekeeper for many years. She hadn't deserved to die like this, and his anger grew thinking of how she must have suffered. Then his thoughts abruptly turned.

Lily! Where was she?

Cautiously, but wasting no time, he searched through the first floor of the house. He found nothing. Taking the stairs two at a time, he bounded down the hall and into her bedroom.

The chamber lay in shadow, as the rest of the house had been, but he saw her lying there as Delcey had been, pale, lifeless, and his first thought was that Lily had met the same fate.

She was lying in the middle of the torn bed sheets, her wrists secured to the bedposts, and she wasn't moving. He grabbed the lamp from the table, lit it with shaking fingers, and hurried to her side. He saw with relief that she was still breathing, but unconscious and barely clinging to life.

Tenderly, Rafe brushed back the snarled silver tangles that had fallen across one pale cheek, and winced when he noticed the ugly purple bruise that had formed below her right eye and around her bound wrists. She hadn't given in easily, he knew, for she would have fought like a tigress. He untied her hands and lowered them to her sides, and it was then he caught the glimmer of brass in her half-closed palm; he retrieved it and held it under the light.

He was staring at it when he heard footsteps ascending the wide staircase. Someone was coming. And he knew what sort of position he was in.

"Lily! Lily, are you up there?" he heard a shout.

Given the dire circumstances, Rafe did the only thing he could.

He blew out the lamp and the room lay in filtered darkness. Only the light from the bright moon slanted through multi-paned windows that overlooked the grounds, and the sultry breeze stirred the frilly Irish lace curtains Lily had so prized because they'd belonged to her mother. A consuming black rage welled up within him. He wanted to find the bastard who'd done this to Lily, and he would, no matter how long it might take him. But he knew if he stayed here, they'd never believe he didn't have anything to do with what had happened here. Lily was a Southerner, and he was a Yankee. He'd obviously been set-up, and he had no idea how the cards might be stacked against him; what evidence might be planted here to incriminate him. Someone had gone to an awful lot of trouble to time everything so perfectly. Rafe looked down at Lily for a moment, then leaning over, he kissed her lips. "This isn't goodbye, sweetheart . . . we'll meet again. They're others coming who will take care of you, Lily."

Silently, he moved through the shadows toward the French doors, and glanced back only once, tenderly and with longing, before he quit the room.

Chapter Five

It was after midnight, and Callie had just finished her shift at the hospital. She walked out on to the street, her eyes drawn irresistibly in the direction of the bayou. The doctors had just informed her there was nothing more that could be done to save Sam Matthews' arm, but she wasn't ready to accept their diagnosis. Although her heart skipped a beat thinking of the perilous journey through the bayou to reach Isadora's, she'd already made up her mind she was going. She only had a matter of hours before someone would discover her bed empty and inform Sister Rose, but she knew she was the last hope Sam Matthews had, so there could be no turning back.

Callie quickened her steps, and by the time she reached the pony trap and untied Butternut's reins from the hitching post, she'd managed to reassure herself that she'd made the right decision. No doubt there would be the devil to pay if Sister Rose found out, but Callie was used to long hours spent in prayer. It seemed she was always seeking repentance for some infraction of the rules and, while she never looked for trouble, it just had a way of always finding her. Snapping the reins against the bay pony's rump she turned him away from the hospital and urged him along. "Hurry, Butternut . . . the sooner we arrive the better."

The little pony plunged valiantly onward, legs stretched out, his hooves flashing in the moonlight. The high wheels of the pony trap rattled along over the deeply rutted road, and Callie sat inside, praying she might make it there and back before anyone discovered where she'd gone.

Callie cautiously guided the pony over the winding road. Inky darkness shrouded the trail, thick stands of trees towered over her, and only the dappled light of the moon showed her the way.

They had gone another mile when Callie knew she'd have to stop and allow Butternut to rest before they went any further. She'd been pushing him hard and he was winded. Choosing a sheltered glen on the side of the road, she drew the pony cart to a halt. The smell of rain was heavy in the air, thunder rumbled in the distance, and the wind caught the strands of her hair and blew it around her face.

Preoccupied with thoughts of reaching her destination before it rained, Callie at first didn't notice that the pony had begun to dance nervously, his ears, which had been drooping listlessly only moments before, now pricked forward. She assumed the wind and the scent of rain in the air was making him uneasy. Stepping out of the cart, she walked around to pat him on the neck. "Settle down, boy, we haven't much farther to go and then I'll see that

95

you get a nice bucket of oats." Yet even her soothing hand couldn't quiet him, and before she could react, he lifted his head and nickered shrilly, the sound echoing through the forest.

Fearing he might bolt Callie grabbed his halter. Then turning her head, she caught a sound that chilled her blood. "Oh, God . . . riders," she gasped, recognizing the sound of pounding hooves heading fast in her direction. She knew she didn't want them to see her, and whirling, she quickly climbed back up into the cart. Slapping the reins hard against the pony's rump, she hung on as he bounded forward with renewed energy.

Callie braced herself as the pony cart careened dangerously around a bend on two wheels, but she didn't even consider slowing the pace. She could still hear the other horses rapidly approaching, gaining on her fast, and the awful truth assailed her. Whatever their reasoning, she knew they were intent on catching her.

Now muffled voices drifted through the trees. It wasn't a moment later that a trio of riders burst out of the shadows no more than thirty feet away, and she heard their triumphant cries.

"I told you I saw a woman!"

"Damned if you weren't right!"

"Well get the lead out boys, we don't want to let the little lady get away!" a jeering voice ordered.

Callie dared a frantic glance over her shoulder, and she realized sickeningly what they might do if they caught her. Her only chance to escape was to outrun them, but she was beginning to think that was wishful thinking. Reacting instinctively, she yanked on the pony's reins and turned him onto a little used path overgrown with weeds. They kept coming, and she knew they weren't about to give up the chase that easily. She urged the pony onward, but she really knew there wasn't much more that Butternut could give. He was tiring fast; soon they'd have her right where they wanted her.

They galloped into the night, and she was unmindful of anything but the exigencies of her situation, and the thought of what would undoubtedly happen to her once they caught her. Images of the night her father had died flashed in her mind and fear, building crushing pressure within her, kept her in mind-numbing flight. Glancing back once again she could see her pursuers, black shadows devoid of features, gaining more ground with each passing minute. With vivid clarity, she recalled the women on that illfated Concord stage, the way they'd been pleading in the end, and how, at first, the savages had taken care not to harm them. They had saved the women for after the killing, when the bloodlust had been running hot in their veins, and then they'd gleefully defiled them again and again.

"Damnit, I'm getting tired of chasing this bitch. Cut her off before she runs our horses to death!" a hoarse voice shouted.

They were right on her heels now. Callie's heart thundered in terror. They meant to close in on her and block her path of escape. Another mile dragged past, and Butternut was failing rapidly, his coat foam-flecked and his sides heaving from the exertion.

Suddenly, her worst fears materialized. She caught a peripheral movement. A horse and rider came at a brisk gallop, the creak of saddle leather and the animal's labored breathing, too close, too frightening, and Callie's hopes sank.

"There isn't anywhere to run darlin', so you might as well save us the trouble of chasing you down," the hulking rider taunted her, his horse's hooves sending spongy moss and mud high into the air.

"Go away and leave me alone," she hissed, frightened, certain there wasn't any way she could fight off three men and hope to win.

"Now I just don't think I want to do that," he sneered. He was wearing a tattered Confederate uniform, and dirty blond hair fell over one eye. She caught a brief glimpse of his profile, and shuddered when she noticed a jagged scar that marred the left side of his face.

In the next instant, tired of the chase and ready to claim his victory, her pursuer dug his heels into his mount's flanks, and the horse pulled ahead to outdistance the pony. Callie barely had time to react when he suddenly jerked his mount's reins sharply, throwing him against Butternut. The poor pony almost stumbled and fell, but Callie reacted quickly, yanking back on the reins to prevent their colliding with the larger horse.

As her wide-eyed gaze locked with her tormentor he gave a triumphant cry, and that awful, leering grin filled her vision.

"This is the end of the line," he snickered, moving in closer.

"Look . . . I don't have any money," she blurted, eyes wide with fear.

The other two riders had joined him. There was a man with a dark, unkempt beard, and the third rider was rail-thin, and had a gaped-tooth smile fixed on thin, cruel lips. But she couldn't seem to tear her eyes from the scruffy soldier who'd ridden her down. He was dirty and unkempt looking, and the puckered scar across his cheek gleamed pale in the moonlight, giving him the appearance of some frightening monster that prowled the night shadows. Her flesh literally crawled just thinking about these men putting their hands on her.

"It isn't your money we're after, sweetheart," the scarred man said, laughing, taking delight it seemed in how cornered and alone she appeared.

"Please . . . just let me pass. You don't want to do this," she implored him, trying to prevent her voice from wavering.

"Yeah, I do, gal, and there ain't no one around going to stop me neither," he retorted.

Callie shrank back against the seat. "I won't allow you to touch me," she said tremulously, her fear becoming almost overwhelming.

"Don't think you're going to be able to stop me," he said, eyes piercing her. "We can make this easy or difficult, it's up to you sugar, but there's no gettin' away. You see, the boys and me really don't want to have to hurt you. We been hiding in these woods for weeks now, and the gals we've had since that time

99

ain't nowhere near as sweet-looking as you." He swung down off his horse and strode purposefully toward her. "So I expect you're gonna fight us like a real hell-cat, but to tell you the truth, I'm kinda looking forward to the tussle."

Truly frightened, Callie shrank away from him, but in one quick leap, he'd jumped up into the cart and grabbed hold of her arm.

"Please . . . leave me alone," she pleaded.

"Now that ain't any way to be, gal." He jerked her roughly against him. "Just wait 'til you see what we got for you. You're gonna end up liking it real fine."

Callie's mind whirled. She couldn't believe this was actually happening to her; the one thing she'd feared the most and there was no way of escaping it.

"Guess this is our lucky day," the bearded rider chortled. "We had us a dark treat this morning, and now we get a little sugar tit before bed. A man just couldn't ask for much more."

Lusty laughter erupted. Sweat ran down into her eyes; her palms were so moist that she had a difficult time maintaining a firm grip on the leather reins, but she wouldn't relinquish them — she couldn't — for they were her last tenuous grasp on sanity. Instinctively, one hand pressed against her gown, where the amulet lay concealed against her breasts. She didn't know why, but she felt as though the amulet had saved her that one other time with the Indians, and she prayed it might do so again. Please, please, I'll never give Sister Rose cause to worry again, she pleaded desperately. Just make these men go away.

"Time's a wastin', sweetheart, and I can't wait to have you any longer," her accoster rasped in her ear.

When he tried to drag her out of the cart, Callie feinted right, and swung her arm as hard as she could. Her open palm cracked against his cheek, but he only seemed to take pleasure from her struggles. He grabbed her by the hair and yanked her head back. He was ruthless, hard, and she knew then her fate was inescapable.

"Go ahead and fight, but if you smack me again I'll crack your jaw for you," he snarled, spittle running down one side of his cruel mouth.

The skinny one tried to kiss her, and she bit down on his bottom lip. He fell back with a cry of pain. "The little bitch about took off my lip!"

The other two men found his distress amusing.

"She's a little spitfire, but that's all right. I like a feisty gal every now and again," the bearded man cackled.

Her assailants reminded her of mad hungry wolves. In a frenzy of lust they began tearing at her clothes.

She began to scream, but even that only seemed to excite them more, and as they pawed her, she began to grow strangely cold and withdrawn. Panic was beginning to overwhelm her.

Suddenly, a shot rang out, and at first, she thought they'd grown tired of her struggles and had decided to end her life. Paralyzed with fear, her head jerked around and she saw something that almost made her swoon. The threatening shadow of another man loomed ahead through a break in the trees that lay dappled with moonlight.

Callie was numb with shock, but she'd noticed that her tormentors were staring in the same direction, and their frantic groping had blessedly ceased. Her skin still crawled where they'd viciously mauled her, and her nostrils quivered at their revolting stench, but at least she'd been given a minute to draw an even breath. An ominous silence settled, but the atmosphere felt no less charged.

"I think you boys better let the lady go," the voice from the shadows demanded.

"Don't think we want to do that," the gaunt man said.

Another man quickly flung back his duster, his hand reaching lightning fast for the butt of his gun. Clearing leather, he snarled, "Yeah, like hell! We done saw her first and she stays with us. We might just have to kill her if you try and interfere."

"I don't think I'd try that," came the reply. "In fact, I wouldn't so much as move that gun hand another inch," the voice warned calmly, but there had been no denying the threat behind that cool exterior.

"And what if I do?" the bearded soldier taunted.

"Then I'll have to kill you."

Callie held her breath. Her nerves were at the breaking point, and her eyes strained to determine who it was waiting in the trees several yards ahead. But the darkness concealed his identity. Still, it seemed she recognized that voice. Or was it perhaps just wishful thinking?

"There's three of us and only one of you," the bearded man ventured. "I don't think I'd be making them kind of threats unless you're prepared to take on all of us."

It wasn't a moment later that her rescuer stepped further into the moonlight, and Callie gasped. He was dressed all in black, but there was no denying that raven hair blowing in the wind, or the deadly gleam in those dark eyes. She could only stare at him in wonder.

"I am," he drawled.

"Mighty foolish of you," the man said cockily, his gun clearing leather.

Callie screamed. The night exploded violently around her.

Men cursed.

Birds nesting high in the treetops winged upward in startled flight.

Finally, she heard only one man's strangled groan.

Staring in horror, Callie saw that one of her attackers, the bearded one, lay dead on the ground.

The realization snapped the small measure of control she had left and she began screaming, "No . . . please, no more killing!"

Numb with shock and fear, she spun away, and found herself running into the surrounding forest, wanting only to escape this place of madness and death.

Chapter Six

"Callie, darling, wake up."

She recognized the voice and knew that she was safe. Callie opened her eyes to find Isadora bending over her, her gaze shadowed by concern.

"I was beginning to worry," Isadora said, a smile lighting her striking features. "You were unconscious for quite a while."

"How . . . did I get to your cabin?" Callie asked, puzzled, not able to remember much of anything but those final, terror-filled moments when she'd been at the mercy of her assailants.

With Isadora's help, she sat up in bed. Everything was wonderfully familiar. Sanctuary and peace. Her heart gave a leap of joy.

"A friend brought you," Isadora replied, handing Callie a glass. "Drink it, *cherie*. It's just something to help soothe your nerves. It's exactly what you need right now."

Callie didn't argue, and when she'd finished the herbal brew, she handed the empty tumbler back to Isadora. "Is . . . he here?" she queried tentatively.

"Who?"

"You know who, the man who rescued me."

Isadora glanced away to set the tumbler on a bed-side table. "Oh, Pierre. *Oui,* he's outside." She turned back at Callie. "You were very lucky he came along when he did *cher.* Those horrible men learned a lesson they won't soon forget, eh?"

"Pierre?" Callie was beginning to doubt what she'd seen now. She could have sworn the man in the bayou had been Rafe. There were no two men who could look so alike.

"Oui, he is a good man, and he knew right away to bring you here."

"And what does my rescuer look like, Isadora?" Callie posed, somewhat bewildered.

"He's a hulking bear of a man with a round face and two chins that rival each other," she replied, smiling. "He lives about two miles down the road. I don't think you've ever had occasion to meet him before." She shook her head. "You gave me a terrible scare! I can't believe you would try and come here alone in the dead of night," she scolded, but there was no denying she was relieved that Callie appeared to have suffered no great harm. "Why did you, *cher?"*

Callie's heart sank. She supposed she could have imagined this Pierre as Rafe. But how could two men differ in so many ways? Shaking off her confusion, she remembered her mission, and replied, "I had to come. I need your help, Isadora." Feeling stronger, she swung her legs over the side of the bed and rose to her feet.

They stood together, one dark and mysterious,

the other all fire and willful determination.

"You still seem distraught, *ma petite,*" Isadora said soothingly, her caring hands reaching out to smooth back the snarled hair from Callie's face. "Of course I will do whatever I can. Now, tell me what it is that has you so concerned?"

Callie carefully explained Sam Matthews' dire condition. Isadora listened quietly, and after she'd pressed another cup of hot herbal tea into Callie's shaking hands and motioned for her to follow, she approached the long work table that stretched across one wall, and reaching upward, jerked a batch of fragrant leaves from the overhead rafter where they'd been hung to dry.

"Of course, I will do what I can, but there is never any guarantee." She sighed. "I wish these doctors would learn to trust us as well. We might be able to save more than we do."

Callie set the teacup aside, and joined her. "Please, let me help," she offered.

Isadora nodded. "Very well, if you're sure you feel up to it. I know you can't sit still when you have something pressing on your mind. You know what to do then." She'd already crushed the dried leaves within her palm, and had dropped them into a stone mortar. Picking up the small pestle, she began to grind them into flakes.

"I'm fine, and I'd like to help." Beside her, Callie had managed to calm her jangled nerves and was once more filled with renewed purpose. Opening an earthen jar, she scooped out handfuls of rich, dark mud to mix with the crushed mimosa leaves, which helped to minimize pain and inflammation. It was

106

effective in fighting the sort of infection that threatened Sam Matthews' life. Although Callie knew the physicians at the hospital would frown on this method, the Indians had successfully used the treatment down through the centuries, and she knew that they really had nothing to lose by applying the treatment, and possibly everything to gain.

Neither woman paused in their work, and finally Isadora swept the crushed leaves into the jar of mud, mixing the two as thoroughly as she could.

"I know you can't stay the night and are anxious to return, but I insist that one of the men go back with you," Isadora said. "Like Pierre, he is a man you can trust. You won't have anything to fear."

"Thank you, I'd be grateful for his company," Callie replied.

When Callie emerged from the cabin she heard the drums still thrumming in pulsing rhythm. Unconsciously, her eyes were drawn to a clearing in the center of the tall live oaks fluttering with Spanish moss, where a bonfire lit up the night shadows.

The air was hot and sultry, with the damp night mist clinging to the moss-draped trees. Reed torches had been touched to flame and flickered over bare limbs and writhing, twisting bodies.

The drums, pounding out a primal beat, seemed to stir something long forgotten in Callie's soul, and she couldn't keep her feet still, or her body from yearning for the freedom the dancer's movements suggested.

There were willowy forms, some dark, some light, circling slowly, their faces masked, their suggestive movements disturbing, but sensual and undeniably fascinating to Callie, who'd never seen anything quite like it before. The breath caught in her throat, and feeling Isadora standing next to her, quietly observing, Callie sent her a questioning look.

"It is the dance of life. The people here seem to know when one of their own is in desperate need. They hope to enlist the aid of the benevolent spirits . . . and after all, it is Mardi Gras, a time when anything might be possible," the healer explained.

"Do you believe in those superstitions, too?" Callie asked.

Isadora's expression was nonrevealing as she gave a little shrug. "I say if you believe enough, anything may happen . . . anything your heart desires."

Callie couldn't seem to shift her gaze from the dancers.

"The dancers make you think . . . and the drums make you feel," Isadora said, eyeing Callie intently. Then she gave Callie a hug. "I must leave you now. There is no time to waste. I must go find Jean Paul for you. Wait here, I'll be back shortly."

Callie had barely heard her. She stood feeling the dull throb of the drums, like a heartbeat, watching the fire blazing higher, hotter . . . the dancers whirling . . . sweat-sheened bodies surrendering to pleasure as they swayed against the backdrop of orange flames that lit up the night sky.

Her eyes flickered over them. A delicious quiver raced over her skin, and she suddenly felt this reckless and powerful yearning. Was it longing, or something more that had guided her to this place? It was an overwhelming feeling, and the only thing she could do was surrender to it.

Her gaze focused on one figure who seemed to move with such grace and surety. He was amidst the dancers, but there was just something about him that made him stand out among the rest. Wearing a black half mask, and stripped to the waist, he was tall, the muscles in his arms and legs rippling beneath bronze skin, and he danced fluidly, with slow insinuating movements and the heat of passion in his eyes. The firelight leaped along the length of his sinewy arms and across his chest, changing from light to shadow, light to shadow, and it was then she saw the scars striping his muscled arms and chest.

She was transfixed by his male beauty and the markings that seemed so out of place on such a strong body. She had the urge to go to him, to ask him, "Why? How did you come by those?"

His dark head rotated from side to side, and caught by the spellbinding drumbeat, he glided gracefully through and around the other dancers. He seemed oblivious to Callie's presence, or to anything that went beyond the fiery circle.

That strange, disturbing sensation returned, and she was all too familiar with it. The dreams, the encounter with Rafe in the hospital foyer, she remembered the same urge, the overwhelming and confusing emotions, and she wondered now, as she'd done then, why this should be happening to her?

Her breath suddenly catching in her throat, she observed a lithe, honey-skinned woman motion to him with her arms outstretched, firm, uptilted breasts, tapered waist and slender hips shifting sinuously. Surrender danced in her eyes.

Beneath her cotton shift, the beauty's skin glowed golden and bare and unrestricted. There was nothing to hinder her movements or desires.

But in looking closer, Callie noticed there was something disturbing about her as well. Something lay draped around her like an opaque shadow. The woman's long dark hair, silken as a spider's web, cascaded out around her, and it was then Callie glimpsed, or thought she did, the long dark shadow flutter.

When Callie finally realized what it was wrapped around her shoulders and upper arms, she almost turned away, but she was so stunned by the startling realization she could only stand transfixed as though caught in a spell.

A snake. A black snake clung possessively, tongue flicking in and out, and then it slowly slithered forward . . . over her right breast . . . her flat belly . . . its head with those eyes glowing red from the firelight, coming to rest against one bare thigh.

Her body trembling, Callie's gaze flitted back to the dark-haired man. He'd seemed to have read the message in the beauty's eyes, and accepted her invitation. Stretching out his hand, he caught strands of her wildly flowing tresses and laced it through his fingertips. He drew her into him, and she bowed her head as though in supplication.

Cupping her chin, he turned her face upward. He assessed her dreamy expression, and his eyes, his movements, seemed to be saying "Tonight is the night for secret desires . . . tell me what you want . . . tell me what you long for . . ."

Callie didn't know how much more of this display she could stand; it was obvious that the woman was dancing only for him now, and he only had to say the words and she would yield.

But suddenly, another man emerged from the swell of bodies, and pressing ever closer behind her, savoring the feel of her against him, and slowly, as if they were moving through water, the men enfolded her, pinning her between their virile hard bodies. Thrusting . . . parrying . . . luring her to surrender, they fluttered in the firelight like wild night creatures paying homage to the starry night and the bright full moon that had broken through the clouds.

Over and around them, the branches of the towering oaks, whipped by the wind, flailed frantically against a thousand stars, and Callie's fingers opened and curled, opened and curled into the folds of her skirt. She could feel their excitement, their heat, and the staccato drumbeat of her heart as her own breathing accelerated. She didn't realize she was holding her breath until it rushed from her in a rasping groan.

Moments later, the dark-haired man whirled away and disappeared into the heavily shadowed bayou. But she could feel his eyes, watching, waiting. And didn't she hear him calling her name?

Without thinking clearly, abandoning reason, Callie walked across the clearing. When she reached the outer circle of dancers he was waiting, and when she hesitated briefly, he held out his arms.

"Dance with me, angel," he said huskily.

"I'm not certain I know how," she said, but her

feet and body were already responding to him, to the night, to the allure of the drums.

Drunk on the emotion she felt pass between them, she seemed to absorb his thoughts, his passion, and their gazes locked.

"Yes, you do . . . you were born for a night such as this," he said, and his body encouraged her to follow, to let him show her the way. He held her lightly in his arms, but she knew he would let no other man intrude. She was his; the blood pulsed hotly through her veins and a quick shaft of desire pierced deep within. Between her legs a moist dew opened the fragile flower and invited his possession.

Gracefully, she began to glide and sway, head rolling just a little, her arms reaching up like slender reeds yielding to the summer breeze. Firelight hued her pale ivory skin a warm golden apricot, and when she undulated back, arching her body, her long crimson hair flowed like liquid fire, and her lips half parted in readiness. Her eyes were blazing with excitement.

He moved closer . . . closer . . . until she could feel desire roused, and the power of his strong body. Watching the play of his beautiful muscle in the firelight through slitted eyes, she felt heat overpowering her. It wasn't an unpleasant sensation, nor was the taut, painful aching around her nipples that seemed to spread throughout her body.

She knew things were getting out of control—at least out of *her* control—and she should stop this before it went any further. But she didn't want this moment to ever end, or the keening heat rising up within her to cool. This feeling was so new and went far beyond anything she'd ever known before. She wanted more and more—craved it like an opium addict needed the potent poppy seed. She wasn't certain what it was she wanted from him that might appease her, or perhaps she just didn't want to acknowledge it, even to herself.

As if equally powerless to turn away from her, her partner gathered her in his arms, and rising up on her toes, she slipped her arms around his neck.

"I . . . I shouldn't . . . be here," she whispered.

"Shhh . . . love, you aren't doing anything wrong," he soothed, "just think of the music . . . how it makes you feel . . . put everything else out of your mind."

That was exactly the problem Callie thought. It was his body, and her own, that were sending her brain all the wrong messages. Like touch me . . . hold me . . . show me what men do to women that ignites passion and forsakes reason. Her arms hugged him of their own accord and her fingers laced across the back of his neck. She kept trying to resist, fight the urge even as she leaned into him and pressed her swelling, throbbing breasts against that bare wide chest.

He dipped his head. "Kiss me," he ordered softly.

And she did, her lips tasting, her tongue boldly thrusting against his. She was drowning in emotion, and his tender assault only confused her. He taught her the age old rhythm that man had been teaching women since the beginning of time. At first, she was uncertain, fearful, and almost drew back. But his firm hands held her imprisoned, gentling her, deliciously kneading her shoulders, enjoying the warmth and the smooth velvet texture of her skin. His deep masculine voice murmured soft sensual words. Husky words uttered in a guttural foreign tongue that she could not understand, but that, for her, needed no interpretation.

When his mouth once again slanted hard over hers, and his teeth nipped her bottom lip, Callie felt the heat all the way down her center to her toes. She bit him back, not hard, but firm.

"Bitch," he breathed, but the way he'd said it made her blood heat, and had not been without affection.

Her head fell back against his shoulder and her head swam dizzily. His seeking lips, his skillful hands, told her everything she ever needed to know about this man. Locked in the protective fold of his arms, with her world draped in ghostly light and the rumble of drums blotting out everything but the soft sounds of their passion, it was like the residue of a dream that Callie never wanted to end.

Her world was spinning crazily and she could do nothing to stop it. Without her being aware, they had moved, and Callie's back was pressed against the trunk of a wide oak tree. She liked the way that he tasted very much, like warm brandy and cigars, and it made that hot sweet feeling in her secret place burn like a firebrand. Instinctively, her hips arched against him and something hard and unyielding pressed into the juncture of her thighs. Her breath almost left her. So this was how a man felt just before he entered a woman, she marveled, having never imagined that it might feel so consuming. There didn't seem to be anything that she could do to control her body's response. Her hips met his thrust and eagerly followed his motion.

"You aren't afraid?" he asked.

"No . . . at least I don't think so . . ." she breathed.

"Good." He nuzzled her neck. "Everything is all right now. This is how it's supposed to be between a man and woman. There's nothing sinful or frightening, and all men aren't animals like those bastards you encountered back in the forest." His lips moved over her skin, leaving her moaning softly, and he pressed his mouth along the curve of her neck, and lower still. His lips sought one pebble-hard crest through the material of her dress, suckling her, drawing her closer and closer to the flame.

She realized after a few moments what he'd revealed, and she drew a shaky breath. "It . . . was you who saved me . . . it was you." And she knew that he'd followed her to Isadora's and had kept her safe. Knowing that Isadora would never lie to her, Callie suspected that Rafe had had the Cajun man take her to Isadora's. That would explain why their stories differed.

Still, he hadn't confirmed her suspicions and he didn't seem as if he was going to. His tender assault began forcing every other thought but one from her mind. She gulped in a rush of air. "Oh . . . I . . . don't know if you should do that," she attempted to protest, but the flesh was weak and it felt so right to be in his arms. Her skin was on fire where he touched her, and she felt as though she would burst aflame if he continued. But she couldn't seem to find her voice again to tell him to stop. She had thought she'd feel fear the next time a man came near her. After all, she had almost been ravished by those horrible men, but with him there was nothing but a sense of calm, a feeling of rightness. An odd languor spread throughout her limbs, making it impossible for her to brush his hands away.

He framed her face in his big hands, and her eyes sought his. "You're not as safe right now as you think," he said, and he gripped her shoulders. "Tell me to leave you alone and I will," he ordered softly, but she could barely speak she was so overwhelmed by her feelings, by him. With a muffled groan, he cupped her breasts and gently rolled the sensitive nipples between his thumb and forefinger.

Spasms of pleasure stabbed through her, her eyes wide with wonder. "I . . . never knew it would be this way . . ." she breathed tremulously.

"Remember, love, and know it shouldn't feel any other way when a man touches you," he said, gentling her, teaching her, his hands, tender but demanding at the same time.

She felt the proof of his need rigid against her belly, and even though she really hadn't realized before tonight, just discovered that women, too, held a power over men. It was called desire. He desired her as much as she wanted him. The knowledge was as heady as his kiss.

A thrill shot through her. Bold as brass, Callie reached out and slipped an arm around his narrow hips, her own taunting him with the motion that he'd taught her.

"I think you may have learned the game too well," he gritted.

"I want to please you," she replied throaty and low. "Tell me . . . show me what to do."

"You really haven't any idea what you're saying," he said hoarsely. "And I shouldn't have started something I knew we damn well couldn't finish."

"Don't . . . please," she quickly objected. "Not now, when we've found something so wonderful."

A dark voice warned him he was getting in over his head. With Callie, there was danger of the worst kind. The kind that tore out your heart and caused unbelievable pain. He didn't want that . . . things were happening too fast, too soon. Once with her would never be enough, and he wanted her so damn badly it shocked him to realize just how much. Hell, a lifetime with a woman like Callie couldn't assuage his want and need of her. She was the most beautiful, desirable female he'd ever met. What would she do if he slipped his hand beneath her skirts and pulling aside her undergarments, cupped the tight copper curls he longed so to fondle, and pushed his finger up inside her?

He could almost feel her warm, wet silkiness; the tightness he'd encounter. His groin ached from just imagining what it would be like, but he knew this was something that couldn't happen. If he took her further, there'd never be any turning back. Pressing his forehead against hers, he swore softly under his breath. "Damnit, don't go confusing things on me. What you feel isn't love, angel. A man and woman don't have to share love to make love. But for a woman like you there can be no other way."

"Rafe . . ." she started to protest, and was silenced when he placed a finger to her lips. She swallowed, and realized that what he said was true. She didn't know exactly what emotion she felt or what her body yearned for, and being with this man, letting him kiss her, touch her anywhere he chose, was an indiscretion she shouldn't have allowed.

Callie suddenly felt confused again. The music had reached a crescendo, and the drums gradually played out, and stilled.

She heard someone calling her.

"Callie! Where are you, *ma petite!*"

"Isadora," she gasped, having almost forgotten.

His hands fell away from her body. "Go to her, angel, and don't look back," he told her, his eyes behind the mask, unreadable once more.

Callie ran to the edge of the trees, then hesitated.

"Go on," he urged.

Callie sprinted forward and never looked back, for she was afraid that if she did she might never return to the world she'd left. She'd go away with him instead. As she ran, his name whispered like a litany in her head.

Savoring the sound of it, even as she joined Isadora and the big Cajun trapper next to the pony trap, her heart sang and her lips whispered.

Rafe . . . Rafe . . . I know it was you.

There was no longer any doubt in her mind. She was in love with him.

Chapter Seven

The days passed in a blur for Callie. She spent long hours at the hospital, and almost every free moment she could spare away from her regular duties was devoted to nursing Sam Matthews back to health. To her joy, he was rapidly regaining his strength. Lately, she'd begun encouraging him to exercise, and they'd been taking short strolls around the grounds together.

The doctors continued to give her encouraging reports regarding his recovery, but not one of them would admit it was due primarily to her skill and dedication. That didn't surprise her, but it didn't matter to Callie. Nothing they said or did could bother her anymore.

On the other hand, Sam Matthews couldn't seem to stop singing her praises. He had told her how grateful he'd always be that she gave him the will to fight for his life. She knew it was only a matter of time before he was released, and she realized she'd miss his warmth and easy laughter when he was gone. He'd become a dear friend, and they'd promised to try and keep in touch with one another.

She was glad she'd kept busy since that night in the bayou, she thought, on her way to the Mother Superior's office. It prevented her from constantly thinking about Rafe, but she still couldn't help wonder why he'd suddenly stopped visiting Sam. It seemed he'd simply disappeared, and even Sam couldn't provide a clue as to where he might have gone, although he'd explained that Rafe had a tendency to come and go as he pleased, so he wasn't surprised in the least.

Callie was. After their shared intimacy, she had expected that Rafe would seek her out once again, gather her in his arms and tell her that he loved her madly and couldn't live without her. It irritated her that he seemed to have dismissed their encounter so easily, and she frowned in sudden indignation. There were other women, she'd known that beforehand, but she didn't want to believe that she'd been just another conquest like the rest, and as easily forgotten.

Pausing to rap lightly on the heavy door, she waited until the nun bade her to enter.

"Come in, child, and sit down, please," the Mother Superior called out, and Callie entered her office.

Callie did, but became immediately uneasy when she noticed the two Union soldiers sitting in chairs next to the nun's desk. Casting a furtive glance in their direction, she was startled by their silent, appraising looks, and she only wished she knew what their presence indicated.

Turning to the Mother Superior, she felt there was something wrong, yet she found no hint of trouble in the nun's eyes. "Sit down, Callie," the nun offered.

"You sent for me, Mother?" Callie inquired, gingerly taking the only remaining chair, staring at the Mother Superior of the Convent of the Ursulines with wide eyes.

The nun peered over the top of her wire-rimmed spectacles at the slender young woman. "Please, don't be alarmed, dear. These men just have a few questions they'd like to ask you. I told them it was all right as long as I was present. Do you mind?"

Callie shook her head, but she began to worry even more. What if they'd found out she'd been in the bayou that night? It was difficult to keep her voice level and her thoughts to herself. "No . . . of course not," she managed to reply.

"*Merci,* I assured them they could count on you for the truth," the nun said. Her long thin face, framed by a snow white wimple, was serious, but not unkind.

One of the men, the officer obviously in charge, introduced himself and went on to explain. "I'm Sergeant Major Allen Brighton, miss. I want you to know this isn't an interrogation, we hope you understand that?"

"*Oui,* I will take your word for that, Sergeant Major. Now, tell me, what is it you wish to know?" Callie asked him.

He nodded. "We have reason to believe that you have knowledge of a Captain Rafael Santino. We'd like for you to tell us if you've seen him in the past week or so?"

She was completely stunned, but she tried her best to conceal her frantic emotions. "I . . . may have, but I really know very little about him," she replied softly. There was a tense silence, and she sat feeling as though she were unable to breathe. Finally she managed to ask, "Something's wrong?" She quickly searched their faces. "Is . . . the captain in some sort of trouble?"

"He could be in a *lot* of trouble," the officer replied solemnly.

"Oh, my," Callie gasped. "But really, I . . . don't know him well enough to be of any help to you," she said, her tone now stiff and cautious. "I met him when he came to the hospital to visit one of my patients. He and I discussed the lieutenant's condition, and Captain Santino was concerned enough to check in on his friend a number of times until the patient's crisis passed. Once the lieutenant's condition improved and he was out of danger, Captain Santino didn't come around again. I haven't seen or heard from him since." She held her head high and hid her nervous hands in her lap. "That's all I can tell you."

"Don't know — or refuse to tell? Which is it?" the Sergeant Major interceded gravely, his expression tense.

Callie had heard the suspicion in his voice, and she began to realize that he didn't want to believe her. "There *is* nothing more," Callie stated, annoyed. "And I'd like to know before we go any further, why you are asking me these questions? I hardly think this line of questioning proper, gentlemen."

"We have a warrant for his arrest," came the flat reply, "except we can't seem to locate him anywhere."

"Arrest? You did not explain yourself to me, sir," the Mother Superior interjected, her hazel eyes shadowed by concern. "You should have informed me of

122

this before I called the girl into my office. I can tell you right now that Callie would never be a party to anything criminal. She is a godfearing girl with high morals and values."

"Perhaps . . ," the Sergeant Major said, "but this is a serious matter, Sister," he added more sternly. "The captain is wanted for murder, as well as several other charges, and we have reason to suspect that he might not have acted alone."

Callie blanched. What were they insinuating? And it couldn't be true—she didn't want to believe for a moment that Rafe could be capable of such brutality! "No .. that isn't possible," she stammered, and forgetting herself, shot to her feet.

She felt all eyes focus on her.

"The evidence we have certainly points to him," the Sergeant Major said. "We even found some of his personal belongings in the victim's room, and there's a witness who can substantiate our theory."

"Rafe wouldn't have any reason to do such a thing," Callie said, her voice rising angrily.

Eyebrows raised at her familiar reference, and the silence was sudden and meaningful.

"Rafe, is it? You just told me that you're barely acquainted with this man, so how come you suddenly sound as if you might know him better than you'd like for us to believe?" the Sergeant Major queried.

Callie swallowed. "Honestly . . . I . . . don't," she stammered.

His expression had become more doubtful by the minute. "I'm sorry to tarnish your image of this man, Miss Angel, but he beat two women so severely that one died, and the other has yet to regain con-

123

sciousness," the Sergeant Major stated bluntly. "A witness can place him near the house on the night in question. It seems the LaFleur woman has been involved in political matters of one sort or another since the war began. She had us fooled for a while helping those runaways and all, but we finally traced a stolen trove of religious artifacts right to her door—no doubt money she was planning on using to help the Confederacy. Of course, the treasure vanished right under our noses, right about the time Santino did as well."

He watched her carefully, and she had the feeling he knew something more that he had been saving for just the right time. She didn't have to wait long to find out. He cleared his throat. "You have a chance to prove to us that you have no knowledge of this man's whereabouts, and that you're not withholding any information. So, why don't you tell us about the night the two of you spent in the bayou?" he ventured. "And don't lie anymore about how well you know this man. We have someone who saw you together, and they're willing to tell us everything if you're not."

Who was this witness who seemed to know so much about her and Rafe? Callie felt like sinking to her knees and weeping in despair. The Mother Superior was staring at her as if she couldn't believe what she'd just heard.

Callie felt as though her life had just ended. Certainly, her reputation was ruined forever. She had never known a time when she'd been more humiliated. And if someone had seen her with Rafe, then these men were aware of what she had done that night, how she'd teased and flirted like some wanton trollop off the streets. No doubt, if she pressed them, they'd be more than happy to tell the Mother Superior every detail as well, although she wasn't going to offer them that. She'd rather go to jail than mention the dance and their shared intimacy; she considered it worse than facing a firing squad, and they would just have to hear the details from their own source, she would never tell them herself. But she'd tell them everything else.

Rafe had left her to face them alone; she didn't owe him any loyalty. At that moment she hated him for the shambles he'd made of her life. She would have to leave New Orleans; maybe she'd go abroad. God, why did it seem like she was always running from something? She stared at the soldiers, their somewhat triumphant faces, and wanted to turn and flee. Another sin to blacken her soul. How these Yankees loved to discredit Southerners whenever they could. Especially their women. Bravely, she held her ground.

Everyone sat waiting. She took a deep breath, and began. With each word the Mother Superior's face paled even more, until it was pasty white and lined with sorrow.

When Callie had finished, the two soldiers seemed satisfied for the moment that she'd been nothing more than an innocent bystander drawn into a tangled web of lies and deceit, but she knew what they really thought of her — how they imagined Rafe seducing her and then casting her aside. Despite everything they'd revealed about him, and even in remembering how he killed the man who'd accosted

125

her in the bayou, she still couldn't accept that he'd done such terrible things to those women.

Lily LaFleur, the woman who'd been victimized by him, was even now a patient in the New Orleans Hospital. Callie remembered her as soon as they'd mentioned her name. She tried not to recall the night that she'd been admitted, or how badly she'd been beaten, the vile way her attacker had debased her, but given the circumstances, it was impossible to dismiss from her mind.

Even worse, she didn't want to think about who it was the soldiers had accused of abusing her. The poor woman had been unconscious for ten days now, and even the doctors couldn't say when she might recover. Callie hadn't been the nurse assigned to her floor, but the incident was the talk of the city at the moment, so there were few details that she hadn't heard. She recalled the LaFleur woman's sister arriving from Illinois, and how she'd been keeping a constant vigil at the woman's bedside. It was such a tragic and senseless crime. Even Sam Matthews had been an acquaintance of this Lily LaFleur as well, and he'd been visiting her at least once a day, but he'd never mentioned to Callie, or to anyone for that matter, that Rafe had apparently known her as well. Was Lily perhaps the reason she had not seen Rafe again after she'd gone to the bayou. She'd also learned that he'd been visiting Sam on the day she was off duty. Suddenly, she felt like such a fool, although it was still difficult to reconcile Rafe as a killer. A more outrageous flirt had never been born, but he adored women too much to have committed this type of horrible crime.

The soldiers were brutal in their questioning. By the time they were finished with her, Callie was almost weeping, and every one of her dreams had been shattered. She had grown quieter and quieter under their condemnatory glares, and she couldn't wait until she could flee the room.

The Mother Superior remained outwardly calm, her hands folded on top of her desk, but Callie knew by the look in her eyes that she was terribly distressed and had lost faith in her.

When the Sergeant Major finally told Callie that she could go, the nun dismissed Callie without further comment. She sent her directly to her room, but, far worse, Callie realized later, she'd felt compelled to relieve Callie of her duties at the hospital.

The soldiers came to their feet, and Callie forced herself to move toward the door, feeling them watching her, knowing they suspected she'd become another of Rafe's women, just like the others, and pitying her for it. But they'd never hear her say the words. Her legs felt wooden as she walked away from them, and after shutting the heavy door quietly behind her, she sagged back against it for support.

She felt betrayed.

She felt violated.

The last thing the soldier had said was that there were going to be Union guards stationed around the outside of the convent, and she knew it was because of her. Everyone would wonder why, and soon, they'd all know. No, it was because of him this had happened, that deceitful Yankee! It was Rafe who'd left her reputation in doubt, and had deserted his regiment as well. If she ever saw him again, she knew what she would do. She'd gladly turn him in, and not shed a tear when they sent him to prison. He'd left without trying to warn her, with no concern for her welfare or her reputation.

She replayed the humiliating scene in the Mother Superior's office, and thought it would be forever etched in her mind. Her eyes glistened with unshed tears. She knew the Mother Superior would have little choice now but to inform her mother of this indiscretion — and the possible scandal that would follow — and she'd have to ask Estelle to quietly withdraw her daughter from the convent. It couldn't be helped. The Ursuline Convent could not afford to have their good name ruined because of her indiscretion.

He'd done this to her, and she'd trusted him! She vowed then if they ever met again to teach him that all women weren't taken in by his charm. She had not been. She had not!!

With bitterness, and perhaps a twinge of regret, Callie dismissed him from her heart, but she knew if they chanced to meet again, somehow, she'd make him feel exactly how she felt at the moment.

She sighed, and closed her eyes, trying her best to put the image of his face, his dark eyes, and the way his body had felt so right melded against hers. Salty tears slid from beneath her tightly shut lids, and she pressed the back of her hand against her mouth to keep from crying aloud. "Rafe . . . how could you have done it? Why did you use me?"

The Prophecy

"The only good Indians I ever saw were dead."
— General Philip Sheridan

"It is too late . . . We wish only to wander on the prairie until we die . . ."
— Par—roowah Sermehno (Ten Bears),
Medicine Lodge, Ks., 1867

Chapter Eight

The Comancheria

The shaman of the Quohadi Comanche sat before his campfire on the warm summer night, his hands folded across his chest as he stared into the roaring flames. It was the time of day when cooking fires sent up tendrils of fragrant smoke all over the village, but Owl Man, his extraordinary black eyes veiled with sadness, was too intent on his peoples' uncertain future to even give notice.

It seemed lately that everywhere he looked there were increasing signs of the white man, and although the Quohadi fought bravely, this enemy could no more be stopped than the wind and rain. Even worse, the People now had to battle another form of killer, a silent invader, yet another curse of the white man. Cholera, spotted fever, killer viruses. Diseases the Comanche had never heard of before, and this unwelcome visitor had stayed to claim more lives than from any warfare fought between the white man and the Indian.

"For the first time that I can remember my power and medical knowledge are not enough," he murmured, feeling bereft and isolated, even though the Comanche people went about their evening chores all around him. His family had been shamans for countless generations, but none of his ancestors had ever faced a more bleak future. He sighed heavily.

The year eighteen sixty-eight was proving a difficult one for the Quohadi Comanche, and he didn't know when they might expect things to change for the better. He did not like to think that old ways were finished, but the path for the future no longer looked as bright to him. Treaties had been made, and his people had tried to adhere to their promises, but the white man continued to enter the Indians' territory in violation of their agreement.

Since the close of the War Between the States, the Indians were facing increasing pressure to give up their old ways and conform to the rules laid down by the white man. They were constantly being told that they could not stop the roads and rails from crisscrossing their hunting ranges, and that they should accept what they could not change and learn to live like the white settlers, taking up farming and learning how to grow crops.

The Quohadi were insulted and outraged. They were not weak and blind like pups, but strong like the bull buffalo and just as determined to protect what they felt rightfully belonged to them.

In October 1867, the great council tribe had spoken at Medicine Lodge. The American Peace Commission, shielded by a large escort of soldiers in full dress uniform, sat among the many chiefs who were resplendent in their gaudy paint and costumes. The chiefs represented the various Indian tribes and they ratified a new treaty. So many of the People attended that at night the lights from their campfires glowed softly over the rolling hills for miles in every direction.

When the talks ended, and both sides had aired their grievances and voiced their concerns, the council had ten chiefs make their mark on a document presented to them. This treaty paper restricted the Kiowas, Comanches, and the Kiowa Apaches to a section of land so small that they would be able to do little more than farm for a living, which they knew nothing about and certainly didn't wish to learn. These proud men were hunters, and they were aware that the terms of the treaty excluded the richest hunting land, the Texas bison plains, which they rightfully considered as theirs.

The chiefs had only signed the paper in hopes of receiving promised gifts, but they'd never actually agreed to any of the other specified terms. This contract was also binding on over one third of the People who had not attended the meetings, or made their mark on the treaty paper.

The white man had promised to help the Indian nations to reform their ways and become more like civilized men, but the Quohadi, who had adamantly refused to attend the gathering, knew this was a lie. The Quohadi tribe had made it clear from the beginning that they were going to continue to live their lives as a free people governed unto themselves.

It was a brave decision, and the only decision as

far as they were concerned.

Behind the brooding shaman heat lightening flashed across the plains and the air shimmered in the wavering firelight. It was oppressively hot and the dust, carried on the incessant wind, covered the village with a fine, brown grit that stung the eyes and nose.

Willow In The Wind, the shaman's youngest granddaughter, approached his lodge. She was just returning from the nearby river and was carrying a buffalo pouch filled with water. Waving, she walked over to stand beside him. "Good evening, *Ap,* Grandfather. I have come to prepare your dinner."

He glanced up at her and returned her greeting warmly. *"Hi. Kaku, nei mataouo?* How are you, Granddaughter, my little one?" She was a beautiful child of twelve summers, with long straight black hair she parted in the middle and plaited into two thick braids wrapped in otter fur. A thin red line was painted along the part, signifying her long journey in life and ties to the Mother Earth. It also represented the woman's desire to be fruitful and bear many children. He remembered her mother, his only daughter, who had lived to bear only this one child. But she was a very special child, and every time he looked into Willow's soulful dark eyes he thought of his daughter. She had been a casualty of the spotted fever, and while it made his heart sad to remember his loss, he saw his daughter every time he looked upon Willow's face. So the Great Spirit still tried to give him a reason to smile.

"You take very good care of your old *ap,*" he said. "You are a thoughtful girl, and I know your mother would have been very proud of you."

He would never again speak his daughter's name aloud. It was considered taboo to mention a dead person by their earth name, but in the Peoples' hearts she lived on and always would.

At mention of her mother, Willow's face clouded briefly, but only momentarily. She was adjusting well to her loss, but she accepted that the hurt inside of her would never completely go away. "I enjoy looking after you, *Ap*," she said, and dipping her hand into the rabbit skin pouch that she wore around her slim waist, she withdrew a handful of the dried tree fungus that she had collected that day especially for him. "See here what I've brought you. I know how you never seem to have enough to treat burns and toothaches. You are a great healer, wise one."

Her thoughtfulness made his heart lighter. He indicated a place next to him for her to sit down. "Come tell me about what else you discovered today," he urged her. "What did you see and learn?"

She smiled. "I was hoping that you would ask me to join you for a while," she said, and happily folded her brown coltish legs beneath her.

They shared a meal together, and as the night deepened, the harmony of sounds that signified the day's end—the women's idle chatter, children laughing at bedtime stories, warriors regaling each other of their battle prowess—wrapped around them like a warm embrace.

The village quieted and settled in. Willow watched the smoke rise up from the campfire and drift away on the wind. "Our people are saying that

135

this summer has been the worst that they can remember. They say that many more of us are going to die from the white man's disease." She drew her knees up and wrapped her arms around them. "Is this true, *Ap?* Are we all going to die?"

A flicker of pain passed over Owl Man's face. "Every night I pray to the Great Spirit and ask this same question. I have pleaded for a sign that will give us hope, but as yet, none has come to me. I say, Oh, Great One, the women of my village wail for their dead husbands and children. The tree limbs in our burial grounds are bowed to the ground with blanket-wrapped bodies, and when the wind blows and the branches sway, you can hear the rattle of many bones. The white man's sickness stretches across the plains and will soon touch every tepee in our village. Please, Spirit, let me find a way to help those that I love more than life itself." His expression was long-suffering. "So far I have no answers, but I will never give up trying."

The child, aware of his grief-etched face, wanted so to ease his sorrow. "I'm sorry . . . I did not mean to imply that you were in any way to blame. You have done everything possible. It is the white man who are to blame." Her eyes sparked. "Black Raven says they are vermin and should all be killed. His way is right, and this talk of peace is foolish when everyone knows it is never going to be."

"It is all right to speak the truth, Granddaughter. I hear what is being said. The People say that if my medicine was still powerful I would have been able to save my own daughter. Since her death, they have begun to lose faith in me." His shoulders lifted; lowered wearily. "I really can't blame them." He glanced over at her. "But I think Black Raven speaks too freely of war. It is not easy to fight when the long knives are many and our warriors become fewer with every battle fought. I can only pray it is not too late for us."

Reaching over, Willow gripped his withered hand, and squeezed reassuringly. "As I do as well."

Moisture formed behind his hooded eyes, and he looked away. "Go now," he told her, his voice gruff with affection. "It is late, and I have yet many things to think about this night."

Realizing his need for solitude while he prayed, Willow reached over and picked up a fringed leather bag that belonged to her grandfather. She handed it to him, and from within it he withdrew a well-worn medicine pipe.

After carefully filling it with tobacco from a small beaded pouch, he placed it between his lips. Willow stuck the tip of a long stick into the fire until it glowed. Then she withdrew it to light the pipe. Owl Man closed his eyes, drew the bitter smoke deep into his lungs and exhaled slowly.

Willow In The Wind rose to her feet. "May the spirits hear your prayers this night, *Ap,* and bring our people hope for the future." She then quietly slipped away to her own lodge.

Owl Man studied the heavens. He puffed on his pipe and blew again. Afterward, he began his incantation. Far off in the rolling hills and winding canyons, coyotes bayed at the moon, and seemed to join Owl Man's prayer song. He implored the coyote to carry his words to the spirits. It was a good night to seek their aid. Everything pointed to the right signs. Mother Earth, Father Moon and the position of the stars foretold a prophecy that would be foretold. The old shaman was in no hurry. He smoked his pipe and waited patiently.

It was almost dawn. The man who had entered the quiet village without detection moved silently and with a warrior's practiced skill. He stepped into the light of Owl Man's campfire. When the shaman saw him, his eyes widened in disbelief. He hardly recognized him as the warrior he'd once known, but there was no denying his own flesh and blood. It had been many years since he'd walked this land, but at long last the spirits had brought him home.

"My eyes can hardly believe what they see," the shaman exclaimed.

"How are you, Owl Man?" Night Of The Hawk asked, waiting politely to be invited to sit by the fire.

The shaman studied him curiously, then he said, "Come, join me, Night Hawk, and we will smoke the pipe together."

"I would be honored to smoke with you," the warrior replied, and took an honored place beside the shaman.

"Night Hawk, my sister's son, we have not heard from you in so long that we feared you might be dead." He was studying him in the firelight. "Does your mother know that you have returned?"

"No, you are the only one. I thought it best that we talk first."

Owl Man picked up several cedar branches and

tossed them on to the smoldering fire. The flames crackled and sparks showered upward against dark clouds billowing against a gray sky. "It has been many moons. We have a great deal to discuss. A lot of things have changed since you last lived among us."

"Yes, I know, and I have returned because the part of me that is Comanche heard my peoples' cries and have felt their pain," the warrior said. "I couldn't stay away knowing this."

"The spirits led you back, Night Hawk. There wasn't any way you could have refused," Owl Man stated solemnly. "It is men like you that we need in our camp right now. For too long now, Black Raven has incited our young warriors to fight recklessly. Many good men have been lost in battle, their women and children left to mourn them. We need leaders who are powerful, but also knowledgable of the white man's ways. Who better to teach us these things than you?"

Night Hawk reached up and rubbed the back of his neck to ease the tension that knotted it. "It's been a long, hard journey back, *nu ara,* my uncle. I am not proud of the fact that it has taken me this many years to return, and I don't know if I'm ready yet to be a leader."

"Still, it is a wise man who sees his destiny, and accepts it. My heart has felt your pain as well. You shall have time here to heal, and then we will see."

Tormented black eyes turned to meet the old man's assessing gaze. "It is good to be home."

Behind the old man's impassive face Night Of The Hawk could see the joy. "Your journey may

139

have been a long and crooked path, my son, but you have returned as I always hoped you would," Owl Man said. "Your newfound strength will help your people in their bitter fight against their white enemies. It was written in the stars long ago, and now it shall come to pass."

Night Of The Hawk stared into the fire, his face immobile. "You have spoken to me of this prophecy before, but I have yet to see it come to pass."

Neither of them said anything for a moment. Finally the shaman spoke softly. "You have known for many years now the road the spirits have chosen for you to walk, but you always refused to let them guide you. It is time. You cannot deny what must be."

The warrior released a shaky breath. "My heart still bleeds for the loss of my wife. I made a promise to her long ago that no other would ever take her place by my side. She is the only woman I will ever honor. There can never be another."

"I understand your pain, but it too shall be eased if you will just open up your heart and set your own spirit free."

"I don't know if I can, but I want to," Night Of The Hawk said.

Owl Man quietly observed the warrior's turmoil, his dark eyes thoughtful. "Our people have always believed in your strong medicine. They have been fighting a losing battle for many years now, waiting, hoping that you would return and lead them from the darkness. I think they know that their old way of life is coming to an end. Those who are strong will survive to carry on our bloodline, but so many will die before this comes to pass that it will seem as though we are doomed to extinction. They are ready to face whatever must be, and I pray that finally, you are as well."

Night Of The Hawk had never felt so tormented as he did at that moment. A tremor shook him. As the sky lightened, he readied himself for the dawn of a new day, and thought about this, his home, and how much he loved it. The only way he would leave it again was when he entered paradise.

"I am ready," he said finally, resolutely. "I will try not to fail you or the People."

"Welcome home," Owl Man said softly. "I will give you all the help that I can."

Chapter Nine

Texas, 1869

It was not quite dark when the carriage drew to an abrupt halt and awakened her. In the early gloom of dusk, Callie, having slept little at the last stop the previous night, had snuggled into the soft upholstery of the carriage and drawn the lap robe over her for a much needed rest. She felt like she'd been on a never-ending journey having come from Paris to the States and then onward to Fort Benton, her final destination.

Since she'd left New Orleans, she had gone her own way, and had been residing in Paris with her Aunt Sophia, her father's sister.

Sophia — never one herself to adhere precisely to the rules of etiquette — was as carefree as a gypsy, and lived in a lovely old chateau just outside of the city. The indiscretion that had prompted Callie's dismissal from the convent was never once mentioned, and the girl was allowed freedom that she had never known before. Sophia reminded Callie so much of her father that it made the girl feel some-how closer to him, and she'd loved the memories that her aunt eagerly shared with her of their child-hood. Sophia did not have Callie's gifted touch, but she knew well the Aztec legacy that her niece was destined to follow. She understood, too, why Callie didn't fit in to the perfect little niche that everyone thought she should.

Sophia was like a refreshing breath of springtime as far as Callie was concerned. She encouraged her niece to pursue her heart's desire however she chose, and she never tried to dissuade Callie from studying the unconventional sciences, but thought it a splen-did way to expand her mind. Sophia, it seemed, was also a woman who chafed at the strictures placed on her gender, and defied them whenever she had the opportunity.

"Live life to the fullest," she would say. "And damn convention to hell."

In her eyes Callie could no nothing wrong. She absolutely never scolded or ridiculed and the girl had welcomed her friendly companionship and the exciting world that Sophia had introduced her to.

There were busy days under the instruction of her tutors, and then exciting nights when Callie had at-tended glittering balls and had mingled with fash-ionable society. To her surprise, her dance card was always the first one filled. For the first time in her life, Callie discovered how thrilling it was to be sur-rounded by ardent admirers. It did wonders for her crushed ego, and she was consistently the last to leave any party. Her fiery beauty seemed to capti-vate the handsome young Frenchmen, and she found their impassioned attention amusing. But in truth, it was terribly flattering and just what she'd needed to restore her shattered confidence.

Callie was to mature in those years, and although some of her defiance was tempered by wisdom, she had never been more independent and sure.

"We're here, ma'am." The driver her stepfather had sent to fetch her from the way station announced their arrival, popping his head inside the window.

Still drowsy and flushed from sleep, Callie stifled a yawn, and sat up. She'd come a long way from the naive convent girl. "Thank you, Private, you don't know how glad I am to hear that," she told him, then reached for her reticule to try and make herself presentable before her arrival was announced to her waiting family.

Smoothing the wrinkles from her dove gray traveling suit trimmed in black velvet, Callie brushed the dust from her skirt and sleeves, and adjusted her cape around her shoulders.

The door of the coach was opened. "Please, allow me," a tall, lean soldier said, assisting her from the carriage.

Clutching her carpetbag and reticule, Callie accepted his hand and stepped down. A brisk Texas wind stirred the thick red dust around her feet, and she smiled wistfully. "Some things never change," she murmured. Glancing up, she noticed at once the barren, almost bleak landscape caught in the last dying rays of the sun. It wasn't Paris, but it did feel rather good to be standing on Texas soil again.

"Welcome to Fort Benton," her driver said, and

handed her luggage over to another man who stood nearby. "I hope your stay will be a pleasant one."

Callie followed behind them, and as they drew closer to the small house that sat apart from the other buildings, the door opened, and there waiting, was a dark-haired Mexican woman, round as she was tall, her flat features and black eyes alight with pleasure.

"It is so good you arrived at last, *Niña,*" she said enthusiastically, ushering Callie, and the soldiers toting her luggage, inside. "Your *mamacita,* she been so worried about you." Her eyes widened fractionally. "You not have any trouble along the way?"

"No, everything was quiet," Callie assured her.

Rosita smiled. *"Bueno, bueno.* Now we can all relax and have a nice evening together."

Callie looked around at her new home. Candlelight glowed softly in the main room and flickered against cool adobe walls. It was furnished in dark wood, and brightly colored rugs covered the tile floor and hung from the walls. Near a fireplace at the far end of the room, were two deeply carved wooden chairs upholstered in leather, and on a table under the window sat a gilt-edged vase filled with wild prairie flowers.

The Mexican woman bustled about issuing instructions to the soldiers. After they'd deposited Callie's trunk and left, the housekeeper turned back to Callie almost shyly. "I am Rosita, and I hope you be happy here with us, *Senorita.*"

"It's a pleasure to meet you," Callie replied, "and I am glad to be home. It's been a long time, but I'm here at last"—her eyes brightened with anticipation—"and now I'd very much like to see my mother."

Rosita nodded, pleased. Then she barely gave Callie time to shed her cape, before she was ushering her along a dimly-lit hallway, and they were standing before a door, faint light spilling from underneath the frame. Rosita knocked softly.

"Yes, come in. Come in," a familiar voice urged.

Rosita opened the door, and Callie followed her over the threshold into a large, airy room that was furnished by a large four poster bed, a frilly-lace dressing table, two upholstered chairs, and an armoire. She motioned for Callie to step into the small room adjacent to the bedchamber. "She wait for you in there," she said.

Callie entered the room. With the light from a smoldering fire playing about the shadows, she saw books, wire-rimmed spectacles and reading papers littering a table sitting between two chairs. A thin, frail looking woman, a shawl draped around her shoulders, rose with difficulty from one of the chairs and extended her hands.

"Mother . . . how wonderful to see you again," Callie said, reaching out to take her hands in her own.

"My dearest Callie, I can't tell you how happy I am to have you with me at last," Estelle Grant said, the joyful transformation in her face as she looked at her daughter bringing tears to Callie's eyes. "Thank you for coming, child, I know it wasn't easy for you to leave Paris, but I do hope you'll be happy here with us. How splendid we'll be together as a family at last."

Callie leaned forward to press a kiss on her mother's pale sunken cheek. "Nonsense, Mama, I wanted to come . . . and I'm very grateful to the colonel for letting me know that you haven't been well lately." She studied her mother's face. "Why didn't you send for me sooner? I would have come home, you know that."

"That's precisely why I didn't. There isn't anything the doctors can do for weak nerves and a faint heart, although many have tried. They all have . . . even the priests, with their prayers and holy water, but nothing helps. I know how much you loved Paris. It sounded like you were very happy there with your Aunt Sophia. I didn't want you to return to Texas until you felt ready. And Fort Benton can be a rather dreary place for a young woman of your experience. I do hope you won't find it a stultifying existence once you've settled in."

"Oh, nonsense, my dear. Callie Rae is going to feel right at home here in no time," a stern, authoritative tone admonished, and both women looked up as Colonel Jeremiah Grant strode into the tiny room, filling it with his power and energy. His gaze did a quick assessment of the slender woman standing before him. "You're even prettier than the daguerreotype you sent your mother last Christmas," he said. "It's a pleasure to welcome you into our family, Callie Rae. I hope you'll be happy here."

"Thank you, sir, I'm sure that I will be," Callie replied, but she had her doubts. On the long journey by coach, she'd experienced some anxiety, but the trip had proven uneventful. There had been no signs of Indians, for which she was eternally grateful, but even in Paris the reports of the increased hostile uprisings following the war had been a frequent topic of discussion.

"My daughter Rosanne, should be along any minute," he went on to explain. "She's a few years younger than you, but I know the two of you will get on just fine." His brown eyes gleamed with pride. "She rearranged her room so there'll be equal space for you both, and she's talked of nothing else but your impending arrival since the day you sent the wire telling us of your decision to come home."

"I've been looking forward to meeting her, and you as well," Callie returned.

"Jeremiah, will you find out what time Rosita is serving lunch?" Estelle inquired. "Callie must be famished. I know the food at the way stations leaves a lot to be desired."

"Of course, right away," he said solicitously.

When the two women were alone once more, Estelle turned her attention back to her daughter. "I know how painful the memories are for you here. Tell me the truth, Callie Rae. Are you sure you made the right decision in coming here?"

Callie hugged her mother. "It's going to be wonderful, Mama," she sought to reassure her. "And I've been away far too long as it is." Leaning back and smiling at her mother, she added, "I'm here to take care of you, and I intend to have you back on your feet before you know it. Just you wait and see."

Estelle's face beamed. "Seeing you is the best medicine anyone could ever prescribe, darling. Now, why don't you help me to my feet and into the dining room? We'll have lunch together as a family."

Callie linked arms with Estelle, and for the first time in a long while, they were again mother and daughter together and looking forward to the future.

The next several weeks passed with predictability. Standing in the small bedroom she shared with Rosanne, Callie contemplated her newfound life. She'd managed to get along well with everyone so far, even her stepfather. Of course she couldn't forget that the women in his household followed his perfunctory rules to the letter, or that might not continue.

There was no denying that Jeremiah Grant was a strict authoritarian, his men could readily attest to that, but so far she'd avoided any unpleasantness by managing to keep her own usually outspoken opinions to herself. She'd been tempted to speak out several times, but she'd refrained for her mother's sake most of all.

Callie knew that Estelle wasn't a well woman, her heart was weak and she'd always been very nervous, which only aggravated her condition. Callie wasn't sure how much could be done for her mother, but she was determined to remain at her side, so she overlooked many of the colonel's shortcomings, and her own frustrations, and tried not to complain.

She looked up at the sound of Rosanne's voice. "What did you say, dear? I'm afraid my mind was wandering."

Rosanne's lips thinned. "I said, I don't know how

149

you manage to do it."

"What?" Callie inquired.

"Keep smiling while Daddy keeps pushing you."

"He doesn't really bother me as much as he does you," Callie replied, wondering just where the conversation was headed. She knew Rosanne well enough by now to expect she had something sticking in her craw that she needed to get said. She stood quietly, and Rosanne plunged ahead.

"He just sets my teeth on edge sometimes the way he treats us," she complained, sitting before her dressing table, watching in the mirror as Rosita arranged a coronet of shining brown curls on top of her head. They were to attend a dance being given by the officers' wives, and Rosanne was always the last one ready in their household.

Callie smiled indulgently as she waited patiently for the younger girl. The satiny skin of her shoulders and lush breasts above corseted peach silk were softly luminescent in the pale lamplight. She'd been ready long before Rosanne, but she'd come to expect the girl to take longer to dress.

"He's a man who knows his own mind," Callie exclaimed, "but I think he only wants what's truly best for all of us."

Rosanne's dark eyes, so like her father's, sparked. "Well, he's not going to tell me who and when I can marry," she pouted. "Roy wanted to announce our engagement soon, but Daddy forbade him," she said. "It seems none of us gets to do anything we want. Only what Daddy wants."

"You're still so young, Rosanne. Perhaps he thinks you should wait a while longer before you marry," Callie commented, trying to lighten the girl's surly mood. "You have plenty of time to settle down later on."

Rosanne glared at her. "I really get tired of people telling me I'm too young to know what I want. Just wait until you find out what he's got in mind for you as well," she blurted, and her expression had turned gloating.

"I know he is very fond of Captain Hamilton, and I expect he may have prompted him to escort me tonight. I don't mind . . . I like the captain well enough."

"For your sake, I hope you like him more than that," Rosanne drawled.

"Why?" Callie asked, puzzled by the girl's sudden smug expression. She reached for her lace silk fan.

"Oh, I guess you're the last to know. Daddy's seeking to match you with Captain Hamilton. He has the idea he'll make you a fine upstanding husband—one befitting of a colonel's daughter." When she noticed Callie's stunned expression, she said, "I told you how he is, now do you believe me?"

"But . . . I don't have any desire to marry anyone," Callie said, clearly dismayed. "And especially a man I don't love."

"Well, I do want to get married, but Daddy says it wouldn't be right for me to marry before you. I overheard him talking to Estelle the other evening. He's convinced the captain is the right man for you, and he thinks it's time you married and had babies instead of playing Florence Nightingale."

Callie's eyes narrowed suddenly. "What did my mother say?"

"She seemed to agree with him. I know she said she wouldn't mind seeing you settle down and have children while she was still well enough to enjoy it. I think she rather likes the idea herself."

"They have it all planned it seems, and no one even bothered to ask my opinion in the matter."

"I told you . . . that's how Daddy is," Rosanne said smugly, satisfied she'd managed to disturb Callie's calm demeanor for once.

Her toilette completed, Rosanne critically appraised her image, her fingers automatically rearranging several curls before she gestured dismissively at the housekeeper. "I think it will do, Rosita. You may leave us now." Turning on the round, upholstered stool she glanced up at Callie. "He doesn't like it that you've begun spending so much time at the hospital, you know. But since Doc would rather tend to the bottle than to the men, Daddy's been forced to look the other way and rely on you to take over his duties for him. It wouldn't look good on Daddy's record to have the soldiers neglected, and that's the only reason he's allowed you to work there in the first place."

"Rosanne, I don't think I care to hear any more of this."

A brisk rap at the door halted their exchange, and Callie was relieved.

"Yes, what is it?" Rosanne inquired sweetly.

"I hope you ladies have your dancing slippers on. The gentlemen are here to escort both of you," Colonel Grant's deep voice intruded from just beyond the door.

"Thank you. Tell them we'll be right out," she replied, then lowering her voice, whispered to Callie, a malicious glint in her eyes. "Just remember, Daddy is never indulgent, and when he is, there is usually a motive behind it. I love him — he's a good man, but he hasn't excelled in the military without having learned a great deal about strategy and silent maneuvering. Just don't you forget that."

Callie was to remember Rosanne's words, and in the evening that followed, she pondered over her future, and how she might avoid her stepfather's intentions for her. It seemed as though someone, usually of the male gender, was trying to orchestrate her life. And she was growing weary of their meddling. She really had no interest in marrying anyone as yet, even though she'd already had several offers from infatuated beaus when she'd been in Paris.

Captain Hamilton wasn't a bad sort, but he was rather dull compared to the other men of her past experience, and she could barely stand having him hold her in his arms when they danced. He talked of nothing else but his own aspirations to become a high-ranking military officer. She'd known after the first hour that she had to find an excuse to escape him or scream.

Finally, there came a break in the dancing. Some of the older ladies retired to the food tables to begin serving the sumptuous buffet, while the men stood in line to fill plates for their ladies who waited outdoors on the veranda, or sat on sofas and chairs about the room, carefully balancing their china plates on their laps.

Callie wasn't hungry and pleaded a headache, although she did assure the captain that he should go on and have supper without her. "Don't worry, Lance, I'll be fine once I get some fresh air. You go on, and then join me later on the veranda."

"Well, I am hungry, so if you really don't mind?" he asked politely.

"Not at all." Callie smiled up at him. "If you'd like you can bring me a glass of punch when you're ready to join me."

"I won't be more than twenty minutes," he said, and she almost breathed a sigh of relief when his hand dropped away from her waist.

After he strode off, she turned and slipped through the crush of people to the outside veranda of the officers' hall. She knew he'd probably become engrossed in conversation with the other men, and no doubt they'd discuss politics and lose track of the time. Indians and the sad state of the economy since the War Between The States were the favorite topics here. At least she could hope that it might deter Lance for a while, and give her some time to herself.

Even though she'd adjusted well to her life here, and had enjoyed quite a social life in Paris, she still found there were times when crowds of people became somewhat overwhelming and she simply needed to escape by herself for a few minutes where she might think without having to make polite conversation and dance until her feet ached.

Alone at last, she thought, the noise, heat, and swell of bodies on the dance floor momentarily forgotten. She stared up at the moonless sky and observed the stars winking brightly. Fireflies flitted past and crickets chirped in the nearby shrubs. A flourishing vegetable garden lay off to her left, and she was one of those who helped tend it daily. Fresh vegetables were hard to come by this far from civilization, and after she'd reminded the colonel of the health benefits, he'd agreed to their having a garden for the fort community. It had only been a small accomplishment, but in a settlement where men ruled by the book, she was proud of this small victory.

At that moment, she heard a woman's soft laughter, and Callie's gaze automatically sought out the source. A young couple stood some distance away from her under the trees. It was dark, and she barely gave them a second glance until she suddenly observed the young man grip the woman's shoulders and crush her against him in a passionate embrace. It seemed innocent enough, until she heard the woman protest, although weakly, "Darling, you know this isn't the time or place. What if someone should see us?"

But she still let him kiss her several times before she extricated herself from his arms, and then picking up her skirts, the woman hurried away from the scene and back toward the officer's hall.

"Serena, please come back, we must talk," the soldier pleaded impassionately, but she didn't pay him heed.

Callie was so stunned by this disclosure that she no longer stared after the man, but at the woman of his affection, and she realized shockingly that she looked very familiar. "Serena Richards, you little witch, just what have you been up to?" she wondered to herself. She followed Serena's hasty return through a side door, and could only wonder if the major realized what was going on right under his nose. Of course, it was common knowledge that Serena was nothing more than a camp follower who had somehow managed to charm her way into the major's bed, and soon after, became his wife. There probably wasn't a man in a hundred miles who didn't know her name and more, Callie thought, and it appeared that her recent marriage hadn't brought about any changes in her lifestyle. It seemed that she was still as free with her favors as she'd always been. Some women never learned.

Staring out at the yard, quiet now except for the guards milling around the gates and the soldiers going about their duties, Callie was caught in her unspoken thoughts, and the memory of another man and time. Despite her best intentions to forget the black-hearted scoundrel, she never had managed to completely dismiss every thought of Rafe. She wondered what had become of him.

No one had heard from him since that night in the bayou five years before. At least that was what Isadora had mentioned in one of her last letters, when she'd written with the news that Lily LaFleur—who'd recovered but still had no memory of her attacker—and Sam Matthews had been exchanging letters since she'd gone to live with her sister, but even they had no idea where Rafe might have gone. Although they both firmly believed he had nothing to do with what occurred at Lily's mansion that long ago night. But it seemed that many people in New

Orleans who still remained doubtful, felt rather certain that he must be to blame or why would he have disappeared?

Moments later, one of the sentries high on the wall fronting the fort, gave a sharp cry, and Callie was jerked rudely back to the present.

"Lone rider coming fast . . . It's okay, let him pass!"

The soldiers scrambled to swing open the gates, and Callie heard the sound of approaching hoofbeats, and a frantic voice.

"Help! I need help!"

Callie was down the stairs and running toward that wavering plea even before the lathered horse came to a skidding halt, and the dust settled.

One of the soldiers grabbed the horse's reins, and a lad of no more than sixteen slid from the animal's back, almost crumpling at their feet. Even in the moonlight, she could see that his face was flushed with fear and urgency.

"You have to get Doc," he gasped, pausing only to draw a quick breath. "My family . . . my ma and sisters . . . they're sick with the spotted fever, and Doc has to come back with me or they're for sure going to die."

Callie knew that Doc wasn't going to be of much help to him tonight, or to anyone for quite a while. He was on another drinking binge—no one knew where he might be found or if he'd even return—and it looked like this latest one was going to last for days. They had been expecting it, and the soldiers had warned her beforehand of the signs. She liked Doc, and he was a competent practitioner when he

157

was sober, but that wasn't a great deal of the time. Callie shook her head at the soldier who stood ready to inform the boy of the unfortunate situation. There wasn't any sense in making the lad aware of the hopelessness.

"You're from the Henderson settlement?" she asked the lad.

Tears glistened in his eyes, and he bravely willed them away. "Yes, ma'am, what's left of us. The fever hit us last week . . . took Pa quick, but the girls and Ma are fighting to hang on." He sniffed. "I don't know why I was spared, but I knew I couldn't save them on my own. They're so terribly sick . . . I . . . need help."

The soldier standing nearest to the boy patted him on the back. "Mighty brave of you riding through Indian country by yourself to reach us," he said, admiration and sympathy in his voice.

"I had to . . . my family's dyin', mister . . . and I had to find help," the boy said, his slender frame shaking with exhaustion.

Callie gripped his elbow and turned him toward their quarters. "It's okay now . . . they'll be taken care of. Now, why don't you come inside with me and we'll get you something to eat, and then we'll find a place for you to rest."

He tensed and pulled away from her. "Thank you kindly, ma'am, but I can't rest. There isn't a minute to spare."

"I know . . . I know . . ." she repeated soothingly, "but you won't do them a bit of good if you fall over where you stand. I promise you I'll see that they receive medical attention, but only if you come with me now without a fuss."

Solemnly, and with reluctance, he followed her quickened stride to the house.

Later, placing him in quarantine, she'd made him promise to remain at the fort under Rosita's watchful eyes until they made certain he wasn't carrying the disease. He glowered at her, but finally he'd agreed if Callie would see that his family was taken care of properly

Callie lay in her bed that night and worried over what she knew she must do. A family was in distress, and there wasn't anyone else who possessed enough medical knowledge to save them but her. Doc might have been able to help, but where was he? Dear God, she didn't want to travel the outskirts of the Llano Estacado in order to reach the Henderson settlement, but she was beginning to think she would have to.

Indians . . . their image taunted her, frightened her, and almost made her think of telling the boy the situation couldn't be helped. But she remembered his desperation, how much he feared for his mother's and sisters' lives.

"Callie . . . you have to go," she prompted herself. "You don't have any other choice." But within, a voice cried out in fear.

Chapter Ten

*The early morning mist swirled and sifted through
the undulating sea of buffalo grass . . .*

*In its midst, a bronzed mass of bodies, feathers
bobbing and rimming their lances, rode beneath the
pastel of sunrise at a steadied pace . . .*

The flame-haired beauty seated in the colonel's
prized black landau, blinked in surprise, the flurry
of movement riveting her gaze. Suddenly, her throat
felt cottony. What was that out there? Lifting one
hand, shading her eyes against the rising sun, she
scanned the brightening horizon uneasily. And saw
nothing.

Whatever she'd imagined had been there, seemed
to have vanished, and there was nothing but the early
morning sun peeking welcomingly through low-ly-
ing clouds and gilding the leaves of the pecan trees.
Just a trick of the eyes, nothing more, she told herself, a frown of anxiety still knitting her brow. There
was no denying that Indians were a constant worry,
but she tried to remember that she had the colonel's
best men accompanying her, and they were experi-

enced Indian fighters. With the threat of hostile attacks an ongoing concern, the colonel had tried to discourage Callie from making the arduous journey to the Hendersons', but she had been adamant, reminding him it was a life or death mission, and in all good conscience they could not ignore their plight.

To her surprise, Captain Hamilton had agreed and offered to personally escort her. Finally, the colonel had relented, but he had insisted they travel under guard, and to insure their safety, he had assigned a heavily-armed detail of soldiers to ride with them.

"Is anything the matter Callie?" The captain's soft inquiry intruded on her thoughts, and she swung around to gaze at him.

"No . . . at least I don't think so," she replied somewhat hesitantly.

"All that talk last night at the dance about the Comanche in the area have you a bit on edge?"

She smiled sheepishly. "A little I guess. I keep remembering the colonel saying that just because you don't actually see Indians doesn't mean they're not around."

"That's true enough, I suppose, but I have our best scout riding point. The Comanche won't get past him without our knowing about it."

"That's reassuring to hear," she replied. Still, her adrenaline kept flowing, and with her eyes slightly narrowed, she searched the distant hills one last time. She then acknowledged to herself that the captain had been right; there wasn't anything for her to be concerned about. She had only been imagining she'd seen something.

His gaze had followed hers, and his mouth spread

into a wide grin. "See . . . nothing. Now will you quit worrying so much and just sit back and enjoy this fine day."

Callie smiled apologetically. "I'm sorry. I must sound like I don't have much faith in you or your men."

"You don't have to apologize, Callie. I understand exactly how you feel," he said. "This country seems even bigger and wilder beyond the walls. Even when you get used to it, you can be out here, and suddenly you start feeling as though it's going to swallow you up the deeper you go. Makes you begin to wonder if anyone will ever find a trace of you again."

She laughed lightly. "I don't think I could have said it better myself. I guess you do understand after all."

"Sure I do. You aren't the only one who's ever gotten the jitters out here," he said. "But then they tell me a man's dreams are always bigger and better in Texas." He chuckled softly. "I suppose a woman's can be, too, but as a rule, most of the gals I know don't dream about anything but getting married and having babies."

"Perhaps . . . but there *are* exceptions to the rule," she countered.

A flush crept up Lance's neck. "Ahhh, yes, there are indeed," he stated wistfully, glancing at her out of the corner of his eye.

"I've never tried to hide the fact," she retorted defensively.

His head swiveled, and he stared down at her until Callie shifted uncomfortably in her seat.

"I have to say you are the most intriguing woman

I've ever met Callie Rae," he said. "But I hope you won't make me wait forever to set our wedding date."

Lance had been pressuring her to marry him since the colonel had given him permission to court her, but her resistance to settling down in wedded bliss was as strong as ever.

"Guess I've gone and said the wrong thing again," he gritted.

She shrugged. "Not really. Your thinking isn't any different than the rest of the men in the world. I don't know a man yet who doesn't believe every female has her heart set on getting married even before she's out of the cradle. You're just frank enough to say what's on your mind," she said smoothly.

He winced. "Ouch! My big foot isn't feeling real comfortable in my mouth right at the moment. All I want to know is if you think we might get married sometime in the near future?"

At the moment she had other concerns, and she just didn't feel like being pressured. Now she understood why Lance had offered to accompany her today. "I don't even know yet if I want to remain in Texas, Lance. I'd like to wait before I make a serious commitment . . . see if I fit in . . . if there's a place for me."

His brows furrowed. "I've already told you, there is as my wife."

She cleared her throat. "You're a fine man, Lance, but just being someone's partner in marriage won't be enough for me. I have dreams, Lance, just like you, and — "

His grin was almost too cocky. "I know. I know. You want to have your own medical practice someday. Well I have to hand it to you, Callie, that is about the biggest dream I've heard come out of Texas so far."

"*Yes* that's exactly what I want," she replied, bristling.

He ignored her censure, and said softly, hopefully, "I'm not a patient man. Don't make me wait forever."

Their eyes locked for several moments, and she had the strangest sensation that he was going to lean over and kiss her. Then she almost shook her head at the thought. The sun must be getting to her. The captain would never do anything so impulsive, and despite the brief flare of heat in his eyes, he wouldn't make any sudden overtures toward her. She didn't know why, but she almost wished he'd step out of character for once and do something she didn't expect. Grab her, kiss her madly, make her head spin from his heady assault, anything. He was so predictable, so controlled. Why couldn't he be just a little reckless, maybe even daring; and then her pulses quickened as she caught herself remembering the wicked gleam in another man's jet-black eyes and the hard angles of his mouth. *He'd* been reckless. *He'd* been daring. And she'd do well to remember what her association with him had cost her. To her dismay, her limbs grew weak and her heart fluttered as Callie trembled with the acknowledgment.

Starling her, Lance queried, "Callie, are you all right? Did I upset you?"

She hadn't noticed that her thoughts had been drifting again. The past faded and blended back into the present. Guiltily, her eyes focused on Lance once again and she tried to smile kindly. "I'm fine. I just felt a little light-headed, that's all."

"You seem flushed. Maybe it's the sun. We can stop and rest for a while if you'd like," he offered solicitously, his expression one of immediate concern. His eyes held hers, glinting, watchful, and she felt pinned beneath his gaze.

"I'd rather not," she replied, uncomfortable under his close scrutiny. She didn't know why it should bother her, but it did. "It's kind of you to ask, but I'd really like to push on in order to reach the Henderson settlement before dusk. It sounded like they're in desperate need of medical attention."

He nodded. "That's what we'll do then. It sure is a shame about the Hendersons. They're a real nice family. I'm dreading what we're going to find when we get there."

"I can only pray we'll be able to prevent the worst," she said solemnly. "Smallpox is a devastatingly swift disease, but sometimes with prompt medical attention, we can save those in the earliest stages." She knew, however, that only time would tell, for she had no idea how far the disease had progressed, although Billy Henderson had carefully described his family's symptoms: the fever, the cough, and finally, the rash that appeared on the skin at the last. His father had been stricken first, then his mother, and finally, the little girls, and them so young. Children were the most tragic victims.

She'd sat with young Billy while he'd wolfed down a hastily prepared meal, and listened as he told her how his folks, Buck and Florence Henderson were of the few who'd stayed on after the government had pulled every able-bodied soldier off the frontier to fight in the War Between The States.

It sounded to her as though it had been a nightmare for them, what with the Indian uprisings, and the suffering they'd endured through scorching summers droughts. Even so, Callie knew they'd never confronted anything as deadly as this silent, merciless killer. It invaded without distinction for race or class of people. Even the fierce Indians had become fallen victims, and it was said the disease had killed off more hostiles than the white man had. Callie sat quietly, overwhelmed by the thought.

Beside her, Captain Hamilton was consumed by other concerns. He stared off into the distance, his astute gaze sweeping over the far reaching landscape as he'd done regularly since they'd left the fort right before dawn. He'd never let Callie realize he was anxious about this last leg of their journey. It afforded them minimal cover. The Comanche were known to wait at the rocky cutoff ahead, keeping well concealed on top of flat outcroppings of red-gold sandstone; and then, at the right moment, they'd spring down on the unsuspecting travelers. It was a frightening prospect, but he was going to make certain nothing like that happened to them.

He made a mental note to remain sharply alert, and most certainly, he couldn't allow Callie's intoxicating beauty to distract him again. It had become the most difficult task on this journey. She was extremely lovely, but he kept reminding himself that he was a man who didn't allow distractions. Every action had a motive — he followed the rules to the letter, and he didn't make a move unless it was certain to further his military career.

At twenty-three, Callie had blossomed into a beautiful, desirable woman, and she could have had her pick of any man on the post. Lance *knew* he was going to be the one to claim her for his bride. Both the colonel and Lance had plans for Callie's future. The Captain intended to see them carried through.

"This is just between us, son. But you convince that gal to marry you, and you'll have my undying gratitude," the colonel had told him in his office the day before she'd arrived. Winking, he'd added, "She's a mite stubborn at times, and she'll need a firm hand, but I know you're the man who can keep her in line. It will be more than worth the investment, I assure you."

Lance had known then that if he married Callie he could write his own ticket, and he'd always been an enterprising young man. "I'll do my very best, sir," he'd replied, but he'd actually dreaded their first meeting. He hadn't known what to expect, particularly after hearing those rumors that she'd been involved in some scandalous affair in New Orleans and had been forced to withdraw from the Ursuline convent to hush everything. Then, of course, his mother would be horrified if she knew he was considering marrying a girl whose shady past might one day catch up with her, with both of them. He didn't want to think where he might end up then. But why borrow trouble?

Hell, what Mother didn't know wouldn't hurt her, Lance always figured. Then there was the colonel, but most of all his own career to consider. Lance damn well wanted that promotion.

After he'd met her, Callie's beauty had been an

added incentive. He'd decided he wouldn't give a damn about those rumors any longer. She was indeed one of the loveliest women he'd ever seen, and she had the most expressive amethyst eyes. Ever changing like her temperament, it seemed, they could sparkle with gaiety or cloud with brooding emotions, whichever suited her particular mood at the time. It was *really* her mouth that kept Lance obsessed with tantalizing visions every night.

Soft and full, her lips invited kissing, although he hadn't yet worked up the nerve to taste their sweetness. He had promised himself he would do so real soon or he damn well would never have a good night's sleep again. Despite his best efforts to win her affection, however, Callie seemed only devoted to her work at the post hospital, and if she found anything beyond those drab walls that proved of greater interest to her, Lance would have been amazed. She didn't seem to trust him, or any man, for that matter. He wondered again about those rumors and the scoundrel who shadowed her past. He longed to know, too, what had happened between them to have made her so wary?

He stared down at her now. He wanted to reach out and touch her hair, which like her spirit, never quite seemed tame. In the heat, her tresses spiraled in rebellious flaming curls about her face. He swallowed over the lump in his throat and tried to divert her attention back to him. "Just a few more miles and the worst leg of our journey will be over," he said. "We shouldn't have any trouble getting there before nightfall."

"That's good to hear," she replied. Stretching the

soreness from her muscles, Callie leaned back in her seat.

Hours and miles had passed slowly, and her neck and back were aching from jostling over the rutted road which was little more than a cattle trail. She hadn't had any other disturbing visions, so she was grateful for that at least. Since she'd returned to Texas, the only Indians she'd encountered were the pitiful bands of refugees from the reservation who often turned up at the fort gates seeking food and blankets.

It seemed the war between the white man and the Indian nations had taken its toll. There were few hostile bands who roamed free of the reservations, and those who did, would never come begging. The proud Comanche would rather starve than ask for handouts. They'd sworn to take a stand against the white man, and had certainly been causing their share of unending trouble.

The War Between The States had been over for four years, but another, equally devastating conflict, had resumed across Texas and everyone who lived here was on the defensive. The Nermernuh, Comanche, rode the plains against the flood of white immigrants, seeking to halt the tide of humanity who'd slowly encroached upon the Indian settlements.

Within the Comanche's raiding range it wasn't uncommon for them to appear without warning as if they'd somehow been conjured up from a terror-filled nightmare and had become a frightening reality. Riding forth to raid the countryside, they'd sweep confidently across the plains and down into Mexico — striking terror in the hearts of their enemies and taking goods and human chattel, whatever so suited them — these lords of the southern plains.

This was their kingdom.

The Texans hated the Comanche and wanted nothing more than to drive them from the land. It was their belief that the Indians were all ruthless killers devoid of human emotion. Hadn't she heard the Colonel say many times that the Indians accepted the treaties that were offered and swore to end the bloodshed, then turned around to go on the warpath before the ink had time to dry on the paper. "You can't trust a one of them. The only good Indian is either dead or secured on the reservations," the colonel had vehemently declared.

At first, Callie had unhesitantly agreed with him. She well knew of the Indian's treachery, how they scorned the white man and wiped out entire families of innocent settlers. She'd also begun to notice a startling change among the Indian bands, and having witnessed it firsthand, knew the truth could no longer be denied.

Once the Indians were a fierce, independent people, but now there seemed to be a new and different breed emerging from the nomadic bands. They'd begun turning up regularly at Fort Benton's gates begging for handouts, and they certainly didn't look like the killers she'd long retained in her memory. They seemed tired and hungry and a far cry from the inhuman beasts the colonel described.

In the beginning, Callie always regarded the Indians warily. She didn't trust them, couldn't even stand the sight of one without remembering how her father had died. Lately, though, she'd found herself intently watching the grim-faced braves and haggard looking squaws who came to the fort, and she'd been forced to acknowledge a new, startling emotion. Compassion. She actually felt pity for them. It was simply impossible for any caring individual to ignore their sad plight.

Driven by desperation and hunger, they'd stand clustered together at the gates. Fathers pleading with upraised hands. Mothers hovering protectively around their children, scrambling for any sort of handout that was tossed their way. Mostly, the Indians begged for scraps of food. One incident in particular had left a lasting impression on her, and to this day, still lingered in her mind.

The colonel, fed up with the endless stream of Indians milling about the fort gates, issued an order that there wouldn't be any further handouts. He wanted the hostiles to understand they were not to come back again.

Later that week, a group of Kiowas had come seeking food, and the guards, in response to the colonel's order, had brusquely refused them.

When the Indians wouldn't leave, the guards quickly became surly.

"You can plead till the sun comes up tomorrow, Injun, but you ain't getting anything more from us," one soldier called down from his guard post, his face darkening with fury. "Now git, before I fill your mangy hide full of buckshot. Then you won't ever have to worry about food again!"

"I do not ask for myself," the somber-faced Indian persisted unflinchingly, "but for my wife and children who haven't eaten in days. Please, you must spare us something . . . anything."

The guards banded together and were actually laughing at the Indian's plight. Finally, one of the soldiers called out in a sly voice. "Wait a sec, I think we might find you some vittles after all!" He moved away, only to return a moment later. "Here — we can spare this, Injun!" the guard chortled, tossing out a pail full of rotting, stinking garbage. "Now take it, and git the hell outa here!"

Hearing the commotion, Callie climbed the ladder to stand at the wall. She watched with shame, then horror, as the garbage rained down upon the man.

The startled Indian stood covered in the reeking filth, but he maintained his regal stance, never even blinking as the maggot-infested garbage dripped from his hair and clothes.

It had been heartrending to watch, and Callie heard a terrible scream and saw one of the squaws, a papoose strapped to her back, rush the locked gates to pound on the rough wood with her bare fists until they were bloodied. The woman's anguish, her raw emotion, was a universal language that everyone watching clearly understood. Even so, the guards remained unmoved, and continued to howl with laughter.

Defeated, perhaps weak from hunger, an older Indian woman had fallen to her knees, clutching two small children to her breast. She sobbed bitterly, her copious tears shattering forever Callie's belief that the Indians were heartless creatures.

Callie tried to deny her new awareness, but she really knew it was useless. The little group was so tragically sad, so hopelessly doomed. She wondered, too, where were the mad killers and beasts? Of course, in thinking this, she immediately felt disloyal to her father's memory. The compassion she felt for the Indians should be inconceivable, but she still could never forget the cruelty of those soldiers.

Truly, if the Indians were so cold and callous, why did they appear so loving, seeming so worried about their children's welfare, she'd thought many times since then. And why were they resistant to living on the reservation, when everything they needed to survive was allotted to them? Surely those stories of tainted meat and lice-infested blankets couldn't be true? The government wouldn't allow such a travesty of justice. Even the colonel reassured her many times that the Indians were well treated and wanted for nothing. It was only a few troublemakers intent on rebellion that she'd been hearing about, he'd said convincingly.

"But even those devils will have to conform eventually," he'd stated with conviction. "Or they'll face extinction."

At the moment, Callie's memory was held prisoner by the colonel's chilling prophecy. Deep in troubled thought, she barely noticed the frantic soldier racing toward them.

Captain Hamilton was well aware, and he recognized the message in the corporal's eyes, knowing his worst fear had been realized.

Chapter Eleven

"Scout's riding hard this way, Captain!" the trooper on horseback shouted.

Callie had felt Lance go rigid beside her. Reaching up, she nervously tucked a wayward strand of hair back under her flower-trimmed bonnet, trying not to think about the unease that flickered within her.

Suddenly, a dust devil whirled past the team of matched bays, and the horses shied away with a snort of surprise. A flock of cawing black birds, startled from the tree-tops, took flight overhead. Callie's gaze automatically followed their flight. The birds scattered and dipped lower across the horizon. It was then that she saw the hazy cloud spanning across the distant skyline. Great plumes of dust swirled, and she felt a prickle of fear and knew this was danger.

"Captain?" she swung her head around and noticed with a sinking feeling that he was staring solemnly in the same direction. She felt light-headed, and her hand clutched at the seat for support.

Beyond the sloping prairie, the tall buffalo grass,

much of it already scorched a dull brown from the summer sun, seemed undisturbed, but far off in its midst she saw what rode boldly toward them under the blazing Texas sky.

"Indians," she gasped and could do nothing but sit and stare transfixed at the magnificent vision of clustered riders thundering toward her; feathers plaited into their flowing hair, sunlight glinting off their breastplates and garishly painted faces.

That single word rippled through the troop of men, and then a hush seemed to settle.

"I know, I see them," Lance stated tensely, grabbing hold of her trembling hand. "Try and stay calm."

"What can we do?" she asked, praying he'd have the right answer, needing just a glimmer of hope.

"We can't outrun them. They'd only ride us down. But you don't have to worry, I'll never let them take you," he stated darkly, and she didn't like the ominous sound.

Those visions of her father and the women on the ill-fated stage began dancing in her head. A frightened scream bubbled in her throat, but she managed to restrain it. "Oh, God! Lance, are we going to die?" she gasped, paling as his eyes pierced hers. What she read in his gaze made her feel as though she'd stopped breathing.

"I pray not, but sometimes there are things far worse than dying, Callie," he said, his voice intense. Desperately, he began to assemble a plan in his mind. He'd never thought the Comanche would challenge them on open ground, but he should have realized that the Quohadi had no fear of the white man at any time. They rode where they pleased and considered this their land. In their eyes, the captain and his men were the trespassers.

"Trevler, sound the call to arms. We'll take a stand!" he ordered. "And remember, no matter what, we mustn't allow Callie to fall into their hands!"

Lance knew full well that their horses, as well as the beautiful white woman, were powerful enticements to a hot-blooded warrior fresh off the raiding trail, and drunk with conquest, they'd come after them with a vengeance. Despite their seemingly even number of men, it was going to be a bitter fight, with heavy losses on both sides. He gnashed his teeth in frustration at their vulnerable position. They didn't stand a chance in hell of outrunning the swifter Comanche ponies, especially when there was a beautiful woman as an added lure.

He realized what he must do, had to do, if he were to protect her, and his heart ached. It was the only decent thing he could do. Blessed relief. The unwritten code in the West. Every seasoned Indian fighter knew what the Comanche did with the white women they took as their captives. It was unspeakable and more horrible than anything a woman like Callie might imagine.

The Comanche actively sought captives — needed them to reproduce future warriors for the People — and kept their victims as slaves until they no longer served their purpose. Then they might trade them or kill them, whatever their particular whim. He knew well that capture by the Indians generally meant torture and death. The worst was the shame visited on

176

the women they kidnapped.

At that moment, he could only think of lost friends and loved ones killed at their hands, or worse, those who had wished they'd died before falling victim to this cruel enemy. The Comanche gave no quarter when it came to warfare, and Lance Hamilton could see only one way to deal with the desperate situation.

"God help us, we can't outrun them, Callie—" Lance's voice caught. "Stay close to me, and I'll do my best to protect you."

"Maybe they don't mean to harm us. Maybe they're just a hunting party?" she posed desperately.

He stared grimly at her and shattered her hopes. "Comanche bring nothing but trouble, and we'd best expect the worst."

Callie tried to recall everything the colonel had told her about the Comanche, and she seemed to remember how he'd said that Indians respected courage even in the face of death, and above all else, how you should never show them fear. "They make it worse if you cower," he'd said. But cower was exactly what she wanted to do now. These Indians looked as fierce as the ones who'd killed her father, and a far cry from the gaunt, starving bands who'd come begging at the fort gates. This time, there was no place for her to hide.

She wished she might blink, and when she opened her eyes again, find they'd disappeared like those in her bad dreams. Yet she knew it was a vain hope. They weren't going to vanish. They were real. They were deadly.

It came to her then, how her mother had always

said that Callie just had something about her — perhaps only an expression in the depths of those haunting violet eyes, or a certain way she smiled up at a man — that would draw all manner of beaus, wicked and gallant alike, to seek her favor. Although the girl had always been somewhat reluctant to take up such a suggestion before, at the moment she was more than inclined to agree. She was luring them. They were coming for her. She could feel them, knew them for what they were.

Murderers! Inhuman beasts!

Hooves thundering, images distorted and shimmered on heat waves. Dark figures slowly emerged, wavering on the distant plain, an apparition from hell that had somehow sprung to life.

She brushed back a strand of hair from her cheek, then moved her hand to shield dark-lashed amethyst eyes from the glare of the sun. The Indians rode ever closer, bright red ribbons on their ponies' manes and tails fluttering in the wind; the tips of their sharp lances gleaming silver in the sunlight, and the warrior's painted bodies, gaudily dressed and ornamented like revelers in a parade, and yet Callie's eyes saw only one man.

He was riding a sleek black horse at the front of the group, and he sat a good head taller than the rest. His long jet-black hair tumbled in the wind and his bronze skin glistened in the sun. His flowing hair and painted face made him terrible to behold, but she was disturbed to find that she was entranced by him as well. She found herself staring intently at the ribbons in his wild-eyed horse's mane. They were red, except for one. A glimpse of lavender satin blew freely, and she experienced a startling shock.

"No," she gasped. But that fluttering length of satin held her spellbound. She didn't have any time to consider it further for Lance had brought the team to a halt. He quickly jumped to the ground and reached up for her.

"Callie, listen closely to me." He was shaking her none too gently. "Do you hear me? You must do exactly as I say."

"Yes . . . yes, I understand," Callie replied, although she was still dazed and confused by the unexpected turn of events.

Lance swung her down on the ground in front of him, and then began shouting orders to the soldiers. "Take cover, men, and we'll give them a fight they won't soon forget!"

Callie saw that the Indians were almost upon them. She clutched at Lance's arm. "Please, give me a gun," she begged him, determined to fight if need be. "I must have something to protect myself."

He stared at her with a stricken expression. "Don't worry, Callie, I'll never let them take you alive," he stated with burning conviction.

"What . . . do you mean?" Callie posed shakily, and experienced yet a new horror when she noticed his right hand snake downward to reach for the Navy Colt strapped on his hip. Survival. There wasn't any other thought as powerful at the moment. She would do whatever she must to stay alive.

"I promised the colonel I'd never allow you to become some Comanche's prize," Lance said, enfolding her in his arms, tightening his grip until she was firmly trapped. "I intend to keep my word."

Her stomach started quivering. Her eyes filled with tears. "No, you don't know what you're saying!"

Callie felt the stranglehold of terror invading. Vaguely, she watched the men running with weapons drawn, scrambling into position, determination and fear etched on their faces. Callie didn't know how she was going to escape, but she must, and her mind, while numb, was trying to search frantically for the means to do so.

But Lance, his arm cinched around her waist, was making it impossible, and she could only stumble blindly along beside him as they ran toward a stand of trees that skirted a marshy riverbank. She caught the sound of pounding hooves, and the Indians' bloodcurdling war whoops. She didn't want to die, had never even considered her own mortality until this moment. The whole scene was like a part of a dream sequence rushing toward a grim conclusion, but she knew this wasn't fantasy. This was real. Lord, what was she going to do?

"Take aim . . . and fire!" Lance ordered the soldiers who'd fanned out around them.

A deafening explosion followed, and the air filled with the acrid smell of gunsmoke. Lance kept Callie secured against him, and he couldn't help but think, sadly, he might never get to taste her lips as he'd imagined since first meeting her. Very likely they'd both end up dying here. Even in the pandemonium, he noticed that the shimmering strands of her burnished red hair had come loose from the pins and tumbled around her shoulders. At that moment she had never looked more beautiful to him.

Over her head, he saw their time was running out.

The reigning lords of the plains had come to pay Callie a Comanche welcome, and he knew what he must do.

"We're outnumbered, but we'll hold them off as long as we can," he told her, his voice suddenly breaking, crackling with emotion. "I'm sorry. I failed you."

Every muscle in her body screamed for her to take flight. Callie stared up at him. She read the intent in his eyes. "Oh God, please Lance," she sobbed, but there didn't seem to be any way to reach him. His mind was set. She felt powerless to stop him.

Callie was startled when he suddenly enfolded her in his arms and bending his head, kissed her lips with a longing that would never be fulfilled. Then, he pressed his cheek against hers, and murmured brokenly, "Forgive me, Callie. I pray you won't feel a thing."

There was no recourse for her, nowhere she could turn. All of her life she'd been in such terrible fear of the Indians, but in that moment she realized that no one man was better or worse than the other. In everyone, man or woman, there was that dark side. She saw it in Lance Hamilton now.

Her eyelids fluttered closed. She heard him lever back the hammer on the Colt and felt the cold barrel as he pressed it against her temple.

She couldn't believe it, but it was true. God have mercy, she was about to die.

Chapter Twelve

Callie had thought she'd known fear before, but she'd never experienced terror like this. She felt cold sweat trickle down her spine, and her knees might have buckled if Lance hadn't held her pinned in his arms. She couldn't remember ever having swooned, but she was certain she might faint at any minute. Her head was spinning, the blood was pounding in her ears, and her heart felt as though it might explode in her chest.

The metallic sound of the hammer on the Colt energized her numb limbs, and her instinct for survival overrode her debilitating fear.

"No, I don't want to die like this!" she cried out, and with a sudden sweep of her arm, she knocked Lance's gun hand aside.

"Are you crazy?" he growled, grappling with her. "Do you know what they'll do if they capture you?"

"But I want to live. I want to live!" she sobbed, amazed that she had found courage she hadn't known she possessed.

"Your life won't be worth living with them!"

They were locked in a violent struggle. "I don't care! You have no right!" Callie screamed. She would fight for her life until the bitter end, but she was finished begging, and she could take care of herself. If indeed she were about to die, she didn't wish to end her life with pleas for mercy, but valiantly, with her head held high. She would never again expect others to protect her. And she damn well wasn't going to die by Lance's hand!

Everything blurred and narrowed in her vision. She saw the stark land around her, barren, brown, filled with hideously painted Comanches. At least in heaven there wouldn't be any Indians. Or would there?

The soldiers ran, firing, cursing the Indians who never seemed to stop charging past, shrieking like all of hell's demons. Men screamed in agony and fell wounded, others already lay dying around her, their blood slowly staining the sandy ground at her feet. The sickly stench of death was overwhelming, and she had difficulty thinking clearly, but when she finally managed to wrench free of Lance, she didn't hesitate.

Quickly, she yanked up her skirts and took off running, her petticoats flying up around her. She didn't know where she might turn, but she felt as though she'd just been granted salvation. At least, for those few precious seconds, she'd never felt more alive!

"Callie, no, please, you mustn't!" she heard Lance's anguished cry.

But she wasn't listening. Before her lay a frightening destiny. If she even had one at all. Her eyes desperately searched for sanctuary, but there was none, and for a moment, she almost gave in to her fear. She stretched her legs as far as they would go, punishing muscles she'd never known she'd possessed before. Praying fervently, she ran blindly. And then her eyes met the most terrible sight she'd ever encountered.

The broken prayer dying on her lips, she saw a Comanche warrior bearing down on her, his mouth open in a howl like that of a mad wolf. His evil looking face was painted for war in bold colors that stood out against his swarthy complexion. The feathers and ribbons attached to his mount, whipped madly in the wind, and she could only stare in disbelief as he raised his battle standard overhead and pointed the gleaming lance in her direction.

"I am Nerm, one of the only People!" he shouted in the Comanche tongue, "and I, Black Raven, will have this *herbi* for my own!"

There was no doubt in her mind that she stared death in the face, and she could scarcely breathe. An anguished scream tore from her throat. The stories she'd heard were pale in comparison to this horrifying vision before her. For an instant she seemed suspended in time. She remembered the women on the stage crying and whimpering as they'd been tortured and raped repeatedly. Then she knew what she must do. Damn them all! she thought bitterly. She'd rather die quickly than slowly, agonizingly, and with her pleading for the end.

With a wild cry, she sprang forward. If need be, she'd use her teeth and nails as weapons against him.

Black Raven's indigo eyes slitted with hatred as he bore down on her, and his lips turned back in a hideous smile. *"Meadro,* let's go, little wildcat," he snarled. "We shall see which one of us survives."

Callie ran onward. "I'll never, never surrender," she whispered fiercely.

"You will make this Comanche a fine slave!" Black Raven shouted.

Callie well imagined these were the last few seconds she had on earth. For a moment, her eyes blurred with tears, but when she blinked them away and looked again, another Comanche had bolted across Black Raven's path, and it seemed now that both warriors were caught up in a race to reach her.

"Aahe, I challenge you for the right to claim the *herbi!"* she heard the tall, dark warrior shout, though she didn't understand the words spoken in Comanche.

"It is the better man who will win!" Black Raven roared out, and kicked his mount's heaving sides. He wanted this flame-haired *herbi!* Such courage he'd never before seen in a white woman, and he knew once he'd broken her spirit she'd please him immensely.

Callie watched them with bated breath. She saw the tall Comanche lean low over his stallion's neck, and he appeared to murmur something in the beast's ear. It took only a split second longer, and then Black Raven was no longer in the running. The night-black stallion stretched out into a smooth rolling gallop, and he easily left the smaller pony behind. She watched the bronze-skinned warrior thundering toward her, heard his mount's hooves pounding staccato and felt the rhythm deep within her soul.

Thrum . . . thrum . . . thrum . . . The stallion bore down on her.

Dazed, she stood spellbound, her eyes locked in the Comanche's dark gaze. His piercing eyes were as volatile as the storms that raged across the plains, his proud form, the body of a conqueror who would never acknowledge defeat.

Horse and rider seemed a blur of motion and as one powerful entity. As the Comanche drew closer, she found herself watching him in bewilderment, for she knew there had been something oddly disturbing about his profile. He was almost too starkly handsome, too lithely graceful, unlike the other shorter, stockier brave whose features were bluntly carved like granite.

Callie felt the earth beneath her feet tremble as the stallion surged past, and she reacted instinctively, however foolishly. The Bible had taught her that all men were equal in God's eyes; Callie could only pray that women were as well.

Stretching out her hand, she felt strong calloused fingers connect with hers, and effortlessly haul her onto his horse in front of him. Her rounded buttocks slammed against his hard, muscular thighs, and her body seemed to burn with a physical reaction beyond her control. She smelled the greasepaint, the wildness, and tasted the salt of her own tears. There was no turning back now. She'd made her choice. Before her, however uncertain, lay her destiny.

And behind her in the flying dust and death, Lance Hamilton fought for his own life. Around him, his men lay sprawled grotesquely, their bodies mutilated beyond recognition. An Indian took the scalp of a soldier not more than ten yards from where he stood, and the man's screams were chilling to Lance. At any moment, he expected the same fate. Still, he kept a single vision and fought to remain calm. Then, feeling as though his heart was breaking, he took careful aim at the red-haired figure in the distance, and squeezed back on the trigger.

The shot reverberated across the plains.

Callie barely caught the warrior's muttered snarl. "The bastard, he'd rather see you dead than with me."

There was no denying he'd spoken English, and with a jolt, she knew that she'd heard that voice before. Her chin snapped up, and she found herself staring into a face that was all too shockingly familiar. He looked so much harsher than she remembered; his full lips set in an uncompromising line. She didn't doubt that he was capable of extreme violence. Still, she couldn't quite believe it was him; didn't want to believe it possible. She'd rather have thought him dead than to know he was now one of them.

"Hang on," he ordered her, "we've a long, hard ride ahead." Raising his battle standard, he signalled to the line of Comanches who were riding back to rejoin him, and shouted, *"Suvante!,* it is finished!" And the cry passed along from man to man.

Nudging his moccasined heels into the black's sides, he wheeled the stallion around, out ahead of the other warriors, leaving the grisly scene behind them.

Then they were riding across the prairie into uncharted territory where few white men had gone before and ever returned to tell their story.

Racing away, they left Lance Hamilton overwhelmed with anguish, watching Callie carried off in the arms of the Comanche. He knew what the night ahead of her would bring.

It wasn't so. It couldn't be! Callie was stunned into silence, but her mind was still frantically searching for answers. She kept telling herself it was absurd, he wasn't who she had first suspected. She wished she had the courage to lean back and look up at him again, but she'd done so once and had quickly glanced away when his eyes had cut right through her.

Since taking her, he'd remained aloof and uncommunicative, his harshly-planed face masked by ghastly black war paint. The dark eyes that stared back at her were devoid of emotion. He appeared implacable and angry. She suddenly had the urge to take her chances and throw herself from his horse.

At that instant as if in answer to her thoughts, his arm tightened like a steel band around her waist, a warning for her not to do anything foolish. She realized then that she couldn't expect to challenge him and win. She'd have to wait until they stopped to attempt her escape when his back was turned.

As they rode onward, she tried not to think about the tales she'd heard of Comanches capturing white women and turning their lives into a hell from which there was no escape. She was fast losing her newfound bravado, and thought herself a fool for even entertaining the notion of escape. He'd ride her down on that black beast, and then God only knew what he'd do to her. No, there was a better way. She must first learn what he planned for her. Then she could form a plan.

She took a deep breath, his features blurred, and she knew she was staring at him through her tears. "I . . . think I have a right to know where you are taking me!" she said, then clutched frantically at him when as he let the stallion plunge down an arroyo, sending dust billowing.

"I told you to hang on," he clipped. Reaching for her arms, he clasped them around his neck, keeping her wedged firmly between his shoulders and thighs.

She really didn't like the strange reaction she was experiencing at that moment. She felt safe, she was protected. But in the next breath, her thinking crystallized. *You fool!* she mentally chastised herself, he's not going to protect you. Later, he'll probably trade you to the highest bidder, perhaps to that other Comanche, who even now watched her and made her feel like one of those poor butterflies whose wings had just been pinned to velvet.

"And at the moment, the only rights you have are the ones I decide to give you," he stated coldly and articulately. "And if you value your life, you'd better keep your mouth shut and learn to do exactly as you're told."

She sniffed, but refused to submit to tears. Better that she die right here. "I must know if you're going to do . . ." she stubbornly persisted. "If you intend to . . ." She couldn't say the words, and she could barely hold her tears at bay. She didn't want to cry in front of him, didn't think she could stop if she once began. "I . . . I won't be treated like some Indian squaw," she choked out. There, perhaps now she'd made herself perfectly clear.

He glanced over her head to where Black Raven rode in front of them, his spine straight as an arrow. The brave was mad enough to challenge him, he knew, but he'd have to take that chance for Callie's sake. If she fell into the others' hands her life wouldn't be worth living, and he wouldn't want to see what she would become. "It would be considered an honor among my people if you were treated like a Comanche's woman," he said. "But a captive is never given such a privilege unless she proves herself worthy. In their eyes this shall remain to be seen. You will hold your tongue and do what I tell you. Let them know you're brave, but don't give

190

them reason to think you more trouble than you're worth."

So much for reassurances! She swallowed over the tightness in her throat and no longer felt quite so sassy. He didn't try and deny that she might be turned over to that mad pack. Dear Lord, she couldn't even bear to think about that, not now when she'd managed to survive after all. "Am I *your* captive then or will you let *them* decide my fate?" she felt compelled to ask.

His gaze collided with hers. As in the past, the impact was strongly felt by both.

"That choice is up to you. You can be mine or Black Raven's. He would be the next one to claim you."

His expression didn't change whether he was being threatening or silent, but she knew by the look in his eyes that he had meant every word.

She liked the ruthless gleam in the other Indian's eyes far less, for whenever Black Raven felt her staring at his back, it seemed he instinctively knew. He'd turn at once to smile jeeringly at her, reminding her of a jackal. It was a gesture that made her flesh crawl. The lesser of two evils, and which one the more deadly, she could not readily say!

Still, she remembered how her captor had saved her from Black Raven, and for that matter, from dying by Lance's hand. She would just have to take the chance he wouldn't abuse her, even though she'd sworn she'd never place her trust in another man again.

"I shall remain with you," she replied quietly,

hating herself for saying the words, but vowing to make him regret them. The colonel would send out a search party, and they'd find her, and these savages would pay in the end, she thought fiercely. She only had to stay alive long enough to be rescued. It was that single focus that kept her sane. Then her thoughts returned to earlier that morning. She recalled the feeling she'd had of their being watched, the strange images in the dawn mist, and she knew he'd been stalking her. She cast him a condemning glare. "How could you have led them to us, allowed them to kill those innocent men?"

"They are always the innocent ones, aren't they?" he sneered.

"We weren't the ones looking for trouble. You attacked us without provocation."

"I won't tell my people they shouldn't fight for what they believe in, even though I know that war is never the answer to anything. It was unfortunate that you had to be with the pony soldiers. There was nothing I could do but make certain you weren't harmed."

The horrible realization of what lay behind them made her gag in revulsion. Her brilliant violet eyes were brimming with tears, and she was unable to halt a rush of overwhelming emotions. Her words stabbed him like a knife. "Oh, Rafe, how could you have become one of these wild beasts?" she half sobbed, remembering once again the terrified death cries of the soldiers, their lifeless bodies littering the plain and her own helpless fury.

His voice was low and strangely taut. "You don't

understand yet, do you, angel?"

Her eyes spilled over at the familiar endearment. But he remained unmoved by her tears. She felt breathless all of a sudden. It had been so long since she'd heard him call her that. "No . . . I don't," she could only stammer.

"The man you knew is dead. My people call me Night Of The Hawk, and I do not belong anywhere else but with them."

"But you can't be Comanche," she gasped.

"I *am* Comanche, my mother is one of them," he bit out, scowling at her. "And your people brought this on themselves. They should not be on Comanche land."

"We had no choice," she snapped, wiping furiously at her damp cheeks with the back of one dirt-smudged hand. "We were on our way to a settlement nearby, and now, because of you, the people we sought to help will probably die without the medicine I had for them."

"I am sorry for that," he said, "but the White Eyes were on our land." Their gazes clashed. "You hate me for saying that, but do you know, or even care, that the White Eyes' sickness is destroying my people as well. We do not have medicine, and for us there is no one who cares." His eyes hardened like flint. "I have no sympathy for trespassers. They only get what they deserve."

"You are worse than the cold bastard I remember," she hissed. "This savage you've become doesn't even have a heart."

His lips curved into a smile, but his eyes were

wintry. "It has allowed me to survive, angel. You will see, and soon you will know what I mean." He was glad she'd matured, even turned into somewhat of a little hellion, it seemed. She would need every bit of that fiery spirit to survive where he was taking her. The Comanche would make her prove her worth before they accorded her any respect, and for a while, just getting through one day at a time was going to be about all that she could manage. He could only afford her so much protection. If she refused to conform they'd demand she be traded, or perhaps even be killed. It was the Comanche way, and he would not defy them and bring dishonor on his family. Because of their loyalty, he was alive today.

As if she'd somehow read his thinking, she shuddered. She seemed to stare blankly ahead of her. "I thought there was nothing worse than dying . . . but I was wrong," she stated softly, contemplatively. She looked up at him again.

Only his eyes changed fractionally, then narrowed. "It's too bad that you feel that way. It's only going to make it more difficult to accept what you cannot change."

"I'll never submit to any man against my will."

"Those are brave words, angel. But even if you could escape me, although I doubt that you can, I'd come after you no matter how far you might travel, and I'd bring you back."

"Why?! I have a family who will worry about me, a mother who'll grieve thinking I'm dead. They will pay you whatever you ask them. Why . . . Why would you wish to hold me against my will?"

"I sympathize with your feelings, but I also have people whom I care very much about, and I couldn't take the risk that you'd lead the pony soldiers back to my village. Do you know what happens when a regiment of bloodthirsty soldiers bent on retaliation can do?"

Numbly, she shook her head.

"They'd rape, maim and kill. Young and old . . . women and babies. They do not discriminate. They do not consider us human."

Her eyes filled. Yes, she knew this much was true. She drew a shaky breath. "So you don't intend to ever let me go?"

"You're the only person who knows that Rafe Santino is still alive."

"But sooner or later someone else will find out. My stepfather will send out scores of men to track me down. He'll find me eventually and he'll see your people punished for kidnapping me."

"Perhaps, but it will be no easy task to locate us. Until then, I have bought more time for the Quohadi. I intend to use it well. We can also use your medical knowledge."

Feeling somewhat dazed, she lapsed into silence. She prayed silently, desperately as they covered mile after mile, but she could find no real comfort in the learned-by-rote scriptures that had sustained her through every other trial she'd faced in her life. Overcome with exhaustion she fought against drifting off.

Finally, after miles of silence and uncertainty,

she couldn't hold out any longer. As she slumped forward over his arm into a troubled slumber, her last thought was to somehow escape. She did not realize when he gently drew her back against him, and cradling her tenderly, he inhaled deeply the tantalizing, flowery scent of her hair.

"*Toquet,* it is well, sweet angel. Sleep for a time and forget everything that you've been through," he whispered.

Chapter Thirteen

She awoke to silence, and Indians. Her captor shifted her in his arms, and she trembled with the force of her emotions. He had saved her life, but Lance had felt certain that death would have been preferable to life with the Comanche. So what had he saved her for? How could she expect these savages to treat her once they reached their village? So many questions without answers, but she had to admit she wasn't sorry that she was alive. She only hoped she might remain brave despite the trials that lay ahead.

"You're awfully quiet, angel." The unexpectedness of that deep voice startled her from her silent reverie. "You know you might relax. I'm not going to bite you." He tried drawing her stiff form back into his arms, but she shrugged away from him.

"Don't do that," she snapped, lurching forward and swatting at his hands.

He sighed. "Look, it's a long journey home, and you'd do both of us a favor if you'd just accept the fact that the two of us are going to be sharing this horse for quite a while."

"I don't intend to accept anything where you're concerned," she retorted heatedly. "I seem to remember trusting you once before, and it was the biggest mistake of my life."

He wrapped an unrelenting arm around her waist and jerked hard. Callie's back slammed against his chest. "It's too bad you feel that way, but it really would make it a whole lot easier if you'd behave yourself. If you don't, I just might decide you're more trouble than you're worth and let you walk the rest of the way."

Overwhelmed by rage, she tilted back her head and stared up at his shuttered features, her eyes narrowed. "Go ahead, anything would be preferable to riding with you."

He kept his eyes fixed straight ahead. "Believe me it's tempting, but then the others would think I can't control you. That being the case, they might demand that I turn you over to someone else. I don't have to tell you who that would be. Black Raven would love nothing better than to become your master."

She swallowed, never having felt more humiliated. He was treating her no better than a slave! How could she have ever thought that these people bore any real emotions? Her hatred festered and spilled over. They only knew how to hunt and kill. The white man was their favorite prey. She might fear them, but they would never break her. "You . . . bastard, I'll never forgive you for this!" she gasped out a series of stinging insults, and was barely able to restrain herself from reaching up and clawing at his dark face. "You despicable half-breed, I hope when the soldiers come for me that you're the first one they shoot."

With a grim set to his mouth, he said, "That would be unfortunate for you, but it's unlikely the soldiers are going to find you where I'm taking you, so I wouldn't get my hopes up too much."

Callie's tongue was momentarily silenced, but he knew it wouldn't take much to further provoke her. She was the only woman who'd ever made him envision turning her over his knee and whaling the daylights out of her. "You've added a few new words to your vocabulary since the last time we were together," he stated with a slight quirk of his mouth. "Who taught you such colorful phrases, angel? What was his name?"

Incensed, she quickly replied, "It's just my being around you! You bring out the worst in me."

"So there's no one special man in your life. Now that surprises me. I'd have thought a beautiful woman like you would have had a number of marriage proposals by now."

Her pride stung, she shot back, "I've had a number of beaus. *They* were every one gentlemen and knew how to treat a lady."

"I saw how one of those fine gentlemen treated you today," he sneered. "And you're right, I'm nothing like the other men you've known. I miss the mark by a mile. I'd never consider shooting a helpless woman in the back."

199

Callie stiffened at the memory. "Given the circumstances, the captain was only doing what he thought was best."

"It seems you two weren't of the same opinion. As I recall it, you were only too eager to ride away with me."

"Of course *you* would see it that way!" The heated flush on Callie's cheeks deepened, and she jerked her head around to stare ahead of her, unseeing. She was tempted to cover her ears with her hands she was so angry with him. "Just shut up! I'm not in the mood to listen to any more of this."

Lazy-lidded ebony eyes stared at the back of her copper curls, the proud tilt of her head, and he was suddenly weary of her trivial harping. "It seems to me that you're not in the mood for much of anything except giving me hell, and I'm getting real tired of haggling with you. If you keep it up I just might decide to put a gag on you."

Gagged! She lifted her head, and in the reflection of the moonlight, her eyes spewed flames. "You wouldn't dare!"

"Wouldn't I?" he shot back. He'd meant what he'd said. He was a Comanche warrior, and he could feel the other braves curiously watching, wondering why he would allow this white woman to address him with such disrespect. He didn't know why himself. He'd never allowed anyone to talk to him as she had, but even though he could not justify it, neither did he want to see her proud spirit crushed. She refused to be cowed, and he knew she'd gained a measure of respect from the other Comanche, himself included.

Still, he was relieved that it seemed some of her anger and resentment had been vented, and although her expression remained unflinching, blessed silence soothed his ears.

Peace at last, he thought, but he could only guess how long it might last. They would be stopping to rest and set up camp soon, and he could only wonder how his little tiger-cat was going to respond when he told her she was going to cook for him.

Once they reached his village, she would be expected to conduct herself respectfully and in accordance with tradition. The other women would make her life intolerable if she gave them as difficult a time as she had given him so far. He almost sighed aloud. Of all the women in Texas that he might have taken captive, why had the spirits deemed to have given him this one? Hundreds of miles had separated them, and still fate had managed to connect their paths.

At least for now, she'd settled comfortably into his arms, perfectly calm, and feeling every bit as if she'd always belonged there. He liked the way the curve of her shoulder and one softly-rounded hip, conformed to the planes and angles of his body, as if she'd been made just for him. The scent of her hair, her skin, and her sweet womanly smell, stirred him more than he even liked to admit. Unbidden, the desire he'd kept checked pulsed to life, fire raced through his blood, and he felt her back go rigid with the acknowledgment of his restless passion.

Even through the many layers of her clothing she must feel the hard, muscular planes of his body with each move the stallion made, and he didn't think it was fear that made her heart pound against his arm that was secured beneath her breasts. She was really extremely beautiful when she was angry, he decided, and although he knew those kind of thoughts were the most dangerous of all, he couldn't halt them. He didn't fear her wrath, but her allure. Making love to her would be something he'd always remember.

He could barely recall his first woman's name, but with this one, everything about her was burned into his brain. He slid his hand across her rib cage, stroking her just beneath her breast. His heart beat in rhythm with hers, and something he didn't wish to acknowledge stirred inside him. Against her it seemed he had no defense. It was a humbling admission for a Comanche warrior to make. Even to himself.

Despite his resolve to retain his baser emotions, his gaze was drawn downward to the steady rise and fall of her creamy breasts about the decolleté of the yellow gown she wore. Even though the garment was dirty and torn, it provided a man with a hint of what was hidden beneath all those frills and lace. But just a hint, nothing too revealing. And he liked that, too. It allowed his thoughts to run wild. He smiled faintly. He'd always had a damn good imagination.

He could tell by the arm he held around her waist that she had her corset cinched up far more than she needed. Although she was slender as a reed and didn't even need to wear the thing in the first place. It made him wonder how in the hell she'd managed to stand the heat for this long without passing out on him by now. Surely, it had to be almost impossible to draw a breath encased in such a ridiculous contraption. It seemed white women had this infernal obsession to make themselves absolutely miserable before they could assure themselves that they were beautiful. It never did make much sense to him.

Indian women wore soft doeskin dresses and leggings with nothing underneath to encumber their movements or constrict their breathing. He held no doubt that Callie would be in a much better mood if she'd shed some of the hardware she was trussed up in. And what a pleasure it would be for him to help her with the task, he thought.

He found himself envisioning peeling off each article of her clothing . . . one piece at a time . . . using the sharp blade of his knife to slice through the damned stays of her corset . . . leaving her bare-assed naked, her pale body his to do with as he pleased.

Desire twisted like an arrow in his belly. He wanted to jerk her skirt up past her knees and feast his eyes on her pale naked thighs. Then with just a few minor adjustments of both their clothing, and lifting her, turning her body so that she sat straddling him, he could show her things she'd never dreamed could be done on a horse. He'd touch her everywhere; look into her eyes, see the passion rise up within her and kiss her lips until she was whimpering for her release.

Christ, he thought, if these thoughts go on much longer he was going to have a difficult time continuing their ride, but he could see no relief in sight until they stopped to make camp and he could put some distance between them. It was going to be a helluva long night.

Suddenly, he wanted to shout out the most vile curses he could think of, for the stallion's steady, swaying gait rocked Callie's body against his, and wedged her hips even tighter between his legs. The hard length of him strained against his breechcloth, burning through the material and nudging her backside. There was nothing he could do to will his body from responding otherwise. It was a natural reaction, and it was just too damned bad if she was shocked by it, he thought.

The next hour dragged by interminably with little relief for his torment. He was caught in an intoxicating state of misery, and he began casting around in his mind, seeking ways to make her seem less attractive. But even though he decided she was too tall, too thin, and too outspoken, he was forced to admit that he'd never felt two rounder, more delectable globes of perfection stirring against his thighs.

He wanted to reach down and press his hands up underneath her bottom, squeezing gently, filling his palms with that glorious mass of womanly flesh. He wondered many other things about her as well, and ended up dreaming far too intently about what it might feel like to have those long, lithesome legs wrapped tightly about his hips.

For her part, Callie raged silently, and couldn't even begin to fathom what was going on in his head. Although she felt certain he was enjoying this latest humiliation he'd enforced on her. He liked taunting her, making her aware of just how easily he could take her anytime that he wanted. And she absolutely hated the way his arms held her so snugly, as if he had every right to do so. Of course, two could play his game. There were ways of making him miserable as well. She knew by his labored breathing, and the unrelenting rigid swell pressing intimately against her, that the languorous heat spreading throughout her body was also consuming him as well.

She was feeling a hot sweet ache there between her legs, and in her breasts, making her nipples grow taut, and leaving her longing for him to touch her, kiss her. She resented the way the close proximity of his body brought to mind everything forbidden they'd done that night in the bayou. Still, she wanted him to know just how easily their roles might be reversed, and she couldn't resist flirting with danger. Settling herself more comfortably across his lap, Callie's hips stirred deliberately and she settled back against the hard length of him.

His body tensed, and he swore softly. "Dammit, you're playing a dangerous game, *mao tao yo,* little one. I think you know it, too. I only hope you're prepared for the consequences later." His mouth was close, and his warm breath brushed against her ear.

She shivered at the seductive warmth of his voice, felt his arms tighten around her, and his long fingers splay intimately against her belly. Her breathing became more labored, and she began to feel extremely peculiar. She recognized what was happening to her, and remembered what it had been like to have his hands stroke her breasts, his mouth suckle her nipples, and her tongue mate with his. Why did she only feel this way with him? He was nothing more than an untamed savage who would probably ravish her the very first chance that he could. Just thinking it prompted that curious tingling to stir in her belly once again.

He nudged the stallion into a brisk trot, and Callie gasped. His muscular thighs rode firm beneath her, and she couldn't prevent her bottom from bouncing against him. Even through her clothing it felt as though that other part of him were invading her, eliciting goosebumps along her spine.

"There's something you seem to have forgotten," he murmured huskily. "I know your needs as well." Those fingers began stroking, teasing. "Feel them stirring?" he suggested softly, and held her wedged firmly between his thighs. "Ah . . . yes, I think you do . . ."

Callie was lost in the velvety darkness of that suggestive voice.

"I can make you do things you've never dreamed of," he whispered, "but I think I'll wait until you come to me. You're going to have to ask me to make love to you. And when you do I promise you it .will be a night unlike anything you might have imagined."

When his hands fell away from her and the spell of the moment was broken, she almost sobbed with relief, but it wasn't because of her fear of him. She didn't even want to admit what she'd been thinking about doing right there on his horse, and for the first time that she could remember, she didn't feel safe from herself.

Hours passed with little verbal communication between them, only the universal message of their body language, which she tried to ignore as best she could. They'd been riding forever it seemed. She wondered if they ever got tired, if they'd ever stop again. They just rode onward.

As much as she told herself she despised him, she needed to hear the sound of another voice like her own. The Comanche tongue was deep, guttural, and frightening to a young woman who couldn't understand their meaning. What were they saying, planning? He'd been questioned by several braves and could only wonder if they'd been discussing her. Was he telling them she belonged to him, or letting them know she was his to barter, and he'd consider any offers later, once they arrived at their destination?

The moon lay obscured behind a cloud bank. The darkness was consuming. Tree limbs reached out like jagged, skeletal fingers, snagging her clothes and hair, making her cringe against him, but his arms quickly swept them away. He seemed determined to keep her from harm, but then she caught herself, and almost laughed at the notion. He just didn't want damaged goods. Just as the horses they'd stolen from the soldiers, she imagined herself being traded for the right price.

When her spirit sunk so low she didn't think she could stand the uncertainty another minute, she'd try to recall how strong and secure his hand had felt when he'd reached out for her in the middle of the melee. He'd saved her from death back there on the plains. Glancing around at the war-painted faces, she thought they appeared very much like the Indians she'd always dreaded meeting. A deep melancholy gripped her. Dear Lord, would she ever hear the sound of her own peoples' voices again?

Once in a while, one of the warriors must have found something amusing to talk about, and there would follow much laughter. She only stared blankly at them, thinking it was the strangest sight she'd ever seen. She'd observed them when they'd been sad, tired, hungry, and crazed with the killing fever, but never like this. It seemed out of character for the ruthless murderers of earlier. After witnessing it first hand today, she was more inclined to believe the stories of their cruelty and torture. She had no idea what their rules were, or what her life was going to be like where they were taking her. She only knew that the tales of their kidnapping women and children, even raping little girls, and when they disobeyed, burning their noses off with live coals, no longer seemed just a cruel white man's joke. Bewildered, she could only listen, and then heard his words, but they did nothing to soothe her fears.

"Look closely, angel. Are we really so different from you? We laugh, we cry, and we protect our own, just as your people do."

"You murder wantonly, you torture the innocent, and I hate everyone of you," she choked out. "I will never forget the senseless killing I saw today."

"Ask yourself who opened fire first?" he posed moderately. "Search for an honest answer this time."

"I *know* what I saw —" she insisted.

"What you want to believe you saw," he snapped, temper flaring. "Now let me tell you what *I* saw. It was not a Comanche, but a white man who was going to take your life. How could I stand by and allow him to do this? I had to stop him the only way that I knew how."

"If you murdered the soldiers because you felt compelled to save me, then I wished Lance would have succeeded and you had failed," she replied acidly.

"Enough!" he snarled, and his dark eyes held a murderous gleam that evaporated some of her anger.

Callie didn't think it wise to continue bating him when he looked at her like that, so she rode in stony silence over the hours and the miles, and could only wonder if they'd ever come to the end of their journey.

Fatigue once again overrode Callie's elemental concerns, and she drifted to sleep once more, although she remained stubbornly resistant to his embrace. She tried to sit without allowing her head to rest against his shoulder, and she jerked forward whenever she felt herself begin to relax. But she couldn't keep this up, and it didn't take long for her chin to droop. She was only vaguely aware of gentle, callused fingers lacing through her tangled hair and drawing her head back. She struggled only briefly, but he held her firmly until she quieted against him.

For hours Callie drifted in that netherworld of slumber, hearing sounds that were in some ways familiar and reassuring. She dreamed that she was back at the convent sleeping in her own bed.

From outside in the long hallway came the sounds of pans clattering as the cook prepared their breakfast. She smelled chicory coffee brewing and could almost taste it thick with cream, but still biting on her tongue.

In her sleep, her nose twitched at the spicy scent of roasting meat. She found she could imagine fluffy biscuits rising in the old cast iron oven, and saw herself dabbing golden butter in the center before she'd munch down two or three.

The smell of horses, burning mesquite, and Indians, sent alarm bells off in her head. Her eyes half open, glazed for that instant by panic.

She saw long braided hair and fringed leather, feathers, and heard bells tinkling softly. There were Comanches moving all around her. Her first instinct was to rise up and defend herself, but then she noticed that they didn't seem to care about her at the moment.

It was time to make camp and relax. Some of them were off in the distance testing their riding skills, hanging half off their ponies or standing atop their mounts' back, their long hair sweeping across the ground as they raced past upside down beneath the waning moon. Laughter was free. A sense of merriment permeated the air.

The Comanches who weren't at play were sorting through their packs and putting together the makings of a camp. Once they were settled and the ponies hobbled nearby, they too became like playful boys, running back and forth, exchanging stolen plunder with each other, and arguing good naturedly it seemed. Surely, these could not be the same murderers she'd been with earlier?

Her captor slung one leg over his horse, and holding her securely in his arms, he dropped to the ground and carried her to a place beside a roaring campfire. She shivered. The evening was chilly, or maybe it was just her blood feeling like ice in her veins that made it seem that way.

She didn't think he would even notice her discomfort, but when he knelt on one knee, and she saw that he meant to drape a blanket around her shoulders, she felt almost grateful. Glancing past him, she noticed Black Raven watching from a place across the campfire, and he didn't seem to appreciate this gesture of kindness. She grasped the ends of the scratchy woolen material and pulled it tightly around her. When Night Of The Hawk started to turn away, she couldn't help herself, her hand shot forward to grasp him about the wrist.

"I . . . can feel Black Raven watching me," she whispered, looking up through thick lashes into his dark eyes. "Please . . . don't leave me alone with him."

In this strange new world, he was her only security. She needed him near to remain brave, and even though he'd never appeared more threatening than at that moment in the firelight with the flames reflecting off his harshly painted face, Callie wanted to cling to him.

He held out his hand. *"Keema,* come, and we'll find a place where you can rest."

She didn't really wish to obey him, but she was uncertain what might happen if she did not. Rising to her feet, she stifled a gasp as needles pricked her legs, and her world seemed to tilt crazily. Callie stumbled and almost fell, but he was beside her immediately, his arm slipping around her waist. "Here, lean against me . . . you need to get the blood circulating in your legs again."

Before she had time to consider this act of kindness, she noticed what dangled from his hand, and shock and outrage exploded in her eyes. The muscles along her throat constricted until she felt she could barely breathe. He was carrying a lengthy rope of rawhide, one end fashioned in a slip knot. Callie shied away from him. "Damn you, I'm not some animal! If you try and put that leash on me you'll have a fight on your hands."

He didn't seem surprised at her reaction, but he didn't sympathize either. "Would you rather be secured to me—" he gave a jerk of his head in the direction of the other warriors "—or have them watch your every move, maybe even issue a challenge that I'd have to honor?"

After considering the alternative, her arms fell limply to her sides. Tears of indignation burned her eyes, moistened the tips of feathery lashes, and the blood roared in her ears.

Indeed, she felt the others staring after them. No doubt, it was time to divide up the spoils, and if she had to belong to any one of these savages, she supposed she'd rather it be him. She closed her eyes. It was the only way she could keep the tears checked as she felt him drop the loop around her neck.

Seconds dragged by with neither of them saying a word. She imagined him feeling smug and victorious having conquered her, and had no idea that he really was experiencing a surge of confusing emotions.

He had to fight the impulse to reach out and brush the teardrops from her cheeks. He silently cursed her, then himself, for the range of emotions he was experiencing at that moment. He remembered how he'd sworn no other woman would ever make him feel like that again.

None had. Until now. Until her.

Just to look at her made him feel as though he betrayed the memory of Morning Star. She made him angry, but she also stirred so many memories he found hard to deal with. Most of all, he refused to consider the fact that this *herbi* with her red hair and violet eyes, was just like his vision had predicted. He studied her, and his lips tightened. Yet, he felt sorry for her, too.

"Ka taikau, toquet, mah-tao-yo, don't cry, it's all right, little one," he wanted to whisper, but he would not allow himself to do so.

Her silken hair lay wind blown and smelled of smoke and the wild sage that had been tossed into the blaze. She felt him free her hair from the tether, but with her eyes downcast, she couldn't know that he watched it sift through his fingers and catch in the firelight, shimmering like liquid flame, and reflecting in his luminous black eyes.

"Aahe, I claim you," he said loud enough for the other braves to hear him, but his voice sounded empty and there was no joy in his heart.

Callie understood by the look in his eyes what the words must mean in Comanche. She felt her face burn, and when she glanced over at the group huddled around the fire some distance away, she noted Black Raven's smoldering glare, but he did not object. She turned her head to stare up at Night Of The Hawk. She had never felt more like killing anyone, and she was ashamed, but nonetheless furious. At that moment if she would have had a weapon in her hand she did not honestly know what she might do.

As if he read her thoughts, his gaze locked with hers, his eyes hard as jet.

"You are now this Comanche's woman," he said, his voice carrying across the camp, "and no matter what I tell you, I expect you'll obey me as quickly as that." He'd snapped his fingers before her eyes.

They stood there for a moment, and then he tightened the knot around her throat, and tugging on the end of the tether, forced her to follow along behind him.

Callie could only stare at his back in disbelief, and refused to answer him. He didn't seem to care that she didn't respond. He'd made his point and she was expected just to listen and obey. Her darkened gaze settled on a place between his shoulder blades. She heard the Comanche's chuckling in the background, and one of them must have made a ribald comment, for their guffaws deepened.

Something hard and mean stirred inside her. Her eyes fell on the hilt of his knife strapped to his firm thigh. She didn't even consider the fact that she would be committing murder when she imagined grabbing it and plunging it into his back. She knew then she would do whatever she must in order to escape him. And she would run away, she promised herself, just as soon as he gave her the slightest opportunity.

Savoring the tiny spark of hope that burned brighter than ever before, Callie walked on, proudly flaunting her honor and courage in the face of her enemy.

Chapter Fourteen

It was her contempt that gave her a single focus and she was able to stare up at her captor, a challenge gleaming in her eyes. He was crazy if he thought she'd do his bidding, she resolved. She drew a deep breath and forbade herself to tremble. "No, I won't do it."

A muscle along his jaw tightened. "This is our way and you'd better get used to it. It is expected that you will cook the meat," he said in a clipped voice, holding two sharpened stakes of skewered venison before her.

Broad, brown shoulders filled her vision. He'd been away for over an hour, but upon his return he had immediately sought her out. She hadn't been hard to find. She'd been sitting exactly where he'd left her, terrified the entire time he'd been away that his two companions who'd stayed behind would approach her.

To her relief, Black Raven had gone hunting with the other braves, but her guard was just as intimidating, although he'd yet to say a word to her. He was big and barrel-chested, with a huge shaggy head. He reminded Callie of a bull buffalo. Thankfully, he had remained at a distance, and she'd quickly decided not to give him the slightest provocation to doubt her intentions. Escape had seemed impossible at any rate. There had been a young Indian standing watch over the ponies, and the buffalo man had seemed intent on her every move.

At the moment it was Night Of The Hawk commanding her attention. Having stated her mind, she'd clamped her jaw tight and stared up at him.

His eyes narrowed. "You *will* learn the ways of our women. One of your tasks will be to prepare meals. I've killed the deer, the fire is hot, and you *are* going to do as I've asked."

The tangy odor of the freshly killed game made Callie's empty stomach roil and she drew back from him. She knew it was foolish of her to keep defying him, but her emotions seemed out of control. Dangerously so. She wanted to hurt him and to make him feel the confusion and pain she'd felt since he'd taken her. Her eyes gave no quarter. "I won't."

A hush fell over the group sitting around the campfire. She could feel them watching her, waiting to see what would happen next. Callie felt surrounded on all sides by the enemy.

Night Of The Hawk hunkered down in front of her. There was a message clearly visible in his eyes. He understood her rage, her feelings of defiance in the face of the enemy, but she would survive only if she conformed to their ways and proved her worth.

"If you keep this up, angel, you're only going to

make it harder on yourself," he said, then lowering his voice, added, "Take the meat. It isn't that much to ask."

"I don't give a damn how difficult you and your friends make my life. I'm not going to become some Comanche's squaw," she spat. "And you can't make me."

If looks could kill she knew he would have murdered her right there. "I have no patience with foolish white women." He grabbed her wrist and shoved the stake at her, clearly in no mood for a battle of wills. "Take it, and cook it. And do not ever argue with me again before my people. I am finished trying to explain the rules to you. You're just going to have to learn the hard way it seems."

For a full minute she couldn't breathe her throat felt so tight. She gave serious thought to taking the chunks of meat and throwing it on the ground at his feet, but she wisely decided otherwise. The look in his eyes clearly indicated he wasn't going to tolerate her further defiance, and she knew that for now he had won. Still, the smoky gaze she turned upon him was clearly indicative of how she actually felt, even as she snatched the stakes out of his hand and stalked over to the fire. There would be another time, and he wouldn't be able to bully her into submission.

Feeling the other men smiling, hearing their smug grunts of approval, she had this overwhelming urge to stand over the blaze and drop his damned dinner into the flames. Her eyes glittered with impotent fury. For an instant, her hand hung there suspended, and she had never been more tempted to do anything in her life. He must have interpreted her thoughts.

"*That* would be a very foolish mistake," he stated tersely.

She never turned to acknowledge him. A confused rush of feelings; fear, hatred, humiliation, defeat, assailed her. She drew back her arm and without a word, knelt down on the ground by the fire and pushed the stakes into the earth at an angle so that the meat would char slowly without overcooking. She'd remembered this from the times her father had taken her for long rides out on the range, and they'd camped out beneath the stars and lived off the land.

Soon afterward, she heard him walk away to rejoin his friends. She sat with her legs curled beneath her skirts, watching the venison roasting above the fire, her thoughts a million miles away. When the meat was finally crispy and golden on the outside, she withdrew the stakes.

Glancing around, she noted his tall frame silhouetted in the moonlight near the riverbank. She walked calmly over to where Night Of The Hawk stood with several other braves, smoking cigarettes they'd fashioned from leaves they'd plucked from the cottonwoods lining the riverbank and had filled with tobacco. He glanced up at her, his ebony eyes unfathomable. But when he noticed the succulent pieces of venison she held out to him, and realized how proficiently she'd managed on her own, he couldn't help but smile.

"You have done well," he said. "I hope you intend to join me."

"I'm not hungry," she replied, with easy defiance, knowing it was her only means left to strike back at him. Suddenly feeling overwhelmingly tired, she averted her eyes and started to turn away, acutely aware that his gaze was still riveted on her.

"If you don't eat you'll make yourself sick. We're all anxious to get home. I can't allow you to slow us down."

Won't allow you, can't let you, God, she was sick and tired of hearing his voice. In subtle ways, and with his ever persistent demands, he was breaking down her barriers one by one. The only thing she had left was her pride, and he was sure trying his best to rob her of that. Tired, hurt, even intimidated, she still intended to show him that she wasn't his damned squaw, and she'd never be as long as she had any breath left in her body.

She whirled and glared at the arrogant, insufferable savage. "Do you really think you can make me sit down to supper with this pack of heathen murderers when the blood from the white scalps they've taken is still fresh under their fingernails?" she retorted harshly, and not waiting for him to reply, she spat at their blank faces. "Well, I wouldn't eat with the likes of you if I were starving!"

The Comanches hadn't understood what she'd said, but they well knew the look of condemnation in her eyes as her gaze had swept over them. Black Raven was on his feet instantly, and stalked over to confront Callie, his expression murderous and his fists tightly clenched.

"This *herbi* has no respect, and I for one think it is time that someone taught her how she is supposed to act in a warrior's presence," he snarled, and grabbing a length of rawhide from his parfleche, he unfurled it with a snap. "Let her feel the bite of my lash against her soft skin. That will take the fight out of her."

Callie instantly froze at the threatening inflection in his voice.

"*Kee!,* No, Black Raven, you will not touch her," Night Of The Hawk declared. He'd sprung to his feet, but he didn't so much as make another move toward them. No one dared breathe for several tension filled moments.

Black Raven came to a rigid halt several feet away from Callie who stood her ground. Lowering his raised hand, he sneered at her. "*Ai,* I'm disgusted, and you are going to find out she is not worth it, Night Hawk. She will betray you the first chance that she gets . . . just you wait and see," he stated curtly, and clearly finding it difficult to repress his rage, he stormed off, leaving Callie trembling with the near violent encounter.

As angry as he'd been, she had no doubt that if Night Of The Hawk hadn't intervened, Black Raven would have taken great pleasure in doing something awful to her. He was a vile, evil man, and she had made a bitter enemy. Clearly, the battle lines had been drawn between them. Closing her eyes for a second, she reached down deep within herself and summoned the reserve strength that she so depended on to keep her strong. It wasn't as easy this time, and a quiver of uncertainty intruded.

"Callie, *keemah,* come with me."

She opened her eyes, and her captor was standing over her. She recognized that familiar hard expression and knew he was terribly angry with her.

"Your sharp tongue is a better weapon than anything this Comanche could ever hope to equal," he

221

said tersely, and when he saw she didn't look as if she wanted to go anywhere with him, added, "You'd damn well better follow me unless you wish to stay behind and let my friends teach you a lesson in manners. I'm sure they'd like nothing better at the moment."

He was back to issuing threats again, proving to her that he was the master. Their gazes locked. Without another word, he walked away from her. Callie quickly decided that for once she wasn't going to argue the point.

The situation was out of her control for the moment. She stood in the darkness facing a deadly enemy, feeling very much like an uninvited guest, and thus, did the only thing she could. She quickened her pace and followed behind her captor to the riverbank.

Callie sat on the ground and leaned back against the trunk of a cottonwood tree. Her bearing remained stiff and proud, but in truth, her spirit was in chaos. At least it was cooler by the river, and quiet, which allowed her to force her confused emotions into some order.

Night Of The Hawk had barely spoken to her in over an hour, but she relished the solitude, using the time to try and analyze her situation. She really wanted to weep with frustration when she considered the hopelessness of it, but she wouldn't allow herself to weaken in front of him. Surprisingly, he'd removed the tether from around her neck just as soon as they were away from the others. Although she'd been relieved, she hadn't so much as inclined her head in a small gesture of thanks. She wasn't grateful. How could she be when she was in this awful situation because of him?

The delicious aroma of brewing coffee wafted to her nostrils. Her stomach rumbled, reminding her that she hadn't eaten the dried meat that he'd offered her earlier that day, and after refusing the venison, she wasn't surprised to find that she was famished. But it was the rich smell of the coffee that almost crumbled her firm resolve. She could almost taste it, but she wouldn't give in.

Her gaze strayed to the big Comanche who was crouched before an enamel coffeepot warming on a flat rock at the edge of the crackling fire. It was a disconcerting vision. Red Buffalo had poured himself a cup of coffee from a pot just like the one found in her mother's kitchen. Realizing the significance, mixed feelings surged through her. She found herself wondering how the Comanche had come by the coffee pot. What white homestead had they raided, how many lives had been lost in the process? The thought tore at her insides.

She watched the outline of the man moving against the flickering light of the fire. He was big and frightening to behold, but yet his actions were so typically human. It was a quick and disturbing realization. She saw him shift the cup to his left hand, and hurriedly blow on his right palm.

"*Anaa!* Ouch!" he cried. Muttering under his breath, he was careful to balance the tin cup so that it wouldn't spill over as he slowly rose to his feet. He turned around, and his eyes searched out her shadowy retreat. He grinned broadly, and called out to her captor. "Night Hawk, *Huuba,* coffee!?"

"Haa, yes!" Night Hawk answered.

Her pulse skittered nervously when she noticed the big warrior head toward them. He moved without haste but with purpose. The ground seemed to quiver beneath his feet, and Callie's gaze pondered each step that he took. He brought with him the fragrant smell of coffee, but also, of grease, smoke and horses. Indian smells. All things she detested. Callie stared at him in waiting silence and quite openly studied him. He was indeed the biggest, fiercest looking man she'd ever seen in her life.

He came closer, gazing down at her intensely. Night Hawk joined them, and Red Buffalo swung his head around to his companion.

"This is for your woman, Night Hawk," the warrior told the raid leader, handing him a tin cup filled with steaming brew, speaking in that harsh, sharp tongue she found impossible to understand. "Make her feel better to have something hot in her stomach, eh?"

"Thank you, friend," Night Of The Hawk replied. "But just try convincing *her* of that."

His gaze fixed on her. "Take it, Callie," he urged her. "Red Buffalo makes the best coffee you've ever tasted."

"I'd rather not," she replied stiffly, turning her head and giving an irritable tug at her sleeve.

Red Buffalo laughed down deep, and the full-hearted sound shook his huge chest and belly. "That's why I tell you. I think *this* Comanche would have better success convincing his horse to fly than to get your woman to take anything from me."

Both men chuckled, and a hot lump felt wedged in Callie's throat. She had misinterpreted their laughter, assuming they were making fun of her. She felt like human chattel. His possession to toy with, laugh at, trade when he tired of her. While the two warriors continued talking, Callie became aware of another sound. One that ignited a spark of hope inside her.

Behind her, a horse had nickered, and it was then she remembered that the animals had been turned out to graze. By the sound, she reasoned they couldn't be very far away. Hopefully, within running distance. Freedom was within her grasp. Maybe. It really depended on her timing and speed once she managed to put some distance between herself and the dreaded Comanches.

Cautiously, she cast a quick look over her shoulder, and sighed inwardly with relief. The horses were even closer than she'd assumed, and now there wasn't anyone standing near them. Tilting her head to one side, she slanted a look at the two warriors in front of her, and said a quick prayer that Night Hawk would turn his back for just a minute. It would have to be enough time for her to reach the horses. Just thinking about what she was going to do made her chest feel as if it would burst. She decided that first she would have to try and make them think she'd decided to accept her plight and make the best of her situation.

Her heart was pounding in a cadence of fear, but she had to remain as calm as possible. Holding out her hand, she said to Night Hawk, "I've changed my mind. The food smells very good. I've decided I'd like something to eat after all."

She noted a wary glimmer in his eyes, but he said nothing, merely told her he would go and bring her back some of the leftover venison. He returned a short time later and handed her a stick speared with venison. She contemplated it, not quite sure if she should eat it with her fingers or nibble it off the stick.

To her surprise, the strapping Comanche with the gravely voice wandered back over to stare curiously at her, then hunkering down, his mouth split in a huge grin that seemed nothing but teeth. He reminded her of a giant grizzly contemplating dinner, and Callie had an hysterical urge to scoot backwards out of his reach. He merely nodded his head several times, and then he took an enormous bite out of the piece of venison he held in one hand and chewed lustily.

"Haa tsaatu. Yes, it's good," he said, rubbing a hand across his round belly. By the tone of his voice and his gestures, she could only assume that he was trying to convince her it was all right to eat heartily.

She bit in to the meat, but she had to force herself to chew.

"I'm happy to see your appetite's improved," Night Hawk told her. "There's more if you're still hungry when you finish." He glanced around them, then turned back to her. "If you need to take care of other needs"—he indicated by a motion of his head the nearby brush—"you can do so in private over there. But first you'll have to promise me you won't try and do anything foolish."

She raised her chin with a cool stare, and nodded slowly. "I promise." She wasn't lying, she thought, for she considered gaining her freedom the wisest thing she could do.

"Go on then. But make it quick. I don't want to have to come looking for you."

Just at that moment, one of his friends who was engaged in a lively dice game, let out a joyous war whoop. Curious, he turned away to stare after them. Then he and Red Buffalo strode over to join their circle.

Callie watched him go. Freedom was never closer, but she knew not to make any sudden moves. She sipped the strong coffee from the cup and took another bite of the meat, but it tasted just like sawdust on her tongue. Her only thought was to escape, and it was difficult for her to make herself move slowly.

Now was as good a time as any, she figured. The Indians were intent on their gambling, and for the first time, no one seemed to be paying her much attention. Just before she set her cup and the stick aside, and thought about how she was going to slip off into the dark shadows, she had an instant of clear rationalization. If she tried and failed, Night Hawk would probably punish her severely. She was shaking and her knees felt weak, but her mind had never been more set on anything. She couldn't afford to pass up this opportunity. Thank God she'd ridden her father's horses enough times that she felt certain she could ride bareback.

When she moved, needlelike pain shot through her legs once again, but she merely winced and was careful not to make a sound. She thought with sudden concern of how she'd have to survive in the wilderness on her own, but she would hope that by now the fort would have learned about the attack on the regiment, and of her abduction. Surely they were already out scouring the countryside in search of her. She only had to hang on for a little while longer before they found her.

Despite the pounding of her heart and her cold, clammy fear, Callie began to make good her plan. She strolled casually toward the bushes and away from the faint glow of the firelight. When she was concealed by mesquite brush, she made an attempt to hitch up her skirts. Just in case someone was watching and might see her. But as soon as she saw that no one seemed interested in her activities, she bolted toward the horses. She smiled then. It was a faint smile, but nonetheless triumphant.

Her ankles were weak from her inactivity and she stumbled over the rocky terrain, twisting her ankle, prompting her to bite down on her bottom lip to keep from crying out. She was a bundle of nerves by the time she reached the small herd.

Choosing the first pony she'd come upon, a black and white pinto with long legs, she grabbed his halter. To her bitter despair, she noticed that the Indians had twisted rawhide hobbles around the ponies' front legs, and she knew it was going to require precious minutes for her to work the knots free. Holding back sobs of desperation, she fell to her knees and began to yank desperately at the knots.

It seemed to take her forever, and she kept thinking that one of the Indians could look over and see her at any moment. Finally, she was able to free the pinto's legs, and she breathed a sigh of relief. Leading him over to a rock where she could then mount him, she scrambled up onto the boulder and grabbed a handful of the pony's mane. He stomped his hooves in agitation, but she managed to pull herself onto his back just as he sidestepped away from her. However, before she could gain her a firm seat on his back, the beast took off at a gallop. She was unmindful of anything after that but trying to remain astride. They tore across the darkened terrain, and Callie felt her first sense of freedom since her nightmare had begun. The wind caught her hair, whipping the flaming tresses back from her face. It shimmered like newly-minted copper in the moonlight.

Hearing the sound of pounding hooves, Night Of The Hawk whirled just in time to see Callie racing away on the pinto; her red hair drew his eyes like a beacon.

"Callie, no!" he shouted, but it was too late. There would be no turning back for Callie, he knew.

Behind her, she heard the Comanches' frantic shouting, but she didn't hesitate for fear they would catch her, and digging her heels into the pony's flanks, she urged him onward. Faster, they had to go faster if she were to gain enough ground so that the Comanche wouldn't catch her. When she heard the pounding of hooves behind her, she chanced a hurried glance back over her shoulder.

There was no mistaking the dark forms of the Indians on horseback, and she noticed Night Hawk at their lead, the others following closely behind. She nudged the pinto onward, speaking softly near his ear as she'd seen the Comanche do before. Responding to her tone of voice, he plunged ahead at a smooth, rolling gallop. She hung on tightly, praying he would be able to keep up the speed.

She began to envision how she would get away, and riding through the night, she would find her way back to the fort and safety. Precious freedom was close at hand.

She couldn't remember her concentration straying for more than a moment, but before she realized, the pony had carried her beneath a sweep of low-hanging tree branches, and a startled scream bubbled in her throat. Twigs and leaves whipped past and tangled in her hair. Suddenly a tree branch loomed up before her eyes. Callie barely had time to throw her arm in front of her face before the world seemed to explode around her. She was thrown off the pony's back and tossed effortlessly through the air like a leaf in the wind.

The last thing she remembered was her life blurring before her.

Chapter Fifteen

Night Hawk was one of the first to reach her. His stallion had barely slowed his pace before the Comanche was off his back and hit the ground running. Reaching Callie's crumpled form, he fell to his knees and carefully turned her over.

Cradling her in his arms, his eyes scanned her face and form. His own heart was beating so erratically he could hardly catch his breath. In the moonlight her pale skin looked ghostly white and she lay so still that he feared she was dead. It was a terrible moment, filled with confusing emotions. She was certainly more trouble than ten women, but she was worth it, he decided. It was a realization that left him bewildered.

The other warriors had quickly gathered around him, their faces grave.

"Is she alive?" Red Buffalo asked, a muscle spasming in his face.

Night Hawk smoothed her hair away from her face with a tenderness that surprised his close friend. Red Buffalo watched as Night Hawk leaned over her, and he noticed his friend's face was etched with worry.

"Haa, yes, she is breathing, but I don't know yet how badly she's been injured," Night Hawk replied, and his eyes gleamed hopefully. Red Buffalo's face split into a relieved smile.

Night Hawk ran his hands over her, assuring himself that she bore no broken bones. He found a nasty bump on her head, swollen to the size of a walnut. It could be serious; it was hard to tell. But she was alive and that was what mattered to him most. Scooping her up in his arms, he hurriedly carried her to his horse. The slow ride back to their camp seemed like it took him forever, but he was afraid to press his stallion beyond a walk for fear of aggravating her head injury.

He dismounted as soon as they reached camp, carried her over to the fire and gently lowered her to the ground. He studied the ugly purple bruise forming near her hairline.

When Callie regained consciousness with her head throbbing, the first thing she saw were his black eyes glittering down at her and she knew he was angry, but concerned as well. She blinked, and it seemed a great effort just to keep her focus on him. He leaned one arm on his knee as he studied her with unwavering intensity.

"You could have been killed," he stated hoarsely. "I really didn't think you'd try something so foolish. Can't I trust you out of my sight for even a minute?"

Tears welled in her eyes but did not spill over.

She wouldn't allow them to. "I told you I would never surrender to you, and I meant every word."

Black Raven strode across the campsite, his expression murderous. Callie was afraid to think what he had in mind for her. She didn't have long to find out.

"This captive does not know her place. She was trying to steal from this Comanche. She failed, but it was my pony she tried to take. Now I demand that she be punished," he growled, standing next to Night Hawk.

Night Hawk leapt to his feet and whirling, placed himself firmly between her trembling form and the furious Comanche warrior. "She is my woman. I will decide whether or not she did anything that merits punishment."

Once again, their exchange was in Comanche, but Callie knew by the harsh tone of their voices, and Black Raven's furious gestures, that they were arguing over her fate.

Black Raven stabbed a finger at her. "It was my pony, therefore it is my business as well. He has an injured foreleg because of her and now will be of no value to me. I will have to turn him loose and ride one of the horses we took from the long knives. This *herbi* should be disciplined the Comanche way."

"Only if *I* say that it is to be," Night Of The Hawk replied, taking a threatening step forward, backing Black Raven down.

"She has made you blind, Night Hawk," he spat. *"Ma burnitui nu,* I will see that you punish her

233

when the time comes. It is only right, and you well know it."

Night Hawk fixed a steely glare on the scowling warrior and his white teeth flashed in a sneer. "Maybe you shouldn't place too much blame on the *herbi*. If you treat your pony in the same manner as you do your women I can well understand why he was eager to run with the woman."

A strained silence fell over the group huddled around them. Black Raven seemed ready to challenge him, but after several tense seconds, he cursed under his breath, and spinning on his heel, stalked away.

Night Hawk knew there would be another time and place. Black Raven would not forgive so easily. He also realized that every man there was wondering, just as Black Raven, why he tolerated this flame-haired woman's insolence. She had lied to him and she did deserve punishment. But he had never laid a hand on a woman in violence. He didn't agree with other men that a cowed woman made a far better companion. It was his experience that the female gender responded far better to a different, more pleasurable, method of persuasion. Callie would prove no exception. He just needed more time to convince her.

Feeling the warriors' steely gaze, he quickly raised his arm in a dismissive gesture. *"Suvante!* It is over. Leave us now. The woman is my responsibility."

Black Raven stormed away, kicking up dust with the toe of his moccasin like a little boy in the throes of a tantrum.

Turning back to Callie, he knelt down next to her. She watched him closely, wondering if he'd given Black Raven his word that he'd kill her for what she tried to do. Somehow, she didn't want to believe he would do such a thing.

His eyes studied her by the light from the flames, and she flinched when she felt him run his hands along her arms and legs, her body quivering expectantly. He did not like it that she was waiting for the blows to fall. What kind of a man did she think that he was? Very gently, so as not to frighten her more, he raised his arms. He slowly burrowed his fingers in to her hair to probe her scalp.

She tried to jerk away from him, but he held her firmly.

"Damnit, I'm not going to hurt you," he stated gruffly. "I just wish to hell that you would accept what has to be and save us both a lot of trouble."

She wanted to brush his hands away, but everything was still so fuzzy and she didn't seem to have the strength necessary to lift her arms, let alone fight him off. Bitterness blocked out the light of reason. "I . . . want my freedom," she rasped fiercely, "and I'll never give up trying to get away from you."

"You'd better if you know what's good for you," he ordered, ignoring her cold rage. After another lengthy scrutiny he was satisfied that she had no broken bones, just a bump on the head that was probably sore as hell but not life threatening. He shifted his weight and sat back on his heels. "You have courage, angel, but it did not serve you well this time. Black Raven is very angry. It was his pony that you tried to steal, and among my people this is a very serious offense." He sighed. "He's demanded restitution. Sooner or later I'll have to think of some way to appease him."

She laughed contemptuously. "Just give him my scalp, Night Hawk. That would undoubtedly please the bastard to no end." Furious, she pushed herself to a sitting position. "After all, what's one more? Especially when you've undoubtedly lifted so many that it probably wouldn't bother you in the least."

"Enough!" he snarled, and she noticed that she'd succeeded in making him visibly angry. It gave her enormous satisfaction to have shaken even a fraction of his iron control. "You think you know so much about us. Well, you don't. So I'll thank you to keep your opinions to yourself."

"I know what I've seen, and I've concluded that you're nothing more than a ruthless killer, just like the rest of these savages you call your people." She had lost the last shred of her reasoning, and words spewed from her without any consideration of their impact. "Although you're the most despicable because you're not full-blooded Comanche, yet you act just like one of them."

"You have a lot to learn about us before you can pass judgment," he snapped, his face inches from her own, his simmering rage plainly evident on his face. He swallowed a biting remark, and an almost satanic smile spread across his lips. "But there will be plenty of time for that later. It's been a long day. I'd say it's about time for bed."

Callie bit her lip, and tried her best not to shrink back from him. "I'm not tired yet."

"Well I am," he drawled, and before she could fend him off he was reaching out for her, grabbing her hands, trapping them between his. He called out something, and one of the warriors hurried to do his bidding. A moment later, she stared in disbelief while he wrapped a length of rope around her wrists and hobbled them.

"You . . . you tied my hands," she exclaimed incredulously.

"I'd say it's a damn good idea and about the only way of ensuring that I'm going to get any sleep." He secured the remainder of the short rope to his own wrist and stood back from her. "That should do it. You even flinch, and I'll feel it."

"You bastard!"

He laughed cynically. "Is that the only swear word you know? Remind me to teach you a few more. I'm getting real tired of hearing the same one over and over." He was watching her in that way she couldn't stand, as if something intimate was about to happen between them, and she felt her cheeks burn. "Don't worry, I never was much into bondage," he added snidely.

She raised a mocking brow. "Given what I know about your past, I find *that* very hard to believe."

Surprising himself, he laughed. "Whatever you choose to believe, I did secure your wrists for your own good. If you tried anything again, and one of

237

the others got to you before I did, they would make you pay in ways that even I might think were exceedingly cruel." Then as though he were suddenly weary of dealing with her, he slipped his hands beneath her and effortlessly hoisted her into his arms.

"I can walk on my own," she hissed, palms pushing against his chest.

"Don't fight me, angel. I've had about enough of tussling with you for one night."

Callie knew well that he wasn't bluffing. Once again, he took her beyond the firelight and the inquisitive stares. When he came upon the dark area secluded by mesquite bushes and large rocks, he strode over to the pallet of soft, luxurious fur that had been spread out on the ground.

"This is where we'll be sleeping tonight," he said matter-of-factly.

She stared at him as if he'd taken leave of his senses. "I . . . I am *not* about to sleep with you."

He jerked his chin in the direction of the other warriors. "Either you can bed down with me, or one of them will be glad to oblige you."

Callie released her breath in a rush. "So *this* is how you intend to punish me. I knew you'd find a way."

His lips twisted in a sardonic smile, and he stared back at her through heavy-lidded eyes. "Leave it to you to think so."

She tensed. The moment she had been dreading was about to happen. He would take her against her will and the others would know and no doubt they'd gloat over the fact. She wished she had grabbed his knife as she'd considered. Only to kill herself, not him. Better to die by her own hand than to suffer this degradation.

He went down on one knee, placing her on the pallet. Then reaching forward, he grasped her left ankle, and with deft fingers, he unbuttoned her ankle-high kid boots. Pulling one off, then the other, he set them on the ground next to her.

Perhaps sensing her trepidation, his dark eyes cut into hers as his fingers lingered on her foot and seemed to burn her skin through her cotton stockings. "It is not an easy time for you. I understand how you must be feeling. And while you may have angered Black Raven, you have managed to earn the respect of the Comanche by your show of courage, *mah tao,* little one. We call such bravery 'Comanche heart.' Do not let it fail you now."

"Why should you care?"

"Trust my words," he reassured her. "You have nothing to fear from me."

"Is that the same thing you said to Lily?" she queried coolly. The words were out before she'd had time to halt them.

He froze for a moment, stunned, then his hand clamped onto her wrists and jerked hard. She was on her knees before him and her body slammed against his bare chest and heavily corded thighs. His fingers lifted her chin, but she had her eyes closed and she couldn't seem to force the lids open. "Don't ever speak to me of Lily in that tone of voice again. You can't even begin to know what she and I had together."

Her lids slowly opened, and she forced herself to look up at him. There was pain etched across his harsh features. She frowned, confused.

Echoing her thoughts, he said tersely. "You still wonder if I was responsible for that night, don't you?"

"I never used to believe you capable of such violence."

"But you do now," he said.

"I've glimpsed a side of you I never realized before."

"I'm not a murderer of women and children," he stated abruptly, cutting into her thoughts.

"I'm not sure of that any longer," she retorted with frank honesty.

He muttered a low and frustrated curse. "Damn you. You speak of the Comanche's cruel torture, but you're better at it than any Comanche could ever hope to be." He pushed her back down onto the bed of furs. Looming over her, he ordered, "Don't get up. I'm through trying to win your trust. As far as my people are concerned, you belong to me. From now on you'll do exactly as you're told. I'm telling you to stay there. You'd better listen."

She'd never seen him so angry, and she bit her lip, suddenly unsure. Not trusting her voice, she merely nodded her head.

When he dropped down beside her and drew her into the curve of his body she did not try and fight him. He pulled the fur over their bodies. She huddled with her back to him, but the rope tied at his wrist prevented her from moving as far away as she would have liked. He slipped one arm beneath her neck to cushion her head.

Callie lay like a block of wood and waited for what she felt certain would follow. He only held her. Tenderly. Protectively. It was not what she'd been expecting.

After a while, she relaxed and let the steady sound of his breathing, and the sensual texture of the fur against her skin, lull her. She didn't know if he were sleeping, or lying awake wondering, as she was. What was this raw emotion she was feeling at the moment? It felt so right lying here like this with him, but she was certain it had to be wrong. Of course it was wrong! Hadn't his kind murdered her father, tortured and raped those women, and today, killed again? He was her enemy, wasn't he?

As if he'd somehow sensed her thoughts, he said, "No one will hurt you. Go to sleep, *mah tao yo*."

How in God's name was she ever going to sleep!? All she could do was lay here and pray for strength, but most of all she wanted to forget everything that had happened to her this day. Some innate sense kept telling her to trust him, but she was still wary and felt that it wouldn't be wise to let down her guard. But just before her eyelids drifted closed, she felt his big hand tenderly stroke the back of her head.

Callie finally drifted to sleep clinging to the hope that in the morning she might somehow be able to convince him to let her go.

A frightened scream shattered the predawn quiet, and Night Of The Hawk was awake in an instant.

"No . . . no . . . please don't kill them," he heard someone sob, and knew that it was Callie caught in the throes of a bad dream.

He reached over to wake her, but when he touched her shoulder she thrashed violently and struck at him.

"Papa . . . don't leave me all alone," she whimpered.

"Shhh, everything's fine, it's nothing but a bad dream," he tried, soothing her as best that he could."

She opened her eyes and stared out at the darkness unseeing, still trapped in painful memories that she'd never been able to put to rest. Her spine tensed. She was dazed and in emotional shock. In her mind she was back on that ill-fated stage. A sob bubbled in her throat. She didn't realize she'd even made a sound, but suddenly there were strong arms enfolding her, lifting and turning her gently, providing a solid, comforting shoulder to pillow her cheek against. He just held her, nothing more, and the shaky grasp Callie had on her emotions weakened even more.

She needed him more at that moment than she'd ever needed anyone before. His body was warm and vital; he made her feel far removed from the horror she'd just experienced. Her close brush with death earlier in the day, and the effects of her dream still lingered in her mind. It was that darkest hour just before dawn, and it was the time when fears loomed out of proportion.

Burying her face in the curve of his neck, she wanted him to reassure her with his warmth and touch. Nothing else mattered but holding her terror at bay. "Please make them go away," she whimpered.

"Talk to me, angel. Tell me what frightens you so," he urged her. He understood how she was feeling, and simply held her shuddering body into his and finally when she felt ready, he listened quietly while she spoke of her fears.

"I've never been able to forget that day. My . . . father was killed by Indians . . . I can't help but remember what they did to him, and to the women who were on the stage with us," she murmured brokenly. "I have always hated and feared the Indians because of it. And today . . . there was more killing. Always it seems there is bloodshed and death to haunt my dreams."

"I am sorry that our people must make war against one another," he whispered against her hair. He drew her against his chest, absorbing the tremors of her body, crooning tender words that she could not understand, but needing to say them to her nevertheless. *"Toquet,* it is well. Rest now, no one will bother you, the dreams won't come again, I won't let them."

He saw that Red Buffalo, alerted by her screams,

243

stood several yards away and appeared watchful. Behind him, a few of the other warriors had thrown off their buffalo robes and were milling about, but they advanced no farther. He waved them away, and when they realized there was no threat, they soon returned to their pallets, and the murmur of voices finally faded once more.

For a long time, Night Hawk listened to the sound of her soft weeping, and felt the burden of her sorrow. She lay cuddled against him, her back pressing against his chest, the curve of her rump and long, lithe legs keeping him wide awake and caught in his own torture.

Damn, he wanted her. He longed to bury himself in her sweet, scented body and lose himself in her warmth. She would be soft and welcoming and ready for him by the time that he was done with her. He knew there was no better way to chase away bad memories of darkness and death than to reaffirm life with loving.

Slowly, so he wouldn't frighten her, he sifted his fingers through her hair, and savored the silky-soft texture between his thumb and forefinger. He wanted to bury his lips in the gleaming mass and inhale deeply the fragrant perfume that was hers alone. He was aware of everything about her, but most of all, how she fit so perfectly in his arms. There was no denying she was the woman from his vision, but until this night he'd never before wanted to admit it. He'd known it in New Orleans, perhaps even from the first although he hadn't wanted to face the reality.

His arm lay draped over her, and his fingers resting against her abdomen began a gentle kneading motion, while the other hand he'd slipped beneath her cupped her breast.

When she tried to pull away from him, he tightened his hand on her midriff, and she dared not move. It was not a threatening gesture, and it wasn't her fear of him that prompted her to lie so still. There were those confusing emotions to contend with again. The ones she felt whenever he came near, and set her blood tingling in her veins.

Liquid heat seemed to pour from his fingertips. She inhaled sharply. "You . . . you mustn't . . ." but the protest died on her lips. His hands had already begun to work their fiery magic on her skin and his lips stirred the buried embers of her desire. Heat, burning sweet flames, seemed to consume her flesh.

Callie moaned and stirred restlessly against him. She half-heartedly mumbled a protest, but it ended in a blissful sigh as her hunger for him sharpened in intensity. She moistened her lips, inexperience making her tremble. "I really think—"

"Don't think, angel, just let yourself feel," he crooned.

He drew her over onto her back, and just before he dipped his head to nuzzle her neck, she glimpsed the raw hot need in his eyes and remembered having seen that look once before in New Orleans. In that brief moment she felt connected to him as she had then.

His hand moved down, his fingers searching,

finding. He palmed her gently curved mound through the layers of material, and her hips arched up to meet his caress.

"You are so beautiful," he whispered. "Let me soothe you."

Sensual voice, skillful hands, and she *did* like how he set her afire. Far too much, she startlingly realized, but she'd never let him know it.

"I told you I wouldn't touch you unless I thought you'd welcome my caress. If you want me to stop, I will," he said.

She couldn't seem to make herself say the words.

He slowly drew the hem of her gown and ruffled petticoats up past her shapely knees, and higher still, discarding layer upon layer of clothing, discovering a lace trimmed garter that held up cotton stockings; quieting her protest with soothing words and seeking hands. Allowing his mind to envision every way in which he would enjoy making love to her. But the single most thing he found himself imagining, was how smooth her skin above those stockings, and how satiny soft it would feel beneath his fingertips.

It was a visual feast for his mind's eye, and his body longed to take possession of hers. But he had never taken a woman without her consent, and he did not intend to do so now. He'd have to hear her say the words to him before he'd satisfy his own need. There were plenty of women who could satisfy his hunger, but there was only one to cool his fever.

He recalled that long ago night in the bayou, and

her uninhibited response. There was no doubt in his mind that he could make her want him like that again, but he wanted more from her than just her passion. Although he didn't think she was ready to give herself to him yet. He would wait, and she would come to him. Until then, there were ways to gentle a wild filly and ignite a slow yearning that she would not easily forget.

Chapter Sixteen

Callie moaned and stirred restlessly against him. She half-heartedly mumbled a protest, but it ended in a blissful sigh as her hunger for him sharpened in intensity. She moistened her lips, inexperience making her tremble. This wasn't love; it was nothing more than seduction. So, why wasn't she drawing away from him?

As if he sensed her confusion, he pressed a kiss behind her ear and murmured. "I'd never do anything to hurt you. Trust me, sweet, just let me show you how good it can be."

Still, it seemed only natural to arch her back when he took her into his arms and his mouth closed over hers. After that, rational thought was abandoned, and she only wanted more of what he'd promised her. With a sigh, her lips parted under his, and she eagerly met the bold thrust of his tongue when it teased her lips apart. The kiss seemed to go on forever, and she felt consumed by a surge of hot need.

His hands, never still, were skillful and set her

afire in places she'd never been touched before. His kisses were a heady assault on her senses. The bunched folds of her gown were up around her thighs, and she could feel the hard length of him pressed against her. She wanted what his body promised, but there was still a part of her that felt uncertain. A tiny whimper of unease escaped her lips, and he captured it on an inward breath, along with her concerns and fears.

He drew his mouth from hers, his lips seeking the softness of her neck, and she felt his hand seek her breast, rub the nipple taut between his fingers. She tried telling herself she should stop him, but she didn't let herself listen.

His hand moved down, his fingers searching, finding, holding her a prisoner of desire. She wanted this, needed it to forget what had happened earlier, and how close she'd come to death. Surrendering to the magic of his touch, she felt desire curl within her. Yet there would always be the remembrance of those other poor women who had been dragged screaming from the stage to intrude harshly. They had been raped, then left torn and bleeding, begging for mercy. Her captor could easily overpower her and do the same horrible things to her. Perhaps this would even be his way of punishing her for stealing Black Raven's pony.

Because of her terrible memories, Callie found it almost impossible to think of surrendering her body to any man. She enjoyed the preliminaries, but even though she longed to know what it was like, she dreaded finding out that it was painful, humiliating, and more horrible than anything she might have imagined.

"Easy," he murmured, gentling her, feeling her heart skittering against her ribcage. "I won't hurt you. We'll go slowly, and when you're ready, you tell me. I won't ever force you, angel."

Sensual voice, skillful hands, they had robbed her of all will. She tensed slightly when she felt the cool night air against her bare breasts, but he reassured her with his voice once again. She stared up at him in the darkness, saw the fierce desire that lit his eyes and noticed that for the first time since she'd known him the hard, reckless lights had dimmed. Reaching upward, she impulsively outlined the fullness of his bottom lip with one finger. His teeth grazed her fingertip, sending shivers scurrying along her spine.

Whatever they shared together at this moment was unlike anything he'd experienced in a long time, and he couldn't honestly say he welcomed it. It was intense and consuming. He thought of nothing and no one but her whenever they were together. Like now, envisioning every way in which he would enjoy making love to her. Had there ever been another woman he'd wanted more than this one? He didn't honestly think so. There were plenty of women who could satisfy his hunger, but there was only this one to cool his raging fever. But this time he'd forego his need and pleasure her. She'd obviously never been with any other man before and he knew she found the idea of surrendering herself degrading. But there came a point, if he were patient, when all sense of fear and reason vanished and she would want him beyond anything else. Only then would she become his.

His kisses probed deeper, hungrier. She felt his desire, hot and hard, return her thrust, and between her thighs a need longed to be satisfied. His lips, never still, moved across her skin, and downward. When he pressed a most intimate kiss against the downy vee of fire-red curls, Callie tried to draw her knees upward, but he held her still.

"You can't mean to—" Callie broke off, terribly embarrassed.

"I intend to do even more than that," he teased, his hands cupping her buttocks, lifting her, positioning her legs where she couldn't twist free of him. He nuzzled the soft flesh between her thighs and nipped gently, surprising her.

"Oh . . . please, I don't think we should do *that*," Callie pleaded, her voice thick and low.

He wouldn't allow her to do anything but surrender to him, and finally, after long, deep kisses that scorched her swollen flesh, every barrier she'd erected against him came tumbling down, and the fire in her veins exploded.

She lifted her hips, allowing him to taste the sweet nectar of her love. There were only his hands and mouth touching every part of her body. She was swept into a whirlwind, feeling lost, uncertain, then suddenly, she found what she'd been seeking. "Oh, God . . . I never knew," she rasped, fingernails digging into the fur pelts beneath her.

Of course, he realized she didn't really know but a fraction of what he intended to teach her.

Caught in an intense, trembling release, she could only go with the throbbing, wavering sensations of pleasure that she'd never imagined possible. When the tiny pulses in her body slowed at last, and she'd quieted in his arms, she thought about what he'd just given her. There hadn't been any taking; he'd wanted nothing for himself, only for her.

Tears sprang into her eyes and washed the bitter hatred from her heart. He'd tried to tell her with words how much he regretted the events that had brought them together. She hadn't wanted to hear him, so he'd found another way to reach her.

Scooping her up against him, he rolled over onto his back, taking her with him. She lay quietly subdued, and even though his body burned with his need of her, he knew his own fulfillment would have to wait. She'd given enough for one day. He stroked her sweat-dampened hair, brushed the back of his hand across her cheek, and wondered if somehow their roles hadn't become reversed. Callused fingers trailed along her spine. It was a question he didn't think he wanted to answer.

Callie lay with her chin tucked against his shoulder, and nothing in her life had ever felt more right than at that moment. She only wished she might hang onto it forever, but she knew with the morning light, that her position would be no different. She'd be little more than a fool if she allowed herself to think otherwise.

"Wake up, angel, the sun's coming up and we have to be moving on."

His voice was the first thing she heard when she awoke the next morning. What they had shared between them only hours before now seemed like a distant memory, and she could hardly force herself to open her eyes and face him.

He made it easy for her. Leaning over, he took hold of her wrist. "Come on, *bella,* we've lost enough time. You'll feel better once you've had some breakfast."

She felt his gaze drift downward to her breast thrusting above the line of her corset. Remembering her state of undress, she grabbed at the buffalo robe and covered herself as her eyes impaled him. He loomed over her, seemingly a completely different man from the one who'd come to her in the darkness and had held her through the night. "Will you just hold your horses a minute," she snapped, refusing to budget another inch. "Unlike you, I prefer to wear clothes. And I'm not about to move until I find my dress and put it back on."

He shot her a quick, amused look. "There isn't any need to keep that blanket pulled up to your chin. The others have already ridden out ahead of us."

He stood before her, filling her view with copper muscle and bare, long limbs. She noticed for the first time that the only sound was their voices. Everything else lay quiet.

"Red Buffalo didn't think it would be wise if Black Raven was around when you woke up."

"I'm not sorry I tried to steal the horse," she said, her chin tilted obstinately. "I just happened to pick the wrong one, that's all."

"Don't underestimate him, angel," he warned her, his expression serious. "You tried to take his most prized possession. He will not easily forgive, and I won't be able to watch over you all the time."

"I can look after myself just fine," she assured him, but a lump rose in her throat.

"I intend to make certain of that," he said. "As soon as there's time I'm going to teach you how to defend yourself."

She glanced up at him, and felt her emotions immediately spiraling out of control. Perhaps after the intimacy they'd shared he might feel differently about setting her free. "You could just let me go and then you wouldn't have to worry," she ventured, trying to keep the hopeful note out of her voice.

"You wouldn't stand a chance in hell out there alone," he replied, dashing her scant hope of freedom.

Callie clamped her lips shut, and her expression turned mutinous. She thought she'd be better off anywhere other than here with him. Now she even had a bloodthirsty Comanche just waiting, it seemed, to exact his revenge. And she so needed to get away from Night Of The Hawk. She could barely stand to think about last night, and the way he'd made her behave. Her face was burning, and she wished more than anything that he would just go away and leave her alone so that she might restore her dignity. What little he'd left her, that is.

He didn't move, but for a split second his hand gentled on her wrist. "There's a stream a few hours up ahead. If we leave within the next half-hour we'll have time for you to bathe before we reach my village."

"Alone, or will you be joining me?" she queried testily.

"If you'd like privacy then you'll have it."

"After last night, you'll have to forgive me if I find that statement a bit hard to believe," Callie replied frostily, turning away.

"Look at me," he demanded sharply.

Her gaze snapped up.

"You wanted me to make love to you last night, so quit trying to deny it, and for God's sake, don't feel guilty either. I damn well enjoyed what I did, although I would have liked to have done a helluva lot more, but it wasn't the right time or place. Although, *I* made that decision, not you. And if you'd look past your prejudice, you'd realize you weren't taken advantage of. You were made love to."

While he was talking, she found herself staring, thinking, and finally, blushing furiously. What he said was true, but she didn't want to hear him speak of it in the daylight. It made it all seem too real, and she couldn't even think about the fact that he might even have gone further, and she would have let him. He was an Indian, and he'd become her first lover. The realization stirred pangs of conscience, but she couldn't help herself. Every fiber of her being had wanted him, still wanted him, but she knew there could never be a next time.

He was watching her studying him, but she didn't care. She found once she'd feasted her eyes on him it was hard to turn away. That was what she'd feared, why she hadn't wanted to let things get so out of hand last night. It was too late now. His lean face was starkly visible in the pearly morning light, and she marveled at the beauty of sculpted cheekbones and those incredibly sensual eyes, and how his lips had given her such pleasure.

In viewing him closer, with his face washed clean of warpaint, and the rising sun streaking his long raven mane with blue-black lights, she thought that, yes, he was different from her in almost every way, but it made him seem even that much more appealing. It startled her to realize this. She didn't want to remember anything but how her father, and then yesterday, the soldiers, had been murdered by men just like him. But now she had other memories as well and, even though it made her feel like a traitor, she felt a surge of heat every time she recalled them.

He'd even tied his hair behind him and it hung down his back, making him look less frightening and more like the man she'd once known. She thought she'd feel even more reassured if he'd just put on some clothes, but she didn't say what she felt, she only glanced away and began gathering her hairpins that lay scattered on the pallet. Everywhere she turned there was the truth staring her in the eyes, and she didn't want to think about anything; not who he was, what he was, only how she was going to escape him. "Please . . . just go away, I'd like to be alone for just a few minutes," she stated softly.

As forthright as ever, he asked, "Can I trust you not to run off on me again?"

She squared her shoulders. "For now," she replied, wanting no more lies between them.

He nodded. "That's the answer I was expecting," he said, and straightening, he turned away knowing she'd keep her word. "There's a pot of coffee on the fire, but we don't have time to cook anything so I'm afraid breakfast will be rather spare. I hope you like pemmican because that's what we're having," he called back over his shoulder.

She scooped up several hair pins and tried to do something with the tangled tresses cascading down past her shoulders. "I'm hungry enough to eat anything," she replied.

Hunkering down by the campfire, he rifled through his parfleche and withdrew a chunk of dried meat that had been pounded thoroughly and mixed with dried nuts and pieces of fruit. It was a staple of the Comanche diet, called Indian bread, and when it was sliced and dipped in honey, even the most finicky palate usually found it delicious.

Reaching for the gourd that he'd filled with honey, he remembered how earlier, while he'd been scouting the area, he had walked beneath a tree and heard the bees hovering ominously over his head. After some effort, and not without a few painful bee stings, he had managed to knock down their hive. He had been thinking about how little she'd had to eat the night before, and the meager breakfast he had to offer her, and that's when he'd decided to bring back the honey. He almost chuckled aloud recalling how once he'd gotten the honey, he'd had to run like the devil with the bees swarming angrily behind him.

He'd barely made it back to his stallion, and they'd still had a time outrunning the bees.

Of course, she would never hear of it from him, because he couldn't even explain his actions to himself. What was there about this woman that made her so different from any of the others? So many questions. The answers didn't flow quite as easily. With a frustrated sigh, he set about putting together the makings of her breakfast.

"I've told you before, I am not your squaw." Callie rode several feet behind Night Of The Hawk on a little sorrel mare, and while she'd been thrilled when she'd discovered that he'd thought to have his friends leave a mount for her, she'd quickly lost her enthusiasm after he'd tied a lead onto the horse's halter. "I know how to ride very well, and you're making me feel foolish."

"I'm not going to remind you to quit using that white man's term around me again," he cautioned her. "And while I might trust you on foot, I don't on horseback."

She bristled at his gruff rebuke. "I've already promised you I won't try and run away." She despised having to speak to his back, and she was sick to death of him ordering her around.

"We'll be riding into my village within the next hour. It will be a welcome sight for me, but I know how you feel about my people and I know you're not going to be overjoyed to see them. There will be a great deal of confusion and excitement. You might feel it would be the perfect time to make good an escape. Don't try it. The end result wouldn't be pleasant."

For the first time, Callie gave serious consideration to where they were headed. No man's land, the home of the Comanche—and he was one of them. She had never felt so alone in her entire life. There were no more thoughts of a quick rescue. She didn't think that anyone would ever see or hear from her again. Tears blinded her, and right then she was glad that his back was to her and he couldn't view her shame.

Ten minutes later, she heard the sound of rushing water far below them. They'd been riding along a narrow ridge overlooking lush, green lowlands that seemed a world apart from the flat, dry plains. He drew rein beside a rock-strewn ledge path that seemed to plunge straight downward.

He half-turned and his eyes met her questioning gaze. "Just let your mare have the lead and you'll be fine."

"We're . . . going down there," she said incredulously.

"I'll go first and you can follow behind Shadow."

"But I hate heights," she squeaked.

"Almost as much as you do Indians, I bet," he declared.

Her biting reply died in her throat. He'd already begun their descent, and she felt her stomach lurch. She knew it wouldn't do her any good to protest, so she decided she may as well listen and do as he said. Squeezing her knees against the mare's sides, Callie buried her fingers in the animal's silky mane and closed her eyes. She'd rather face a hundred Indians than have to endure this fiendish torture.

"If you're a good girl, when we get to the bottom I might reward you and wash your back for you," he said cheerfully.

"You don't have to do that," she retorted hotly.

"It's the least I can do after everything you've been through."

Suddenly, after his glib announcement, Callie wasn't so certain she ever wanted their ride to end.

Chapter Seventeen

The place where he took her to bathe was ruggedly beautiful. Surrounded by wind-shaped bluffs of red, pink and gold sandstone, they'd ridden into a ravine shaded by massive trees and thick, wild foliage. It was like a private paradise; quiet, calm, and far removed from the world.

Reaching up to help her dismount, he made it impossible for her to slip away from him, and she was forced to endure his arms around her. She kept telling herself she didn't like the way he so casually molded his long naked body against her every curve, or the musky scent of his sun-warmed skin that mingled with her sensual fragrance, but it was an outright lie and she knew it.

"Watch yourself so you don't slip," he cautioned. He led her across moss-covered rocks and then, several yards deeper, against a backdrop of plummeting ravines, she gasped in awe. A rush of water cascaded down some fifty feet over boulders into a wide, clear pool that emptied into a nearby stream. Callie caught her breath in surprise.

"It's beautiful," she sighed, breathing in the fresh air that felt so much cooler at the base of the canyon. Flashes of blinding color, like fluid sunshine, rippled across the sandstone, and overhead, the sky was bright turquoise and tufted with high, white clouds. It seemed far removed from where she'd been.

He seemed pleased that she approved. "I thought you'd like it." Gesturing toward the pool, he said, "You go ahead, I'm going to tend the horses, then I'll be back."

"Will you be gone long?" she queried, glancing away from him into the glistening pool. Her voice sounded tremulous.

A slow, wide smile split his lips, and heat was beginning to flow through him. Just the hint of suggestion could make him forget everything else but how much he wanted to possess her, to make sweet love to her the rest of the afternoon. Last night he'd only had a sample of her uninhibited passion and it had heightened his desire. There wasn't one curve or hidden charm that he hadn't already explored, and recalled now with almost savage delight. He pushed a stray curl away from her eyes. "No, and I won't be far away if you should need me for anything . . . anything at all."

There was a question in his eyes, and she almost didn't know what to say, but after having the hard assurance of his arms around her throughout the night, she wanted—no needed—to feel the security of his embrace again soon. Right or wrong, there was more than just a physical attraction between them. They came from two different worlds, and even though his was a forbidden culture that women like her were supposed to abhor, he'd suddenly become closer to her than anyone had ever been before.

She felt him watching her. Looking up at him, she said, "I'll be waiting. Don't be gone long."

He walked away thinking that when he returned, there was going to be no turning back for either of them. Today, like this, just the two of them, the world was in balance and trust within reach.

Callie watched him stride off, her heart thudding. This was the first time she'd been allowed a measure of freedom since he'd taken her captive. She could hardly wait to remove her soiled gown and torn stockings. She planned on washing them before he returned and then spread them on some nearby chokeberry bushes to dry in the sun.

Nothing had ever felt better than to step out of her gown, strip her stockings down her legs, and let the warm breeze caress her bare skin. But suddenly, she was embarrassed to think of herself cavorting naked in the sunlight. Despite last night, she didn't yet feel daring enough to remove her chemise and pantalets. And she wasn't about to shrug out of her corset. That was absolutely unthinkable. After all, hadn't she worn it religiously for as long as she could remember? The only time she'd ever taken it off was at night before she went to bed. Yet, she'd never been more tempted than at that moment. She wanted to remove it and draw a long, deep breath. But in the end, her modesty won out. Callie waded into the pool in her undergarments.

The water felt delightfully cool against her sunburned skin. Earlier, before they'd ridden away from the campsite, he'd tried to smear some wet mud over her face and neck, but she'd absolutely balked at the prospect. She was beginning to doubt the wisdom of her vanity when she winced just wrinkling her nose. Cupping her hands, she dipped them into the pool and sluiced water over her neck and shoulders, letting it trickle down her arms.

Still, it wasn't quite satisfying enough. There had to be a way to enjoy herself even more. Groping around with her right foot until she found a large flat rock she might sit on, she gingerly lowered her body into the water, and sighed as it lapped up around her breasts. Oh, now that was truly heavenly, she thought. She sat there for a moment in contentment, the breeze blowing strands of her sweat-dampened hair against the back of her neck. Removing the pins, Callie dipped her head back and smiled with pleasure when the water flowed over her tresses.

She didn't know how long she sat there with

her eyes shut, her thoughts drifting as a relaxed languor stole over her. She wished the moment might last forever, for she didn't want to think about the end of her journey. Later today they'd ride into his village and she could expect her life would change dramatically. She was desperately afraid, and even though she was beginning to trust Night Of The Hawk, he was still a Comanche, and unlike anyone she'd ever known before. Yet, wasn't that part of the attraction? She couldn't deny that he fascinated her and held her enthralled, even as she feared what he represented.

"Do you mind if I join you?" His familiar voice broke the silence.

Her head came up and she quickly crossed her arms over her breasts. She stared at him in surprise, and noted his lazy-lidded gaze, then the bar of soap he held in one hand. He'd removed his leggings and moccasins, but he still wore his breechcloth. There was a knife with a turquoise-studded handle strapped against one firm thigh, but it was the invitation in his eyes that made her tremble. Facing him, and her emotions, had been so much easier in the dark. Here, with the sun streaming down, the look in his eyes was all too visible. She found answering him the hardest thing she'd ever had to do.

Eyes lowered, she was barely able to raise her voice above a whisper. "If you'd like."

He waded into the water, his gaze feasting on

the drops of moisture that clung to her face and shoulders, the hint of her breasts above her arms. He didn't think she'd ever looked more desirable, or beautiful, with her hair flowing out behind her in the water like wet silk, and he wanted to go to her and fill his hands with it.

When he'd covered the short distance that separated them, he positioned himself on a rock directly behind her, and placing his hands on her shoulders, he slowly drew her back between his legs. At first she stiffened, but his voice gentled her.

"Don't fight me, sweet. I'm just going to help you wash your hair."

"Nothing . . . more?"

"If that's how you want it to be."

"Everything has happened so fast." She began to relax against him. "I suppose you think me awful the way I acted last night?"

"No, I understand how you must feel. I know how difficult the first time is for a woman."

Callie felt herself blushing. "You . . . do?"

"Yes, but nothing will happen until you absolutely feel certain that you're ready." While his voice soothed her troubled cares, his hands kneaded the tense muscles along her back and neck.

Slowly, she began to respond to him, and soon her body felt weightless and light as a feather. Tiny tremors shook her spine and he let his hands absorb them as his palms slid along her back, savoring the feel of her in his arms.

She closed her eyes, and he watched the play of emotions on her face. It pleased him that she'd slowly begun to relax her guard. "Stop talking now. Just let yourself relax." He worked the soap between his big hands until he'd built up a lather, and then he spread his fingers and laced them through her hair. Rubbing the fiery strands of copper between his fingers, he cleansed her hair until it felt as slick and smooth as the finest satin. His fingers moved over her, kneading her scalp, massaging the dull ache from her temples.

A soft sigh was his reward, and the sound filled him with immense pleasure. He hadn't touched a woman in this way for many years, and even Morning Star had never liked for him to bathe with her. She'd been terribly shy when it came to revealing her body, even to him, and she'd preferred to join the women of their village, who would gather every morning to bathe in the river. He'd tried to understand her need for privacy, but he'd always been a man who appreciated the differences between the sexes, and he had missed sharing the experience with her.

He always thought there wasn't anything more alluring than a woman's body. Tall, short, lushly endowed, or willow-slim with long coltish legs. They were all beautiful in their own way. Physical perfection didn't matter to him, but a woman seemed to think that it did. It really hadn't surprised him to discover Callie sitting in the water wearing her underclothes but he had been startled to find her still wearing that damned corset. He should have gotten rid of it last night, but then she probably would have protested that action more than anything else that he'd done. She was one of the most extraordinarily lovely women that he'd ever met, but he'd be willing to bet that she never went out in public without that infernal contraption strapped around her midsection.

Glancing down, the enticing pulse beating rapidly at the base of her throat was luring him, and he wanted so to bend his head and press a kiss there. He was hot and hard for her, but he fought the need to take her swiftly there in the water because he never wanted any regrets between them.

"Lean back so I can rinse the soap from your hair," he told her, but he was really thinking how he'd like to see her standing before him in the sunlight with nothing but her red hair against that smooth skin. He was thinking about this and much more as he placed his arm around Callie's shoulder. She never even flinched as he eased her back into the water, and cradling her, rinsed the last traces of soap from her hair.

Callie was enjoying herself very much. She'd been taking care of other people for so many years that she really couldn't remember the last time anyone had offered to tend to her needs. She'd never known a man so attuned to what gave a woman pleasure, certainly none in her experience — only this one. The man she'd thought had become a barbaric savage possessed more heart and soul than any of the fine gentlemen of her prior acquaintance. His gentle touch amazed her, for she'd seen the strength in those hands and remembered only too well how they could kill as well as give pleasure.

She found his solicitude more unsettling than when he was making demands on her.

Callie's eyes opened. Before she even realized it, her hand slid up around his neck, drawing his head forward to allow her lips to press against the hollow of his throat, breathing deeply of his clean, masculine scent. The salty male taste of him was like an aphrodisiac to her. She wanted only to be somehow closer to him, and she could only imagine doing so in one way.

If he was stunned by the invitation he'd glimpsed in her eyes, his confusion quickly spun away when she pressed her body close in his arms. Forgotten were their differences, her contempt for his race. Here, right now, there was nothing but the two of them. They had been through a lot in the past twenty-four hours. She needed him, he needed her. The very fact they were alive after the fierce battle yesterday was a sweet victory. He was thinking how damn good it felt to be alive, to hold a beautiful, willing woman in his arms, and his need suddenly blotted out every other factor.

He had wanted her since the first time he'd laid eyes on her, and this time she was going to become his. His blood coursed like wildfire through his veins, and there was a certain savage urgency gripping him. God, she felt good, so vital and eager to help him forget.

He needed her to help him calm the bloodlust that at times came very close to overwhelming him. Out here in the wild, where survival became a foremost concern, it was very easy to forget there was a part of him that was supposed to be civilized. He heard her plaintive sigh, and his fingers tangled in her hair.

"I want you so damn badly, and I've waited long enough," he said, soft but implacable. His senses were drugged by her. At the moment all he wanted to do was lose himself in her arms. Skin as soft as rose petals met his sure touch. Beneath his hands she felt all woman, and he yearned to tear away the barrier of clothing between them. Freeing one of her breasts, he lowered his head and took the puckered crest into his mouth. He suckled her, his tongue circling, wooing the nipple erect. She arched her back and moaned softly, the small sound filling him with heady passion. His mouth couldn't seem to get enough of her.

"You taste so sweet," he murmured against the curve of her shoulder.

With ease, he gathered her up in his strong arms and lifting her, he rose to his feet and carried her toward the bank. She unhesitatingly wrapped her long legs around his waist, and when he unsheathed the knife at his thigh, she wasn't the least bit afraid. Without her being aware, they were suddenly kneeling, facing one another on a bed of cool moss. The leaves overhead in the trees stirred the breeze across their fevered skin, and the zephyr seemed to sigh with approval.

She froze, motionless for only an instant when he raised the knife. The gleaming blade flashed in the sunlight before her eyes.

Wrapping his fingers around her damp hair, he held her firmly while the blade descended over her shoulder. Her gaze penetrated his, and she thought the golden flecks in his eyes had never burned more intensely.

"This is the last barrier we'll ever have between us," he said thickly, and with a sudden downward thrust of the razor-sharp blade, he severed the stays that bound her corset, then literally tore it off her. With a satisfied growl, he tossed it aside.

Her lungs felt free and she gratefully drew in several deep, fortifying breaths, but it didn't calm her racing heart. Only one thing would, she knew. His possession. This time she was ready.

They were breathing hard with pent-up desire that had been held in check far too long. He jerked her up against him, and his hands moved down to palm her breasts.

The feel of his big, sinewy body and the seductive taste of him that still lingered in her mouth ignited a raging inferno within her, blotting out everything but her need. She could tell by his rough, urgent caresses that he was going to make love to her, and she had never wanted anything more in her life. Almost without her being aware, his fingers were on her camisole, then moving downward to her lacy drawers, untying ribbons, long, supple fingers sending the garments gliding unnoticed to the mossy ground.

He found himself marveling that without hesitation, she let him savor every inch of her pale, nude beauty. She was even more woman than he could ever have imagined. Sleek limbs, high, supple breasts, and a slim waist that tapered down to a flat belly and the fiery red triangle of curls that he waited so long to possess. Her legs were magnificent as well, and suddenly he wanted to bury his fingers between them and caress her soft flesh until she was mindless with desire.

"You're the most beautiful woman I've ever seen. I waited so long to love you," he murmured, drawing her within his arms. He took her small hand, felt the slight hesitation of her fingers just before he placed it against the fullness of his erection. "Touch me," he said.

She did, tentatively at first, cupping him through his breechcloth, marveling at the size of him, but wondering, too, how so much of him was going to fit inside of her. She was familiar with men's bodies, having worked at the hospital tending her patients' every need. She'd seen them naked, bathed them, changed dressings, even touched their private places, but never had she thought of how their bodies might feel joined with hers. She'd never even considered it, although there were incidents when she knew that her patient had been aroused, but she'd quickly extricated herself and the situation had been resolved. But Night Of The Hawk was far from wounded, and more than well endowed. She worried, too, if she could please him.

"Untie the rawhide thongs," he ordered huskily. He wanted to be naked in her arms and feel her heated flesh against his. Nothing short of dying could have torn him away from her at that moment. His breath caught in his throat when she did as he'd commanded, pulling the garment away from his body and tossing it aside. "Now, look at me. I want you to know everything, experience everything. We'll never again have any secrets between us, angel."

Curiosity overcame her trepidation. She drew back and shyly lowered her eyes, and the image both calmed her unease and ignited her passion. "You're beautiful, too," she whispered.

He smiled, and caught her back up in his arms. "This time touch me as I have you."

Her hand closed around him, and he taught her the motion that would please him; he thought perhaps too well, and he groaned, "Enough . . . I won't last for you if we keep this up much longer. I want all of you, angel, without any regrets later."

"There won't be any," she replied. "Make me your woman."

He dipped his head and captured her mouth with his, while gently pressing her to their mossy bed. His hands gripped her buttocks and lifted her hips to meet his first thrust, and her thighs parted instinctively. She moaned softly when the velvety tip of his shaft nudged between silky folds, but she willingly accepted the slow penetration of his flesh into hers. She quivered beneath him at the first sharp thrust of his hips.

"It only gets better, love. I'll never have to hurt you again," he murmured, his lips pressed against hers, capturing her gasp of sweet agony.

She didn't realize what the effort cost him to lie unmoving inside her while feeling her wet heat wrapped tightly around his fully aroused member, but he wanted her to set the rhythm. He withdrew, but she surged upward, drawing him back to her waiting warmth.

A rapturous shudder quivered through her as her flesh strove once again to accept all of him, and her legs wrapped greedily around his hips. Her body was taut and unsure, but he patiently brought her along with him. He moved smoothly, powerfully, his senses consumed by her. He couldn't seem to get enough of touching her, smelling her, thrusting into her satiny welcome.

Callie thought the burning need between her

legs would never be satisfied, and her muscles clutched and grasped, holding him prisoner with greedy delight. She felt as if he were absorbing her, all of her. Thought, will, emotions. Never would anyone touch the core of her as he had.

Faster, harder, he moved in and out of her, giving, taking, inflamed so intensely by their mating that his body shook with the force of his emotions. She was so hot and incredibly tight, and he thought with almost boyish delight that she must have been formed exclusively for him. He heard her cry out when she reached her peak, and only then, did he let himself go, quickly joining her and soaring to unbelievable heights of ecstasy.

When it was over, he held her quietly, and Callie thought that right now, like this, their world was in balance and trust within reach.

Chapter Eighteen

It was early evening by the time they reached the outskirts of the Quohadi encampment, and the sun was setting in a fiery orange glow, spilling scarlet-gold shafts down through the drifting clouds onto the busy village.

The day had been long and the ride tiring. Callie had spoken little for the past few hours, and now as she looked down from a slight promontory, she found herself staring at the village in utter amazement.

A haze of fragrant gray smoke from the cooking fires spiraled upward through the air, the aroma of coffee and roasting meat making her mouth water. There were endless rows of smoke-yellowed lodges spread out among the trees, and children and barking dogs seemed to be everywhere. Women were calling their families to supper, and from somewhere in the distance, the sound of drums signaled their arrival.

"They've known we were coming for several miles," Night Hawk said. "I'd better warn you that some of my friends will probably ride out to greet us. They might appear threatening, but you don't have anything to fear from them as long as you're with me. Some of my people understand your language, but it would be best if you let me do the talking." He glanced over at her. "I will introduce you as my woman, and they will treat you with respect."

"I guess I don't have any other choice but to trust you," she replied solemnly.

"Is that still so difficult for you?"

"I'm trying very hard, but it's going to take time."

His dark eyes never left hers for an instant. Wariness crept into his gaze. "I understand, but I hope it won't be long before you feel as one of us."

She dropped her eyes before his steady gaze, not wanting to let him see her uncertainty. He seemed to have a need for her to approve of him and his people. She really wished that she could grant him that, but she didn't know if the wounds from her past would ever heal, and she seriously doubted whether she'd ever feel a kinship to these people. Every time she was confronted with the dark-eyed, bronze-skinned Comanches, she remembered that day in her past. She merely nodded back at him without speaking.

He reined Shadow in close to her mare, and reaching out, he surprised her by taking hold of

278

her hand and squeezing her fingers reassuringly. "I want us to start over, angel. Can we do that?"

She looked up at him, and noted the warm, meaningful gleam in his eyes. "I'd like that very much," she replied.

His mouth split into a heartstopping smile. "You're a brave woman. I've no doubt you'll be just fine here."

Callie didn't answer, but she felt oddly comforted by his words. Not long afterward, she quietly followed behind Night Hawk as they wound their way through the trees toward the village in the distance, and the tempo of the drums increased.

She was startled by a group of riders who came charging out of the trees toward them. Red Buffalo was among them, and as they drew closer, she recognized several others. Then she realized why their appearance seemed less threatening to her. Their faces were washed clean of the scabrous black paint, and for the first time, they were smiling. They were home. There would be no killing. Callie relaxed, but still watched them closely.

"Hi, tai, hello, friend!" was the cry echoing throughout the riders.

Warm words of welcome were exchanged, and Callie kept quiet as she'd agreed while the men conversed with each other on the ride back to their village.

A group of young boys brandishing small bows

279

and arrows ran forward. Darting in and around the horse's legs, it amazed Callie how they managed to avoid being trampled. They were agile and quick, their whooping loud enough to be heard over the men's raised voices. It seemed terribly rude, but no one made any attempt to reprimand them. Then she remembered having heard how the Comanche people loved children, even those they took captive, and would spoil them terribly. She was bewildered by yet another discovery, and could only wonder about the audience that she could see gathering ahead of them. What else would this day reveal? Would she ever again see another white face?

Within minutes, they were riding among the brightly decorated lodges, and the people came rushing forward to call out greetings to them. Callie could hear the announcement of their arrival circulating throughout the camp, and felt the curious stares focused on her. Women were tittering behind their hands, and everyone seemed to be inching forward in an effort to touch her.

Children halted in play and quietly observed her, and all work came to a standstill at their approach. This was the moment of truth for Callie. She imagined that many of the Comanche had never seen a white woman before and they seemed especially intrigued by her red hair. But the women seemed to be the most curious, and they stood huddled together, chattering and pointing in her direction, then giggling as their gazes fell on Night Hawk. Callie was surrounded by a dreaded enemy, but oddly enough she didn't feel threatened as she'd expected that she would.

"What are they saying about us?" she couldn't resist asking Night Hawk.

A smile touched his eyes. "Are you sure you wish to know?"

"Yes, please tell me," Callie urged.

"They said that our babies will be strong and beautiful, but they worry that a boy child born with your fire hair might not live a long life."

She blushed, but she was also piqued, and prompted him. "Why is that? Do they think because I am white that I am too weak to bear strong children?"

A grin overtook his features. "They fear that his hair would be a blazing banner that would alert his enemies of his approach."

"Pooh on such a notion," she exclaimed indignantly. "Our son would be too smart to ride into battle ill prepared. His father would have taught him well the ways of the Comanche. He would have first shown him how to darken his hair with bear grease before he rode to meet the enemy."

Night Hawk grinned broadly, and his chest swelled with pride. She was one fine woman, and her words honored him. He had never desired to sire a child with any woman since he'd lost Morning Star and their daughter, and had given up any thought of having future children.

Suddenly, he realized for the first time that he no longer felt burdened by his heavy mantle of grief, and that his sorrow had eased. He knew it was because of Callie, and the fact that their mind, body, and soul were linked together as one. It no longer angered him to recall the vision that had foretold of the prophecy, but he was consumed by guilt. He did not see Morning Star's face whenever he looked upon this woman. It was hard for him to accept. He still did not know if he could allow himself to know happiness until Morning Star and Precious Flower had been revenged.

Owl Man had once told him, "Keep your face to the shadows and you will never see the sunshine." He had listened, but he had refused to heed the shaman's warning, preferring instead to succumb to his sorrow. But since he'd known Callie he'd begun to desire more in his life than darkness and despair. He had felt dead inside for too long.

His gaze roamed over Callie's lovely face, and he trembled with a new awareness. Was this woman his sun? Would the future remain bright as long as she remained by his side? He knew the days and nights ahead would provide the answers to his questions. It surprised him to realize he was eagerly looking forward to spending this time with Callie.

Drums sounded, and the people continued to gather, the throng thickening as the call went out across the encampment. There were over seven-hundred tepees spread out around the snaking river, but every man, woman, and child would turn out to welcome back their returning leader.

Callie waited patiently while Night Hawk dismounted, and observed a young boy hurry forward to take the stallion's reins. After Night Hawk had helped her to dismount, the Indian boy led both their horses away.

"It has recently become Swift Otter's responsibility to care for the tribe's pony herd," Night Hawk explained to her. "There are few positions more honorable, and his parents are very proud that their son was the one chosen among so many."

Callie barely acknowledged him, her mind and eyes were too preoccupied with watching everything going on around her. Her gaze darted from face to face. There were dark-eyed people moving everywhere, with long hair that was either braided or flowed around their shoulders, and bare mahogany limbs gleaming in the firelight. The men and young children wore little clothing, just breechcloths and moccasins, and the little ones seemed excited by the events.

The women were dressed in fringed buckskin made of elk or doeskin, beautifully decorated with feathers and colorful beadwork. She noticed too that each woman had a red line painted down the center part of her hair, and she made a mental note to ask Night Hawk about it later. Dogs barked and horses whinnied over the loud pounding of the drums, the noise and confusion a bit overwhelming to Callie who had never seen anything like it before.

The group began pressing closer as others came forward to join them, and when a few of the young women reached out to touch Callie's hair with a sense of awe, she instinctively moved nearer to Night Hawk. She was careful not to touch him or reveal how nervous she felt, but she wished that soon she might be alone with him again. There was never a moment when she needed reassuring more.

Casting a sideways look up at him, it suddenly dawned on her for the first time how much a part of these people he actually was. In seeing him here like this, it was hard for her to remember there had ever been a man she'd once known as Rafe Santino. An icy fear suddenly clutched at her heart. What would happen to her now? Would he demand that she obey his every command and expect her to be little more than his slave?

Feeling her uncertainty, Night Hawk placed his hand at the small of her back. "Smile at me, angel. Let them see that you approve of them. It is very important that they know this."

She tried, but how could she, she wondered, when she was standing in the middle of a bunch of savages at war with her own people, the only white face among them? She didn't even know what tomorrow might bring, or for that matter, if they'd allow her to live beyond the next moment. She remembered his cautionary words of earlier, and she sensed that he was testing her, perhaps needing some reassurances from her as well.

The fingers splayed against her back seemed tense, and surprisingly, she discovered that he was as nervous as she was. Perhaps it had been his intention to bring her here in order for her to see fully what his people were like with her own eyes. He wanted her approval as much for himself as for them.

With this new awareness, she was able to nod slowly, and turning her eyes to meet his, her lips lifted at the corners somewhat tentatively at first, then with his gaze holding hers reassuringly, Callie widened her smile. His eyes gleamed with pride, and something else she couldn't quite believe. Her pulse quickened. He was an ever-changing mystery, but there was a warmth in his gaze that she hadn't seen before. Her troubled spirits quieted, and her cheeks colored under the heat of his eyes.

Callie was almost afraid to acknowledge that something very special had just transpired between them, and for the first time since he'd taken her, she wanted to abandon caution and reason and succumb to this new, overwhelming emotion. She could only imagine that this was what it must feel like to be in love, but she still wasn't certain she had touched his heart in the way he had hers. He was an exciting, virile lover, and even now she could hardly wait for the privacy of his lodge, where she might once again become his. She no longer wanted to think about the fact of his being Indian, and belonging to this alien culture, and why she now found herself here. She only wanted to be alone with him. Overcome by emotions she couldn't acknowledge, she ducked her head and waited quietly until he moved them forward through the parting swell of people.

After they'd gone a little way, he stopped, and motioned toward a lodge on their left. "This will be your new home," he said. "I think you will find it quite comfortable." He paused outside the lodge door. "You go on inside and rest for awhile. I'll be back later."

Callie cast a wary look up at him. The last thing she had expected was to be left alone. "Will you be gone long?"

He stepped around her to push the hide covering aside. "I must pay my respects to the civil chief of our tribe and speak with the council. It might take me a couple of hours, but there's nothing for you to worry about, you'll be safe here."

She stepped hesitantly inside, and when the hide was drawn closed behind her, she couldn't help flinching. Nervously, she looked around her.

The interior of the lodge wasn't anything like she'd expected. It was actually very spacious, and everything was arranged neatly along the walls in fringed leather bags. Various weapons, a strung bow, a quiver of arrows, and a war club, feathers dangling from it, were hanging from a rack in the rear. Another rack held various items of Indian clothing: fringed and beaded shirts and leggings, a scalplock adorned with shells and white ermine tails.

The floor was covered with buffalo pelts, and Callie's boots sunk into their thick pile as she stepped farther into the tepee. She saw that there was only a single bed, raised a few inches off the floor, and covered in luxurious black furs.

A small fire had been lit in the center of the lodge, and someone had prepared a meal and left it warming on the rocks that surrounded the blaze. The fragrant aroma of freshly baked bread and roasted corn permeated the lodge, but she was far too nervous to think of eating.

Tilting her head back, she watched the smoke spiraling upward and through a center hole far above her head, noticing the mural that was painted along the curved hide. It was of a hawk, its wings spread in flight, and it covered the upper section of the tepee. Callie stared at it in awe and thought about the hours of work that must have taken to create something so vividly realistic and beautiful.

Glancing down, she noticed the cooking utensils and earthen bowls stacked on rawhide boxes, and several buffalo skin pouches hung from pegs that had been driven into tent poles. Nothing seemed in any way familiar. It was a strange and alien dwelling, but there was no doubt in her mind who lived here. Night Hawk. And it was his familiar scent, that faint combination of wind and sun-kissed skin, that calmed her somehow and made everything seem less intimidating. Her throat constricted. It only took this slight reminder of him to send her senses reeling. He was becoming more important to her with each passing hour. She could see nothing feminine in the lodge and this pleased her immensely. As she'd hoped, he lived alone.

She didn't know for certain whether she would be sharing his dwelling with him but she assumed as much. What would be expected of her, she wondered? He was her captor, but she thought of him as her lover. Would he treat her like a slave, or as his woman? She gnawed her bottom lip, wondering how long she would have to wait before her many questions were answered.

Ten men would decide Callie's fate, but Night Of The Hawk knew the full determination of her future was really in his hands, and that he would have to take great care in explaining Callie's presence in the Quohadi camp to the council.

He had entered the huge lodge which was located in the center of the village and had taken a seat facing the men of the council. A woman entered behind him and deposited a basket full of sweet grass on the hot stones around the center fire, then departed, closing the hide flap tightly behind her. The pungent odor of the burning grass blended with the sharp tang of pipe tobacco filled the enclosure.

The ceremonial pipe was removed from an intricately beaded pouch and lit. After each council member had puffed on the pipe, it was passed to him. One of the men hit on a drum each time that the pipe and bowl was passed and recited a chant.

"We are represented here tonight by the members of the Quohadi council to decide the fate of a white captive. We wish the spirits aid in helping us reach a wise decision."

Each man held a rattle and shook it slowly. Owl Man, their shaman, then turned his face up and gazed at the stars visible through the smoke hole. "I call the stars and the Father moon to this place and ask that all our prayers here tonight will be answered." Lifting a finely-carved bone whistle that hung about his neck, he blew softly. First to the east, then the south, west and north. When he'd finished, he said. "Now we will pray."

At the end of their chant, Owl Man raised up his arms and the voices stilled.

It was Night Hawk's turn to speak. He spoke from his heart, knowing that the council could overturn his decision if they thought the woman he'd selected was not worthy of the honor of joining their people. He would have no choice in the final outcome, but he could do a lot now to persuade them.

"I will speak to you of the flame-haired woman I have claimed for mine," he said. "Her coming was foreseen by me many years ago. She is strong and brave. I do not think she knows what it means to have a faint heart. She has the gift to heal, and can help our people who even now lay stricken with the white man's sickness. I so say that any children she might bear in the future would be tall, proud, and strong enough to bear the uncertainty of our future. Indeed, her sons would help ensure the future of our people." Night Hawk only paused for a moment, then made the most difficult decision of all. He had to make his choice here and now. "I humbly request your permission to groom this woman as the future bride of our next chief. Our blood intermixed with hers is the way to our future survival. It must be so, for it was written in the stars many years before, and the prophecy is a true one."

Owl Man leaned back with a satisfied nod.

The council members seemed content as well.

Night Hawk waited patiently.

To his relief, there were no objections. Callie belonged to him, and there was no man among them who would interfere if he decided to take her for his wife. That decision would remain his.

After they left he would stay to fast and pray.

He must make certain that the gods also approved. If they did not, he would know before the night was over.

The Comanche warrior stared down at the pale beauty before him. It was almost dawn. Callie lay sleeping on his bed, the buffalo robe pulled up around her shoulders, her shining hair spread out against the sable furs.

Her rumpled gown lay on the floor next to his right foot, and just brushing his ankle against her discarded clothing stirred his desire to a fever pitch. His eyes made love to her as they feasted on her gently parted lips. He leaned over and touched his lips to that warm place just behind her ear, and it felt like molten silk. Callie stirred and drew in a startled breath.

"There's nothing to fear, angel," he whispered soothingly. "You must know by now that I would never hurt you."

She sighed in acknowledgment, a breathy sound that made him tremble with anticipation. After leaving the council lodge, he'd bathed in the river and he wore only his breechcloth, which he untied now and dropped on the floor. Then slipping under the buffalo robe, he laid down beside her, and cradled her head against his shoulder. "Sleep, angel, you're safe."

Unconsciously, she reached up to thread her fingers through his thick black hair, never even opening her eyes before their lips met. His warm body felt so right melded against hers, and she wanted to feel more of him, much more. She knew that voice, that touch. Every hard plane of his body was as familiar as her own.

A soft murmur of need escaped her lips and he captured it in his mouth. Their tongues met in a mating dance, and she nuzzled closer to him, pressing her hips against his in offering, luring him closer to her fire.

The moon shone brilliantly down on their sleek young bodies through the center smoke hole and cast them in a silver aura.

He kissed her until her lungs felt tight from lack of air and her head whirled with emotions that were still so hard to accept. Then suddenly, his lips tore free of hers, and she faced him, gasping raggedly, trembling from the myriad of sensations he'd awakened. He held her pinioned against him, and despite her many misgivings about their future, Callie never wanted to be free of his embrace.

"Oh, God, you make me feel so confused," she murmured. "When you're holding me, touching me, it's wonderful . . . you're wonderful, but the other times . . ."

His night-black eyes seemed to consume her. "Shh . . . shh . . . let's forget the other times. I want you, angel, more than I ever thought possible. And I know you want me too. Forget about tomorrow, it doesn't matter right now."

Further words weren't necessary. They devoured each other with their eyes.

To her, he was dark, mysterious, and forbidden. She was already beginning to fear loving him.

She was like a bright shooting star, brilliant and glittering, dazzling him with her fiery beauty. He didn't wish ever to be anywhere else but in her arms.

Their need was intensely fierce and demanding that night. Neither wanted preliminaries, only possession, hot and hard. Vital and wild.

He gripped her buttocks, and entered her in a single smooth thrust, impaling her, drawing her over on top of him and letting her set the pace.

She learned quickly, her own hunger the driving force. Drawing him deep inside her, she thought of nothing, felt nothing but the scalding heat building between her legs. She marveled at the way her pliant flesh ached so sweetly, and how his size and length seemed to carve through her and sear deep inside her belly.

Callie instinctively drew her knees up and rode him. Blood was charging through her veins, heat was burning her from within. Mindlessly, she rose up and arched her back, then balancing herself on the balls of her feet, she twisted and writhed in a grinding dance of desire, her hands like beating wings against his chest. Alone in their shadowy retreat she felt protected and cherished. And she thought how wonderful it would be if reality never had to intrude.

"Angel, I've waited for you for so long," he groaned between wet, open-mouthed kisses that sent currents of desire through her.

His big hands stroked her hips, her thighs, and the juncture where they were joined. To feel himself imprisoned within her body, knowing she willingly accepted his flesh as part of hers, thrilled him in a way that no woman ever had before. She consumed him, but he didn't care. His need of her knew no bounds; he sensed it would always be this way between them. Surrendering his will, he joined her as one. Their souls touched and hearts that had denied, at last became one.

Their release came together in a searing rush, and she cried out his name again and again. At that moment, with her doubts about him rapidly fading, she began to think she didn't want to ever be anywhere else but in his arms. With him, she felt complete.

Chapter Nineteen

They were awakened in the early wash of morning light by the sound of a woman's frantic cries.

"What happened?" Callie exclaimed, sitting up in bed.

Night Hawk was already up, and dressed hastily. "I don't know but I intend to find out. Stay here, angel. I'll send someone to stay with you until I can return." He started toward the doorway.

Her face clouded. "Wait!" she called after him. "I'd like to come along with you. It will only take me a minute to get dressed."

"Not this time," he said, glancing over his shoulder at her. "Your place is here. I'll be back as soon as I can."

Callie pulled the buffalo robe around her, and stared after him. There had been no denying the silken thread of warning in his voice. There was something going on, and apparently he didn't want her to know about it.

She stared thoughtfully at the door cover, then in

the next instant, was startled when an Indian woman stepped through the entrance. With a graceful, fluid motion she crossed the lodge to stand several feet in front of Callie.

"Do not be frightened," the older woman said in broken English. "Night Hawk asked me to bring you clean clothing. I tell him it be my pleasure to do so. I also go with you to the river if you would like to bathe."

"You speak English," Callie said, clearly pleased to find someone other than Night Hawk that she might converse with.

"Yes, I learned your language as a young woman. There are still some words I do not understand, but for the most part I can speak what is on my mind." Her smile was endearing. "Sometimes this not good, or so my son tells me."

Callie had been studying her since she'd entered the lodge, and she saw before her a woman of slight stature in her middle years, with eyes like dark pools warmed by sunlight. Her shining black hair was plaited into a single braid, and she wore a brightly beaded gown that fell past her knees. Callie thought she was lovely, and when she smiled at Callie, the warmth in her eyes set the tone.

"In your language my name is Eyes Like Summer, but you may simply call me Summer. Everyone else does."

An easy smile played at the corners of Callie's mouth. "I am very pleased to make your acquaintance. I am Callie. I hope we'll be friends. There is so much about your people that I don't understand, and perhaps now you can explain things to me."

"If you like Cal . . . lie." She tested the foreign word on her tongue. "It is pretty name," Summer said, handing Callie the soft doeskin dress and leggings.

Callie's eyes brightened with pleasure as she fingered the soft two-piece dress of muted gold, marveling at the intricate beadwork and the beautiful shells that adorned the scalloped neckline. "You . . . want me to wear this?"

"It would give me great pleasure if you would," Summer replied, her smile broadening.

"It's lovely, but the pleasure would be all mine."

"We will be good friends, Cal . . . lie."

When Callie was dressed, she set about showing Callie how to roll the sides of the tepee up off the ground about two feet and secure it with rawhide straps. Once this had been accomplished, a delightful breeze drifted through the dwelling.

Callie glanced around the lodge, a gleam of interest in her eyes. "What can we do next?"

Summer seemed pleased that Callie was so enthusiastic to learn the ways of the People. She went on to show Callie how to prepare a hearty breakfast of buffalo steak and cornmeal mush, and the two women shared the meal, washing it down with freshly brewed coffee.

While they ate, Summer talked a great deal about life in the village, and Callie listened intently. She had hoped she might learn something more about Night Hawk, but it seemed that Summer was careful about mentioning his name. She did tell Callie that he was the next in line to become chief, and her face positively glowed whenever she spoke of him.

"He has many coup-feathers in his honor. Our people, even his enemies, respect him. He is both greatly loved and feared. He will make fine leader someday," Summer told her.

"What does it mean when you say he has many coup-feathers?" Callie asked, setting her tin coffee cup aside.

"It is the way a warrior gets honor from his people." When Callie stared at her perplexed, Summer thought for a moment and proceeded to explain in more detail. "A brave act. It means to touch a live enemy, or to kill and touch a dangerous animal. Stealing tethered horses from a hostile camp without being caught is considered a very high honor as well. It is any brave act against our enemies. Our warriors always seek the greatest coup of all. Tonight there will be a victory celebration for two braves who have first coup. Much dancing and good time. You must come."

Callie's brow furrowed, and a momentary look of discomfort crossed her features. She understood enough to know she could not be a part of this ritual. "I . . . can't join in this celebration, Summer. Your warriors counted coup on some of my own people. They brutally murdered them. I hope you understand how I feel."

Summer stopped her with a raised hand. "You do not have to explain yourself to me. My own husband felt like you when he first came to live among us. Soon, he understood that there was good and evil on both sides. It didn't matter the color of the skin." Her expressive face changed and became almost somber. "Our warriors were killed and wounded in this battle as well. It was a fair fight. I hope you believe Summer."

"I'm sure you see it that way, but I was there and it was the most senseless thing I've ever witnessed."

Summer laid a comforting hand on Callie's arm. "You not ready yet to open your heart to the truth, but I like being with you just the same. We *haitsi,* friends?"

Callie couldn't help feeling warmed by Summer's obvious sincerity and the tenderness in her tone. The two women stared at each other, and smiled earnestly.

"I'd like that very much," Callie replied.

"Good, then this friend take you to join in fun at the river," Summer informed her. Grasping Callie's hand, Summer pulled her to her feet. *"Mea-dro,* mean, let's go!"

Callie eagerly followed behind her, unconsciously putting to memory these first few words of the Comanche tongue.

At the river Callie and Summer joined several other women who were washing clothing and chattering companionably while keeping a watchful eye on their splashing toddlers. Later Summer led her back through the maze of lodges with ease.

The noises of the camp seemed to engulf them after the peaceful serenity of the river. Several dogs charged across their path, growling and barking in play. There were the sounds of children's laughter, babies crying, horses neighing, men and women toiling over daily chores. Hammering, scraping, Indian tools at work. Everything had a purpose, but a very noisy sense of disorder seemed to prevail.

"How can you remember your way?" Callie asked, marveling at each assured turn that took them down another avenue filled with tepees; old men sitting before their lodges, buffalo robes pulled up around their shoulders to protect against the broiling sun that shone down upon them. She'd been expecting at any moment to see the lodge with the great winged hawk painted on its side, but so far she'd passed only those decorated in a host of colors and designs, the meat racks alongside them filled with drying strips. It was mass confusion, and she hoped she never had to find her way alone.

"There are ways," Summer replied. "You will learn to use your senses. Your nose can tell the way home when you learn to trust it. We will close our eyes." She paused, then said, "Now, we take deep breath. Here I smell mesquite bread baking and wild plums simmering over a fire." She grasped Callie's hand in hers, tugging gently. "We take few steps. Yes, I think someone—She Who Speaks Wisely, is roasting pecans today."

Callie was impressed, but still doubtful that she'd ever learn such a feat.

Opening their eyes they walked on, with Summer

still explaining things to Callie. "Later you will learn the village as it is laid out and memorize each detail, much like you would one of your towns. There are identifying landmarks, but it is too soon for you to recognize them. Patience, golden one. You will learn quick, I think."

Callie nodded, and felt elated. She *would* learn, and she was surprised to realize how eager she was to know everything about Summer and Night Hawk's people.

As they were passing by a group of men bent over a heated dice game, Callie heard a familiar voice drift out from the lodge on her left. Her steps faltered.

A sensual young female stepped through the opening, and almost collided with Summer. Sharp words were exchanged. Callie froze, and her breath caught painfully in her throat. Following behind the Indian maiden was Night Hawk.

Callie was torn by conflicting emotions, but she tried not to reveal her dismay. He had a fiery, angry look that was unfamiliar to her, but when he noticed her it changed to one of surprise.

"Night Hawk . . . what is going on?" Callie felt compelled to ask.

He didn't acknowledge her, but swung his gaze to glare at Summer accusingly. "Mother, why did you bring her here?" he demanded, his expression thunderous.

Callie's gaze flew to Summer. "You're his mother?"

Summer stared at Callie and nodded, her eyes pleading for understanding, then she glanced meaningfully back at her son. Her censorious look silenced him immediately. "Cal . . . lie and I were just returning from the river. I had no idea that you would be here," she replied calmly, ignoring his black scowl.

Then turning once more to Callie, she sought to explain. "I was going to tell you, but then I think it best we get to know each other better . . . understand more first. Was it wrong of me to think this way?"

The tension in Callie began to melt. She knew she could never be mad at Summer, who'd been so kind and thoughtful to her. "No, it just came as a bit of a surprise."

"You are surprise, too," the young maiden interjected sarcastically. "You no belong. Go back to your own people, you not wanted here!"

"That is enough, Little Doe," Night Hawk stated firmly, grasping hold of the maiden's arm. "Callie is our guest. You will apologize now."

Little Doe clamped her lips together, her almond-colored eyes still fixed on Callie, her expression mutinous. She was even smaller in stature than Summer, although her features weren't as handsome, but standing between the two Indian women, easily towering over them, Callie felt oddly out of place. She was suddenly anxious to escape from their disturbing presence. She could tell by the look in the other girl's eyes that she was furious with her because of Night Hawk. Why?

Could they have once been lovers? And were they still?

Callie swallowed with difficulty, and found her voice. "It's . . . all right Night Hawk . . . I understand." She looked up at him, seeking some reassurance, but his face closed, as if guarding a secret.

"No, I don't think you really do. She isn't a cruel person, Callie," he said, the corner of his mouth twisting with exasperation.

He seemed eager to explain away the other woman's rude behavior, Callie reflected with some bitterness. It rankled her more than she was ready to admit. Thankfully, at that moment Summer intervened.

"Come along, Cal . . . lie," she said, cupping her elbow gently. "We'd better leave, there is still much to see and do."

Night Hawk made no move to accompany them. Callie could feel her throat closing up. She allowed Summer to lead her away, trying hard to keep her chin erect when what she really wanted to do was vent her frustration on Night Hawk. There was a heavy feeling in her stomach and her legs barely supported her, but far worse was the sharp pain in her heart.

Summer said very little on the walk back to Night Hawk's lodge. Once there, she tried to reassure Callie that her son would have a reasonable explanation when he returned. "Do not think the worst. It is not that way between them," she declared.

Callie exhaled slowly, and sat down on the bed.

"Then tell me what it is like. It certainly appeared to me as if there might be something between them. Little Doe is obviously someone he cares a great deal about."

"Wait and see. He will speak of her when he returns. I wish to tell you, but it is his story and he should explain himself."

"Whenever that will be," Callie muttered, her hands twisting unconsciously in her lap.

"I go now," Summer said softly. "You rest for tonight. Maybe you come with Night Hawk after all."

"I wouldn't count on it," Callie muttered under her breath, feeling miserable.

It was dusk when Callie awoke with a start and turned over in bed. Night Hawk was sitting beside her, his gaze as soft as a caress.

"How long have you been sitting there?" she asked, and couldn't help but notice the tingle of excitement inside her.

"A while," he said huskily.

"You could have awakened me," she said, raising up on one elbow and staring up at him.

He smiled with beautiful candor. "I could have, but I rather liked being captivated."

Callie blushed, and pushed back the heavy mass of hair from her face. "You didn't seem all that enthralled with me earlier. In fact, it seemed to me as if you were rather taken with Little Doe."

"It wasn't what it appeared, angel," he said, an almost imperceptible note of pleading in his face.

"Tell me how it is then," she persisted gently.

He reached out and gathered her close to him. There wasn't any part of her that could resist him. She felt his hand brush the hair from her neck, and the warmth of his personal contact seemed to steady her.

"You've been through quite an ordeal. I had hoped we might have a while longer before I had to confront you with my past. I don't know if you're ready yet."

Callie moved out of his arms, leaned her head back and gazed into his eyes. "Your mother said as much earlier. I am as strong as any other woman here. You must know that. At least you should by now. There may be a lot I don't understand, but I am trying to do so." She was having a hard time getting the words past her constricted throat, but she persevered, her anger softly worded, but plain. "You brought me here against my will, but I have tried not to be bitter toward you or the others. But I am getting tired of being met by a wall of silence every time I ask questions about you. I have a right to know these things. I don't think I can stay here with you unless I do."

He sighed heavily. "God, I wish it were as easy as a simple explanation."

Something was flickering far back in his eyes. Doubts crowded her mind, but she knew nothing could be worse than her suspicions. Reaching for his hand, she interlaced her fingers through his. "Trust me. Talk to me, please. I need you, Night Hawk. I'm ready to listen."

Finally after a long moment of silence he drew a shaky breath, and proceeded to speak slowly. "Little Doe is angry because she feels that you are going to take her sister's place in my heart."

"She was the woman outside our lodge this morning?"

"Yes. I'm sorry you had to hear that."

"Little Doe obviously doesn't want us to be together."

Raw hurt glittered in his dark eyes. "She believes the spirits will lose faith in me because I have chosen a white woman and forsaken a vow I made to her sister."

"Who is Little Doe's sister . . . what vow?" Callie posed quietly, but her mind whirled. Was there another woman in his life? Suddenly she didn't know if she wanted him to continue. His next words tore at her heart.

"She was my wife, and Little Doe's sister," he replied solemnly.

"Your wife," Callie gasped, her luminous eyes widening in astonishment. "You aren't still married to her?"

The muscles of his forearm hardened beneath her fingers. "She was killed many years ago, along with our baby daughter."

"How awful," Callie replied, feeling his pain.

She forced herself to listen calmly while he explained the day of the murders, and somehow she managed to hold her raw emotions in check.

"So you see how it is with me. My life in this world and the next belongs to my wife and daughter. I have been searching for their murderer since that ill-fated day. At the time it was easy to make such a vow. I was young and heartbroken. I couldn't imagine ever loving anyone again." He sighed deeply. "But time passes and eases sorrow. I will never forget my slain family. They were a part of my life, and they will both live on forever in my memories. But I need something more to live for. I spoke of this to Little Doe, but she is still too upset with me to try and understand."

The tension between Callie and Night Hawk began to melt. Her heart ached for him, and for the pain he must have endured at the tragic loss of his wife and daughter. She pressed herself close in his arms. "I'm so sorry you had to bear so tragic a loss. It must have been a terrible time for you."

"Yes, it was, but it was also difficult for my wife's family. Especially Little Doe, who loved her sister very much. She came to our lodge this morning to confront the both of us, but I told her that she could not speak to you in anger. It is why I left with her. She'd needed to hear my words, for she will always be family to me. When Little Doe saw you with my mother she just couldn't control herself any longer." He kissed her on the temple. "I apologize for the things she said to you, but I hope you understand why I could not walk away with you then and leave her standing there alone. She needed me, and I knew that my mother would remain by your side."

"Yes, I understand." She wrapped her arms tightly around him, tears trembling on her lashes.

307

His strong heartbeat throbbed against her ear. "Your heart has room enough for old memories as well as the new. And I want us to make them beautiful and lasting. I love you, Night Hawk, and I believe that one day soon you'll say those same words to me." Tipping her head back, she stared up at him. "But for now, love me . . . show me how you feel."

His eyes darkened with emotion as he took hold of her arms and placed them around his neck. "Hold tight, sweet angel, this might take a very long time."

Their desire swept away the pain and anger as they spent the long, lazy hours ignoring everything but each other.

Chapter Twenty

When the soldiers on guard duty first saw the bedraggled man slumped over the neck of the pack mule plodding toward them shortly after dawn they didn't recognize him, only the Cavalry blue that he was wearing. They could see that his head was clumsily swathed in a blood-soaked rag, and that his uniform was tattered and crusted with filth. His feet were bare, and his face spattered with dried blood. A call for aid went out. "Soldier, open the gates, we've a wounded man coming in!"

The dusty settlement was coming to life, and as the shout echoed through the many buildings, people began to gather in their doorways, staring curiously. Women in rag curlers peered out from open windows, soldiers emerged from the livery and general store, waiting to hear if a call to arms would be issued. On the frontier, nothing was left to chance, and even a lone man might be the first indication of an approaching enemy. Even the bleary-eyed women who worked far into the night in the whorehouse near the fort—women were scarce in the wilderness and the girls were greatly appreciated by the enlisted men—stumbled from their beds to see what the commotion was about.

As the weary rider drew closer, one of the astonished guards shouted, "Christ almighty, it looks like Captain Hamilton!"

Several soldiers were immediately dispatched to assist him.

Captain Hamilton had managed to survive the deadly battle with the Comanches, although he'd lain unconscious amid the bodies of his wounded and slain comrades for over twenty-four hours beneath the blistering sun. At night, he'd had to fend off the wild animals with only his bare fists and the butt of his rifle.

Out of thirty-five men, only a handful had survived the attack. Hamilton had been the only man able to stand without help. His wounds had been minor compared to the other men.

At the moment, hearing the soldiers' voices, he felt almost giddy. He'd found his way back to the fort. He never wanted to go through another experience like that again, and he could only wonder if the soldier who'd gotten trigger happy and had fired first at the Indians was still alive. He hoped so, although no one had admitted the costly mistake to him. He'd known there might be trouble, but he'd hoped to try and avoid the bloody massacre of so many of his men.

Lance would never forget seeing his men fall.

Bodies littered the ground around him like scattered kindling. It was the most horrible sight he'd ever encountered in all of his years soldiering. At the end he'd had to stand and helplessly watch as the Comanche had moved in for a final sweep.

The combat was hand to hand, and the Indians knew well that the soldiers were rattled by having to fight dismounted, with no way to seek a quick retreat. Even though his men were within easy range of the charging Comanche and picked off quite a few of their warriors before they'd come screaming down on top of them, the enemy didn't seem to know any fear. They also had known a helluva lot about fighting strategy, and their leader had intentionally sent them running directly at the grouped soldiers, forcing them to split apart in confusion and thus were unable to sight down on the Indians at close range. Soldiers slashed left and right with gleaming sabers, but mostly they were on the defensive. It took a warrior less than sixty seconds to shoot and restring an arrow. War clubs cracked skulls open like pecan nuts left to dry overlong in the sun.

Lance sustained a nasty head wound, and the impact of the war club had brought him to his knees. But he refused to fall. Just as the brave was preparing to deliver another blow, and the club flashed downward, Lance swerved aside and managed to deflect the worst of the impact, taking the full force on his shoulder. It didn't deter the Comanche. He leapt on Lance with a warlike howl, both men tumbling to the ground. The captain expected at any moment to feel the slice of the knife across his scalp.

Woozy and disoriented, he laid sprawled on his back and could only watch helplessly as the Comanche straddled his prone form, knife in hand, and grabbed hold of Lance's hair. The captain thought for sure he was about to be scalped alive, and he had never known such fear before in his life. It was just at that instant, when the razor-sharp knife had descended toward him that their leader signaled an end to the battle and, in doing so, unknowingly spared Lance's life. It was as if a power that was not his own had stayed the Indian's hand. Lance had never before been a religious man, but in that instant he felt touched by the will of God.

The Comanche, having successfully counted coup on their enemy, rode away, their victory cries ringing in the captain's ears, leaving behind so many of his men dead.

He listened as the sound of hooves thrummed in the distance, and promised himself that he'd one day make that Comanche chief pay for what he'd done. It was the last thing he remembered before a swirling gray mist enveloped his brain.

Sometime later he'd awakened to the shrill cries of the carrion circling overhead, and the overwhelming sight of his comrades, many of them mutilated beyond recognition, lying all around him.

There were moans of pain and cries for help, but the worst was the eerie wind that seemed to wail in grief across the flat plain. Overwhelmed, Lance had doubled over and retched until his stomach had emptied.

After staggering to his feet, he stumbled through the carnage of bodies checking for survivors, listening for any faint sound that would indicate someone alive. Mostly he heard only deathly stillness, but sometimes he caught a slight groan or whimper. He searched persistently through the bodies, and he was able to find several men still clinging to life, some just by a slender thread. He knew they needed medical attention desperately, and after he'd done everything that he could for them, he began to formulate a plan for returning to the fort. He knew it was up to him to make the long journey back. Using a rifle to support his weight, he'd walked for miles under the blistering sun, his thoughts tortured by images of Callie at the mercy of the hostiles, and the wounded men he'd left behind who were probably suffering under the searing sun more than he was. It kept driving him onward.

Lance knew the degrading treatment she'd suffer and he only hoped that she might endure until she could be found. He was consumed with guilt for having failed to prevent her capture, and he kept telling himself that only her panic had caused her to run straight into the arms of that damned half-breed. She wouldn't have done so if her mind hadn't snapped.

Providence intervened to lead the young captain into the camp of several buffalo hunters, where he'd proceeded to explain his plight. The men had made him welcome and provided him his first hot meal in days. They didn't want any part of Injun trouble, they'd quickly told him, but they generously loaned him one of their supply mules, and by mid-morning of the following day Lance had found his way to the gates of Fort Benton.

He'd covered the forty miles in under nine hours, driven by the memory of his men lying dead or wounded back on the plains. As soon as the soldiers heard their captain's urgent message, they sent a man directly to the colonel's office to relay the distressing news.

"Sergeant Jamison requests permission to speak with you, Colonel," the nervous aide informed his superior officer.

Colonel Williams glanced up from his paperwork. "Permission granted, Bailey. Send him in."

The sergeant's face was pale as death as he stood before the colonel's desk, and tried to keep his voice even. "I'm afraid I have terrible news, sir," he said.

Seeing the anxious officer, noting the tremor in his voice, the colonel was instantly on his feet. Bracing his hands on top of his desk, he listened, and with a sinking heart, knew they'd probably never see Callie alive again. Then he felt close to

314

weeping as he heard of further loss of so many fine men.

"Captain Hamilton will have a full report ready, sir, just as soon as he's released from the infirmary."

Swallowing the bile that rose in his throat, the colonel asked, "How is the captain?"

"Compared to the others, I'd say he came out of this the lucky one. He took a blow on the head, and Doc says he'll need stitches to close a knife wound in his shoulder, but otherwise, he'll pull through just fine."

"Good," the colonel replied, then growled, "Those bastards won't get away with this, Sergeant, not as long as I'm in command of this post." He slammed his closed fist against the desk top. "I want those renegades hunted down no matter how long it takes! By God, I'll see that sonofabitch hanged by the neck before I'm through."

"My sentiments exactly, sir," the sergeant exclaimed, eyes narrowing. "How many troopers does the colonel intend to put in the field?"

"Sound revelry. I want the officers to report to my office at once, and every other available man mounted and ready to pull out within two hours. We need to aid our wounded and bury the dead. Then, we'll track those Comanches—into hell if necessary." Walking around to the front of his desk, he added, "And Sergeant, tell the men that their colonel will be going along. I want them to realize the gravity of this situation. An innocent girl's life is at stake. I want her found and returned unharmed if at all possible."

"Yes, sir, I'll inform the men right away," the burly sergeant replied, and pivoting on his heel, he hurried away.

As soon as the sergeant closed the door behind him, the colonel whirled on his assistant who'd been furiously scribbling notes on a pad throughout the exchange. "Listen up, Bailey. Not one word of this goes beyond these walls until I give the okay. No telegrams or correspondence of any sort. Inform the staff, and make certain you make my position clear. I want time to resolve this before we have to give Washington a full report. Also, send some men ahead of our detachment to warn the homesteaders of the danger from these renegades that are on the loose. The families that have a mind can seek refuge here at the fort until the savages are captured. And ask someone to look in on the Hendersons. I only hope it isn't too late for them as well."

The aide was still scribbling notes as he hurried away to do the colonel's bidding.

After his office door closed, colonel Williams strode over to the window, and said shakily to himself, "Now it's left for me to do the worst thing of all. I must tell Estelle her daughter's been captured by Indians. Sweet Jesus, how does anyone tell a mother something like that?"

With a despondent sigh, he ran his fingers through his crisp white hair. Callie had been nothing but a source of anxiety to him since he'd married her mother. He didn't understand her, never had for that matter, but when his Estelle had fallen ill so suddenly and they'd feared she might not survive, she'd longed to see her child, and he'd thought it might speed her recovery to have Callie here with her. He'd do anything for Estelle; he loved her dearly, and now he was afraid that this news might kill her.

She'd probably blame him as well for giving Callie permission to travel to the Hendersons. But hell, Callie really hadn't given him much choice. He had hoped by allowing her to assist Doc in the hospital to keep her busy and out of harms way, and they needed someone dependable to help out when Doc wasn't up to snuff. But he'd been worried that something like this might happen; more than once he'd had to remind his stepdaughter not to ride beyond the gates without an escort, although it seemed that even a detachment of his finest soldiers apparently hadn't been enough to protect her.

He had to admit these soldiers of today were vastly different in discipline and dedication than the brave fighting men who'd served under him during the War Between The States. Those had been real fighting men, and that was a war where he'd served proudly. His lips curved downward in a sneer. But this cat and mouse game they fought with the filthy savages wasn't anything a man could be proud of, or expect to result in advancement in his military status. He'd never wanted this damned post in the middle of no man's land, but he'd been assigned here anyway. He'd reflected more than once on why he'd been sent here, to Texas, to fight merciless heathens who were little better than beasts, instead of receiving a plush assignment in Washington as he'd been expecting. His eyes glittered with outrage.

Already he could hear the din of voices outside on the parade ground where no doubt the men and their families would assemble and wait for the official announcement of the tragic event that had taken place. He ground his teeth in impotent fury. This sort of news spread as rapidly as a prairie fire, and he knew what he must do first — he had to hurry to Estelle before someone else told her. He dreaded this task more than he ever had anything in his life.

By the time he'd arrived home, Colonel Williams had mentally prepared himself for the task of informing his wife that her daughter was a captive of the Quohadi Comanche.

He paused outside her bedroom door, then knocked and entered, his heart heavy. He thought he was prepared, but he could not have expected the extent of Estelle's grief when he broke the news to her. She became a wild woman, and it took both himself and his daughter to finally restrain her and force her back into bed. Her piercing, agonized screams would remain with him for the rest of his days.

"Oh, dear God in heaven . . . no . . . not my

baby girl!" Reaching up, she'd grabbed hold of his arm and pulled herself up until she was on her knees, tears streaming down her face. "Tell me you're going to find her . . . please, Bradford."

"I'll do everything within my power," he replied.

"It's the same as when I lost her father," she sobbed. "This can't be happening to me again." Then as if she'd just realized an even worse horror, her eyes beseeched his. "You've told me yourself what happens to white female captives . . . and she's been so gently reared. She couldn't stand it . . . you must find her before they . . . before they . . ." Her voice broke, and she couldn't go on, but they both knew what she'd been intending to say.

"We'll find her, darling, and we'll wipe out every Indian village in Texas along the way. I've been too easy with these savages. Well, no more," the Colonel swore, gathering his hysterical wife close in his arms. "I've already decided to go with the men. We're leaving within the hour. I'll do my best, that's all I can promise you."

Estelle clung to him as though to absorb strength into her frail body through his, her pale oval face ravaged by tears. "Oh, thank you . . . thank you. I know if anyone can save her you can."

"Please, Estelle, you must try and calm yourself." The colonel patted the back of her golden head, and was finally able to urge her to lie back

319

on the pillows. Murmuring soothing words, he sat holding her hand until she'd finally quieted.

Nineteen-year-old Melanie Williams sat on the other side of her stepmother's bedroom, and nervously chewed the tips of her carefully manicured fingernails until they were ragged. She knew that by the time they found Callie she would either be dead or mad. Everyone knew what sort of bestial brutality white women were subjected to when held captive by the savages.

She recalled the way the other girls related stories they'd heard regarding the unfortunate victims of the Comanches. None of them had ever personally known anyone kidnapped by the redskins before, but they did now. The women often discussed what they would do if they were ever taken captive, how they'd kill themselves before they'd let any Indian force them to do awful, vile acts.

Melanie figured Callie had probably already taken her own life, or was planning to. Everyone knew that sending out a search party was just a waste of time, for captives were rarely returned to their white families, and even when the Comanche did trade them back, the women who returned were never the same as when they'd left.

Indian whores, that's what some of the soldiers called the unfortunate women who became Indian slaves. It didn't seem to matter that they hadn't been willing victims — they'd become tainted — and no one would ever see them any other way.

She wasn't overly fond of Callie—she felt pale in comparison to her stepsister's vibrant beauty—but she'd never have wished for something so horrible to happen to her. Poor, poor Callie. Because of the Comanche, her soul was damned to hell for all eternity.

Lance Hamilton was beginning to feel much the same way about his soul. Twenty minutes after his oratory before his men, Colonel Williams paid a visit to the hospital, and now stood at the captain's bedside.

There was no one else but the two of them in the room. The colonel had made certain they had privacy, and had first ordered everyone else out of the room. There had only been one other patient, a trooper who was recovering from a bout with the flu, and Doc had wheeled him outside in the sunshine.

It was obvious that the captain was more than a bit nervous. His hands trembled visibly, and when the colonel offered him a cigarette, Lance's fingers shook so badly he could hardly place it between his lips. Colonel Williams had to take the match stick from the captain's hands, and light the cigarette for him.

"I know this is difficult for you, but I'm leaving within the hour and I need you to apprise me of the situation," the colonel said. He stared down at Lance's bleak face. "My God, son, how could they have taken you, a seasoned Indian fighter, completely off guard?"

Lance winced, and cleared his throat. "As much as I hate to say it, they just outmaneuvered us, sir." Still, his voice shook with emotion. "It was that half-breed we've been hearing so much about. He was riding with them. I don't know if he was their leader, but I'd be willing to bet you he is. Smart sonofabitch, so they tell me, and he seems to know a lot about battle strategy. He's the one who took our Callie."

A muscle flexed in the colonel's jaw. "I intend to make him pay for what he's done. You can be certain of it."

Lance nodded bleakly. "You'll need to send for reinforcements, sir. They were a large war party. God only knows how many of them they really are."

Colonel Williams glared at him. "You don't have to explain the facts to me, Captain Hamilton. I know how to handle these Indians. And I know I don't have to remind you what with the damn Indians tearing the entire state apart, I've had the brass coming down hard enough on me to round up those renegades. I sure as hell didn't need anything like this to contend with now." He pointedly held Lance's gaze. "If this goes badly, it will be on your record, as well. I don't intend to take it on the chin alone."

"Yes, sir, I expected as much," Lance sighed.

"Now you understand why I want to do everything I can to clean up this mess as quietly and efficiently as possible."

"Considering the circumstances, I'd like to join the search party as soon as I'm able, sir. Do I have your permission?"

The colonel nodded crisply. "Of course, I would have expected nothing less from an officer as fine as you, Hamilton. You realize, too, that if we find Callie Rae, and she's returned to her mother unharmed and her abductors punished, then the tide will turn in our favor. We'll be heroes instead of fools. Perhaps you most of all, Captain. The brave soldier who rode into battle and rescued his lady fair from the savage who'd stolen her away." His green eyes gleamed. "Yes, I like the sound of that. For sure Callie will be forever grateful to you as well. You might yet become my son-in-law, and that would still make me very proud."

"Nothing would give me greater pleasure, sir," Lance replied, but in truth he had to force such a reply, for he was beginning to wonder if he still wanted Callie for his wife. True, he might receive a promotion, but he'd be saddled with a woman whose reputation would be ruined. Not exactly how he'd had his future planned. Marriage to Callie no longer seemed quite as appealing. Lance began having a difficult time focusing his train of thought on the colonel's continuing words.

"By the time I'm finished with him, his people will have learned what will happen to them when they challenge Colonel Bradford Williams. This is a second chance for you, boy. I'm even going to let you have an hour or two alone with the son-ofabitch after we have him in our custody. After-ward, what's left of him is mine."

Captain Hamilton managed a crisp salute. "Thank you, sir! I won't let you down. You can count on me to carry through, and this time that half-breed sonofabitch won't stand a chance against our army."

Lance awoke with a start. It was dark in the hospital room, but instinctively he knew there was someone else there beside him. He didn't move a muscle until he'd waited for his eyes to adjust to the unfamiliarity of his surroundings. The first thing he saw was a privacy screen shielding his bed from view of the room.

A cloaked figure glided through the shadows in the corner and into a shaft of moonlight stream-ing through the window. "Sorry if I woke you," the female voice said throatily.

His face brightened, and he felt his earlier de-pression evaporating. Stretching lazily, he noticed that her gaze was drawn to the muscle rippling across his bare chest and arms. "No, you're not sorry at all. You've never been remorseful over anything in your life, Serena."

"That's not true. I was sorry when I heard that you'd been injured," she replied with a slow, se-ductive smile.

"Mmmm . . . perhaps, but only because you were probably worried over what part of my anatomy sustained injury."

"Well . . . maybe just a little concerned." She leaned into him, and worked her small hand under the sheet draping his body, enjoying the play of hard muscle beneath her roving fingertips. Her searching fingers moved lower, and she smiled. "How nice to find that the Comanche spared your most prized possession," she purred.

"Believe me, I'm thrilled as all hell," Lance quipped, although he meant every word. Little by little warmth and life began creeping back into Lance's body. Thank God there were still women like Serena.

The corners of Serena's mouth twitched upward. "Would you like me to show you how thrilled *I* am?" she asked playfully, but her voice was husky with desire. "I promise you it would be an experience you're not likely to forget."

Lance frowned. "Ordinarily I'd say nothing would make me happier. But the colonel came down hard on me this afternoon. I don't know if what you so obviously have in mind is such a good idea right now. Someone might have seen you come in here and decide to investigate."

She drew an invisible pattern on his belly. "No one saw me. I slipped in by the side door."

He raised one eyebrow and peered at her speculatively. "They lock that door at night. How did you manage to get in?"

"I have other talents besides the ones you're aware of."

He was suddenly filled with a strange, inner

325

excitement, ready to throw caution to the winds. He really didn't mind being the recipient of Serena's restless desire. And the sensation of her fingers stroking him, cupping him, stirring life back into his beaten body, was the best medicine the doctor could have ordered. He watched her moisten her lips with the tip of her tongue. In the moonlight, it glistened with moisture and experience. He squirmed, and his breath came in ragged gasps. He'd known the touch of her lips before. She had an accomplished erotic technique, and the image his mind projected hurtled his passion beyond reasonable control.

Serena slowly pulled the bedcovers aside. "Let Serena make it all better," she cooed, bending over him.

Captain Lance Hamilton soon found it difficult to concentrate on anything but her warm lips, her seeking tongue, and the gentle nibbles that fragmented his thoughts as they went on their hungry search. It was a raw act of possession, but he loved every minute.

"Je . . . sus . . . chri . . . ma . . . nitly," was all that he could gasp, his hips arching upward off the bed as he surrendered completely to her mastery.

When he was solid, and thrusting lustily, she suddenly rose up, and with a wicked gleam in her eyes, declared, "How wonderful, darling. Everything's still in fine working order."

His mouth curved into an unconscious smile as he stared at her.

Her green eyes glittered in the moonlight streaming through the window beside his bed, softening the lines bracketing her eyes and mouth. She was older than he—he guessed probably by at least ten years—but with the sort of relationship they'd mutually agreed upon, age didn't really matter. He knew she wasn't the sort of woman to fall in love with. He'd be a fool when it was well known she slept with whomever caught her fancy.

Gazing up at her in the shadowy light, he thought she looked like a wild jungle cat, and he only hoped she'd remember to keep her claws sheathed. He felt his groin tighten, and in thinking about how close he'd come to never making love to a woman again, whispered a silent prayer of thanks that Serena had looked so kindly on him this evening. His eyes were drawn to her black velvet cloak. He knew that if he slipped his hand inside its soft folds that he'd find she was naked as the day she was born. He reached out with one hand and slid his cool fingers inside her cloak. What he found widened his smile. Capturing a pink crest between his thumb and forefinger, he squeezed just hard enough so that she moaned in pleasure.

His eyelids felt weighted, his limbs free of pain. Just when his body began to spasm and lose all control, she moved up and over him, the heat between her parted thighs more than she could bear.

Impaling herself on his pulsing length, Serena

set the grinding, bucking pace. She demanded the lead, and he didn't have to do anything but lie back and enjoy the ride.

When she'd exhausted herself and him, Serena eased gently over and onto her back next to the blissful, sated Captain Hamilton. "Would you like a cigarette?" she asked.

He didn't even open his eyes, but remained stretched out, every nerve in his body desensitized and feeling no pain. Who in the hell needed Doc when there was Serena? He stifled a sleepy yawn. "Yeah . . . I would."

He heard her open the nightstand drawer and search through it. Slitting one eye, Lance watched her deftly roll a cigarette, and then clamp the cylinder between those talented lips. It shocked him more than her recent performance. "Just what in the hell do you think you're doing?"

She ignored him and took another drag, exhaling smoke through delicate nostrils before answering. "You forget, Captain, that you're not with your little nun. A woman like me has to have vices. The more the better."

"I would have thought you already had plenty," he shot back. "And she isn't a nun," he added testily.

Unruffled, she shrugged one bare shoulder. "She was raised by the nuns, and it's just about the same difference if you ask me," Serena countered. Withdrawing the cigarette from her lips, she offered it to him.

After drawing smoke deep into his lungs, Lance exhaled and blew several smoke rings toward the ceiling. Serena reached up and poked her finger through each one.

"She isn't like anyone I've ever met before," he said. "It's too bad things had to go sour so soon. I rather liked her. She was a little boring, but she had class."

"Eeee . . . gads . . . you're beginning to sound like a lovesick puppy," Serena drawled. "And here I thought I was the only woman in your life."

Lance lifted her hand to his lips, pressing a kiss to the inside of her palm. "If my memory serves me correctly you're already married to the major, although sometime I wonder if you remember."

"Believe me, darling, I think about my dreary existence every moment of the day, and when I go to sleep at night, all I dream about is how I might escape," she drawled, revealing another side of her he'd never seen before. He knew she was cool and calculating, but did she honestly believe that he would allow her to use him to further her own goals? It sounded to him as if Serena was growing restless and looking for greener pastures. Well, she'd just have to find some other poor bastard to help her out. Lance wasn't about to jeopardize his career by being caught in a messy scandal.

So the handsome blond officer just let her remark slide past, and soon afterward, he feigned sleep. Minutes later, he heard Serena tip-toe from the room, and the sound of the door as she closed it softly behind her.

In the future, he thought, it would be wise of him to start weaning himself away from Serena. She was trouble, and he didn't need any more to handle than he already had.

Two Hearts Divided

Doubt thou the stars are fire;
Doubt that the sun doth move;
Doubt truth to be a liar;
But never doubt I love.
William Shakespeare
Hamlet

Chapter Twenty-one

Callie went along with the other women that morning to bathe in the river. Night Hawk had left before she'd awakened, and she didn't like to think where he might have gone.

Lately he seemed to think of nothing else but finding Morning Star and Precious Flower's murderer. She tried to understand how he must feel, but she couldn't help wondering if his vendetta wasn't the most important thing in his life right now. She was beginning to wonder if she shouldn't speak with him about letting her return to the fort. Perhaps he was of a different opinion now that he realized how attached she'd become to his people. She'd never wish any harm to come to them, or to him. With each passing day she was certain she was falling more deeply in love with him. It was something she certainly hadn't wanted to do. Her passion ensnared him, but after his ardor cooled, what remained? Only her aching heart and impossible dreams. She was beginning to doubt that there would ever be a time when they could start building a life together. They were just going through the motions, and Callie knew she was only fooling herself when she thought it might one day change. The future looked vague and shadowy. She and Night Hawk were literally worlds apart.

"You're awfully quiet this morning, Callie," Willow said, eyes questioning. "My cousin treats you well, does he not?"

Callie kept her gaze level, and splashed water over her arms. "He is a good man, Willow. It is nothing like that."

Summer waded over to join them in the shoulder-high water. She smiled to herself. Callie was getting used to their custom of bathing together, but she still sought out the deepest part of the river where she might stand with the water up to her chin.

"I have never seen my son as happy as he has been lately," Summer said thoughtfully. "I am grateful to you, Callie, for I know it is because of you that he smiles more now. I only hope that soon you will be making another announcement as well. My son needs a wife. I would be pleased to have you for a daughter as well."

"You honor me," Callie replied, "but Night Hawk and I haven't even talked of marriage yet. He seems to have far too many other things on his mind."

Summer smiled. "Tonight that will change. You wait and see."

"*Haa,* yes, at the dance where a man chooses the woman he wants to become his partner in marriage," Willow chimed in happily.

Callie did smile a little then. "You two are such hopeless romantics. But I wouldn't count on Night Hawk even showing up."

Summer and Willow exchanged questioning looks, and perplexed, Summer shrugged.

Willow turned her questioning gaze to Callie. "What do these hopeless romantic words mean?"

Callie's face creased into a sudden smile. "It is when a person never fails to believe in love and happy endings. Like the two of you."

"Is this a bad thing to do?" Willow questioned, her expression serious.

"Heavens no," Callie replied quickly. "It's just not always possible to have both. But I guess it never hurts to keep trying. Who knows, one day you just might find you have everything you need to make you happy. That's what really matters. How you feel inside."

"Then I stay this hopeless romantic," Willow exclaimed. "I already very happy with what I have in my life. Who needs to wake up every morning feeling dark like storm cloud. If you think happy instead of sad then you might get good things you want."

"You are definitely an optimist," Callie said without thinking.

"What is this op . . . ti . . . mist?" Willow was quick to ask.

Callie's smile was alive with affection and delight. "Dear Willow, you are just the person I needed to be with this morning."

They shared smiles, and soon after waded from the river to join the cluster of women gathering on the riverbank. They all sat together on the mossy bank, oblivious to their nudity, discussing the evening's upcoming festivities while they'd waited for the hot morning sun to bake their skin dry.

Callie, on the other hand, hurriedly rubbed herself dry with a cloth and quickly slipped back into her fringed skirt and top. She'd never seen so many mirrors flashing in the sunlight, or heard such excited chattering. Then she settled herself beside Summer, and began to comb out her damp hair. She couldn't remember a time when the women had taken such care with their appearance. Long hair had been scrupulously washed, combed and braided, and anxious faces were carefully painted.

She enjoyed spending time with these women, but she still found the idea of communal bathing a bit unnerving. It wasn't easy for a convent girl to shed her inhibitions, but in the weeks since she'd been among the Indians she'd managed to discard more than a few. Of course it had far from boosted her courage the first day she'd joined them and had heard them giggling softly when they'd first glimpsed her bare ivory skin. But that had been over a week ago, and she wasn't pale any longer, she thought. Since she'd been spending so much time outdoors, her skin had begun to turn a rich, golden apricot, and even her hair was now streaked with tawny highlights. She often wore it in a braid, or flowing down her back, feathers tied to the gleaming tresses. She knew it wasn't considered fashionable in a civilized society, but Callie wasn't all so sure she cared about propriety anymore. She

336

rather liked her new appearance and healthy glow, and she could tell by the times she'd caught Night Hawk staring at her, that he was pleased by her transformation as well.

She was also beginning to understand the Comanche language, and spoke in sentences quite well. Although there were still many words she mispronounced, and there were times when she'd had to resort to sign language to make her point known, she was learning more every day. Surprisingly, everyone was patient with her and seemed eager to teach her the simple, beautiful way they lived.

Night Hawk had been true to his word and had taught her well how to string a bow with an arrow and to hit a target he'd tacked on a tree. She could shoot his Colt .45 with considerable accuracy as well, and he'd given her a jeweled dagger that he'd taken in a raid.

In a matter of a few hours, Callie became proficient with it as well, although she'd thought no matter the circumstance, it would be hard for her to take anyone else's life. He'd told her that at least if the occasion ever arose, and he hoped that it never did, she would at least have the skill and courage to know what to do. He'd sheathed the gleaming weapon in a rawhide case and strapped it against her leg, his fingers playing against the fine red-gold hairs of her inner thigh.

When he'd finished looping the straps, they were both flushed, and in mutual agreement that the lesson was over for the day. They'd spent the next hour in pursuit of other pleasures.

Later, he'd gifted her with a long-legged sorrel filly, which she decided to name Wind. She often took long rides in the moonlight with Night Hawk beside her on Shadow. It was a quiet escape from their busy life in the village, and they savored this time together alone.

They spent many hours making love beneath the stars — there was one time that she didn't think she'd ever forget — when the involuntary tremors of arousal had begun, and they'd been swept along in a possessive fervor.

At the time they'd been riding double on Shadow. The surging stallion had been galloping smoothly across the open plains, but they perhaps had been too eager, and their intimacy had become so spontaneous, that they allowed desire to overtake them. But even as he settled her across his hips and they began tearing at each other's clothing, their hands fumbled and their body thrusts were awkward. Making love on horseback was not anything like she might have imagined.

They ended up laughing hysterically, a golden wave of passion and love flowing between them as they found themselves rolling off the stallion's back in each other's arms. Night Hawk had cushioned her fall with his body, and once the dust had settled, the laughter soon died. He'd caught her hair in possessive, fisted fingers, and they'd succumbed to raw passion, the cool earth embracing them as they were joined under the night-draped sky.

In spirit and countenance Callie was becoming more like one of the People with each passing day.

The fear she'd known when she'd first rode into the village, had slowly diminished. In its place was a new awareness. In her heart for the first time she'd begun to know peace.

A full moon rose, pale and splendid, spilling its fiery light over the Quohadi encampment and the people who'd begun to gather in celebration. They assembled around the roaring fire in the center of the village, drawn by the pulsing rhythm of the drums and the hypnotic chant of the love song. It was a disquietingly sensual ballad, signifying the beginning of the ceremony that everyone had been anticipating for weeks. Especially the unmarried maidens of the camp. The event was one of the most significant of their lives.

On this night a man would choose the woman he wanted to become his wife. The single women of the village had been bustling since early morning in preparation. Particular care had been given to appearance, for the maidens knew they had to look their best in order to draw attention from the men during the dance

Callie stood outside of Night Hawk's lodge in the arid night air, staring toward the gathering of people, her eyes searching for any sign of his tall, familiar figure. He'd been gone since before dawn, and although they hadn't discussed it, she had wanted to believe that he would return before the start of the evening's festivities. Perhaps it had only been wishful thinking on her part that tonight he'd finally prove before everyone how much he cared for her.

"Come with us. We are going to join the other women," her friend *Hiitoo,* Meadowlark, called out to her as she passed by with her married sister who had been chosen at last year's dance.

Callie thought Meadowlark had never looked lovelier. She was dressed in a doeskin gown dyed sky blue, and her hair gleamed black as a raven's wing in the moonlight.

"I'll be along in awhile," Callie replied, her composure suddenly like a fragile shell that might shatter at any moment. Where was Night Hawk? Why hadn't he returned as yet?

"The dancers are beginning to gather. Don't wait too long or you will miss out," Meadowlark replied, before continuing onward.

Shortly afterward, the dance began. The golden moon and the canopy of stars overhead soared against a sky like black velvet. Callie's gaze was held spellbound as she watched from the sidelines.

The ring of dancers began swaying to and fro to the pulsing drumbeat, the women rising up from their heels to their toes, arms raised, slender forms fluid and graceful.

She saw the other young braves, all resplendantly dressed, their bodies sleek, firm muscle, watching the circle of women, who were facing outward, glide past. One by one the men joined in the dance, and chose the woman who would become their partner for life.

Callie could almost feel their rapture, the quickening of their hearts, and wished that she might experience such emotions. At the moment, standing alone while the other women were being chosen, she only felt hurt and disappointed.

Glancing down at her new dress trimmed in sable that she'd made with the expressed intention of wearing to this evening's festivities, Callie thought how much time and effort had gone into making the garment. Summer had helped her, of course, but Callie had been eager to do most of the work herself.

Summer had shown Callie how to treat the hide until it was soft as butter, and together they'd sewn on the tiny glistening shells. Callie couldn't remember ever having another gown that she'd liked so well. Whenever she took a step, the swells and curves of her body moved loosely beneath the thin material and the shells chinkled. It was a shame the one person she'd wanted to see wasn't here to appreciate her efforts.

She'd even carefully braided her flaming red hair and wrapped the long plait that hung down the middle of her back in lush sable. Summer had given her a bracelet of tiny onyx stones that she was wearing around her wrist. She felt beautiful and desirable. On this special night of nights, she so wanted to be a part of the sensual, graceful bodies swaying together in the primitive, pagan dance.

The music continued over the next hour, and still the dancers gathered, shapes and faces taking on new contours in shadow and firelight, the perfume of summer inexplicably sweet, wafting on the night air.

Callie found she couldn't take her eyes off the ceremony, nor could she deny the kindling of desire in her loins. Her heart seemed to beat with the pulse of the drums, her body, stroked and enticed by a lover's invisible hands. New wants, needs, sensations, emerged and prickled pleasurably along her skin.

The longer she stood there watching, the more susceptible she became to the magic that seemed so much a part of this night. She ached to see Night Hawk, and perhaps had even spoken his name aloud, for the thought of him burned within her brain with single-minded intensity. Her gaze was drawn to something beyond the circle of dancers that moved among the shadows, and she stared brazenly as a distinctive shape separated from the darkness, solidified, and started toward her.

Everything else around her blurred, and her focus became absolute. He strode through the flickering firelight with the supple grace of a mountain cat. Callie watched the way he moved, and felt her pulses suddenly leap with excitement.

"Night Hawk. You're here at last." She breathed in the heady, captivating musk that was his alone, and felt drugged by his closeness.

"Come with me, angel, let's join them," he said, holding out his hand.

His deep-timbred voice seemed to echo her own longings, but she realized that if she accepted his invitation, it would be expected that they would marry soon. He offered her no explanations for his long absence and expected her to just fall into his arms now that he had returned. Callie had already decided as she'd been waiting, that she wasn't going to marry him until she was certain that he'd exorcised his demons and could set aside the ghosts from his past. And there were still so many other nagging questions. She still didn't know if she could spend the rest of her life among these people, put aside her hopes, her dreams, and live forever as one of them.

It was true that the Quohadi were beginning to accept her, and they even respected her as a healer. Of course, she had Owl Man to thank for that. He believed in her healing medicine, and had often sought her assistance in the treatment of a patient. Because of his faith in her, the people were beginning to trust her judgment as well. And there wasn't one among them who hadn't noticed the amulet she wore around her neck. Owl Man had pointed this out to anyone who would listen. He'd declared that she had great medicine power because of the sacred charm. She'd heard him speak to his people of the spirit power he thought the amulet possessed, and she had to admit that she had always thought as much herself.

For a long moment she stood there, unable to face him and unable to turn away. Night Hawk took a step closer. She felt his hands span her reed-slim waist.

"Join me, *bella*. You won't ever regret doing so."

Her breath was shallow; her senses drugged. She fought to remain clear-headed and slowly shook her head. Tears glistened in her eyes. "If you only would have asked me earlier. I've been thinking, Night Hawk. We come from different worlds. You can't live in mine, and I don't know if I want to remain here and live in yours. We need more time to think about this."

He toyed with a strand of her hair, wrapping it around his index finger. "If you'd search your heart for the truth you'd realize that this is how you want it to be. You must *feel,* angel, not try and analyze everything."

"I do feel. And it hurts too much to be a part of your life," she said softly. The warmth of his skin so near hers was intoxicating, and she felt her resolve weakening. Perhaps it would not be such a bad thing to marry him on any terms, she mused, staring up into his dark face. A face she'd come to love so well. "Night Hawk . . . I want us to be together, but I just don't think it's going to work out."

He put his hand under her chin, turning her toward him. Placing his forefinger against her lips, he murmured low. "Hush, just give me a chance. Trust must come first between us. I thought you were learning to trust me. Was I wrong?"

The soft brushing of those long fingers against her cheek only added to her confusion. "How can I when you keep shutting me out."

His burning gaze held her still. "Then let me bare part of my soul to you tonight. It will be the first step toward our building a life together."

She reached up, smoothed his hair with her hand and loved him with her eyes. Her mouth felt suddenly dry. His bare lithe body was naked, and even though she'd grown used to seeing him in only a breechcloth, leggings and moccasins, she found that he'd never seemed more ruggedly virile than at that moment. His ebony hair was unfettered and hung to his shoulders. In the firelight his eyes shone like bits of gleaming topaz, and the ghostly flickering played across his features and the stark paint that slashed across the chiseled bones of his face.

"I want to, Night Hawk, but from the moment I step into the circle of dancers we will live in only one world. And I'm not sure if there's a place for me in your life yet."

There, she had made her decision, even though she knew she'd just set him free to choose any other woman if he wanted. Her heart would break if he did. She wished she wasn't remembering the first time she had ever danced with him in the bayou; how she hadn't been able to take her eyes off his long, lean body, the play of muscle under his bronzed skin that had rippled fluidly in the firelight. It wasn't any different tonight. Her senses were drowning in his beauty. Whenever he was near she felt this compelling urge to be held close in his arms and forget that anything existed but the two of them. It wasn't right! He shouldn't be so important to her. She had always thought she'd dedicate her life to medicine, and not to loving a man. How could he expect her to live her life in his shadow and never know freedom again? But the foremost question that plagued her had been nagging at the back of her mind for some time. Did he feel obligated to marry her?

He had to know that she could never return to her old way of life and be accepted by her own people. She was caught between two worlds, as he was. At the moment she didn't know which way she should turn. To go forward would mean having him as her husband, and perhaps one day they would love as equals. To return to the fort would bring her heartache, and of course, everyone there would think of her as a half-breed's squaw and pity her.

And she couldn't live here as his wife without a declaration of love. She eased back from him. "I don't think we should join the dancers."

He stiffened. "Then you won't become my wife?"

Pain sliced through her. "Not yet . . . your heart isn't yet free to love me. As far as I'm concerned that's the only reason two people should get married."

He searched her upturned face. "Don't you know by now how I feel about you? Haven't I shown you in a hundred ways?" It was the first time since Morning Star's death that he'd even considered sharing his life with another woman; he only wished that he could tell Callie everything. But he could not. The power that he'd asked for that night in the sacred canyon had been secured through his guardian spirit and revealed in his vision. He had sworn to track down Morning Star and Precious Flower's murderer before he gave his heart to another woman.

The Comanche would consider it a taboo to forsake his vow after he'd become the recipient of such power. He had to find this man first and exact his revenge for his slain family. Then he'd return to the canyon, thank the spirit for his blessing and tell him that he no longer wished to use the medicine power. It would be a night of ceremony and prayer. This would mark the end of his mourning period, and he'd be free to give his love to Callie. Although he'd never considered himself a particularly superstitious man, he could not jeopardize Callie by perhaps angering these spirits.

Callie expelled a long, audible sigh, and held back her tears. "Maybe neither one of us knows how our love's supposed to feel. Maybe we never will."

Burying his face in the flowery perfume of her hair, he said in a raw voice. "Don't say that."

"I'm not afraid of the truth. In your heart you still have only one wife. And it is not me."

Tugging her close, he whispered into her soft hair. "I'm not going to let you get away from me. Bear with me, and when you're filled with doubt as you are now, know that whenever I'm near you I can't think of anything but how much I want to hold you . . . touch you . . . hear that breathy sound you make when your body accepts my flesh deep inside you. With you, I can forget my past and look forward to the future. I want desperately to share so much with you my love." He laced his fingers through her hair and drew her head back. Waves of flickering heat stirred low in his belly as, dipping his head, he brushed his mouth across her lips. "Come with me . . . at least be my love for tonight, and forget about everything else."

Callie's gaze was tender. "And tomorrow?"

"Just love me now, angel. Let tomorrow take

care of itself." His lips came coaxingly down on hers.

She surrendered completely to his masterful seduction, and spent the rest of that night lost in his arms.

But she would not dance with him.

She was firm in this decision, even though her heart was breaking.

Night Hawk didn't insist again, preferring to wait until he could promise her his love forever. He prayed it would be soon.

Chapter Twenty-two

"I'll find that half-breed bastard for you, Colonel," the man stated confidently in a pronounced southern drawl. Leaning back in the chair, he glanced down at the tumbler of bourbon he held in his hand. He swirled the amber liquid around in the glass.

"Why do I need to hire you when I have an entire cavalry regiment at my command?" the colonel posed, sitting with his hands folded on top his desk. Becker Stevenson seemed to take perverse pleasure in tracking down Indian renegades and the colonel had even heard rumors that he had quite a collection of scalps with flowing black hair as proof of his victories. It made his flesh crawl just to think he was sitting across his desk from so vile a man. When he'd turned up at the fort earlier that morning and had offered the colonel a proposition to track down the Comanche half-breed who'd taken Callie over a month ago, the Colonel's first instinct had been to send him away. Then he thought how his wife was slowly grieving herself to death, and how his own efforts to locate the Quohadi encampment had proved futile. Estelle seemed to have lost faith in him. She wouldn't eat, couldn't sleep, and it didn't even seem to matter that he was there for her. She only wanted Callie. Stevenson's voice intruded on his misery.

"No offense, sir, but it seems that half-breed just plain outsmarted your men. My sources have told me that for all the cavalry's efforts, you haven't been able to turn up a thing." He scratched his stubbled jaw. "In the meantime, this savage's got himself dug in real good somewhere, and he's got your lovely stepdaughter to keep him company. The more time you waste, the harder it gets for her." His fleshy lips pulled back from stained, crooked teeth. "I think you know the longer she's with him the harder it's going to be to recivilize the young lady."

Colonel Williams cleared his throat. "Yes, I understand. God only knows what the poor girl's suffered already." His gaze narrowed on the scout's sunburned face, the kind that eventually blistered under the Texas sun. Of course, the grime that covered it would help to protect his fair skin. He reeked of filth and unwashed skin. The colonel tried not to breathe too deeply. "What makes you think you can succeed where an entire regiment of trained men have failed?"

"Because I know something that you and your men don't," he said, before tossing back the rest of his drink.

"Just what would that be?" the colonel asked, frowning with annoyance. The more time he spent with this man the less he liked him.

Stevenson peered over the rim of the empty glass,

350

his lank blond hair partially covering one eye as his gaze met the colonel's. "How these renegades think, what their habits are, and just how far they're willing to go to remain free. Let me remind you that you're dealing with the worst of the lot. A half-breed. They're smarter and more devious than your ordinary hostile. This devil sounds like he's been stirring up enough trouble for more than one army to handle." His gaze flitted downward, as if he weren't quite comfortable looking any man directly in the eyes for too long, and plucked at the dirty fringe on his buckskin trousers with jagged fingernails. "My men and I work pretty reasonable, and we know how to keep our mouths shut when the situation calls for it. I don't imagine you'd want this sort of thing getting around, so that's why I approached you in private. Our deal can be just between us. Nobody else need know why we're here."

"How much are your services going to cost me, Stevenson?" the colonel asked. He had serious doubts about entrusting him with this mission. The man was known to travel in bad company — several other drifters had ridden in with him and even now were waiting for him just outside the gates — and his past was something of an enigma. Although the colonel strongly suspected that if he wanted to take the time to dig deep enough, he'd find that Stevenson shunned civilization because he had secrets of his own he didn't want uncovered. Just about everyone who ended up in this godforsaken country was either running away, or trying to prove something. Still, there was the girl's life to consider, and his wife's precarious health. There was also his own reputation to think about. If the scout could bring Callie back safe, and possibly none the worse for wear, he stood a chance of salvaging his record.

Stevenson gave that some thought, then glanced up at the colonel. "See'ins how you're kinda in a bad light right now and all, I'm gonna give you a good deal." He grinned. "My men and I will work for chicken feed . . . say five hundred now, and another five hundred when I bring back your stepdaughter . . . and that half-breed's scalp."

"My God, man, I don't want the man's scalp," the colonel snarled. "Just return Callie safely to her mother, that's all that I ask."

"It's a deal then." Stevenson proffered a rough, calloused hand, and the colonel accepted it within his firm grasp with obvious reluctance. "Consider it as good as done, sir. But I hope you won't have any objections if I lift his hair as a trophy for myself. It's a nasty habit I just can't seem to break," he added with a leer.

Colonel Williams withdrew his hand and resisted a strong urge to wipe his palms on his shirt. To control the impulse, he ran thick, strong fingers through his hair. Rising to his feet, he favored the man with a meaningful stare. "Let's make one thing clear before you go, Stevenson. I don't approve of your methods, and I can't say that I even like you very much, but it can't hurt to have as many people searching as possible. However, the only reason I'm going along with you is for my family's sake. I still believe in the capability of my men. We'll just see who finds her first."

"Colonel, I'm so certain I'm gonna find that little gal before your men that I'm willing to make you a wager on the side," he declared in a blustery tone. "Call it added incentive. What do you say?"

The colonel had watched the scout drain three tumblers filled with bourbon. He figured it was the liquor talking, but he nodded his head. "Go ahead, I'm listening, Stevenson."

"If your soldiers find her, we only get the first five hundred as total payment. If we bring her back, then you fork over the rest of the money, plus an added bonus of two hundred more paid to me personally."

Colonel Williams, raising his eyebrows, turned away and strode over to stare out of the wide windows at the flagpole with its colors unfurled in the breeze. "You drive a hard bargain, Stevenson. But consider it done if you bring the girl back unharmed, and also, bring me proof that that half-breed bastard's no longer one of my worries. Do I make myself clear?"

"Yeah," the scout replied, pleasure glowing in his eyes and lifting the corners of his thin lips. " I'd say you had second thoughts about my bringing you that souvenir after all."

The colonel didn't respond, he just stood there quietly looking out the window onto the parade grounds where some of his men were beginning to gather as they did every day at this time. As he heard the scout prepare to take his leave, he stated quietly. "Use the back door of my office, Stevenson. The less anyone else knows about you the better."

Dismissing the scout from his mind, he barely paid notice as Becker Stevenson quit the room. He was thinking how every ambitious young officer to come out of West Point had been converging on the

Plains since the close of the War Between The States, hoping to earn himself a name and a promotion. Eliminate the problems with the Indians, and you had a set of gold bars for your shoulder. They made it sound so easy to men who were very much like he had been at one time. Young, eager, determined to get ahead no matter what they had to do. Of course, he was still tough as nails and could hold his own against any of these young pups under his command. But since the attack on his company, and Callie's abduction, he'd begun to look upon the half-breed renegade who'd taken her in a new and different light. Oh, he'd heard enough about him even before. He knew he wasn't just another uneducated, ruthless savage who thought he could hold onto the land and his culture with brute force. He was revered among his people, and feared by most white men. Where he roamed, no man dared trespass without serious consequence.

Capturing him would take strategy and cunning, the colonel felt certain. The Indians would say the breed had powerful medicine on his side, and perhaps this was true. But he was also a lot smarter than he wanted any white man to realize. It was his cunning intelligence that made him so formidable a foe. Who in the hell was he? Where had he come from? Primarily, how might they get rid of him? That was the foremost question plaguing the colonel at that moment. For now, he didn't have the answer, but intuitively he sensed that the battle ahead of them would be intense, and with careful strategy as opposed to brute force, the colonel thought he might yet emerge the winner.

The renegade had taken Callie for a definite reason, and when he decided to make them known, the colonel knew he'd be the first to hear.

"Keep well until then, poor child, but most of all, stay sane. For I think it will be hard for you to do with them," he murmured wearily.

She was no longer the same woman. The weeks had flown swiftly past, and Callie had adjusted quite well to her new way of life. As Night Hawk's woman she was accorded respect and privileges.

The comanche were a proud people, who did not have time to worry about anything else but their survival, and they celebrated life to the fullest, however and whenever it was possible. Social gatherings were always filled with laughter and revelry. When food was plentiful and there were no pressing duties, the people would gather in the evening around the fire kindled in the center of the village, and tell stories or dance until the moon waned in the night sky. Their movements, like their lifestyle, was vivid and natural.

It was impossible not to respond to the people's warmth and sincerity. The women dropped by Night Hawk's lodge frequently to pay their respects to Callie, others came seeking advice for physical maladies that they thought another woman might better understand. At first Callie had been cautious when giving out medical advice, not wishing to offend the shaman. But the shaman, Owl Man, continued to encourage her in every way. Though she did not style herself as a healer among the People, the shaman readily accepted her theories. It wasn't long before

Callie and the shaman realized that they shared a strong belief in the natural remedies obtained from forest and garden and began frequently exchanging advice on procedures and cures.

Life among the Quohadi Comanche was unlike anything she'd ever experienced and she knew she'd never again view life or the Indians as she had before. She wasn't even certain when her attitude had begun to change, or why, but she'd noticed that lately when she awoke in the morning it was with a satisfying feeling, and at night, falling asleep tucked securely in Night Hawk's arms, Callie decided she couldn't think of any other place she'd rather be.

To her delight she had begun to discover the freedom she'd always longed for. She had made many friends, this despite the suspicion that Little Doe and Black Raven still harbored ill will toward her. Even though she had tried to apologize to Black Raven for attempting to steal his pony, it didn't change his attitude toward her. He still remained unforgiving, and Little Doe obviously resented her out of her sense of loyalty to Morning Star's memory.

They were the only two people who did not attend her naming ceremony, but everyone else in the village turned out in their finery to honor her. She was named *Puhawi,* Medicine Woman, by the name giver. It was done. She was truly one of them now.

After the ceremony, they feasted on roasted buffalo and bread that had been freshly baked with pecans and honey on stones before the fire. It was hot and fragrant. She was so excited that Callie couldn't eat very much of her thick buffalo steak, but she munched on several pieces of the bread while the others stuffed themselves until they'd finally managed to eat an entire buffalo.

When they were finished with the meal and the men had smoked the pipe, the real fun began. The drums signaled the men and women, and they began to file together toward the line of dancers who'd begun to gather nearby.

"I believe this is our dance," Night Hawk said, taking hold of her hand.

She didn't object, for she knew there was no significance involved, just pure fun. They slipped into the circle, and he stood a short distance apart facing her. Placing his hands around her waist and clasping hers around him in similar fashion, he led her through the dance routine. With a touch of the devil in his eyes, Night Hawk made it clear to any other brave who came near that she was his, and he expected they would keep their distance. She knew their language well now, and couldn't help but smile shyly.

He made a slight gesture with his right hand. "Stay away, she is off limits," he warned his cousin, Raging Bear, who'd sneaked up behind Night Hawk's back and tapped him on the shoulder.

Raging Bear peered over his cousin's shoulder. "Is your golden one so special that she is worth spending so much of your time away from your other friends? Maybe you would consider a trade of six fine horses for her and then have your freedom once again?"

Protective arms pressed her closer to him. "Not even if you offered me a white buffalo," Night Hawk said with quiet emphasis.

Chuckling, Raging Bear slapped his cousin on the

back, and announced to everyone who was near, "I think that Medicine Woman has been putting love medicine in our brother's food. I have never heard of anyone who would turn down six horses and a white buffalo."

Night Hawk smiled down at Callie. "Now do you believe that everything will be good between us? Surely by now you must?"

"*Haa,* you have convinced me these past weeks. I believe, Night Hawk," she replied, a gentle softness in her voice.

As the pace of the tempo increased, the bodies pressed closer and closer together, but every movement was vivid and natural. Still, she was very aware of Night Hawk's hard body brushing intimately against her, and imagined, how later, she would feel the press of his bare flesh and hungry kiss in the privacy of their lodge.

Loving him seemed so easy now. Not very long ago she'd thought of him as her enemy and didn't think it would be possible for them to look forward to a future together. She still liked to tease him and call him captor, but he was in every way her lover. Despite her efforts to resist his affection, she knew that now and forever she would belong only to him.

Gazing up at him, her smile had a spark of eroticism, and he responded by bending his head and placing his lips near her ear.

In very descriptive detail, he explained how he was going to make love to her later, and she could do nothing to banish the images that flitted ceaselessly through her mind. The surrounding crowd blurred as his words played over her and his thoughts seemed to fuse with her own.

"I'm looking forward to it," she whispered, her body melting against his, the universe suddenly filled with only him.

The next morning she awoke later than usual and lay there listening to the sounds of the village stir to life. Night Hawk still slept beside her. It had been a wonderful night. If not for the fact that her family did not know if she were dead or alive, she might have felt like the luckiest woman in the world. Slipping from beneath the buffalo robe, she rose and dressed quietly.

By the time that she returned from the river and had begun preparing their breakfast, Night Hawk was awake. She had tried to dismiss her concerns. But as always, when thoughts of her former life intruded on her daydreams, she became broodingly silent.

Now she had a different set of concerns. Were they still searching for her? What would she do if they should find her? How could she stand to think of the bloodshed and violence that might transpire?

She'd been helping Night Hawk gather together the things he needed for his hunting trip. It was late summer, and the Comanche knew how imperative it was that they have enough meat before the winter set in. It was becoming harder to find the buffalo herds, primarily due to the white hunters who wantonly slaughtered the buffalo for their hides, leaving the carcasses rotting on the plains; thus the meat the Comanche needed to survive through the hard winter was lost. The People were already feeling the effects.

Everyone wondered what the winter would be like if the buffalo could not be found soon.

"I wish you were coming along with me," Night Hawk said, reaching for the rifle that he kept next to their bed. He took it along for protection, but he preferred to hunt with his fourteen-foot Plains lance, a weapon fashioned after the conquistadores. The Comanche felt it took more daring to bring down a raging buffalo with only a lance, and it was a mark of pride to carry one on a hunt. During the fall it was customary for the entire village to turn out for the hunt. Each family worked with precision timing after the buffalo was killed, moving in to skin and butcher the carcass from head to tail, leaving nothing behind. The People didn't waste any part of the buffalo.

"I'll be here waiting for you to return," Callie replied softly. She began to gather together the strips of *Inapa,* jerky, as the People called it, and wrap it in clothlike rawhide. The jerky was made from buffalo meat cut into thin strips that were one to three feet in length, and carved against the grain so that the fat was evenly distributed. She'd come to realize how important the buffalo was to the People. If this hunt proved successful they'd have enough food until spring. She didn't want to think about what it could be like if the hunters returned empty-handed, as they'd begun doing more and more often lately.

Suddenly, she was in his arms and her heart constricted as she clung to him.

"I guess I've always feared that one day you might not be here when I return," he said. "I want you with me always, angel. I don't think I've ever longed for anything more in my life."

"Are you asking me to marry you, Night Hawk?" she posed, lifting her head, straining back against his arms.

"If you'll have me."

Her smile was radiant and her heart leapt with joy. *"Haa,* yes, my darling. I'd be honored to become your wife."

Claiming her lips, he crushed her to him. Love flowed in her like wild honey, and lowering her back onto the bed of furs, together they found the tempo that bound them together body and soul.

She didn't know why but for some reason her nerves were unsteady. Her hands trembled as she filled the parfleche with the last of the supplies and drew the flap closed. There was nothing left to do but tell him goodbye.

Suddenly, she didn't want him to leave without her. Her fingers grasped the amulet and squeezed tightly. Wrapping an arm around her shoulders, he pulled her against him and kissed her forehead.

"Are you feeling all right?" he asked with quiet concern. "I noticed you barely touched your meal last night and this morning you didn't eat very much breakfast."

"It's nothing to worry about," she replied. "I'll be fine." But she couldn't shake her feelings of unease after he'd left.

He'd become the most important person in her world. If anything should happen to him she didn't think she could bear the pain. She laid her hand upon her flat abdomen. It was too early for her to know for certain, but she hoped by the time that he returned she'd have something important to tell him. Together, they would pray to the spirits for a healthy child. Boy or girl, it did not matter. It would be a part of them and offered the People new hope for the future. Then a sudden thought occurred to her. In which world would their child grow up? Callie knew the uncertain future ahead for the Comanche. But what could she expect if she stayed with the People and raised her child as one of them? Her concerns had become theirs. She didn't know if she could go back to her other life as she'd known it before. In that world there was no Night Hawk, or his People. The time she'd shared with Night Hawk had been beautiful and given her life new meaning. She didn't think she could bear facing even one day without him beside her.

Callie was grateful when she heard Owl Man's familiar voice outside of the lodge door.

"I have come seeking your advice, wise one. One of our people needs our counsel."

Callie indicated that the shaman should enter. While she listened to Owl Man describe the sick child's symptoms, she was already deciding which of her herbs that she might need, and hurriedly packed them in her medicine pouch.

"I do not like to think what we might be facing," Callie told him.

His face bore grave concern. "We both already know what we are facing. The white man's sickness has found the way to our village."

* * *

Night Hawk was uneasy as the Comanche hunting party rode mile after mile toward the giant shadow in the blue sky.

"What do you think it is?" Red Buffalo asked, the lines of concentration deepening along his thick brows and under his eyes.

"I do not know for certain, but I do not think it bodes well," Night Hawk replied gravely.

They rode on in silence, every man's eyes focused on the black stain that spread across the horizon. The hunting party had been gone longer than anyone had intended, but it wasn't something they might have foreseen. There were few buffalo signs for them to follow, and they'd had to search longer and harder for the herd. Still, they weren't surprised, and knew why. The white hunters had reached the buffalo first.

When the trail finally ended, and the heavy mantle of flapping, swirling darkness was directly over them, the hunters found that they could only stare in helpless fury at the dreaded sight that met their eyes.

"My eyes don't believe what they see," Black Raven growled.

"It is what I have feared," Night Hawk said.

The vultures circling overhead, thick as black insects, blotted out the blue sky.

"They are all dead. Every last one," another man exclaimed.

Before the hunters, the plain was littered with the lifeless bodies of hundreds of buffalo. They had been butchered for their hides. The meat, exposed to the sun, had putrefied, and insects swarmed over the bloody mass that was left.

Wolves fed upon the carcass until their bellies had swelled, pausing in their frenzied feeding to snap at the frustrated birds who circled low over their heads.

It was a scene of madness.

Worse, it was a sign of the future.

Chapter Twenty-three

"It's the spotted sickness . . . it is called small-pox," Callie explained to Owl Man and Little Doe, after examining the young child who'd become the latest victim of the virulent epidemic that was already responsible for the deaths of so many of the People.

What the Quohadi had come to fear more than the *tabau-boh,* soldiers, had silently invaded their village, and the People had been powerless to stop it.

Already the other Comanche nations had told of the tree limbs near their encampments that were weighted down with the blanket wrapped bodies of those who had tragically succumbed to the killer disease.

The interior of Little Doe's lodge smelled of burnt offerings and sickness, but the evil spirit seemed to remain.

The holy man had known if the child was to be saved that there was only one among them who might be able to help.

The boy lay shrunken and still as death, his

breathing shallow, but his skin had yet to bear the small red spots that were the last symptom to appear. By then it was often too late to save the victim. Callie felt afraid, but she was also angry. Suddenly, she had never felt more powerless. She heard the boy's mother, who was standing by his slight body, sigh mournfully, and fought back her own tears. She would do everything within her power to save as many as she could, but she knew the odds weren't good.

The Comanche didn't have any words in their language for the white man's diseases, but they were beginning to understand this deadly curse their enemy had visited on them. No white man had ever been able to locate the Quohadi village, but their sickness had. And Callie knew from what she'd been hearing from the other Comanche bands, that the disease was spreading rapidly throughout the various Indian nations. There were already far too many death poles before their lodges, and sadly, she knew more could be expected.

Callie turned her gaze on the child's mother. Little Doe's agonized eyes beseeched her. "I don't know what I can do," Callie exclaimed gently. "If you'd like, I will try to help him, but I cannot promise that he will recover."

Little Doe's voice quavered. "I would like."

Callie nodded. She could see that the boy had already begun to dehydrate; his skin appeared like dry parchment. "Then listen carefully to my instructions. He must have water and broth as often as you can get him to take it. If he can't, or won't do so willingly, then try placing a hollowed out reed in his mouth and blow the fluid gently down his throat. Not too much, we don't want him to choke, but we must keep the fever from drying out his body. Do you understand what I've told you?" she asked the boy's mother and the shaman.

"Yes," Owl Man replied, and falling back, he closed his eyes and began to chant softly, sending his own plea heavenward to enlist the aid of the spirits. He prayed for the boy and his family, and he prayed for Callie as well. Little Doe would be grateful to Callie if the boy lived, but what would the father say if the child succumbed to the disease? He was not a forgiving man. It was something the holy man didn't wish to ponder for long. He chanted fervently, and his voice wavered throughout the camp.

"We do as you say," the grieved mother assured Callie. "You make my son better, and my husband Black Raven, give you anything you ask."

"I don't want anything from you in return except friendship," Callie replied quietly.

Tears sprang to Little Doe's eyes. "I do not know why you want me for friend when I've been so mean to you."

Callie smiled. "Because I know you have a good heart, and I would have probably felt the same had our situations been reversed. You love your sister very much. Please know that there will always be a special place in Night Hawk's heart for your sister and their child. I do not ever intend to take their place. Only to be a part of his future. His past will always belong to them."

"You much good woman, too," Little Doe exclaimed. "We be friends forever more."

Callie agreed they would. The holy man finished his chant, and turned to her.

"Is there nothing more we can do Medicine Woman?" he asked. "Are we to remain helpless against this deadly foe?"

Callie well understood his frustration. "There is very little we can do to help him. A decoction of Indian sage might help lower the boy's fever, but I don't have any more. I'll need to go in search of other medicinal herbs as well. My supply has run low these past few days."

"I will instruct my nephew to go with you. I wish Night Hawk and the other warriors were here. I do not like that they have been gone for two weeks. It is another bad sign." The shaman sighed wearily. "Too many bad signs lately. My heart is very troubled."

"As mine is," Callie said, and stepping around Little Doe, she slipped through the door, the shaman following behind her. When they stood outside, she began to issue him further instructions. "While I am gone you must make the people understand that they must not move about from lodge to lodge. We need to isolate those who are sick, keep the family groups together and away from the others, and burn their tepees. Clothing, blankets, everything must be destroyed. Fire is the only way to contain the illness. It kills the sickness, and the disease cannot spread to the others."

Owl Man nodded his head as he listened intently to Callie describe how the sick ones should be stripped of their clothing, bathed in clean water laced with garlic. He thought this a strange request, but he'd come to respect Callie's judgment — her gifted touch had saved several lives since she'd come to live among them — so he did not question her instructions. His own medical knowledge had failed him. Perhaps hers could still save them.

"It will be done as you have asked," he replied. He had never felt more old or tired. "I will ask the spirits to guide you safely, golden one." A thoughtful smile curved his mouth. "Be careful in your journey for you carry the future of our people beneath your heart. This new life is the greatest hope we have for the future. You will make Night Hawk a very proud warrior when he returns."

Her face brightened at his words, and she smiled up at him. "I don't know how you always seem to realize these things, Owl Man. I've only suspected I might be with child this past week."

The expression in his currant-black eyes softened. "No magic involved. This old medicine man knows the signs. They are easy to read in a woman's eyes. You have fine son, I think. He live a long life and give his people new hope for tomorrow."

"A boy, you say? But that is impossible to predict."

"You see," he reiterated confidently. "You have Night Hawk's son. The future chief of the Quohadi Comanche will be the last of his kind, but he be wise and strong enough to show us new way. We survive through the blood of my people, your people. Soon, we will be as one. It was meant to be."

Callie nudged Wind into a gallop. Brave Eagle rode beside her, her bodyguard and friend. They spoke very little, but concentrated their efforts on searching for the plants they needed to take back with them. This was their second journey. The raging sickness required an ever increasing quantity of the medicinal herbs, but at least Callie had been able to save more of the people than she'd first imagined. She and Owl Man combined their efforts, relying on the mystical as well as her herbal treatments. Since she'd come to live with the Indians she'd found her ability to heal only growing stronger. Perhaps it was because here the belief in the power of the mind, body and soul, had been ingrained deeply for centuries. There were some things that just couldn't be explained. For whatever the reason, she was grateful that Black Raven and Little Doe's boy was one of those who'd survived the illness. But his father still had no idea how perilously close to death his son had been. The hunters had yet to return.

Word of her successful treatments had quickly spread to the other tribes, and she had become much sought after. Callie visited those villages that she could, but there was never enough time to treat all those who were stricken by the illness. She intended to gather more of the yarrow today. She wanted as much of the precious plant as they could carry. The leaves were boiled and used in a poultice for the rash. She wanted other plants as well. There were those for fever, for cramps, and still others for nausea. Her eyes constantly searched the area as they rode along.

She followed Brave Eagle through a natural pass beautifully covered with brush and a blanket of wild flowers. It was quiet and serene, but it was hard for

Callie to concentrate on anything other than her grim mission.

The sun was hidden behind heavy clouds and the smell of rain was in the air. Thunder rumbled in the distance. Callie was glad there was a storm approaching. It would fill the river skirting the village that had become still as glass in the past weeks.

Spotting a group of plants that she needed, she signaled to Brave Eagle. After dismounting, they began to gather them up and place them in their parfleches.

Brave Eagle was no more than twenty feet away from her when she noticed him suddenly look up.

"Is there anything wrong?" she asked him, pausing, shading her eyes against the sun with one hand.

Brave Eagle frowned. "It may have only been the thunder, but I thought I heard riders approaching." Without another word, he dropped to the ground and placed his ear against the earth. It wasn't a moment later that he sprang to his feet.

Callie could tell by his actions that he was alarmed. She was schooled enough in the ways of the Comanche to know she must be very quiet and listen to the other messages that the wind might carry. Dropping the parfleche, she rested the heel of her hand on the hilt of her knife.

"Someone comes. It may be nothing. But we not take chance. You take your mare and ride out," Brave Eagle told her. "I stay behind and make certain no one follow you."

Callie stared at the young brave who'd been a companion to her whenever she'd had to journey far from the village. "I'm not going to leave you here alone."

"You must, for I gave my word to Night Hawk that I would watch over you whenever he could not. You and I are friends. You should not wish to bring dishonor to me." He had already scooped up her mare's reins and was standing, waiting to offer her a leg up.

Reluctantly, Callie bent down to retrieve her parfleche, and then allowed him to boost her up onto Wind's back. "I'll wait for you on the other side of the pass," she said.

He shook his head. "You keep riding until I catch up with you. If I do not, then you know to head straight for our village. Whatever you do, don't look back. If trouble comes to me at least I will know that you have chance to reach safety."

He had barely spoken the words when a rifle shot splintered the air. Moments later, Brave Eagle was hurled forward against the mare as a bullet slammed into his back. His face contorted in disbelief, then pain, but he managed to raise his hand and smack Wind's rump with force. "Go . . . ride as fast and far away as you can. I will . . . hold the attackers off."

Wild-eyed, Callie sobbed out his name, but Wind had already sprinted forward, and Callie could only squeeze her knees tightly around the mare and watch as the ground flew past beneath them.

Three other shots erupted. Stunned, she heard Wind's shrill scream, felt the valiant animal's legs folding under, and could do nothing to prevent the animal falling. The screams choked off in her throat as she was pitched forward.

* * *

"Looks like she's coming around," she heard an unfamiliar male voice exclaim.

With difficulty Callie struggled awake, and discovered that she was riding slumped over, her cheek pressed against the woolly mane of a strange horse. The animal was clearly not her beloved Wind. Her eyes teared when she remembered that her mare was probably lying dead where she'd fallen. Her wrists were bound around the horse's neck and her moccasined feet, looped and tied to the stirrups.

"That sure as hell is a relief," another man replied. "I could just see our money going up in smoke when dumb ass over there decided to shoot her horse out from under her."

"Go to hell, Stevenson. At least we got her," the accused retorted.

"Yeah, we have at that. But I want to get as far away as possible before that half-breed finds out she's gone. He'll come after her and us," Becker Stevenson warned the other three men riding with him. "And believe me, you don't want him to catch up to us."

"If it hadn't been for her red hair I might not have known it was her," one of Stevenson's surly companions, exclaimed. "She's been out in the sun so much she's almost as dark as a Comanch. And look how she's dressed, even got some heathen medicine necklace around her throat. That breed sure didn't waste any time staking his claim, and she didn't seem none too eager to be rescued, so I'd say she's about as wild as he is by now. Her pa and ma gonna wish like hell they'd left her where she was."

"Well, the colonel didn't say how she had to look when we brought her in, only that he wanted her back," Stevenson declared. "What they do about re-civilizing her is their problem."

Callie lay quietly without twitching a muscle, solemn as any brave Comanche woman, her gaze drawn to the man riding next to her. Only her eyes filled with contempt.

"Whoo . . . eee, if looks could kill, we'd be dead, amigos!"

"Yeah, I bet she's a regular little hell-cat when you're between her legs, too," the swarthy Mexican who wore Chihuahua spurs that chinged whenever he moved, said. "Sure would like to have me a go at her before we reach the fort."

Callie felt her flesh crawl. "You even try something like that and I'll turn you into a eunuch," she warned, the note of certainty in her voice enough to make the dark-skinned rider stare suspiciously at her.

Stevenson hooted with laughter. "Guess you better explain to Juan what a eunuch is, lady. Then he might think twice about heeding them brave words of yours."

"Don't need to know," Juan snarled, his face turning as beet red as his neckerchief. "She tries anything, and colonel or no, I'll beat her until she can't walk." Swinging around to stare at her, he growled low. "Believe me, *muchacha,* I know how to do it so's there wouldn't be any telling marks on that purty skin. So you just watch your step. You don't know who you're dealing with."

"Neither do you," Callie spat defiantly. "Night

374

Hawk will find you no matter how much distance you try and put between us. And I wouldn't want to be you when he does. The Comanche don't kill their male captives quickly, but then I guess you already know how they take great care to keep them alive . . . at least until they're ready for them to die slowly."

"Shut up, whore," Stevenson growled. "Your squaw man ain't gonna find us, so you can forget that notion."

"Oh, he will," Callie insisted, speaking to all, but staring only at him. Something about him seemed vaguely, disturbingly familiar, as if he'd emerged from a nightmare she'd once had to haunt her yet again. She wracked her memory, but couldn't come up with the answer. Yet she knew they'd met somewhere before.

He leaned over in the saddle toward her, and raised his hand. "You need a lesson in obedience. That smart mouth of yours don't know when to keep quiet."

Callie bared her teeth. "Touch me and you'll be sorrier than you ever imagined."

Stevenson's arm instinctively drew back. Now she was the victim of his glare. "You're a hellion, that much is for sure, but see'ins how your stepdaddy's paying me to bring you in, I guess I'd better not mark you up none."

"You're never going to see a dime of your money, mister," Callie shot back. "Night Hawk will never let you get as far as the fort."

"Shut the bitch up, Stevenson," one of the men demanded. "All that talk about Indians is setting my teeth on edge."

"You heard the man, Miss Angel," Stevenson said to her.

She fell silent, but it wasn't because of his threats. She had remembered she still had her dagger secured high on her thigh beneath her skirt, and she began to silently plot how she might find a way to reach it. She recalled Night Hawk's words the day he'd given it to her, and how she'd expressed her unwillingness to use it, even to protect herself from harm. She still didn't think that she could, but she could at least free her bonds if she found an opportunity.

A burst of lightning snaked across the sky; blinding and potent. She thought it was surely a sign from her guardian spirit. Then the rains came in torrents, and the thunder shook the earth. Callie's faith did not waver.

Stevenson laughed jeeringly, clearly delighted by the storm's fury. "The half-breed ain't gonna find you now, sweetheart. There's no man can track in this kind of rain."

"Night Hawk will find me," Callie insisted. "You'll see. And I can promise you that when he does you'll be sorry." She did not want to think about the fact that Night Hawk had yet to return from the hunt. In her mind she called out to him, sending a silent plea across the miles.

Chapter Twenty-four

Two hours later the rain was much lighter, but there was a mist that obscured the view of the four men and the lone woman who rode through the pass at a murderous pace. They'd been riding for almost two days, but the end of their journey was near.

Stevenson had smugly informed her that the fort was only hours away. Callie didn't know whether to feel relieved or filled with despair. Where was Night Hawk? What would he think, worse, what would he believe about her when he learned that she was missing. He might think that once she'd tasted freedom she probably discovered that she was glad to be free of him. Nothing could have been further from the truth. She called silently to him across the windswept plains. He had to come soon or there would be no turning back. Once she was behind the walls of the fort he could never reach her.

I need you, Night Hawk, please come before it is too late.

Becker Stevenson led the way, the others following behind him, and Callie riding second to last. Despite their show of bravado, she sensed they were anxious to leave Indian country behind. They only stopped riding to rest the horses, and then never for more than fifteen minutes at a time. The men were well versed in the ways of war. They cleverly disguised their trail, sweeping away any tracks. Callie wondered if even Night Hawk would be able to track them when they left no signs for him to follow.

She'd had plenty of opportunity to observe them, and she had to admit to herself that they did frighten her. If not for her stepfather's reward money, she felt certain they would have fallen on her like wild animals. They were indeed a shifty looking lot—their clothes covered in grime, guns strapped low on their hips, and the look in their eyes one she was familiar with. These were mercenaries, and they swore no allegiance to God or country—only to themselves.

The one they called Becker gave all the orders and was obviously their leader. Callie despised him. He was the most despicable human being she'd ever encountered. He wore a filthy tunic in Union blue, the double row of brass buttons along the front tarnished, a black hat with an eagle's feather tucked in the band, buckskin trousers, and long greasy blond hair straggling down around his face. She knew he kept his head bowed most of the time to conceal his badly scarred countenance, but the jagged flesh was so pronounced that it wasn't something he could hide easily. She wondered if he'd received the disfiguring wound in the war? She feared him more than any of the others.

Sister Rose had always said that you could determine a person's character by their eyes. "They're windows to the soul," she'd said. Callie thought the leader's eyes were cold and expressionless. He was a brutal man, and she didn't doubt that he could kill without an ounce of regret. This thought flitted through her mind whenever she envisioned trying to escape. And there was no sense trying to beg him for mercy. He didn't know the meaning of the word.

Suddenly, hot tears burned behind her eyelids, but she held them in check. With her cheek pressed against the horse's neck and her hands and ankles secured, she felt helpless and vulnerable—but not defeated. She hated them at that moment, and feared the look in her eyes would give her thoughts of escape away.

But the men didn't notice. They were intent on scanning the outcropping of rocks around them, searching for any sign of the Comanche, and little concern was afforded Callie. It was what she'd been waiting for. Working up her nerve, she began to concentrate on the bonds that secured her wrists, her long-simmering anger providing her impetus.

The rope was tight, but also wet from the constant drizzle. She began to persistently wiggle her wrists, and soon she felt the scratchy hemp begin to stretch. Cautiously, she concentrated her efforts and watched her captors from the corner of her eyes. She had to reach her knife. It was her only chance to get away. And she would be free. There was no life for her back at the fort. Her place was with Night Hawk.

Stevenson, speaking in a low tone, said, "Something about this place don't feel right to me. It's too quiet, and that ain't a good sign."

A crack of thunder shook the ground beneath them.

The first man to look up felt his blood turn to ice.

The thick brush amidst the boulders seemed to move, as though magically coming to life before the startled riders. Stevenson yelled to his men to find cover but, trapped in the narrow passage, it was virtually impossible for them to do.

"Grab the woman!" Stevenson shouted, but his words went unheeded.

His men were staring in terror and disbelief at the cliffs above their heads.

"We're trapped! It's every man for himself I say," one of the mercenaries shouted.

The Comanche warriors had camouflaged themselves with warpaint, and had lain hidden behind the scrub foliage and rocks until just the right moment. When their leader had felt absolutely certain of their advantage, he'd signaled to them. They'd sprung forward, their faces and bodies slashed with signs and symbols of war, their battle cries soaring down from the ridge.

"God in heaven, did you ever see anything like

it?" another man said, and reached frantically for his holstered pistol.

Becker Stevenson reacted on instinct. He'd fought in hand to hand combat enough times during the war to remain level headed in the face of danger, but he wasn't leaving his survival to chance. Yanking on the lead secured to Callie's mount, he broke away from the others and dug his booted heels into his horse's flanks, spurring the animal to a brisk trot. He wasn't taking a chance of losing his life, or her. There was the smell of fear in the air, and behind him, his men began to scream in panic. Shots rang out as the mercenaries began to open fire on the Indians.

"You aren't going to escape!" she yelled at Stevenson.

"Like hell I'm not," he hissed, but she thought he sounded more than a little fearful.

Callie wasn't afraid or uncertain. Her people had come for her.

Night Hawk had already anticipated their leader's move. He took off at a run to where Storm had been hidden from view behind the bluffs, and leaping high, he landed smoothly onto the stallion's back. Behind him, over a hundred braves rose up to defend his back. Runners had been sent to bring the warriors their mounts.

Now mounted, brandishing tomahawks and lances, they were the most terrifying vision the mercenaries had ever encountered. The Comanches advanced with deadly purpose, but they did not raise their weapons.

The mercenaries crowded together, their eyes wide and horror-filled.

"Sweet Jesus, they're gonna take us alive," one man cried, his expression bitter and hopeless. Quickly raising his notched revolver to his head, he pulled the trigger.

The Comanches surged over the lone survivors.

Unmindful of the danger, Becker Stevenson drove the horses through the narrow corridors of high, wind shaped sandstone, and Callie could only clench her teeth against the horse's bone-jarring gait.

"I'll kill you before I turn you back over to that half-breed bastard," he flung back over his shoulder, kicking his horse sharply.

Callie's mount was forced to keep up, and she could do nothing to slow their pace. She didn't want to beg, had bitten down on her bottom lip to keep from doing so, but every muscle in her body screamed in agony. Worse, she was certain the violent cramps that had begun down low in her abdomen were not a good sign. Bright motes of color danced in her vision. If they didn't slow down soon she thought she might faint. And she didn't even want to consider that she might lose her baby. The rain on her face mingled with her tears.

They had just ridden through a wide passage when she heard Stevenson's snarl of frustration. Sawing back on his mount's reins, he growled. "Damnit, we're in a blind." He sat there quietly, then muttered. "And I can feel him closing in on us, and getting nearer too with each passing minute."

Callie clenched her teeth against the pain, and finally was able to slip her right hand free. Her skirts were hitched up above her knees. Slowly, her fingers inched their way beneath her skirt and along her thigh, seeking the hilt of her knife. There was no longer any more time to wait for Night Hawk to rescue her. She had to make her move if their baby were to survive.

Countless doubts had tortured Night Hawk for hours after they'd returned to the village and he had learned that Callie had gone with Brave Eagle in search of medicinal herbs, but as yet neither of them had returned. He feared for her, and he'd immediately left to search for her.

Night Hawk's rage had been insurmountable when he'd found his loyal friend Brave Eagle slain. His heart lightened when he hadn't found another body. At least there was every chance that she was still alive. He scoured the area for signs, but there had been few. He also had seen no indication that there had been a struggle. He could not help but wonder if the soldiers had come and she had decided to return to the fort with them. After all, she was from their world; perhaps he'd been a fool to think that he could make her want to be a part of his.

Now, watching from his vantage point high above the mercenary and the flame-haired woman he loved, Night Hawk knew shame for having doubted her. Lifting his face heavenward, he sent a bloodcurdling call reverberating through the canyon passages. He would let no man take away what was his. This man would pay dearly for what he had done.

Callie had a firm grip on the knife hilt when she'd heard the call of the wolf. Night Hawk was out there. She had hoped and prayed that he would find her. But she had another fear. She knew this man would try to kill him before he'd allow Night Hawk to take her away with him.

"What the hell was that?" Stevenson growled, his hand tightening on the Spencer resting in his arm. "Ain't no wolves gonna sniff around a man in broad daylight unless he's loco."

Callie merely stared at him.

Hurriedly swinging down from the saddle, Stevenson approached Callie, his rifle in hand. His face was mottled by rage. "You know what it is, don't you, woman? You think it's him?"

She raised her chin with a cool stare in his direction. "I believe you'll find out real soon."

"Ain't gonna wait around to see if it's him or not," he snarled, and reaching her, he began untying the rope around her left ankle. "I ain't losing that reward. Especially now that the other boys is dead and the money's all mine." He was so preoccupied with mentally tallying his riches and his urgency to find cover, that he never even saw her jerk the dagger from the rawhide sheath under her skirt and raise it quickly.

She actually considered taking his life. It would have been so easy at that moment, but she just couldn't bring herself to plunge the knife into his back. Instead, she swung the knife downward and sunk the sharp blade deep into his hand poised on the cantle of the saddle.

Stevenson's eyes flew to hers, glittering with murderous lights, and he bellowed in pain and shock. "You damned, bloodthirsty squaw!" he cried out, whimpering when his gaze fell on the blade pinning his hand to the leather saddle.

But before he had time to react further, she'd grabbed hold of the barrel of his rifle, and tried vainly to jerk it free of his other hand. They became locked in a struggle, but despite his injury, he was still amazingly strong. Adrenaline surged through her veins. With her heart slamming, fighting back her terror, Callie held on and managed to maintain her grip. She knew that he wouldn't hesitate to shoot her or Night Hawk, and she wasn't about to let him.

With a low snarl, Stevenson wrenched the rifle away from her, and swinging the butt around forcefully, clipped her on the jaw.

A red mist seemed to envelop her. Callie groaned softly and slumped forward over the horse's neck.

"Damn fool, woman, now look at what you've gone and made me do," Stevenson growled. He hoped like hell she was still breathing for he didn't like to think he might lose the reward money he'd been promised. But right at the moment he knew he was in a battle to save his own life. And all the riches in the world couldn't buy him out of this mess, so he had to concentrate on his survival before anything else. Gritting his teeth, he jerked the dagger free of his hand, and whirling, he ran for a cover of rocks.

In the same instant, a high, piercing cry erupted from somewhere above him, and a feathered lance found its mark.

Stevenson felt a sickening jolt, and his leg gave out beneath him. Pain seared through him, and he crumbled to the ground, the lance blade tearing through muscle and bone before imbedding in the back of his thigh. The rifle flew out of his hands, and he forgot everything in his bid for survival. Desperately, he began crawling toward the rocks that would provide him with shelter. Inch by inch he pulled himself along.

Night Hawk's deadly black eyes stared down at the man writhing in agony. He made a quick descent from the cliff, and reaching Callie, he quickly severed her bonds with his knife and drew her down into his arms. He called to her, but she didn't respond. Cradling her against him, Night Hawk laid her gently on a flat area of tufted grass. "They will pay for what they have done to you, *bella*," he snarled, touching her cheek tenderly.

Then, he focused on Becker Stevenson. Eyes burning with an unnatural light, he stalked the terrified man, his steps measured and steady, his voice raised in a death chant.

The mercenary glanced back over his shoulder, and a straggled sob bubbled from his throat. "I never meant to hurt your woman . . . really . . . I only wanted money." He extended one hand in a pleading gesture. "Don't kill me . . . please."

"Oh, I don't intend to kill you . . . at least not right away," Night Hawk drawled, long legs spread as he stood over the terrified Stevenson. It was then he noticed the gleam of gold on Stevenson's little finger, and a shock rippled through him. Grabbing hold of the mercenary's wrist, he peered closer at the ring. "Where did you get this?"

Stevenson misunderstood his interest. He knew how fond the Indians were of beads and shiny trinkets. "You like it, it's yours," he blurted, sweat rolling down his face and streaking his grimy face.

Night Hawk squeezed talonlike fingers around the quivering man's wrist. "I asked where you got it."

"I've had it since the war . . . I have other stuff you'd like even more. Shiny gold, bright stones. It's stashed away at my ranch. We can go there . . . I'd share it with you if you'll spare my life."

"Where is your ranch?" Night Hawk inquired calmly.

"About thirty miles west of Fort Benton. Not far . . . it wouldn't take us long to get there."

Night Hawk's eyes were riveted to the gleaming gold. He twisted the ring off Stevenson's finger, and glanced at the inscribed initials on the inner band. L L. His expression darkened.

Dropping down beside the mercenary, Night

Hawk's hand snaked out and knocked the man's hat off his head. Grasping a fistful of Stevenson's hair, he yanked the man's head back, and stared coldly into his eyes. "It's taken years, but at last we meet face to face. Surely you remember me?"

Stevenson swallowed hard. "You're mad. I've never seen you before in my life."

"Take a closer look, you bastard. I'm the man who took the blame for you in New Orleans after you murdered Delcey and damned near did the same to Lily."

The mercenary's eyes looked glazed and desperate. "I don't know what you're talking about."

Night Hawk's eyes swept over the tattered Union tunic. He remembered the brass button that Lily had been clutching in her hand when he'd found her. He knew this was the man responsible. "I'd be willing to bet you're lying. That patch on your shoulder tells me just about everything I need to know. Your company was in New Orleans a lot during the occupation. And the ring on your finger belongs to a friend of mine. You were there all right, and you left a trail of violence and death behind you."

"Lily was a whore!" Stevenson spat. "She used men. They couldn't see past that lovely smile and perfect body. I watched the two of you together. I knew what she was . . . how she'd used you, too." His eyes took on a maniacal gleam. "Her husband was a prisoner of war before he died. I was his guard. LaFleur caught lung fever, and he rambled about this treasure of religious artifacts that he'd found in a mine shaft while he'd been hiding from the enemy. He found a way to get it back to New Orleans before the occupation, and he hid all of it in the crawl space under his house. She knew about it, and after he died, she managed to smuggle some of the pieces abroad and sell them. Then she'd turn the money over to the Confederacy. I couldn't let her do that . . . so I found a way to finally stop her. Better that the treasure belonged to me than to southern dogs who would have used it against us." He shrugged indifferently. "She really didn't matter. She was only one whore among many that I managed to stop. Everything went as planned that night at the LaFleur mansion, except that I needed someone to take the blame and throw the suspicion off me. You just happened to come along at a convenient time. It wasn't a personal vendetta. Just necessary. So I planted some of her things in your quarters, and the brass took it from there." He scowled. "I didn't plan on this . . . wouldn't have thought something so unlikely could be possible."

"Well this is a personal vendetta," Night Hawk said, pressing the razor-sharp blade against the quivering man's scalp. "You see, I know that Lily and Delcey weren't the only women you've attacked. There were many others. You left a trail of bodies behind you." He made a tiny motion with his hand, and the blade drew a thin line of red across his scalp. "I know because I've been tracking you for years. Ever since the day you happened upon the Indian woman and her baby by the pool near the Comanches' summer camp. They became your victims too. You killed them without a single regret, but I swore you'd know and remember who they were before I killed you. For a while the war got in my way. That was why I finally enlisted. I had hoped to be able to track you down and learn your identity. It wasn't easy, and you seemed to have all the luck on your side for awhile. I'd begun to give up hope of ever finding you." He smiled chillingly. "Looks to me like your luck has just run out."

"Have mercy . . . have mercy!" Stevenson wailed, imagining how the sharp skinning knife would slice cleanly across his scalp.

Raising the blade, Night Hawk held it aloft and stared coldly down into Stevenson's face. "The same mercy you showed my loved ones?"

"I didn't kill your wife," Stevenson blubbered. "I swear!"

Night Hawk took the blade of his knife, and grasping a fistful of hair that lay across Stevenson's brow, he hacked away.

Stevenson's eyes squeezed closed. "Oh, sweet Jesus . . . don't do . . . it . . . don't take my hair."

Night Hawk had sliced off the long hair that had fallen over the mercenary's face, and now he stared at the jagged flesh bared to his gaze, his blood beginning to pound. "That scar tells a different story. It was the last message my wife left me before you murdered her," he said darkly. "I always believed that one day the spirits would lead me to you. Your day of reckoning has come, you sonofabitch." He tossed aside his knife, his gaze filled with painful memories. "You will know how it feels to die slowly, and with your last breath, see my face, and hear your soul cursed for eternity."

Stevenson saw his own death mirrored in the warrior's deadly black eyes, but managed only a garbled scream before steellike fingers enclosed around his throat.

"May you never know paradise and spend eternity walking in darkness," Night Hawk said with cold finality.

Stevenson's face began to tinge blue, his breath rattled in his throat and his mouth dribbled foamy spittle. He tried desperately to draw air into his lungs, and clawed at the fingers that continued to slowly apply crushing pressure against his windpipe.

His struggles were in vain.

Chapter Twenty-five

Lance Hamilton rushed from his quarters just as soon as he'd received the news from the excited recruit, and knew a dull ache of foreboding. He'd told him that a Comanche Indian was riding toward the fort, and he appeared to be holding a white woman in his arms. Could it be Callie, Lance had wondered? It wasn't a thought that brightened his sullen mood. In fact, he'd never felt such overwhelming fury.

All of their efforts to find her had been in vain. He wasn't in the colonel's favor and he'd been relieved of most of his duties. His own men barely paid him an ounce of respect. Serena had even started avoiding him. And now that damned half-breed was going to bring Callie in on his own—he was probably bored with her already—and would expect them to trade with him for her. Lance ground his teeth in frustration. The colonel would probably welcome her back with open arms, and then allow that breed to ride out again. Lance knew that Estelle's health was failing rapidly, and that the colonel was ready to meet any demands just to see Callie safely returned.

"Guess I'll still be expected to marry her, too," Lance muttered, his voice hardening ruthlessly. "Well, maybe I will and maybe I won't. It's going to be a cold day in hell when that bastard dumps her off on me, and walks away without a care. I swore he'd pay, and by God he's going to."

His starkly chiseled face set in determined lines, Night Hawk rode through the open gates of Fort Benton, a white cloth fluttering from the tip of his lance. It was a sign that he came in peace, but he didn't know whether it would be honored.

Blue-coated troopers rushed forward and began to close in on him. He showed them no fear; he really didn't feel any. If they killed him, then so be it. His only concern was that Callie received the medical attention she so desperately needed. He cradled Callie's inert form, and prayed to the Great Spirit that he had done the right thing by bringing her here. He hadn't any other choice. The ride back to the Quohadi village would have taken them over two days. Callie wouldn't have been able to withstand the gruelling trip through the canyon, so he'd chosen the easier trail across the flat plains. She was only semi-conscious, but it wasn't the blow she'd received that was responsible. For several hours she'd been in terrible pain, twisting and writhing in agony, choking back her sobs.

"I . . . think I'm . . . going to lose our baby," she'd murmured brokenly to him when the pains had first begun.

He had been stunned by her disclosure, but he'd wisely withheld questioning her. The only thing that mattered to him at that moment was to save her life. She'd meant more to him than anyone else in the world. "Hang on, sweetheart," he'd whispered lovingly. "I'm taking you where you'll receive the proper care you need."

Dazed, she'd stared up at him. "Yes . . . take . . . me back to our village, Night Hawk. Take me home."

His eyes had blurred with moisture. "I can't. It's too long a journey, darling. We must go on to the fort."

Her gaze had widened with alarm, and she'd tried to convince him otherwise. "They'll kill you! No, you mustn't go there! Please, turn back. I wouldn't want to live if anything should happen to you."

"Shhh, be still, love." He'd tried soothing her for he was afraid she would cause further harm to herself and the unborn child. "I'll be fine. And so will you. Trust me?"

"I do trust you," she whispered unhesitatingly. "With all my heart."

But he couldn't help wondering as he glanced

down at her ashen face, if he might already be too late. She'd told him several miles back that she thought she'd begun to bleed. He'd held her while she'd sobbed softly, and his heart had cried with her. The child she carried would unite their bloodline, and his people would live forever through each generation to pass. It was a good thing. Soon, the old ways would be gone and the People with them. Children were the only guarantee of a future for his kind. It didn't matter if he died this day. There would be new life to secure them a rightful place.

Not that he welcomed death. He did not, for there was so much he wanted to live for. He wanted this child, and to be at her side when she gave birth, to see his son or daughter in her arms, and know that their love had created a precious life together. But perhaps that wasn't to be. At the moment, it didn't seem likely.

The soldiers pressed closer, and a big man stepped out of the crowd. He held out his arms. "Give my stepdaughter to me," he ordered Night Hawk in a firm voice. "Then you'd best dismount slowly, and don't make any sudden moves. If you do, I guarantee you won't live to make another."

Night Hawk rendered a grudging nod, and reluctantly lowered Callie into the colonel's uplifted arms. He felt as if he'd lost a part of his soul. "She's with child, sir, and needs immediate medical attention," he said quietly.

The colonel's eyes flashed fire, but he merely

nodded curtly, and spun on his heel. "Sergeant Major, see that this man is placed under arrest. I'll tend to him later. Right now, get the bastard out of my sight."

Callie stirred, sensing she was no longer secure in Night Hawk's embrace. Her eyes opened, and she craned her neck to catch sight of the man she loved. "Don't let . . . them separate us . . . please don't . . ." she pleaded hoarsely.

Something flickered in Night Hawk's eyes, and he spoke in Comanche. "I love you, angel. And no matter what happens I always will."

Callie mouthed the words, hoping he would see, but an explosion momentarily stunned her.

Night Hawk felt something hard and white-hot slam into his chest, and he was unable to prevent his body from pitching forward. His limp form tumbled from the stallion onto the ground, not more than ten feet in front of Callie.

She saw the red stain seeping across his chest and staining the dust where he lay. her soul cried out in anguish. *They've finally killed him!*

The colonel half-turned, and noticed a small cloud of wavering black smoke to his right. He glimpsed the fleeting image of Lance Hamilton, Navy revolver still in his hand, darting back into the shadows of the buildings. He said nothing, merely issued a curt order to have Night Hawk's body taken away at once. Then he hurried in the direction of the hospital. He didn't give a damn about the half-breed or Callie's baby, but he desperately needed to keep his stepdaughter alive for Estelle. She was only holding on by a slender thread. If Callie died, he knew that Estelle would give up her fight to live as well.

Darkness came and sifted through the bars of his cell. Night Hawk lay quietly on the hard bunk, feeling his life spirit slowly draining from his body. He tried to focus on the moon shining through the small window high above him. It was a Comanche moon. Perhaps it was not so bad a night to die after all.

He was dying, he knew it, and at the moment his thoughts were consumed with Callie. The guards hadn't been back to check on him once since they'd dumped him inside the cell, and had locked the door behind them. He wanted to find out how Callie was, but it didn't seem likely that anyone would think to inform him. There was so much left unsaid between them.

So many thoughts and memories. *Callie, my sweet angel, I love you,* his tired brain repeated. He wished he'd said those words to her many times instead of just once. Too late now . . . too late . . . your time here is at an end.

Then he heard Morning Star's voice.

My darling Night Hawk we shall be together again, she was saying. *But I do not think you really wish the time to be now. There is much that you can still do for our people. Go back . . .*

fight for the future. It can be yours.

Night Hawk saw her there waiting for him, her arms outstretched, their baby laughing and happy, strapped into her cradleboard on her mother's back. They were smiling! They had truly found peace!

He smiled back at them, at that moment wanting very much to join them there by the bright white light. He was so tired and he hurt so badly. The light was so beautiful. He could feel the love and warmth that emanated from it. He'd be free from his earthly cares and worries. With a sigh, he felt his spirit slipping free of his earthly form. No, it was not such a bad day to die after all.

"Night Hawk, can you hear me, darling?" Callie placed her mouth near his ear. "I've regained my strength, our baby's well. You mustn't give up . . . fight my darling. We need you." Then taking the amulet from around her neck, she laid it on his heavily bandaged chest. She didn't know what else she might do. This was her only hope.

Everything that could be done had been already. She'd tended him for the past two days, but he had yet to respond as they'd hoped he might.

Earlier, Doc had held Night Hawk's shoulders while she'd carefully scraped away the festering scab that had formed over the ugly wound rimmed in purple flesh. She'd cleaned it, had ap-plied *pouip* juice mixed with boiled yarrow, and then rebound it with clean cloth. Every five hours she'd changed the dressing.

Until this moment, she'd never really believed that the amulet held any powers on its own, but right now she was desperate enough to try anything.

"What are you thinking of doing, child?" Doc asked, with a glint of wonder in his eyes.

"Something I've never believed possible before," Callie replied, then gently laying her hands on either side of the gleaming amulet, she splayed her fingers across Night Hawk's chest. She bowed her head and closed her eyes, her thoughts seeking to fuse with that of her beloved.

Let thine own self be healed. Cast aside your doubt and believe in the power of our love. In the future that we will share. I need you so, Night Hawk. I love you more than I ever thought possible. Please come back to me.

Bending over him, she tenderly kissed his lips, breathing life and love from her body into his.

Night Hawk felt the warm rush of radiant light infuse his body. Slowly, his eyelids blinked, and his heartbeat quickened. Still he had no idea how to find his way. "Angel . . . where are you?" he whispered hoarsely. He remembered Callie, and thought of so much he needed to say to her. He wasn't ready to leave her. He wanted to lavish his love on her. Summoning the will from deep within, he called out for strength.

I know it is not time for me yet, Morning Star. Help me. Give me the strength I need to return and pick up the pieces of my life. The People need me. Callie and my unborn child need me, but I have never felt so weak.

Do not touch the light! Morning Star ordered him. *You must open your eyes, Night Hawk. Do it! Open them now!*

He heard other voices around him. The weakness seemed to pass.

Slowly, he opened his eyes. Harsh light. Confusion. And who was that shouting?

"Damnation, soldier, you'd better allow us to remain in this cell and treat this man!" a stern voice boomed.

"The colonel says the Injun ain't hurt that bad, and nobody was to touch him until we received further orders from him."

"Well I'm the post doctor, and I say that this man is going to die unless we take care of him proper. And I can assure you I intend to file my own report regarding this incident." There was a heck of a lot more that needed to be said as well, but Doc thought to keep it between himself and the Colonel. And there would be time enough for that later, after he and Callie took care of the patient's needs.

The pimply-faced young recruit stared at the graying doctor as if seeing him for the first time. The practitioner's eyes burned with determination and his hand that gripped his black medical

400

satchel were steady.

"I know what you're thinking," Doc said, noticing the boy inspecting him suspiciously. "You can't believe that an old sot like me might have reformed. Well I have. Took my last drink the day Callie was placed in my care. She's done so much for me, that I thought it was the least I could do for her. Don't intend to start up again neither." His eyes seared into the lad. "We're wasting time here, soldier. Now skee-dat. This young woman and I have a man's life to save."

Callie fell on her knees beside the bunk, and took Night Hawk's hand in hers. Tears streamed from her eyes. "I'm here. I'll always be at your side. No one can ever separate us again."

Night Hawk squeezed her hand and favored her with a weak but nonetheless devastating smile. "I love you, little Medicine Woman. I will until the day I die."

"That won't be for a long time, so you're stuck having to marry me because I'm never leaving your side again," she said, in a lower, huskier tone.

He shook his head, and his mouth twisted bitterly. "I don't think that is going to ever happen now, although I would marry you in a minute given the opportunity."

"You're wrong. My stepfather has enough to answer for already. He won't stand in our way unless he wants to risk ruining his own reputation. And I don't think he'll do that. Doc's

401

struck some sort of a deal with the colonel. I'm not certain of the details, he wouldn't even discuss it with me. I only know that you and I will simply disappear. And no one will be the wiser as to where we've gone."

"You're telling me that we are just going to ride out of here and no one is going to try and stop us?"

"That's how Doc put it to me."

Night Hawk trained his dark gaze on the portly sawbones. "Why? You don't even know me."

A faint light twinkled in the depths of his amber eyes. "Let's just say that Callie gave me a chance to find myself, although how she put up with me half the time I don't know." He smiled at them. "I'm also a hopeless romantic. I believe in love. If what I saw here today is any indication, you two young people are going to do a lot to bridge the gap between our people. It's high time we tried to find a way to end the war and start showing compassion for each other. War never solved a damn thing, but love has been known to move mountains. You're both strong, intelligent and compassionate people. The children born of your union will bear these same attributes. They'll strive hard to unite our two cultures and take us beyond the boundaries to carve out a new and brighter future."

"The future . . ." Night Hawk whispered tentatively. "How I would like to have an opportunity to spend all the rest of my days with you, *bella*."

Trembling, Callie went into his arms and laid her head gently on his shoulder. "You shall," she whispered. "I won't have it any other way."

Neither of them noticed that Doc had already slipped out of the cell, leaving the door wide open behind him, or the medicine bag filled with bottles of serum and syringes that he left for them to take back with them to the Quohadi village. It would be enough to vaccinate the people of Night Hawk's village against smallpox.

It was a beginning forged by a new awareness, and love.

Chapter Twenty-six

Palo Duro Canyon, three weeks later

The invading darkness altered the landscape, and a cool breeze carried the chant of a single voice on its ripples. The full Comanche moon, stark and ghostly pale, cast the splendid form of the naked warrior in shifting patterns of shimmering silver as he turned his face heavenward to admire its beauty.

He had come here because this was a place he knew well. He came and went here as he pleased, for his clan understood the land and the wind that spoke to them of many things. But soon, even this sacred place would no longer belong to the Comanche.

He stood on the cliff and gazed down on their once vast territory, and felt the sweep of change. For an instant, his eyes clouded with pain. The Comanche nation was dying. His people couldn't halt the overwhelming tide of settlers. There just were too many encroaching on their land, but even though he felt a terrible sadness at what would be lost, he knew that the People's voices would forever be heard. His children would go forth from this land and spread the word, as would the others to follow.

Through each generation to come, on the drifting wind, in the echo of laughter, the Comanche spirit would always remain vibrant and alive.

So many times, on a night just like this one, they had ridden forth from this canyon to raid the countryside, the lords of the southern plains sweeping confidently across Texas and down into Mexico, striking terror in the hearts of their enemies. Thundering through the thick silver grass that carpeted the plain to the horizon, they'd make their way back here to this sanctuary and into the labyrinth of rock and strewn boulders. Then horse and rider seemingly vanished like phantoms, leaving no indication that they'd been there.

Once, it had been just that way.

Soon, it would be no more.

And he had come here tonight because this was the one place he was certain to receive a clear view of the future, as well as recall the past that had led to this moment.

It was a night when he would ask the spirits to relieve him of his medicine power. He no longer needed their guidance. He had accomplished much, and looked forward more than he ever had thought possible to living out his days with the woman he loved.

The warrior stood with his arms outstretched as though embracing the night, and he sang his prayer in a low, modulated voice. "Hih-yah, hih-yah, hear my voice oh spirit of the People. I have come to this sacred altar to give back the medicine power you bestowed on me. It has served me well, but I am no longer in need. My life, and the lives of the People, have been decided. There will be change in the future, but even though we may eventually lose the land, we will never surrender our Comanche heart to the white man. Our children, and their children after them, will always know who they are, and of the Comanche blood that flows through their veins. Through our offspring the Quohadi band will live on. They will sing our songs and continue to honor our ways. Suvante, it is finished for me. My destiny takes me along another path."

In the flicker of firelight that backlit his powerful form, another shadowy figure moved. The woman came forward, and stood beside him. Lifting her gaze, she noted the fierce gleam in his jet black eyes, and the wolf's rings encircling them. He had painted his face in lines and patterns that signified he was a warrior of many great battles and victories. There was the sweep of a hawk's wings on his chest. She understood, but it never failed to stir the tortured memories. She didn't want them to intrude tonight. This was the first time that they'd been alone in weeks.

"I love you," she said, her gaze roaming over the strong planes of his face, reminding herself that this was not a man she'd ever have to fear.

"And I adore you, angel." Having returned to the sacred bluff and relinquished his medicine power, Night Hawk was free to love and marry again. His heart swelled with the depth of his feelings for this woman. He seized her around the waist, and pulled her into his arms.

Their lips met and she felt buffeted by the winds of a savage harmony. It was a kiss that bespoke his hopes and dreams and love.

He caught her wrist in his hands and drew them behind her back. Instinctively, her body arched against him. Reaching up, he curled long fingers inside the laces on the front of her ivory doeskin shift, and in a single deft motion, rent the soft material from her shoulder to thigh, his gaze following as the garment whispered down her body and puddled at her feet.

Bared to the moon's revealing light, she looked vulnerable and uncertain. She caught her breath in surprise, clinging to the last slender thread of her modesty.

"I promised you that one day I would take away the bad memories. This is the last barrier. Tonight we'll both leave the past behind, and with the dawn, start anew."

They stood together at the edge of the cliff,

their bare bodies awash in the soft moonlight, hearts beating as one. Then slowly, tenderly, he pressed her down onto the towering stone altar, and stretching out beside her, he removed her leggings and moccasins. Drawing her arms back over her head, he studied the image of her lying naked and beautiful, a sensual offering. Dipping his head, he placed a gentle kiss low on the slight swell of her belly, where the new prince of the Quohadi lay nestled safe and secure within her. Then he proceeded to stroke and kiss her flesh, tugging hungrily at the crest of her breast, abrading the taut peak with his teeth.

He raised his head and stared down at her, desire glittering in his eyes. "I love you so much, sweet Medicine Woman, more than I ever thought possible." Then, from about his neck, he took a small pouch.

Callie could only watch him through heavy-lidded eyes drugged by passion, her heart beating nervously.

He removed a small earthen jar, and held it up before her. "I ask that the spirits guide my hand in what I'm about to do. Bestow your blessing on our union and remove any doubt or fear that may linger."

Lowering his arms, he dipped one long finger into the jar, and withdrawing it, brought it to rest against her forehead, where he drew several symbols in bright crimson. As he slashed lines across her cheekbones and along her jaw, he watched the play of emotions cross her face and recited the Comanche belief that the use of vermillion was to denote courage, potency, and valor.

"You have proven yourself worthy to be a Comanche woman," he said. "I want you to remember this night forever, to never again know terror when you are confronted by our patterns and symbols. When you recall this night, it will resurrect memories of a loving like you've never known before. You will remember that other dark time as only a distant part of your past."

He held the jar aloft, and she felt the sticky, wet liquid puddle in the delicate, almond-shaped well of her navel. His hands ran over her body, touching, teasing, arousing. Callie shivered with the rise of her passion.

Then he dipped the tip of his finger into the paint on her belly, and crimson fire suddenly streaked over her stomach and along her ribcage, searing upward, ringing one nipple, before moving on, and encircling the other. The dark red shimmered in the moonlight like fire dancing along her skin, leaping along her torso, greedily lapping at her breasts.

"Close your eyes now, *bella,*" he ordered huskily.

"Is this a customary part of the ceremony?" she asked softly, eyelids drifting shut, as if they were weighted, as if she were mesmerized.

"It's a very important ritual, and you must not talk and distract me or the spirits will be angered and take away my powers," he whispered.

Her left eyebrow rose a fraction, but she didn't open her eyes. "Mmmm, somehow I don't think so."

"Shhhh, you aren't ever supposed to let them hear you question," he murmured, bending over her, running his tongue lightly over her nipples until they were wet and glistening in the firelight.

One hand slid downward to explore her thighs, and began a lust-arousing exploration of her soft flesh. Fire licked at her loins; slow but consuming, working its way up inside her. Callie didn't need his urging to spread her legs and invite his exploration. He settled between her thighs, his fingers sifting through fiery curls, and his eyes watched as the tiny bud that had been hidden in her womanly flesh, became exposed. He flicked his thumb back and forth over it, and she panted her need of him.

"Don't make me wait any longer. I want you to fill me. Come inside me, Night Hawk, be my love." Arching her hips in wanton abandon, she rubbed her moist silky folds against his fingers, then reaching down, she took his hand and placed it to his lips. His mouth opened slightly, and his tongue lapped the sweet, wild nectar from his fingertips. "Taste my need of you. See how badly you've made me want you."

He groaned. Hers was an exquisite offering, and the scent of her beckoned him. Desire exploded in his brain. "God, I want you so badly," he said hoarsely. He grasped her hips, and pulling her under him, he thrust his swollen sex inside her.

Callie cried out in ecstasy. Her fingers twisted in his long raven hair, and she tightened her fists around it. Bodies straining, hips thrashing, they were like two strong young wolves caught in a fierce mating. "Love me, Night Hawk. Love me until the end of time."

He knew that he would, and no matter the trials or adversity that came with the future, they would face it together. As man and wife, as lovers, for all time.

Epilogue

Callie Rae Angel became Mrs. Rafael Santino in a private, but lavish, southern wedding at the beautiful mansion in New Orleans, ending his long estrangement with his Creole family. The elder Santino had been corresponding with his son for many weeks. He'd mentioned his desire to see his son married in grand style, as befitting his heir, and Callie had thought it was the right thing to do. Rafe had agreed.

The ceremony took place at sunset beneath the rose arbor overlooking the Mississippi river. The bride wore a moire silk gown, trimmed in white Brussels lace, seed pearls forming clusters of leaves, spilling down the skirt and along the flowing train. The handsome groom, attired in black formal wear, waited nervously for her to join him before the priest.

Sam Matthews gave the bride away and acted as his friend's best man. He brought a lady with him that everyone was delighted to see. It was evident by the way they looked at one another that they would soon be the next to exchange their vows.

Just as the sun set on the river, Callie and Rafe were pronounced man and wife. For the second time. Owl Man had already sealed their lives in a meaningful ceremony before the Quohadi people. A grateful Black Raven had gifted the bride with many fine ponies, and offered his hand in friendship. Little Doe and their son had looked on smiling. Before they'd departed for New Orleans, Rafe had told Black Raven where the treasure Stevenson had horded might be found.

"We will use it for the People," he had informed a wide-eyed Black Raven. "To buy land and ensure their freedom. I will contact you soon."

The reception on the plantation grounds that evening was joyful. Lily LaFleur caught the bridal bouquet. Beaming at Sam, she favored him with a saucy wink. Sam gave the newlyweds the best present of all. The news that Rafe had finally been cleared of the charges against him.

Later, as the happy couple were whisked away in the sleek black carriage adorned with magnolias and ivory roses, the handsome bridegroom turned to his lovely bride. "No regrets?"

"Not one," she replied unhesitatingly.

"Then kiss me, Mrs. Santino," he urged, enfolding her in his arms. "And love me forever."

"I promise you a lifetime of loving, my darling," she murmured, and reaching up to draw the velvet draperies closed, she smiled seductively. "And I don't think it's too soon to begin the honeymoon, do you?"

FEEL THE FIRE IN CAROL FINCH'S ROMANCES!